Other Books by Amos Aricha

Journey Toward Death
Hour of the Clown
Phoenix

The Flying Camel

Amos Aricha

E. P. DUTTON NEW YORK

Published in the United States by E. P. Dutton,
a division of New American Library,
2 Park Avenue, New York, N.Y. 10016.

Library of Congress Cataloging-in-Publication Data

Aricha, Amos, 1933–
The Flying Camel.
I. Title.
PS3551.R435F59   1987   813'.54   86-13379
ISBN: 0-525-24472-7

Published simultaneously in Canada by
Fitzhenry & Whiteside, Ltd., Toronto

CUSA

Designed by Steven N. Stathakis

10 9 8 7 6 5 4 3 2 1

First Edition

For Anna Dolgin Thaler

My sincere gratitude to Martin P. Levin, Herbert K. Schnall, and Peretz Kidron for their unwavering friendship, faith, and welcome advice.

To Richard Marek, editor and publisher, my appreciation for enabling the winged camel to take flight.

1

Monday morning at five o'clock Charlie called from Washington. Harassment by telephone was an ugly habit he had fallen into since the Iranian kamikaze strike on the U.S. Marine headquarters in Beirut.

"What's doing?" I asked unnecessarily.

"Nothing special." His voice was velvety. "I just wanted to remind you about Beirut."

"I haven't forgotten."

"You mustn't ever."

"How can I," I said, "with you calling me once a week?"

"Everyone has a job to do, Daniel," he responded softly. "We must never forget. Two hundred and forty-one of our boys. Two hundred and forty-one coffins set out in a long line, like an endless freight train."

"I remember." I fought to keep myself under control, to combat my fears. My hand clutching the receiver was covered with sweat, and my heart pounded wildly. Charlie would recognize my symptoms; he had warned me about these signs as part of the risks of the trade—the syndrome that overtakes a headhunter when he loses a hold on his nerves. Charlie inevitably showed little patience with any such loss of control. It may have been the pigheaded pride of a young man reluctant to acknowledge the cracks in his self-image, but I couldn't bring myself to admit my fear to Charlie, the man who pulled the secret strings of my life.

"Accounts will have to be squared." Charlie paused for me to grasp his meaning. "Those responsible must be made to pay. Lousy bunch of crazy perverts," he continued, his voice rising. "Iranians. Syrians. Lebanese. Those creeps have to be made aware that there are still people like you and me around. They'll have to learn."

"I'm sure they will." There was no enthusiasm in my reply.

With tiresome predictability, he turned to his list of prime suspects: five men, all Syrians. One would eventually be pinpointed as the target. "I'm more and more convinced that Rif'at Shishakali is our man."

"Maybe."

Charlie sounded distressed. "You've studied their files, each one. You know those men inside out. Better'n me even. And you say 'maybe'?"

"He's one of five," I pointed out.

"Whenever I mention Shishakali, you get restless." There was a brief pause. "What is it about him that makes you so uneasy?"

"I haven't the faintest interest in Shishakali," I said slowly and distinctly, "nor in any of your other suspects." I flung a glance at the wall clock. "It's getting late."

"I didn't mean to keep you." Charlie's tone became conciliatory. He knew I generally left early for the Manhattan law firm where I was employed as an expert in Mideastern affairs and translator of Semitic languages. It was Charlie, in fact, who had arranged the job as an ideal cover for my missions to the Mideast. "I just wanted to make sure you start your week with a reminder."

"Your reminder has begun to louse up my day," I retorted, and hung up. I knew Charlie's style; he would give me no peace.

2

Once he sank his teeth in, I would never free myself from his jaws. Behind his deceptively mild appearance, Charlie was tough and uncompromising, particularly when it came to matters of national security. His insistence that I undertake the Beirut mission was his way of forcing me into a corner. I would soon be left with no choice but to confess that I was finished, but it would be a perilous step. I would be jeopardizing more than Charlie's good opinion of me; I would also be running the risk of forfeiting substantial monies I was owed by the CIA. It was a sobering thought, yet I could not escape the ominous premonition that any additional mission I undertook would somehow lead to disaster. Thinking again about what lay in store kept me in a cold sweat long after I had laid down the receiver.

It was 5:45 when I left my basement apartment in Aunt Bertha's house. Instantly, my face was flayed by a stinging gust of hail. I picked my way carefully through the grubby snow and paced to the bus stop across Avenue Z. Moments later, I was at the Sheepshead Bay subway station. Together with the other passengers, I pressed against the wall at the end of the platform, seeking shelter from the wind. We huddled there until the express thundered in from Brighton Beach. It was the last train on which I had any hope of finding a seat for the forty-five-minute ride to Forty-seventh Street. All the later trains would be crammed tight with the closely packed press of bodies I have always detested. Another reason I preferred to set out so early.

Before stepping into the train, I cast a swift glance about me, caught by a sudden awareness of being followed. It was a sensation that had recurred several times in recent days, ever since Charlie began stepping up his calls. I speculated whether he'd decided to tighten the screws by having me placed under surveillance. I surveyed the faces about me, but detected no familiar features. I shrugged it off, reassuring myself that it was just my imagination, another sign that my overwrought nerves were playing tricks on me.

I found a seat at the end of the car and stretched out my legs, attempting to relax and banish Charlie from my thoughts. I was determined not to allow his persistence to spoil my mood. This evening I would be joining Ariadne's friends in celebrating her twenty-first birthday, and I turned my mind once more to

3

the problem of a present that would suit her taste. Aunt Bertha had advised me to take advantage of a lunch break to shop Lexington Avenue, where I might find some modest but tasteful piece of jewelry that I could afford. Bertha's suggestion of jewelry had given me an idea: I recalled the long-neglected jewel box that had belonged to my late mother. I then rummaged in her closet and dug out the box. It was encased in green velvet and faded with age; its smooth surface was marred by numerous worn patches. The box was about ten inches by seven and divided vertically into two levels. The upper compartment contained a number of heavy bracelets, fitted with cheap settings. There were also several rings and sets of earrings. In the bottom section, I discovered a string of fake pearls, some gold-plated brooches, and various other items which I barely glanced at. What had caught my eye in particular was a curious-looking headpiece, set in the center with a small winged camel fashioned out of white metal.

I surveyed the jewels before me with embarrassment; I could hardly blame my mother for never wearing them. I turned them over. None was to my liking, but I picked out one ring of somewhat finer form, not quite as shoddy as the rest of the collection. It would do for a present, I had thought, feeling relieved at having solved the problem. I hoped Ariadne would at least appreciate my good intentions. I found a small box to fit the ring, took out one of my cards, scrawled a simple and direct "To Ariadne, from Daniel," and slipped it inside.

But now, as the subway train plunged into the tunnel beyond the Brooklyn Bridge, I remained doubtful about the suitability of my gift. I feared that the tawdry ring would show up my taste—or, to be precise, my want of taste. Undecided, I allowed my hand to rest on the box, which nestled in my overcoat pocket. In the end, I resolved to put the matter out of my thoughts till I finished work. Time enough then to make up my mind whether or not to present the ring to Ariadne. Should I decide against it, I could still manage to buy her a bunch of flowers or a bottle of wine.

Monday, March 5, 1984, was one of those days when so much happens that the workload builds up to double its normal volume. Immediately on arrival at the office, I flung myself into

4

translating the balance sheet of a Florida construction corporation that had been offered for sale to the renowned Saudi businessman, Sheikh Ibrahim Ibn Aziz. I was hard at work long before the appearance of my employers, Sheldon Moritz and Ed Liebman. Their specialty was handling commercial deals, representing investors from Saudi Arabia and the Persian Gulf emirates. Both Moritz and Liebman were Jews, but that proved no obstacle in their work on behalf of Arab governments or other orthodox Moslem clients.

I had not failed to observe the agitation that seized my bosses whenever the name of Sheikh Ibn Aziz came up, so I made a special effort on this assignment. The sheikh, one of the wealthiest men in Saudi Arabia, was in the United States on behalf of the Saudi monarch, who had sent him to mediate in the crisis between Syria and the U.S. administration. Now, on his way back from Washington, he had consented to stop over in New York to be briefed by my employers on the proposed purchase of the Florida firm.

Only moments after I finished making Xeroxes of the translated pages, the sheikh swept into the office, surrounded by his entourage. The guests made an imposing appearance in their flowing headdresses and long white robes, their alien character heightened by Sheikh Ibn Aziz's air of subdued omnipotence. The sheikh was elderly, although it was difficult to guess his precise age owing to the pallor of ill health that marked his complexion. He shuffled in slowly, stooping slightly over the long staff on which he leaned. His face was drawn, the cheekbones sunken and the sharp jaw standing out like the muzzle of a half-starved wolf. His expression was fierce, retaining its harsh lines even as the attorneys introduced the senior employees they were placing at his disposal. He surveyed us all with a sharp, arrogant gaze, declining to shake the hands stretched out toward him.

When it was my turn to be presented, he subjected me to an inquisitive stare. "Kottler," he muttered, his tone somewhere between affirmation and query.

"Yes sir."

"I hope your mastery of Arabic is worthy of our noble tongue." He did not take his gaze off me.

I bowed my head. "I'll do my best to meet your wishes."

5

"It would be well so," he mumbled and shuffled away, heading for the inner office where we convened for our preliminary meeting.

The sheikh was no man for small talk. He confined conversation to the topics for which he had taken the trouble to come. Plunging into the minutest details of the matter at hand, he kept the attorneys riveted; the tension in the office mounted by the minute. It was a startling sight to watch my usually dignified employers falling over one another in deference to the sheikh and his attendants. However, I was soon to undergo my own ordeal. The sheikh's ears turned out to be as sharp as his gaze: catching a minor error in my Arabic translation, his expression froze and he voiced the hope that I would do better next time. Having put me in my place, he went on to suggest that a law firm maintaining such close ties with the Saudi government ought to cater to the convenience of its clients by opening a branch office in Riyadh. My employers assured him that they had already given his request their consideration; they agreed to schedule an immediate visit to the desert capital to set their plans in motion.

By the time the meeting was concluded, I was sweating. It came as an enormous relief to me when the partners escorted the sheikh and his party to lunch. Their departure was my cue to head for my own midday hangout on the corner of Forty-sixth Street and Sixth Avenue.

It was here, one month ago, that I had made the acquaintance of Ariadne. The first time we talked was when she passed by my table looking for a place to sit. The restaurant was particularly crowded and all the other tables were occupied. When I offered her the seat next to mine, she accepted gratefully. That encounter marked the beginning of a friendship that I dearly wished to cultivate in spite of the nearly eleven years' difference in our ages. One day, when I remarked on the disparity, Ariadne broke into one of her pealing laughs. Such a minor difference, she shrugged; her own father had been her mother's senior by thirty-one years. Ironically, her mother died at the age of thirty-four while giving birth to Ariadne; her father was sixty-five at the time.

Ariadne was fond of reminiscing about her family. Like my

6

own, hers had its origins in prerevolutionary Russia, but that was about as far as the similarity in our backgrounds went. My Jewish grandparents fled from the pogroms during czarist times, whereas her Pravoslav forebears left later, during the revolution, when they were persecuted for their aristocratic pedigree, as blood relatives of Czar Nikolai. My family settled in Brooklyn, where their life-style fell into the patterns of the Jewish lower middle class. By contrast, Ariadne's grandfather fled to Paris, where he and his only son became antique dealers. World War Two came and went before Ariadne's father, Prince Alexander, moved to New York. He was a devotee of Greek culture, which, she said, is why he named her Ariadne, after the daughter of Minos, king of Crete. Just as that maiden of antiquity proffered her beloved Theseus the thread that was to become his lifeline, so Alexander perceived the appearance of his daughter—in the autumn of his life—as the thread whereby he retrieved his springtime. After his death, Ariadne decided to perpetuate his memory by adopting Alexander as her family name.

I was captivated by Ariadne's tales, but I could not help concluding privately that she was blessed with an overactive imagination.

Today, as always, I found her awaiting me at a corner table. Over lunch, she launched into one of her family histories, then tried to draw me out about my own ancestors.

"There isn't anything interesting in my past," I assured her.

She studied me at length. "You don't have much to say about yourself."

I smiled. "I'm not very talkative."

"That isn't all . . ." She fell silent.

"What are you trying to say?"

"You're more than just a lawyer's clerk," she declared firmly.

"I am?"

"You bear the traits of some other person, someone who is rooted deep inside you . . ."

I hastened to interrupt. "Whatever makes you think so?"

"I sense it inside." She laid her hand on her bosom. "I feel it here."

"What is it that you feel?"

"I can't put it into words." She broke into an innocent smile.

"You describe yourself as an Arabic translator—but with your talents, I can't imagine you remaining content with a job like that. I sense there's something more."

A doubt ran through my mind, questioning whether she was as naïve as she seemed, but I rejected the suspicion. "I am what I am," I said quietly.

Ariadne laughed. "Of course you are. But you may not be aware of certain aspects of yourself. You may not have discovered all there is." Unexpectedly, she laid a hand on my arm. "Let me see your palm." Obediently, I turned my hand upward, to have it studied with sorceresslike intensity before Ariadne's gaze returned to my face. "You have unusual features," she pronounced finally. "In both hand and face, I divine traces of royalty. You have the blood of a Semitic prince."

My God, I thought, this is too much! "Are you convinced?"

"Beyond any doubt," she said. "Your palm reveals something highly unusual in your past—something exciting." She prattled on about my antecedents, her tone a blend of agitation and enthusiasm, and focused on a tiny spot on my hand, where she claimed to see a fine network of lines. Her green eyes flashed, like those of a fortune-teller peering into a crystal ball. "These lines prove your links with an ancient race. I wouldn't be surprised if you traced your roots back as far as ancient Jerusalem, long before the birth of Christ. You might very well be a descendant of King David."

This was more than I could take. "I'm sorry to have to disappoint you," I said, "but my ancestry—on my mother's side, at least—consists of a perfectly ordinary drab Jewish family which can't trace its pedigree further back than three generations."

"Maybe it's on your father's side," she persisted.

"I scarcely know anything about him. He died before I was born."

"You see!" she exclaimed triumphantly. "How come you know nothing about him?"

I shrugged. "If there were anything about him I ought to feel proud of, I don't suppose my mother would have concealed it. I don't even bear his name—Kottler's my mother's maiden name."

"Why didn't you ever ask her?"

"I did."

"What did she say?"

I hesitated, reluctant to recall that terrifying moment far back in my early childhood when an innocent question about my father had so upset my mother. "Nothing," I said. "She just made me promise never to mention him again."

Ariadne would not give up. "Try to remember," she urged. "Where was he born?"

"In Israel." With a half-smile, I added, "Not far from the spot where Jesus walked upon the waters." Her eyes widened at this apparent confirmation of her divinations. "But that doesn't bear out your fantasy about my royal origins."

Her tone grew aggrieved. "You think I'm making it all up, but you're wrong. The past is the root and source of everything we are. When you come to my apartment tonight, you'll see what I mean."

She rose to leave, but I stopped her. "I don't even know the address."

"You'll have no difficulty finding it," she replied. "It's on Seventy-second Street. I live in the Dakota."

I was astonished. As a dance teacher at an arts college and part-time photographer, she could never make enough to afford an apartment in one of Manhattan's most famous residences.

We walked out into the street, where we parted. I was due back at the office, while Ariadne headed for the nearby arts school where she taught. I stood at the corner, watching her slim figure recede from view until it was swallowed up in the school entrance. Only then did I cross the street, my hand resting in my pocket, clutching the box that held my mother's ring.

I could sense my neck muscles growing taut. The sensation was familiar, a reliable indication that I was being followed. My nerves were frayed, but they were still sufficiently fine-honed to act as a warning. My most primitive instincts now took control. I paced along at a moderate speed, flinging an occasional casual glance at the torrent of humanity behind me, in search of my anonymous watcher. He must have been a professional, because I failed to detect him. That bastard Charlie, I thought, he's beginning to unsheath his claws.

Charlie controlled numerous agents who served as his executioners, dispatching them on missions to far-off places in pursuit of the victims he selected. Whenever one of his headhunters was lost or otherwise became unavailable, Charlie had no difficulty finding a replacement. But this time, he would accept no substitute: it was me he wanted. Me, and no one else.

I was aware of my reputation as Washington's number one hit man in the Mideast, which was why Charlie insisted on saddling me with the mission of retribution against the perpetrators of the Beirut massacre. The operation was far too important to entrust to a less experienced agent. Charlie was intent on proving to his superiors his proficiency in pinpointing the culprits and in exacting vengeance at the time and place of his choosing. But the more he leaned on me to undertake the assignment, the further I plunged into a panic brought on by the certainty that if I accepted, I would not come back alive. I was wrong in disguising my doubts and hesitations. I had to unburden myself to Charlie: there was no way I would undertake the Beirut mission.

Back in the office, I asked my secretary to book me a hotel room so I could spend the night in Manhattan after Ariadne's party. The booking was, as always, at the Warwick, a friendly hotel to whose delights Charlie had introduced me some years back. Since then, I had made it a habit to keep a small overnight bag in my office. It was equally useful for spontaneous missions to distant destinations that Charlie sometimes sprang on me. My secretary got the booking right away, adding the usual request for a room overlooking Sixth Avenue. On my instructions, she was always particular about that detail.

I spent several hours in my office, studying the construction corporation's balance sheet and inserting the Arabic corrections demanded by the sheikh. When the corrections were finished, I instructed my secretary to make a Xerox of several sets; three of the copies were to be sent by messenger to the hotel where the sheikh was staying with his entourage.

I stretched my arms and yawned. The time had come to make up my mind about Ariadne's birthday present, so I extracted the box for a further inspection of the ring. It was actually quite an attractive piece, I thought; it might have been worth no more than twenty or thirty dollars, but even that was no trifling gift for someone like Ariadne, by her own account left penniless when her father lost all his money. But, I wondered, if penniless, how was it that she lived in the Dakota?

When I got to my hotel room, I took a shower and flopped down on the bed to shed my accumulated tension and weariness. At 7:30, I decided to make my way to Seventy-second Street on foot. I strolled along until I reached Fifty-ninth Street and crossed the broad avenue. Turning left, I walked alongside Central Park's gray stone wall as far as Columbus Circle.

Nearing Sixty-seventh Street, I turned my head abruptly; I could have sworn I saw a figure springing over the wall into the shadowy recesses of the park. I froze momentarily, my well-trained reflexes failing me. The CIA combat school would have awarded me negative ratings for that fleeting hesitation; I quickly resorted to a trick learned from one of the instructors. Searing my lungs with a sharp intake of chilly air, I propelled myself into a swift leap toward the spot where I had seen the stranger vanish.

I landed in the middle of a mass of low, shadowy bushes, where I paused briefly to accustom my eyes to the dim light filtering through the undergrowth. As soon as I could distinguish the outlines of the various trees and shrubs, I began to advance carefully, conducting a thorough search. But I discovered no sign of my mysterious watcher.

I worked my way into the deserted depths of the park. Although my ears were attuned to detect the slightest suspicious sound, they picked up nothing but the murmur of the breeze fluttering through the treetops. Encountering no one, I gave up my quest. As I turned and circled back, disturbing thoughts ran through my mind: Had I imagined that shadowy figure? Was my fantasy running wild? If so, it would be yet another by-product of the tension brought on by Charlie's relentless harassment.

Finally reaching Seventy-second Street, I stopped to stare at the imposing facade of the Dakota, shuddering in anticipation of the embarrassment we would both feel when Ariadne's story of living there was shown up for a pretense. Still, I entered the courtyard, where I was immediately stopped by a uniformed guard.

"Can I help you, sir?"

"I hope you can," I grinned awkwardly. "I'm looking for Miss Alexander's apartment."

"Certainly, sir," he replied in an earnest tone acquired, I assumed, by all those entrusted with the safekeeping of so eminent an institution as the Dakota. "What is your name, sir?" he asked, checking a list.

"Kottler," I said. The name suddenly rang dismally simple. "Mister Kottler," I corrected, feeling foolish.

The doorman checked the list. "Mister Daniel Kottler." He inclined his head politely. "Would you be good enough to come with me, sir?"

"Sir" was good enough to escort the guard to the elevator. The riddle of Ariadne's residence was beyond me. The fortunate few who could give a Dakota address were among Manhattan's high society. Where did that place Ariadne?

On the third floor, I took a deep breath to overcome my nervousness and pushed the doorbell to Ariadne's apartment. The door opened, and I rocked back on my heels as I found myself facing a strikingly beautiful young woman. Ariadne, familiar and yet dramatically changed from the form dominating my thoughts these past weeks, stood facing me, shining with the dazzling glamour of a *Vogue* cover girl. Her chestnut brown hair with its occasional strand of red was tied up in a narrow ribbon, giving it the form of a finely wrought coronet. Her long sky-blue gown left her slender arms and shoulders bare. The dress, recalling Viennese fashions of the turn of the century, suited her perfectly.

Ariadne seized my hands, still chilled from their exposure to the cold air outside. "I'm so glad you came."

I managed to mumble some response, but I was stunned by her and by the sight that met my eyes as the door closed behind me. The apartment resembled nothing I had ever seen. Ariadne guided me along the corridor where slide projectors cast images of famous Viennese locations onto the lofty walls. The slides were her own, she explained; they had been taken during journeys with her father, and she made a habit of screening them for her friends. Her collection included over three thousand pictures, shot in places as far-flung as Tibet, the Himalayas, India, China, Egypt, and Greece. The ones being projected now provided the Viennese setting she had chosen for the party, the atmosphere gaining a further authenticity from the Strauss waltzes playing through the rooms.

Ariadne led me past the streets and squares of gay Vienna, until we entered the expansive drawing room, in which about twenty guests were gathered. The air of merriment failed to dispel my sense of being an outsider. Ariadne's friends affected an offhand style, and when she introduced me to one or two of them, they scarcely noticed me. I felt even more out of place when I realized that several of the glamorous-looking women were actresses who had already made a name for themselves on stage or screen. One golden-haired beauty struck me as particularly familiar; I remembered seeing her in *42nd Street*. Everybody seemed to know everybody. I appeared to be the only one whose face no one recognized.

Settling myself forlornly in a corner, I gulped down large amounts of red wine, which soon inspired sombre reflections that my friendship with Ariadne would inevitably come to an early end. I fixed my gaze on her as she flitted about among her guests, a gentle smile on her face. Her chestnut curls bounced about as though possessing a life of their own, and her eyes sparkled joyfully. I could not take my eyes from her.

Finally, I decided to wander about the cavernous apartment, whose large rooms were crammed with relics of czarist Russia. It did not take me long to realize that Ariadne had not exaggerated when she spoke of her family's past. I was struck by the heavy furniture, with carvings representing human forms and animals, and by the huge oils depicting snow-covered landscapes such as I had never seen, with sleighs drawn by powerful steeds, hotly pursued by packs of wolves. I was particularly impressed by an enormous painting of Moscow in winter. It was flanked by photographs from a distant past, when men with flowing mustaches and carefully tended beards preened themselves in ornate dress uniforms and women posed proudly with sharply upturned bosoms. Yesterday's world.

"You're Daniel, aren't you?" A melodious voice from behind jolted me out of my contemplation of the Russian aristocracy. Turning, I found myself face to face with the actress from *42nd*

Street. Her smiling features were highlighted by a thick plait of blond hair dangling over her shoulder. It was a beautiful face, narrow until it rounded at the chin; her lips seemed to have been painted on. "My name is Sheila Griffiths." She extended a hand. "Ariadne asked me to keep you company till she can get away from the kitchen. So you and I had better find a topic we're both familiar with. I suggest Ariadne. We've been friends since we were seven." She halted her breathless outpouring to smile at my intrigued expression. "We first met at dance class with Madame Ludmilla, and we've scarcely been apart since, except when she was off on one of those expeditions with her father."

"She never mentioned you," I said.

Sheila smiled forgiveness at my inadvertently offensive remark. "When she's with you, I think she tries to avoid anything that sounds like name-dropping."

"Because of me?"

"She has the impression you don't quite believe her." Sheila inspected me curiously. "I think she's got a thing for you. She didn't want to scare you off."

"She almost did," I acknowledged.

"I assure you she's one hundred percent genuine," Sheila said. "And an extraordinary person."

I made a clumsy jab at slyness. "Here you are, a famous actress, and yet you sound as though you're jealous of her."

Sheila's expression grew earnest. "I am and always have been. Ariadne was the girl who had everything. Beauty. Money. Talent. Even the pedigree of an authentic princess." Asking my preference, she poured me a bourbon on the rocks before settling herself on the armrest of an antique armchair in whose depths I was already ensconced. "Ariadne," she resumed, "is the sort of girl you can't get out of your mind. She used to arrive at dance class in a huge limousine, a green Lincoln as long as a railway coach, driven by a chauffeur in gray livery; he would wait for her till the class ended. Don't get me wrong—I wasn't jealous of her because of the limo. No, I envied her talent. I didn't want to be Sheila Griffiths—my dream was to become Ariadne Alexander."

"But you're the one who made it."

"Let me show you around—it'll help you to understand."

14

Sheila was thoroughly acquainted with the huge apartment. She took me on a guided tour. I recall nine rooms, but there may have been more. Our tour concluded in the library, whose towering, glass-encased bookshelves must have housed at least ten thousand volumes. Most were in Russian, others were in French, German, and English. One entire wall was given over to family snapshots. My eyes fell on a large photograph of two men; one, middle-aged, was bearded and wore dress uniform; the other also sported a beard, but he was young and very handsome.

Sheila caught my look. "The man in the center is Czar Nikolai. The one standing beside him is Prince Andrey Andreyevitch, Ariadne's grandfather." She led me to a corner hung with more recent photographs and pointed out a little girl, about nine years old, photographed as she executed an arabesque and instantly recognizable as Ariadne. Beside her was another diminutive ballerina, her hair tied up in a pony tail and equally unmistakable: Sheila.

"What talent!" Sheila said. "What promise she had!"

I listened, puzzled. "What went wrong?"

"It all came apart four years back. First, her father died and everything collapsed about her. No more limousine, no property, no money. All she had left was this apartment and a small sum to keep it up. But she still had her terrific talent. Somebody was looking for a couple of actresses for a musical, and we grabbed at the chance. Ariadne was rehearsing with one of our male dancers. She did a pirouette; he hoisted her up. But then he lost his grip on her and she fell. Her left knee was wrenched." Sheila sighed. "It was the end."

She fell still; I too sat wordless, reluctant to break the silence. Behind us, the noisy revelry of the other guests seemed to come from a great distance.

"The end?"

Sheila shrugged. "The kneecap was jolted out of place. The doctors tried all kinds of things, like special exercises to build up muscles which would hold the kneecap in place. You've never seen anyone put in so much effort as Ariadne. But it was useless. Not even surgery could completely repair the damage."

"It must have been a horrible disappointment."

Sheila nodded. "She can still dance—superbly—but she never

knows when some movement will wrench the kneecap out of place."

I wondered at Ariadne's high spirits and the zest for life she retained. We renewed our study of the photographs, which presented an extraordinary blend of epochs and figures. There was Ariadne's father as a boy, dressed in the finery characteristic of Russian nobility; then he appeared as a young man in Paris, sporting the elegant European fashions of the time. Nearby, he was portrayed in the company of a slim beauty almost his equal in height and evidently many years his junior.

"That's Miranda," Sheila explained. "Ariadne's mother."

"She hardly ever mentions her," I said. "What do you know about her?"

"Not much. She was a Bostonian. An authentic American aristocrat, which means a blend of French and Irish. Ariadne doesn't have anything to do with her Boston relatives. When their business empire was in trouble, her father bailed them out. But when Ariadne needed help, they didn't lift a finger for her." Sheila smiled wryly. "Ariadne says you can't expect more from a family who made their money from running whiskey and whorehouses. Anyway, she's proud; she'd rather rot than ask for help."

We returned to the other guests just as Ariadne reappeared from the kitchen. I watched her flit among her friends, exchanging a word here and there before coming over to us.

"You two enjoying yourselves?"

"It's like Latin dancing." Sheila rose to her feet. "One step forward, two steps back. That's how it goes on a first meeting."

Ariadne's eyes glinted humorously. "Sounds like a backward samba. May I cut in?"

"Be my guest."

As Sheila tactfully withdrew, Ariadne laid a hand on my shoulder. "Sorry it took me so long. I hope Sheila kept you entertained."

"She's wonderful."

"I hoped you two would get on."

"She told me about those happy hours you little angels spent with Madame Ludmilla." But I could not maintain the flippant note. "I was sorry to hear about your accident."

"Past history." Her tone was soft.

I admired her self-control. "It's still painful to think—"

"I'll make it up to myself," she said with fierce determination. "I'll get there. I still have my photography."

I wanted to seize her in my arms and never let go. But I knew I was totally out of place in this high-walled museum dedicated to departed czarist boyars. Myself, I was from Brooklyn.

Ariadne must have noticed my sudden rush of discomfort. "Is something bothering you?"

"I've had a long day."

"I'm sorry. I hoped we'd have some time together when everybody leaves."

"Can we take a rain check on that? Just now, I need to be on my own, to get used to the Ariadne I met here this evening." I waved an arm at the imposing surroundings.

Ariadne made no attempt to detain me. I appreciated her consideration, though I suspected she would feel relieved when this ugly duckling waddled away from her lakeful of swans. She led me to the door where she helped me into my overcoat. I slipped my hand into the pocket to encounter the tiny box. Dammit, I thought. I forgot. My confusion swept aside my earlier indecision and I fished out the box. "I hope you like it," I stammered. "Of course, I won't be offended if you don't."

Ariadne gazed at me in delighted surprise. "It's kind of you," she murmured, obviously moved.

Anxious to be gone before she saw the ring, I planted a hasty kiss on her cheek and fled to the elevator, flushed with shame at my cowardice. Out of the corner of my eye, I saw Ariadne standing in the doorway, watching me till the elevator door closed.

With the awesome magnitude of the Dakota behind me, I paused to take in deep breaths of icy air. There was no urgency about returning to my hotel room; instead, I strolled the streets, allowing myself time to regain my composure. Suddenly, I saw Ariadne's features, so near I could almost touch her, and I was swept by a wave of sexual desire that made me ache.

The next morning I arrived at the office at seven. Moments after I entered, my phone rang. I knew who it was, and a cold spasm ran through me. "Yes, Charlie. What is it now?"

He chuckled, "You know only too well."

"I don't owe you a thing."

"That's a matter of opinion. But you owe a helluva lot to your country." He paused briefly. "You and I will know no rest until Beirut . . ."

"Every day now?" I snapped. "Am I going to have you on my back every day?"

My brusqueness failed to put him off. "After all these years," he mused, "suddenly you get evasive. How come?"

"Two good reasons. One, I'm frightened. Two, I'm scared."

"What's gotten into you, Daniel?"

"I'm burnt out. My nerves have gone. You can't make me do it, Charlie. Your time has run out."

I was right, as Charlie knew; my contractual obligations were nearing termination. That left him with no legal way of subjugating me. But he could afford to overlook the legalities because he still held the power. The terms of my contract would soon make me eligible for some very substantial benefits of the greatest significance for my future. The prospect of those benefits had allowed me to indulge in some very delicious fantasizing. Above all, I harbored an old dream of buying a small sailboat and setting out on a long sea cruise. It was a modest fantasy, but even so, my only chance of ever undertaking it depended upon Charlie.

I possessed no written copy of the commitment nor any other formal proof of ever having been employed by an official agency. Consequently, my benefits—and my future—depended exclusively upon Charlie's goodwill. The son of a bitch was perfectly capable of denying any connection with me; he could do so without experiencing the slightest twinge of remorse. If he didn't have that hold on me, I wouldn't hesitate to tell him to go screw himself. But as it was—

I began to feel as though I were imprisoned in some medieval torture chamber, an iron collar gradually tightening about my neck.

"I'll be the one to decide when the time is up," Charlie's voice dropped to a harsh whisper. "We have five suspects, and I'm almost sure—"

"It's Shishakali, I know."

"What more d'you know? About him, I mean."

His deference to my expertise was a trap; I knew that but I fell for it all the same. "Very little," I admitted. "His record is hazy. But he's one of the top men around the Syrian president. Assad's hatchetman, some say."

"And I say that Shishakali is the one directly responsible for the Beirut attack. A mystery man! I hoped you'd know more than that!" He hesitated momentarily. "You're a scholar, a specialist on the Mideast."

"But not a specialist on Rif'at Shishakali."

"Oh, I just thought . . ." He paused again. "But like you said, it could be any one of the five."

"And like I said, I'm not interested." Never before had I known Charlie to be so obsessively inquisitive about a prospective target. He must have had his reasons; but his stubborn pursuit of me was getting on my nerves. "Find yourself someone else," I counseled. "I'm a free man now."

"You're wrong there. You'll be free as soon as you've wrapped up the Beirut affair."

"Get off my back!" I shouted. Sweat trickled down my face.

He ignored my protest. "Don't forget the marines," he cautioned. It was his turn to hang up on me, leaving me with the receiver purring in my ear.

To take my mind off Charlie, I immersed myself in work, which consisted of translating a series of press articles about the prospects for the Florida construction industry; the translations were to be dispatched to Sheikh Ibrahim Ibn Aziz, now on his way home to Riyadh. I was so engrossed that I failed to notice when lunchtime came and passed. At three, my secretary put through a call. Instantly, I recognized Ariadne's soft tones. "I missed you at lunch," she said. "I hope I'm not disturbing you."

"Of course not," I assured her. "And I'm happy you called, because I wanted to tell you how much I enjoyed the party."

"I'm glad you did," she said indifferently, and fell silent. There was an uneasy pause. "Something wrong?" No sooner had I asked the question when a sudden stab of insight made me guess what was on her mind. The ring. My heart sank. She hated it.

"I have to talk to you," she said. Her tone was icy and remote.

19

We arranged to meet at the Rendezvous Bar of the Berkshire Hotel at 5:30. I got there early. Ariadne appeared moments later. At the first glimpse of her slim form, I sensed the pain of the imminent loss; I was about to forfeit something very precious, something I could never replace. She stood at the entrance, her tall figure encased in her old gray overcoat, her gaze wandering in search of me.

I leapt to my feet, with all the grace and agility of a bull. My knee thudded into the table, overturning a glass of water. Instinctively recoiling, I knocked over my chair, watching it fall against a matron seated at the adjacent table. Apologizing profusely, I cursed myself for my clumsiness.

By this time, Ariadne had reached my table. Her gaze, I noted, was chilly and distant. I stepped forward to help her off with her coat, but she turned away. "That's all right. I can manage."

"Being mad at me is no grounds for denying my masculine rights." My stab of humor paid off: Ariadne's expression softened and she made no protest as I drew the coat off her shoulders. But she insisted on laying it on the vacant chair at the side of the table, where it rested between us like some forbidding line of demarcation.

We ordered our drinks: gin and tonic for Ariadne, vodka on the rocks for me. When the waiter left, there was an embarrassed silence, which I tried awkwardly to break. "Last night I was finally convinced that you weren't making it all up—" I regretted the words almost as soon as they were out of my mouth.

Ariadne raised her head. "You didn't believe me, did you?" She broke into a peal of laughter.

"It was—all—so—fantastic," I stammered helplessly.

Her laughter faded, leaving her expression unusually earnest. "You're a riddle," she sighed. "How bizarre that you should doubt me." She placed great stress on "you" and "me." "When the shoe ought to be on the other foot."

I gazed at her in puzzlement. "What are you talking about?"

Ariadne's eyes did not leave my face. Her pale cheeks were flushed with patches of pink, brought on as much by her laughter as by the overheated air and the alcohol. "Credibility, Daniel. Credibility . . ."

"I'm don't understand."

"All this time, you've treated me like an imposter, but I'm not the imposter—you are!" She giggled once more. "Sheila also feels you're putting on some act—and she has a very sharp eye. So here we are. I've established my credibility—it's your turn now. Tell the truth!"

"About what?" I asked.

She subjected me to an accusing glare. "Mister Kottler, you have a gift for inventing plausible stories. Brighton Beach. Sheepshead Bay. Coney Island. Bobbeh and Zeideh. Danny Kottler grows in Brooklyn. You really broke my heart with your stories. And I fell for them."

"What are you talking about?" I was amazed at her insinuations.

"I don't want to offend you—" Her hand delved into her purse and brought out the little box into which I had placed the ring.

This is it, I thought. I goofed. The worthless little ring was no fit present for someone like Ariadne. "I'm sorry about the ring—" I began.

Ariadne leaned forward. She laid the box on the table. "Now look," she said firmly, "I only wanted your friendship, nothing more. But you had to go overboard with this expensive gift, and you've ruined everything. Everything! On top of which, you confirmed my suspicions that you aren't the humble little attorney's clerk you pretend to be."

By this time, I was thoroughly baffled. "What on earth—?"

She sighed impatiently. "As I told Sheila, this ring is the work of a master. The stone alone is at least three and a half carats. Sheila knows very little about jewelry. She laughed and said I was mad. So I took the ring to an expert, a friend of my father's. He confirmed what I already knew—he even told me I was right about the weight of the stone."

Ariadne fell silent, her face set in a triumphant expression. But I was overcome by sadness. She had lost her grip on reality. Having convinced myself of her truthfulness the previous evening, I found myself facing renewed manifestations of an overworked imagination. How should I treat her fantasizing? What could I say?

In a bid to gain time, I opened the box to examine the ring around which she had woven her latest fiction. It was, beyond any doubt, a fake, though I had to concede it was a convincing one.

"That's the strangest thing I ever heard," I said, meeting Ariadne's gaze without flinching. In her whole life, my mother never owned anything worth more than a few dollars. "I'm sorry to disagree with you, but you're wrong about the ring. No matter what a so-called 'expert' says!"

Ariadne sat bolt upright, staring at me fixedly. "Daniel—"

I silenced her with a raised hand. "I know nothing about jewelry. I couldn't tell a million-dollar ruby from a hunk of colored glass. What I do know is I'd love to give you a valuable present, but that's out of the question for the simple reason that I can't afford one. So, if you don't want the ring, all you need say is 'thanks but no thanks.' There's no need to come up with such an elaborate fabrication—"

I fell silent abruptly. She was staring at me as though I were the one who had gone out of his mind. "Jesus!" she cried unexpectedly, clapping her hand to her mouth as though to hold back her laughter. "We're not on the same wavelength." She dropped her hand on my arm. "Daniel, everything I told you about the ring is the truth. I swear . . ."

I took my time before replying. She was clearly speaking in earnest. If so . . . I shook my head, refusing to consider such a crazy notion. But nevertheless, just supposing she was right? If so, I thought, my mind reeling, if so, there was something about the ring of which I had not the faintest inkling. I tried to speak, but my throat had suddenly turned dry. I took a long slug of the vodka. "That expert of yours, he . . . ?"

"He's tops," she said. "I could be wrong, but Paul Oppenheimer? Never!" Ariadne glanced at her watch. "His office isn't far. If we hurry, we can catch him before he closes."

"Let's go," I croaked. I could scarcely recognize my own voice. I was already on my feet, flinging down a bill on the table before hurrying to help Ariadne into her coat.

2

We stepped out into the darkness. The weather had worsened; a snappy breeze lashing in sideways off the river forced me to bury my head in my overcoat collar. Ariadne and I did not link arms; we strode along, side by side but separately, like two strangers.

I sought some thread to help me unravel the riddle facing me. It was inconceivable that Ariadne could be right about the ring; but if she were . . .

We had only walked one block when I was once again jolted by the familiar feeling of being followed. I glanced about, trying to locate my shadow, but in vain. In my frustration, I experienced a sudden rush of hatred for Charlie. It was humiliating to feel that I had become one of his targets.

It took us ten minutes to reach the corner of Fifth Avenue and Fifty-seventh Street, where we entered the building and rode up to the seventh floor. I found myself facing a sliding steel door, electronically controlled. I picked out the eye of a closed-circuit television camera, probably with a direct hookup to an alarm at some private security agency. The jeweler's office enjoyed all the protection that technical ingenuity could provide.

When Ariadne had been identified, the door glided soundlessly to one side, admitting us into a kind of cage, its far wall made of highly polished reinforced glass. The steel door slid to behind us, whereupon the glass wall folded into its housing, and we paced into a splendidly ornate office.

I might have been forgiven for believing myself to be in the head office of some late nineteenth-century shipping line, for the room was designed to resemble a clipper captain's cabin. The dark wood paneling on the walls carried large oils depicting famous naval battles. I looked around in vain for any sign of jewelry display cabinets. It did not take me long to grasp that this Victorian opulence served as nothing more than a waiting room. Within moments, an attractive young woman dressed with elegant simplicity welcomed us with a smile and beckoned us to follow her into Mr. Oppenheimer's private office.

As we stepped through the doorway, a short, bald gentleman in his late sixties rose from his seat behind an antique carved desk. His shoulders were rounded, as though he spent much of his life peering through magnifying glasses. Behind his gold-rimmed spectacles, a pair of tiny eyes examined us; when we approached, he inclined his head in greeting. His secretary introduced us, her voice lowered to a whisper, as though she feared violating the sanctity of this inner shrine.

"I'm glad to make your acquaintance, Mister Kottler," the jeweler beamed. "As for Ariadne, no need for introductions, is there?" He flung a swift glance at his secretary, who departed. He bade us be seated and directed an impish look at Ariadne. "I see, my dear, that you are still concerned about the ring."

"It belongs to Mister Kottler, and I thought he should come here in person to hear your valuation. He finds your figure a little off."

Feeling ill at ease, I hurriedly qualified: "I don't question your professional judgment. It's just that I've never had anything to do with jewelry. The ring belonged to my late mother, and I have no idea of its value."

"Most people know little about jewelry," Oppenheimer pronounced with a note of self-satisfaction. "One of my jobs is to instruct and enlighten."

At Oppenheimer's request, I laid the box on the desk, thinking as I did so how embarrassed we would all feel when a further examination by the jeweler showed up his error. I watched closely as he studied the ring without removing it from the box.

After a moment of silence, broken only by the sound of breathing, Oppenheimer raised his head to regard me. "This ring," he said, "is far from being new. I would estimate its age at about seventy to eighty years. I find two indications to help establish its date: one, the cut of the stone, and two, the imprint of the renowned Zurich master craftsman Marcel d'Orly." He intoned the name with undisguised admiration. "Three years ago, a similar ring was sold in England for one hundred and seventy-five thousand dollars." The elderly connoisseur fixed his gaze on me, his expression inscrutable.

I sat in my armchair, frozen.

Oppenheimer continued his exposition, maintaining the same passionless tone. "To the best of my judgment, this ring would fetch a considerably higher price. Should you wish to sell, I would be happy to be of service."

I stared at his rounded features, which seemed to loom at me from beyond the bounds of fantasy. To my feverish gaze, his face appeared to stretch and contract by turns, like some surrealistic vision.

Finally, with a conscious effort, I managed to find my voice. "Thank you," I said slowly, trying to adopt the tone of grave deliberation that I sensed was appropriate to the occasion. "I confess that your valuation comes as a surprise to me."

Oppenheimer's unblinking eyes did not leave my face. "Should you entertain any doubts as to its accuracy, you may request an additional opinion. Any expert would be able to submit an estimate for a d'Orly creation."

I flushed, fearing that I had offended him by voicing my doubts. But Ariadne hastened to my rescue. "I'm sure Mister Kottler trusts your judgment."

"That goes without saying," I said. My voice seemed to boom from a remote depth, and my mind once again seemed to detach itself from my body, soaring to some external vantage point from which it could contemplate my own frozen figure. Perched in my imaginary observation tower, I saw Ariadne exchange glances with Oppenheimer, their expressions indicating that they dismissed my show of consternation as nothing more than a pretense.

Oppenheimer nodded slightly, as though to acknowledge my submission. He leaned toward me: "With your leave, Mister Kottler, may I ask a personal question?"

"Go ahead." The blood was throbbing at my temples and a dull ache spread downward from my forehead, as though a rope looped about my skull was being tugged by some remorseless hand.

"I understand you discovered the ring among your late mother's jewelry." Oppenheimer cocked his head to one side. "Do you have any knowledge as to how it came into her possession? Was it an heirloom or a present?"

"I have no idea." Indeed, having been convinced that the ring was as worthless as the rest of my mother's baubles, I had not given its origin much thought. Now, the jeweler's startling pronouncement as to its value left me too dazed to answer his question with anything but an evasive "My Aunt Bertha may know more."

"It would be wise to find out," Mr. Oppenheimer smiled. "If you wish, I could help by soliciting details about its history."

"How can you do that?" I asked. My headache was getting worse, and my lips were dry.

"D'Orly's heirs continue to do business in Zurich. They have sales records going back to the establishment of their company in 1868. I could at least learn the identity of the first purchaser." He sounded eager to undertake his assignment. "There are instances when one comes across the most amazing stories."

"I'm sure," I said. "Would they know anything about its most recent buyer?"

"Only if the transaction was for some reason conducted under their auspices." There was nothing more to say, and Oppenheimer rose to escort us to the door. "Should you wish to have the rest of your mother's jewelry examined, I shall be pleased . . ." He shook my hand and bowed in farewell.

Ariadne and I stepped out into the street. We had not exchanged a word since leaving Oppenheimer's office, and the silence lay between us, heavy and dense. I was too dazed to take it all in; Ariadne too seemed withdrawn.

"I'd give anything for a drink," I said.

"And I," she linked arms with mine, "have got a thirst that oceans couldn't quench."

We walked down Fifth Avenue as far as Fifty-fourth Street, where we turned left toward Madison Avenue, finding a quiet little pub on the way. The far end of the bar was vacant, allowing us to sit at the corner facing one another. Ariadne elected to stick with her usual gin and tonic, and I ordered a double vodka. She sipped her drink, but I tossed mine down. When she was halfway through her first drink I had disposed of my third. The alcohol did little for my headache—on the contrary. But the liquor helped wonderfully to focus my mind.

I thought about my mother. Ever since her death, I had wondered how well I really knew this strange woman, so detached from the present, so deeply immersed in distant times and remote places. Above all, I was haunted by the memory of her tireless efforts to transpose me into an effeminate misfit, sending me to ballet classes, piano lessons, and needlework courses. The mere thought that I might follow my natural masculine instincts was enough to drive her to distraction. I was humiliated by her obsessions and terrified of her fits of madness that often led to her being hospitalized.

She never told me the story of her tragic love for my father; the mystery surrounding this man who constituted the sole pivot of her world was compounded by her refusal to even mention his name. I only knew that he died while on a secret mission for his country and that my grandfather referred to him as "der Spion"—the spy.

Indeed, in one very tangible way, he remained the staff of her life, since her only income was the pension she drew as his widow. But that precisely pinpointed the present riddle: the monthly payment was no more than a pittance, a sum that could never add up to the price of the damned ring.

Abruptly, I turned to Ariadne. "I truly had no idea," I said without any preface.

"How do you suppose the ring came into your mother's possession?" she asked.

"I wish to hell I knew. Maybe my Aunt Bertha can help.

I'm not sure. My mother was more than halfway crazy, and she could endure life only by withdrawing deep into her shell, where no one could get at her, not even Bertha."

I could no longer think straight, nor could I stand the pub. After dropping Ariadne at the Dakota, I indulged myself in a rare luxury: I hailed a cab and told the driver to take me out to Brooklyn, to Avenue Z.

Wednesday, I arranged to meet Ariadne after work, for a second visit to Paul Oppenheimer's office. I intended to take the jeweler up on his offer to inspect the rest of my mother's collection.

I wrapped the velvet-bound jewelry box in a brown paper grocer's bag. Slightly embarrassed, I clutched the bag under my arm as I rode the early morning subway. When I reached the office, I stuffed it into the closet. That done, I seated myself at my desk and worked without respite. My assignment was another translation for Sheikh Ibrahim Ibn Aziz, and in view of that gentleman's insistence on flawless Arabic, I intended to give the task my complete attention. Nevertheless, I caught myself making repeated errors. Ordinarily, I would have taken a short break to clear my mind, but such self-indulgence was out of the question today: in one week, I was to accompany my employers to Riyadh, and the translation had to be completed in time to allow for corrections. I flung myself into my work, trying to drive my other concerns out of my thoughts.

When I finally left, darkness had fallen. I set out toward Fifth Avenue, trying to keep warm by walking quickly. It struck me that my swift stride would present a challenge to my ever-present shadow, but I made no attempt to single him out: just this once, his presence did not bother me.

I spotted Ariadne standing at the entrance to the building, bundled up against the cold. She saw me coming and raised an arm to greet me. Her hair glistened in the street light, and my heartbeats accelerated. There could be no further doubt about the place this young woman occupied in my life. She represented the appeal of the unknown, and I sensed that wondrous things would befall me in her company.

I apologized for my lack of punctuality, blaming it on my

work. Ariadne glanced at her watch and grinned: "You're right on time—I just got here." She steered me into the office building. "I'm excited," she confessed. "Something important's about to happen."

"Second sight?"

"My heart tells me." She laid my hand on her breast in the most natural way imaginable, totally indifferent to the people about us. "Do you feel it beating?"

I nodded, my cheeks glowing. "Don't pin too many hopes on dime-store trinkets," I said.

"What a pessimist you are. A person can't live without faith in something. No one belongs exclusively to the present; there's always something that transcends the time dimension. You have to seek answers to the riddles as they arise. It's like fitting the right key into each door to allow yourself to advance further."

"Maybe."

Her regard was critical. "You're on edge."

"That's hardly surprising. This business is unnerving."

I was relieved when the elevator stopped on the seventh floor, putting an end to our exchange. The same elegantly clothed secretary received us, showing the way into Oppenheimer's private office.

The jeweler welcomed us with the courtesy reserved for honored clients, though when his eyes fell on my brown paper parcel, his face took on a slightly disdainful look. I could hardly blame him.

"I see you've brought the collection." His tone was polite. In my skeptical mood, I was sure he regretted the encouragement he had given me the previous day, which now obliged him to waste his time on a pile of cheap rubbish.

But it was too late for regrets: I hauled the old jewel box out of the paper bag and laid it on the desk. "Sorry to put you to so much trouble."

"It's no trouble," he replied mildly. With an unhurried turn of the wrist, he opened the box. He did not immediately extract its contents; instead, he bent forward, scanning the trinkets where they lay. His gaze was sharp and penetrating; his lips were pursed. After several minutes of silent inspection, he opened a drawer in his desk to produce a roll of black velvet, which he spread out before him. Then he brought out a set of magnifying glasses of various sizes, arranging them on the desk with great deliberation. Next, he reached for what resembled an articulated reading lamp, which turned out to be a self-illuminating enlarger of the type used by stamp collectors. Oppenheimer directed its light at the various pieces of jewelry, laying each one in turn on the velvet material for a better view. He took special care in examining the coronet with the strange winged camel. My impression was that he didn't think highly of the design or of the value of the piece. But his expression remained inscrutable, his silence giving no clue to his observations.

I exchanged a nervous glance with Ariadne, who seemed equally on tenterhooks. Like me, she must have been thinking that the prolongation of the jeweler's examination foreshadowed some unexpected revelation. Most of the collection was worthless, that was indisputable; but who knew, I speculated, it might include one or two pieces of value, in addition to the ring.

Oppenheimer now picked out the last of the trinkets, submitting it to the same searching examination as its predecessors. Then, with smooth, unhurried movements, he flicked off the enlarger light, folded up the velvet, and replaced it in its drawer, together with the magnifying glasses. He raised his head, offering me a glimpse of the tiny beads of perspiration clinging to his forehead and upper lip. The inspection could not have taken more than twenty minutes, but he looked exhausted.

The jeweler was in no hurry to pronounce his verdict. Drawing off his gold-rimmed eyeglasses, he polished the thick lenses with a piece of soft hide, simultaneously subjecting first Ariadne and then me to a pensive gaze I found difficult to interpret. He now cleared his throat, evidently in preparation for his pronouncement. I tensed on the edge of my seat, waiting. "Fascinating . . ." he said and fell silent once more.

I endured several more moments of this suspense before the oracle spoke again. "Mister Kottler, what we see before us is a stunning collection of rare creations, the likes of which I have not often seen. Their design is of the finest, and they are set with stones of unusual quality."

I stared at him thunderstruck, the blood rushing to my face. I wanted to say something, but all I could get out was "You mean it isn't just the ring?"

"Precisely."

"All of them—the whole lot?"

"Every single one." He glanced at the collection. "Not all are by d'Orly, though I did pick out four pieces of his. The others are contemporary."

"Could you put a date on them?"

"Ten to twenty years, more or less." He paused. "What lies beyond any doubt is that you are to be congratulated, Mister Kottler. You are a wealthy man."

"How wealthy?" I asked, my voice trembling.

"I cannot yet offer a precise valuation of each piece—that will take another day or two. As a cautious estimate, however, their combined value is around five million dollars."

My grin must have been inane. I sensed the perspiration on my forehead. "That's impossible," I muttered. "I just can't take it in. I walked in here a poor man, and now you tell me I'm a millionaire." I turned my gaze toward Ariadne. "Isn't it—unbelievable?"

She nodded, her eyes sparkling. "It's fantastic!"

"It'll take some time to get used to the idea," I mumbled foolishly. I flung a wary glance at the jeweler. "Mister Oppenheimer, you're an expert, I know, and I trust your judgment. But all the same—could there be some mistake in your valuation?"

His smile was mild. "There could—but it would be in your favor. I hope you find that gratifying."

Gratifying, I thought, of course it's gratifying. My God, this ought to be the happiest moment of my life. Why, then, am I on fire; why is my stomach turning over? I sat motionless, endeavoring to give no outward sign of the ferment. Things would never again be as they were in the past. "What do I do now?" I inquired helplessly.

"I suggest you deposit the jewels with me until you decide how to dispose of them."

"Certainly."

"You may leave them with me as long as you wish," the jeweler proposed. "The charge will be reasonable. Our premises are well protected; our safe is under electronic supervision more sophisticated than the systems used by the major banks."

He went away to make the necessary arrangements; in the

31

meantime, his secretary entered, summoned by the press of a button, and poured us drinks, which we consumed in a silence broken only by the notes of a Chopin nocturne from hidden stereo speakers.

An hour later the heavy door opened and Oppenheimer reappeared, apologizing for the delay. He brought a slim blue folder, engraved in gold with the name Oppenheimer, and a pair of keys, which he extended to me. "These belong to your safe. And this," he opened the folder at the first page, "contains the formal receipts for your valuables."

I leafed through: each page was devoted to a different piece, with a precise specification of the metal, the gem settings, and other identifying marks, supplemented by a photograph of the item.

"It's very impressive," I said, "practically a pedigree certificate."

Oppenheimer promised to contact me as soon as he completed his valuation. As we stood up to leave, I remembered something. With a muttered apology, I turned to the desk, leaning over it to pick up the paper bag. I saw Oppenheimer and Ariadne staring at me. To my relief, I detected no smile on either face. Unsure what to do with the bag, I stuffed it into my overcoat pocket. In its way, it was a last souvenir of Brooklyn. When we got to the street, I yanked it out of my pocket and dropped it into a garbage can.

I had not uttered a word since leaving Oppenheimer's office, and I paused now on the sidewalk, confused and helpless.

It was Ariadne who finally broke the silence. "I guess you don't want to talk about the jewelry."

"Not now." I shook my head vigorously. "Later, maybe."

"Is there anything you'd like to do?"

"I'm starving," I said. Indeed, I had not eaten all day, my appetite dulled by the suspense. Now, it returned with a vengeance. "Let's go somewhere really fancy."

We opted for a restaurant nearby, where we were ushered to a table in a shadowy corner. My thoughts wandered back to the scene in Oppenheimer's office. Only now was I beginning to take in the full significance of his pronouncement about my mother's jewels.

Yet, in the back of my mind, another thought was stirring, sending out warning waves of unease. If Oppenheimer was right, the serpent whispered, then my mother must have . . . No, I told myself resolutely. No! No! No! All that matters now is that I'm rich.

"You're a wealthy man, Daniel." With her hand pressing my arm, Ariadne must have read my thoughts. "But it's more than the money," she went on earnestly. "The jewelry is somehow linked with some secret of enormous importance to you. It has to do with the man you've been till now and the man you will be in the future."

"Those premonitions of yours are beginning to frighten me," I said.

Slowly, I seized her hand and kissed it. I lowered it, continuing to gaze into her eyes where I read a curiosity I fully shared. Like her, I too sensed that the discovery of my mother's treasure was no mere instance of an unexpected windfall. Certainly, I was experiencing an earthquake.

"Do you know—" I began, but broke off. The thought gnawing at the back of my mind was beginning to emerge from its lair.

Ariadne eyed me sharply. "What were you about to say?"

"I'm just wondering." I tried to keep my tone casual, but I could hear the tremor in my voice. "About my mother."

"Your mother?"

"She was a gentle lady with an obsession for cleanliness and purity," I said, taking a gulp of my drink. I mumbled a curse under my breath, but Ariadne heard.

"You never use that kind of language," she said. She was wrong, of course; it was merely one habit of mine with which she was as yet unfamiliar.

"All women are whores," I growled. I laid a hand on my chest. "I sense it here."

"Daniel!"

"Fuck it!" I roared suddenly. "My mother was a whore. A fucking whore!"

Embarrassed, Ariadne cautioned me gently. "It's your mother you're talking about."

"Sure I am, and I'll tell you what my conclusions are." Unsteadily, I leaned across the table. "My mother had a lover. Two or three times a year she went off to Miami to make a fast buck in a few days of fucking with some millionaire. And me"—my voice rose in sudden fury—"and me she fed some story about visiting a sick relative. Fucking lies!"

Ariadne stared at me with a blend of dismay and pity. "Let's not talk about the jewelry," she said. "You've become rich overnight. That's good grounds for celebration, so come on, forget all the rest and let's celebrate."

She was right. I dismissed my doubts and we proceeded to make a night of it. After our meal at the restuarant, we went pub-crawling along First and Second avenues, then took a cab to Sardi's, where a ten-dollar bill in the headwaiter's palm got us a table for two, well placed for a good view of the celebrities. By eleven, the restaurant was packed. Our table attracted a continual stream of Ariadne's friends. I shook hands with some and exchanged a few noncommittal phrases with others, all the time hoping that I was not putting Ariadne to shame.

"What a surprise!" I heard a familiar voice. Raising my eyes from my glass, I encountered the shapely presence of Sheila Griffiths. She was standing over our table in the company of a tall man who looked like a movie star. Ariadne whispered that he was Sheila's regular date, here from the West Coast for a few days in her company. They managed to retrieve a couple of chairs and seated themselves at our table. I listened with silent disdain as Kirk—the golden boy from California—detailed the list of stunts he was expected to perform in his forthcoming movie.

Sheila suggested we go dancing, and we all agreed at once. Enthusiastically, we set off, starting at Studio 54 and ending up at the Red Parrot. Ariadne was taken by my skills as a dancer.

"You're very good!" she cried.

"That's not surprising," I replied cheerfully, holding her tight, "after three years of ballet classes."

She halted momentarily. "I thought you were kidding."

"I wasn't," I replied. "Nor was my mother."

The music was soft and slow now, and I wanted it to go on and on so that I would not have to release my grip on Ariadne. She leaned her head against my chest, where she could probably hear the thumping of my heart. Her breasts pressed against me, and my knee brushed her inner thigh. I wanted her with a longing akin to physical pain.

The slow music faded away, to be replaced by the thunderous tattoo of a disco beat. Picking up our coats, we walked out and stood on the sidewalk, undecided what to do next. It was after midnight, though the rumble of traffic indicated that the city was still wide awake. Kirk proposed a nightcap at a bar not far from Ariadne's apartment. But I thought it was time to get some sleep: the dancing had sobered me up sufficiently to recall that, my newfound wealth notwithstanding, the following morning would require my punctual appearance at the Park Avenue office. I asked Kirk and Sheila to take Ariadne home.

"What about you?" Ariadne said. "Where are you going?"

"Don't worry," I replied airily. Someone was prowling in the nearby unlit alleyway. Instantaneously, the mist in my head cleared; my nerves and muscles went taut.

Sheila came over to me. "You can't walk the streets alone. You're drunk."

"Oh anyone can see I'm a g-good guy," I bellowed. "And everybody loves a good g-guy." My drunken clowning was intentional, staged for the benefit of my unseen watcher. Meanwhile, I was measuring distance. I couldn't take any chances; when I moved, it would have to be fast.

Sheila appealed to Ariadne. "He isn't fit to go anywhere."

"Of course not," Kirk said. "He'll get mugged." He turned to me. "Don't forget where you are, man. This is Manhattan."

"Ain't you all a bunch of nervous nellies," I giggled. I had the distance about right now. "I can take ex-exshellent c-care of myself."

Ariadne looked at me. "They're right, Daniel, you know they are." Her concern was evident; she must have suspected me of being knocked off balance by the day's events. I lurched forward, but she propped me up. "You've had a little too much."

I responded with a sharp battle cry, which made her draw back in alarm. Without warning, I flung myself into the air to complete a backward somersault, landing on my feet in a karate combat stance. "How was that?" I grinned.

She looked stunned. Before she could respond, I repeated

my reverse flips until I disappeared into the alleyway. My unknown tracker was there; I could sniff his sweat. I picked him out as he pressed against the wall, completely disconcerted by my bizarre antics. Before he could regain his equilibrium, I completed my final somersault by driving my right foot into his groin. He uttered a soft groan and crumpled to the ground.

Swiftly, I bent over to inspect him in the half-light. His eyes were shut and he was breathing heavily. He was, I saw, about my own age, with smooth, flat features. I picked out his wallet and discovered the ID testifying that he was one of Charlie's men.

The entire tussle had taken no more than a moment or two. Now, straightening up in the dark alleyway, I let out another cry, then flung myself into a renewed series of flips, until I emerged from the alleyway and came to a sharp halt in front of Ariadne. "You shee," I mumbled, "I'm perfeckly . . ."

Ariadne reached the appropriate decision. "Okay, I'll stay with him," she told Sheila.

Sheila came over and gave me a hug and a kiss. "I'll see ya. You're an utter maniac and I like that." Kirk laid an arm around Sheila's narrow hips, and the pair marched in unison down the street.

When we were left alone, Ariadne turned to me. "What now?"

"I dunno." My tongue was swollen, as though from a bee sting. My voice was strangely thick. I'm high, I thought. Not before. Now.

"You don't look well."

"I'm not used to that kind of celebration." My stomach was churning. My attempt to evade the facts had left me with nothing more than a sense of nausea. Nothing had changed: I stood at a crossroads, uncertain whether to turn left or right.

"You don't have to talk if you don't want to," Ariadne said.

"I need to breathe." The cold air hit my lungs. "And walk," I added, taking one step forward.

"Let's get a cab," Ariadne proposed.

"I'd rather walk." I would have fallen had Ariadne not been there in time to catch me.

Arm in arm, we walked slowly along the deserted streets,

while I told Ariadne about that day when I was fifteen and stayed on in school to train for the long-jump competition. When I got home, I expected hell from my mother for getting back so late. I excelled at athletics, but she never showed the least pride or interest in my achievements; she didn't say a word. I found her on edge and restless; I thought she was on the verge of one of her sporadic attacks. She was all dressed up in a gleaming white outfit, with long gloves reaching up above the elbows and a white hat bordered with a narrow green velvet ribbon. She was pale with agitation. "I've got to go to Miami, to Cousin Reizel," she told me rapidly, her voice unnaturally loud. "I'll be back in a few days."

"That was the first time," I told Ariadne. "After that, for five straight years, right up to the time she was killed in a car accident, she went away regularly, once or twice a year. To take care of her cousin. Some cousin!"

In spite of the early morning chill, my face ran with perspiration. I felt sorry for myself, mourning the home I had lost, the parents I never had, and the woman in white who once lived in Brooklyn.

"Let's make love," I said.

God bless her, Ariadne did not hasten to reply; instead, she examined me at length, her expression displaying greater understanding than anyone had ever shown me. She smiled wanly. "We can make love anytime." She paused. "Anytime, but not now."

"Why not?"

"Because," she replied gently, "you'll wake up in the morning and you won't remember a thing."

3

When I opened my eyes, I found myself surrounded by the eminent faces that once adorned the court of His Imperial Highness Czar Nikolai. On all sides, I glimpsed the distinguished features of men and women whose corpses were later to litter the bloodstained ascent of Lenin, Trotsky, and Stalin.

I was particularly taken with an oil on the opposite wall, in which a thick-bearded figure, sporting the epaulets of high rank, laid an elegantly languorous hand on the sword girded at his waist. I bowed a deferential greeting to Ariadne's noble grandfather, Prince Andrey Andreyevitch.

On the upholstered armchair at the side of the bed lay my clothes, neatly folded as though my mother had sneaked in during the night to make sure her son's life-style remained decorous and orderly. I had not the faintest recollection of how I was brought here to Ariadne's apartment; it must have been difficult to get me up here in the state I was in.

I raised my head warily, fearing that an abrupt movement

would send a stab of pain through my temples. But to my surprise, my head was clear and light. Tossing aside the blanket, I found myself dressed in blue silk pajamas—probably an heirloom left by Ariadne's father. I sat up, stretching my arms, and stepped over to the window, to survey the building's inner courtyard with the stone basin of its fountain, gray from long disuse. I glanced at my watch. Five on the dot. I had awakened precisely at my regular time.

I found a bathroom obviously prepared for me, with fresh towels, a razor, and a toothbrush. I finished my toilet and set off in search of Ariadne, discovering her in an enormous bedroom adjoining the library, where she was stretched out in a huge canopy bed. I tiptoed over, eager to see her asleep. She lay there like some Snow White sunk in a bewitched slumber that preserved her youth for all eternity. Her head seemed to hover over the pillow; she breathed lightly. Bending over with great care, I let my lips brush lightly over hers. Instantly, I turned and left the room, hastening into the kitchen where I boiled up some water for coffee.

That Thursday morning of the most bizarre week of my life, I reached the office at seven. When my secretary arrived two hours later, I told her to hold all calls; I was in need of time to myself. I did not want to see Ariadne, and I was sure she would understand: I had to digest matters in my own way. I studied my American Express receipts and was horrified to learn that I had spent over three hundred dollars in a single evening. I must have been out of my mind to waste such an enormous sum. I had the disconcerting sensation of housing two separate personalities within me: one more or less familiar, the other only recently emerging. I was shaken by this sense of a dual personality; I could only hope it was merely another symptom of the stress I had endured in recent weeks, ever since Charlie began hounding me with his calls about Beirut.

My first confrontation with Mike Donnevy, a.k.a. Charlie, flashed before my eyes. It came at a time I would not easily forget. I was just beginning to work on my master's degree, a few months after my mother's accidental death. An examination of her bank account showed I had been left with nothing. Aunt Bertha toyed with the idea of raising the money for my tuition by taking out a second mortgage on the house, a proposal I rejected out of hand. Instead I turned for help to my department head, Professor Oreseley. Oreseley was sympathetic to my problem and said he could easily find a sponsor to finance the rest of my education.

In spite of my naïveté, it did not take me long to grasp what my professor was up to: Oreseley was a recruiter for some arm of the federal government; particularly favored targets were those students in difficult financial straits. The realization gave me a thrill of hope. I had heard of certain official agencies that underwrote tuition for students who met the agencies' qualifications. For their part, the candidates signed a long-term service contract that came into effect immediately upon their graduation.

A week after I had spoken to him, Professor Oreseley notified me that a meeting had been arranged for me, in the bar of the Warwick Hotel, with a man by the name of Charlie. Precisely at noon on the appointed day, I walked toward the far end of the bar to a table that was occupied by a thin, lanky figure reading *The Washington Post*.

As I marched up, he laid down his paper and nodded a greeting. His was a horse face if ever I had seen one. Rarely had I encountered a human countenance of such disproportionate length: his cheeks were sunken and his jaw stood out strangely, as though he were continually munching hay.

Folding up his newspaper with precise, measured movements, the man studied me closely. "Mister Kottler?" His voice was soft, almost a whisper, and I thought I detected the trace of a sneer.

"That's me."

"Come and sit down, boy."

Without any preface, Charlie steered the interview toward my personal biography, asking for a description of my upbringing. I told him about Avenue Z, about Bobbeh and Zeideh, about Bertha and Sam, about going to the temple on Saturdays and Jewish festivals. Assuming he had done some preliminary research on me, I saw no grounds to conceal my mother's eccentricities and medical history or the fact that my late father had been an Israeli who was killed while on some intelligence mission for his country.

40

Charlie seemed to be enjoying my account of our run-of-the-mill Jewish family, which, like others of its kind, blended Eastern European cultural roots with a natural curiosity and sensitivity about Israel. Then suddenly he broke into my words. "I understand you speak good Hebrew."

Taken off guard, I blurted out an imprudent reply. "Like a native-born Israeli."

Charlie's eyes narrowed. He obviously found my reply significant because he took a moment to digest it before resuming. "Some Americans believe that if Israel were in trouble, the Je-e-ews," he drawled out the word, "would help in any way, even at the expense of their allegiance to the United States." With no change in his expression beyond a certain glint in his eyes, he added: "And you, boy . . . ?"

I decided to meet his challenge head on. "I'd find it easier to reply if you simply asked what I'd do if I had to choose between the interests of Israel and of America."

He eyed me with appreciation. "What's your answer?"

"My attitude toward Israel is reserved, but that's where some of my roots lie; the rest lie here, in this country."

Charlie looked reflective, and I thought he was succumbing to weariness as his eyelids drooped. But he reopened them swiftly, and his gaze was alert. "Suppose we were to decide that you are the kind of material that could interest certain officials . . ."

My imagination soared. From the hint Charlie had thrown out, I guessed the job was in the intelligence field. Perhaps the CIA wanted to call upon my knowledge of Semitic languages by putting me to work on cyphers at some embassy. I was elated at the prospect.

Charlie further reinforced my assessment. "We may want you to sign a long-term contract," he said.

"I'm ready to try." I sensed a further wave of elation. It was the hand of destiny reaching out to touch me; it was as though providence had made my path cross that of my father's. The thought of following my father's footsteps into the field of intelligence work filled me with excitement—an excitement that testified finally and convincingly to my mother's failure to mold my character to her crazy ideas.

In mid-February 1975, I got a message from Charlie summoning me to Washington for a stay of several days. Reporting as requested, I found myself entrusted to a row of experts in various fields who subjected me to dozens of tests aimed at pinpointing any defects, physical or psychic. It was an exhausting procedure, and by week's end I felt I had been squeezed dry. Charlie drove me to the airport, seeing me off with a handshake, but not a single word of encouragement.

Weeks passed before I heard from him again. This time, he called me to Washington to sign a contract with the CIA. My ordeal was ended; I had achieved my goal. My gratification might have waned had I been able to peer into the future. For the moment, the feeling uppermost in my mind was elation at my first success in attaining a common denominator with my father, by finding my way into the shadowy world that had always fired my imagination.

I returned to my studies, thankfully freed of financial burdens. My tuition was paid directly to Columbia's bursary, and my modest bank account was enriched by a remittance that permitted me to share in the upkeep of our Avenue Z home. At the time, I was unaware that the Washington experts had found me gifted with all the high endowments required for an efficient hit man.

In fact, as I was to discover later, it was Charlie alone who made the final decision to have me trained as an assassinator. By then, I was so deeply indoctrinated in the CIA and so beholden to Charlie that I didn't have a choice. The bastard had found my weak spot and had played on it by placing himself in the role of the father figure I never had. He brought me to such heights of admiration and emulation that I was even willing to kill in order to win his respect.

But no more.

I left the office without asking my secretary whether any calls had come in for me.

At 6:15, I got out of the subway station at Sheepshead Bay where I headed for the anchorage that housed a handsome thirty-foot sailing dinghy, a single-master I occasionally rented from a Polish friend, Jazhek Dizma. Jazhek kept a small store, selling fishing tackle and bait, and I stopped by to tell him I would be coming in the following day to rent the sailboat for the weekend. I then continued on my way, dropping into Angelo's for a dish of my favorite seafood. It did wonders in restoring my jaded spirits.

As I walked down Avenue Z, a rapid glance picked out Aunt Bertha perched in her upper-story window, awaiting me. Her daily vigilance was an expression of her loneliness. Bobbeh and Zeideh had died within a year after my enlistment into the CIA. Uncle Sam passed away a few years later, in 1977, the year I presented my doctoral thesis. Just the two of us were left, Bertha and me. Unless I called to tell her not to expect me home that day, she would sit there, dividing her attention between what went on in the street and the Sony television set strategically situated at her side. Never once had she missed my return home, sometimes waiting for me until the early hours of the morning. Whenever I arrived, she would summon me for a cup of coffee and a chat.

Bertha greeted me in the kitchen. "How's things?"

"Everything's fine," I said. She recognized instantly that I was lying.

"You ate?"

I nodded. "At Angelo's."

"You want some coffee then." She knew I didn't drink Angelo's coffee, just as she was tolerantly aware of my weakness for his ritually impure shellfish. Bertha ran a kosher household, though less from adherence to Jewish religious ritual than out of loyalty to tradition. Bertha was no ordinary aunt: in many ways, she had taken the place of my mother. She was adept at keeping a conversation going, rambling on about all kinds of unconnected topics until she found an opportunity to pinpoint whatever was troubling me. This evening, she declared herself profoundly dissatisfied with the White House. The President's meeting with Mubarak and Hussein was not at all to her liking. It was going behind Shamir's back, and Bertha had no sympathy for such underhanded dealings. Not enough the President decided to pull the marines out of Lebanon; suddenly he's on buddy-buddy terms with the Saudis, at the expense of relations with Israel. Bertha was eternally anxious about the security of the Jewish state.

43

"It's a pity you aren't more concerned," she complained.

"I used to be," I shrugged, unwilling to be drawn in.

She regarded me reproachfully. "And you speak such good Hebrew, just like an Israeli. If you ever went there, you'd feel at home right away, like one of them."

This was my cue and I leapt at it. "That's hardly surprising. After all, I was almost one of them." Laying great stress on my words, I added, "Just like my father."

Bertha stared at me in wonder, evidently taken aback by my temerity in touching on a subject that had always been taboo. "Your father?" She scrutinized me sharply. "How come you're suddenly interested in your father?"

I avoided her eyes. "Don't you think I want to know about him?"

"What is it you want to know?"

"All kinds of things. I don't even know how he and my mother met."

A gentle smile softened Bertha's wrinkled features. "In a way," she said, "it was your grandfather's fault they ever came near one another." The occasion, she recalled, was the 1936 Levant Fair, a commercial exhibition mounted to promote the economy of the Holy Land. Her father, being an ardent Zionist, decided that this was the perfect opportunity to take his family on a visit to the land of the Jews.

After a two-week cruise, their ship anchored about a mile offshore, unable to approach any closer to Tel Aviv's tiny new port. The passengers were ferried ashore by boat.

Tel Aviv was less than thirty years old at the time of the fair, and construction was going on feverishly. Jews were pouring in at that period, refugees from Nazi Germany for the most part, often highly educated people who made the city into a vibrant, vital center. "It was like an ancient prophecy coming true before our eyes." Bertha dabbed at her nose with her handkerchief.

The Kottlers stayed at the Savoy, a small hotel near the beach, built in Levantine style—all arches and reliefs—its facade painted a dazzling white. The day after their arrival, they went to visit the exhibition, set out in large pavilions to the north of the town. "I'll never forget it as long as I live. It was a turmoil of sights and sounds, like a costume parade. The young Jews wore light-colored shirts and knee-length khaki shorts. The local Arabs wore long flowing robes, and rich Egyptian effendis came in European suits with red tarbooshes on their heads. Here and there we saw some elderly Jews, new immigrants, elegantly dressed as though they'd just come from some diplomatic reception."

The first feature of the fair to catch their eyes, Bertha recalled, was a thirty-foot-high pillar. "And at the top stood the emblem of the fair, a flying camel."

"A flying camel?" I recalled the curious headpiece in my mother's jewel box.

Bertha nodded. "It represented the East awakening from its slumber," she explained. "It was rearing up, its hind legs attached to the pillar, while the front pair were folded up beneath its belly, and the wings were stretched out in flight."

She was describing exactly the mounting of the white metal coronet. There was no room for doubt. And no coincidence could be that farfetched.

Bertha was too immersed in nostalgia to notice my agitation. "And that," she said, "was where we met your father. I remember like it was yesterday. Suddenly, I saw this young man pacing about near the entrance, not far from where we stood. He was tall, almost as tall as you are. He had a slim build, and he moved with a light, agile stride. He had hair like yours, the same texture—but pitch-black, as though it had been dyed. And even from that distance, twenty paces maybe, I could pick out the piercing gray of his eyes." Bertha smiled. "I noticed his eyes instantly, because they were fixed on Rachel. Staring at her without shame or embarrassment, with total concentration, like there was no one else in the whole wide world but Rachel. And Rachel . . ." Bertha shook her head, even now, forty-eight years later, still enraptured with the wonder of that moment. "She was staring right back. I was startled. It was the first time I realized that my kid sister wasn't a little girl any longer. I turned to Zeideh and suggested that we find someone to take a snapshot of us beside the flying camel. And quickly, before he could say anything, I walked over to the young man and held the camera out to him. That was how I started the ball rolling."

"Maybe you just provided a shortcut."

"Maybe." Bertha's eyes glinted. "But it did speed matters

up. The young man introduced himself as Yosef Dur. Yosef offered to guide us around the exhibition. For three hours he took us on a tour of the pavilions, and all the while he scarcely took his eyes off Rachel. When we stopped off at a restaurant, Zeideh naturally invited him to join us, and it was equally natural when Yosef asked Zeideh's permission to come around to our hotel that evening to take 'the girls,' as he called us, to the first concert of the new Palestine Philharmonic Orchestra." It was much later before the Kottlers learned how Dur came to have the tickets: he had been delegated by the Hagana underground to act as bodyguard to Arturo Toscanini, who had come to the Holy Land to conduct its inaugural concert.

"Orchestral violins providing background music for the first date," I said teasingly. "It sounds very romantic . . ."

Bertha flung me a reproving glance. "That's just the way it was—romantic. That was how your mother and father began their love affair."

"Why did they take so long to get married?"

"On account of the wars," Bertha replied, her use of the plural mystifying me. When that summer came to an end, the Kottlers returned to New York. Yosef Dur must have realized there was nothing he could do until Rachel reached seventeen. In the meantime, he wrote her regularly and made plans to come to the States in the late fall of 1939. That plan, of course, came to nothing.

When World War Two broke out, Yosef Dur enlisted in the British army. He served in combat throughout the war, emerging uninjured. After his release from the army, he finally managed to come to the United States. "That was in October of forty-seven. I was already four years married to your Uncle Sam, may his soul rest in peace. What we saw then was like the eruption of an extinct volcano, an outpouring of molten lava scorching everything that lay in its path. That was the way their love re-kindled, like a fire, after eleven years with nothing to hold them together but the letters they exchanged. A bridge of paper, but it was stronger than steel."

"How old was he at the time?" I asked.

"He was the age you are now—thirty-one, thirty-two maybe. He was thinner than I remembered him, his eyes a more pronounced gray. He was more withdrawn and wary, like some ferocious jungle beast. He walked like a beast too, with a light tread, and constantly on guard. The war had affected him, though I know very little about what he did, and we didn't ask questions. He was a loner by choice. If Yosef Dur held back about his personal experiences, he was outspoken on his commitment to the Jewish nation. 'The supreme duty is to serve your people,' he always said."

"I admire men like that," I sneered. "The nation uber alles. Shit!"

Bertha showed anger at my disrespect. "Don't be in such a hurry to put him down. When you were with him, you felt safe. He was like a rock."

"And—my mother?"

"Blossomed like a flower! She burst into bloom with the ecstasy of her love. A few days after Yosef Dur's arrival, they decided to get married. The date was fixed for December. But a few weeks earlier, on November 29, 1947, the United Nations voted to partition Palestine, with one-half allotted to the Jews. That night, the Arabs launched their first armed attacks."

"And that was his cue to gallop off into the fray—so bang went the chosseneh."

My flippancy evidently irritated Bertha, but she overlooked my interruption. "Your mother wanted to go back with him. But Zeideh wouldn't hear of it. He didn't want his Rucheleh mixed up in a war. Your father assured him that a Jewish victory was certain, but Zeideh refused to listen."

"It sounds like a battle of wills."

"It was—between Zeideh and Rachel. But she won. Six or seven months later, she took a plane to Europe and reached Marseilles. From there, she boarded a ship carrying immigrants to Haifa—concentration camp survivors. She arrived one month after Israel's independence, but Yosef wasn't there. He had just left on a mission to Yemen to organize the Jewish community there for its airborne exodus to Israel. Nobody could tell her when he'd be back. Time passed and we didn't hear a word from her—until one night she called, yelling for joy, to say that Yosef had returned from his mission and they had just gotten married at his family home in Tiberias. She was the first bride ever to

47

stand under the canopy surrounded on all sides by Jewish spies—"

"Spies?"

"Your father's colleagues from the Mossad. What a chosseneh, with each pole of the canopy held up by a Jewish James Bond . . ."

"And after the wedding?" I prompted gently.

"Those first few months of married life must have been glorious." Bertha's eyes were distant and dreamy. "Rachel's letters overflowed with happiness. Bobbeh and Zeideh were overjoyed. And then, late March 1952, Rachel sent word that she was coming home. When she got here, she gave no explanation. Not a hint. But she told us she was three months pregnant. She looked half-dead. I could sense that something terrible had happened. We all held off from asking, waiting for her to tell us. One day, when we were sitting in Zeideh's lounge, she broke down and poured it all out. He—your father—had gone on a mission, but had never returned. And wouldn't come back ever, she screamed, because he was dead. Dead! She gave no details; she never referred to it again. That evening, she just sat there hugging her belly, as though already cradling her baby, already protecting it from a savage, cruel world."

Bertha paused, staring into space. There was a long moment of silence. I said nothing.

"That marked the onset of the most agonizing period of her life." Bertha's voice dropped to a somber whisper. "Rachel had to live with her loneliness and her bereavement. It was heartbreaking to watch her." She glanced at me. "When you were born, I went to see her in the hospital. She held you in her arms and told me she hoped you'd take after her. She didn't want you to resemble your father. She didn't want you to remind her of him. That's why she went to such trouble to bring you up totally unlike—"

"Totally unlike a man," I broke in harshly.

Bertha pursed her lips. "She hoped for a girl."

"And instead, she got a boy. A boy who was a good athlete. But she never wanted to accept that."

"Of course she didn't. It was a trait you inherited from him."

"She tried to erase all trace of my father."

"She tried and failed. He couldn't be erased; she herself never came to terms with his death. To her, he was immortal." Bertha closed her eyes wearily. "Every time she relived his death, she was overcome with horror. Her sufferings were frightful. I can understand her desire to build a wall around you, to protect you from coming to resemble your father. She dreaded the day she'd lose you, too."

Bertha knew what she was talking about. One day, my mother found me in Bertha's bedroom, reading a book about Israel's War of Independence. She snatched the book out of my hands. "I won't have him becoming like his father!" she screamed.

That incident signaled the onset of one of my mother's periodic bouts of insanity, which led to her committal to a private nursing home in Connecticut for several months. A thought struck me. "Those treatments must have cost the earth," I said. "Where did the money come from?"

"The Israeli government paid. Whenever she got sick, we notified the Israeli consulate in Manhattan, and they got us an allotment from their Defense Ministry."

"Their help must have been a godsend."

"Without it, Sam would have had to sell this house. Those hospitals are expensive, and we just didn't have that kind of money."

"Didn't my mother have any?"

"Your mother?" Bertha was incredulous. "She barely had a cent to her name."

It was an opportunity I couldn't let slip by. I made an effort to keep my tone casual. "Suppose you were to learn that she owned a considerable amount of valuables?"

Bertha eyed me sharply. "Out of the question. When she was killed, all she had in her bank account was three hundred dollars."

I decided to probe in a new direction. "This cousin in Miami—"

"Reizel? What about her?"

"There are a few questions I'd like to ask her," I said slowly. "About the presents she gave my mother. Some jewelry, for example."

"You can't ask Reizel any questions because she died last year. And she left all of her jewelry to her daughter Sandy.

49

Anyway, your mother wouldn't have taken anything from Reizel because Reizel's taste was abominable, and your mother wasn't that crazy about jewelry herself. Did you ever see her wear any?"

I evaded her question by asking one of my own. "So she got nothing from Reizel—you're sure of that?"

"Positive."

One by one, each hypothesis was being eliminated, forcing me back to my original conclusion. A rich man who doted on my mother, probably plying her with gifts, even commissioning a specially designed coronet with a tiny winged camel set at its center . . .

"In short, when my mother died, she left nothing?"

Bertha shrugged. "Her personal possessions. A few old photographs. Papers and documents. Your father's letters . . ."

My father's letters . . . Of course! I remembered having once stumbled upon them. It could not have been long after the death of my mother. One day, I was rummaging through her closet, idly inspecting her few possessions, when my eyes fell on a bundle neatly tied together with colored ribbon. The letters were arranged in chronological order, each one carefully preserved in its original envelope. Casually, I drew out several of the yellowing pages and glanced through their contents. The few lines I deciphered were a seemingly meaningless jumble of amorous outpourings and political jargon. I replaced the letters, and from that day to this, I never gave them a second thought.

But now, I seized at Bertha's hint with the eagerness of a drowning man clutching at a lifeline. "Letters," I mumbled, making a mental note to find them again.

Bertha was studying me with a blend of concern and curiosity. "Daniel, what's happened to you? Why all these questions now?"

"I want to learn everything you know about her." I flung a challenging glance. "Was she candid with you?"

"No one was closer. I knew almost everything there was to know."

"Intimate matters?"

Bertha's eyes arrowed. "Like what?"

There was no holding back now: I had to know the truth. "Did she have a lover?"

Bertha's smile was wan. "Your mother had only one man in her life. One man, and one love. There just wasn't room for anyone else."

"You're certain?"

"I haven't the slightest doubt."

I felt a twinge of disappointment hearing Bertha's pronouncement. Her absolute insistence that my mother had been true to my father led me to suspect that she was hiding something from me. There was some chance that she wasn't aware of all of the dark corners of my mother's existence, but my gut feeling was that she was trying to protect me from some hurt.

There was nothing further to ask. I rose from my seat and headed for the door, bidding Bertha good night.

I reached my basement apartment and shut the door behind me. Only one corner of the apartment was preserved as it had been during my mother's lifetime: her bedroom. That was my destination now. When I opened the door, I regarded the room with entirely fresh eyes, as though I had never been there before.

The room was not large. On the north side, a window looked out on the tiny garden; in springtime, it showed the struggling wisps of greenery, a source of rare delight to my melancholy mother. At such times, she would spend hours gazing out, lost in her memories and private thoughts.

On the opposite wall hung a Renoir reproduction, flanked by snapshots of Bobbeh and Zeideh, taken at their prime. Bobbeh was seated upright, her gaze vigorous; and Zeideh regarded me through his round eyeglasses, eyes twinkling.

But it was a photograph on the bedside table that caught my attention. The picture was of a man on horseback: my father. There were days when my mother reclined on the bed, her chin resting on her hand and her eyes fixed on the picture with an intense stare. Alongside stood another framed snapshot depicting a charming child with fair, shoulder-length curls, Shirley Temple style. It was a portrait of me, taken as my mother would have me.

As I opened the doors of her closet, my gaze fell on a shelf filled with the clothes I wore in my early teens. I reached out a hand and picked up a pair of shabby, well-worn jeans. That zipper, I thought with a wry grin . . .

Our next-door neighbors were the Fishers, an Orthodox Jewish family with four daughters. The youngest, Moria, was delicate in appearance and demure in her ways; no one would have suspected her of being passionate. Screwing her was the dream of all the kids in the neighborhood, me included. I turned out to be the lucky one. At twelve, I was nearly two years her junior, but I must have looked older, because she picked me out unabashedly as her prospective partner in sin. She began hanging out at our house. My mother could not have helped noticing the overheated glances we exchanged. Realizing what was in the wind, she delivered an impassioned harangue, warning me to keep my distance from Moria; she accused her of wicked designs that would leave me maimed for life.

The great day came. Taking care not to be overheard, Moria whispered to me to come to their basement; she went ahead to wait for me, and I followed a few moments later. I was aglow with excitement, breathing heavily. Moria was already slipping out of her clothes, and I flung off my shirt. Then I reached down to unzip my jeans—and the fastener stuck. I heaved and struggled until I got it free, but a couple of precious minutes had been wasted. At the precise moment I finally yanked it down, the basement door flew open and my mother stormed in. I never discovered how she found us with such unerring precision: it must have been some primitive maternal instinct. She stood over us, white as chalk, screaming at me as I had never heard her scream before. "You're worse than an animal!" she yelled. Her onslaught frightened me, but it also filled me with a strange joy, as though I had succeeded at long last in asserting my true self.

Finally, accompanied by the unconcealed grins of fascinated neighbors, my mother dragged me home. With an unexpected display of physical strength, she shoved me into the shower, where she forced me to soap myself thoroughly before making me stand under alternating streams of hot and cold water.

Late that night, when I was sure my mother was asleep, I slipped into my clothes and crept out of the apartment, flitting along the deserted streets to the anchorage, to seek haven in one of Jazhek Dizma's sailboats. It was morning before my mother discovered my disappearance; as I foresaw, she almost went out of her mind. Everyone set out to search for me; by midday Aunt Bertha had ferreted out my hideout. She said nothing to me, but after she brought me home and supervised the tear-stained return, she took my mother aside for a long talk. From then on, my mother eased up in her restrictions upon me. As for Moria, I thought it prudent to steer a safe distance from her, at least for a few months.

With a shrug I returned the shabby jeans to the shelf and continued my rummaging. There was a drawer filled with lingerie, neatly pressed and sorted, pervaded with the delicate aroma of rose water. Another drawer contained belts, in a surprisingly large assortment. I opened yet another drawer and shook my head in disbelief. It was full of gloves, dozens of pairs, black and white. There were gloves for everyday wear and gloves for festive occasions; some were of ordinary material, a few bore elaborate embroidery; some were short, others long enough to extend beyond the elbow. I stood gazing down at them and remembered another evening.

It was shortly after the incident with Moria Fisher. The shock and agitation my mother experienced that day must have pushed her beyond her thin hold on sanity. She had always been a stickler for cleanliness, but from that day on, she went overboard. Her obsession led her into an unbridled frenzy. She conducted a relentless campaign to preserve our little apartment as an island of unsullied purity in a world she perceived as an open sewer.

One evening, seating myself at the table for supper, I found a pair of white gloves beside my plate. I stared at them in perplexity, unable to grasp what they were doing there. When I finally raised my eyes, I encountered my mother's firm unblinking gaze. "You're growing up, Danush," she explained with inexorable logic. Her own hands were encased in a pair of long white gloves, as had been her habit for some time. Indicating them, she went on: "You must follow my lead, if we are to safeguard the purity of our nest."

"Nest?" I wanted to yell. "It's a cuckoo's nest!" But I said nothing beyond an obedient "Yes, Mother," for fear of arousing her anger. Resigned and humiliated, with my stomach turning over, I pulled on the white linen gloves; and then, under the overjoyed gaze of those demented eyes, I picked up my knife and fork.

My mother was ecstatic at her success in drawing me into her fantasy. The following day, she bought me half a dozen pairs of gloves to wear around the house. She conducted regular inspections, and whenever she found the pair I was wearing to be less than spotless, she insisted that I change them for another pair. I must have changed three or four times a day. Every night, she would take the used pairs and drop them into boiling water to disinfect them.

I closed the drawer with a shudder. I remained standing there for a long moment before my heartbeat slowed down to its normal tempo and I could continue my search.

I reached the bottom drawer before I turned up what I was looking for: a packet carefully wrapped in faded green paper. I picked it up gingerly and found myself holding a thick bundle of letters, a hundred or more at least, each one resting in its original envelope, each one addressed: *Miss Rachel Kottler, 851 Avenue Z, Brooklyn, New York*. The handwriting was unusual, the letters large and uneven, as though laboriously formed by someone whose native language was not English. On the reverse side, the envelopes bore the name of the sender: *Yosef Dur, Tiberias, Palestine*. Some, dating from the war years, bore military addresses.

Picking out an envelope at random, I opened it carefully and slipped out the sheet of paper doubled up inside. Reverently, I unfolded it and laid it on the bed. With that first glance, my pulse raced: the letter was unsigned. Instead of a signature, it bore the skillfully executed sketch of a winged camel.

I sat there scanning the forms of the words. The Hebrew handwriting bore little resemblance to its English counterpart. The Hebrew letters were small on the whole, though a few were extended, and others ended in a sharp flourish. In either language, my father's handwriting hardly qualified as elegant, but that was not what struck me at that particular moment. What seized my attention was the characteristic shape of certain letters and the sudden realization that, had I not known they were in my father's hand, I would have sworn it was I who had written them.

54

My excitement grew the moment I actually began to read. Soon, however, my intrusion into the intimacy of my parents' relationship became too disturbing, and I could not continue. I was suddenly tired and emotionally spent.

It was all too much for me. I thrust the bundle of letters back into its place in the drawer and stumbled out of the room. For the first time since my mother's death, I locked the door, as though fearing that some alien foot would enter and defile the room.

The following day, Sheldon Moritz instructed me to translate an urgent telegram to Sheikh Ibn Aziz, confirming that our party would reach Riyadh on Wednesday, March 14. Ordinarily I would have been excited at the prospect of visiting that exotic capital. But my mind was not on Riyadh, nor on any other place on earth.

Having completed the translation, I decided to go home. I was already at the door when I heard my telephone ring. I hurried back to lift the receiver; the voice I heard was Charlie's.

"I'm sorry I picked up the phone," I said.

"Have no regrets," he advised breezily. "We've made great progress. I think we have something solid to go on. Our man in Beirut just called with some information of interest. He's located the missing link. It won't take long to squeeze the source for the information we need. With your help, we'll get the right name from our list of five."

"You'll get no help from me!" I protested.

"You and no one else," he insisted. "I'll make you an offer. If Rif'at Shishakali doesn't turn out to be the one we're gunning for, I'll let you off the hook."

I did not reply immediately. There was something about the way Charlie spoke of Shishakali that made me suspicious; his interest in the Syrian went beyond the obvious issue of punishing the man responsible for the marine headquarters attack.

"Well?" Charlie asked.

"In view of past experience," I said, laying great stress on each word, "I'm wary of your propositions. I never know where you're aiming to go. But as for me—I'm going to Riyadh next week on business."

55

"That fits in perfectly," Charlie purred. "From Riyadh, you'll have easy access to the rendezvous we've set up." He paused. "It's about time you and I met face to face. You'll hear from me shortly."

Before I could reply, the line went dead.

I continued to speculate on our conversation on my way home. The unexpected windfall that made me a rich man overnight brought with it a newfound freedom. Compared with the millions that had tumbled into my lap, the benefits accruing to me with the imminent termination of my contract had become insignificant. There was now no financial reason not to tell Charlie to go take a running jump. But I had to be prudent. I didn't want him to have any inkling about my mother's jewelry; I had a sneaking fear that he might turn up something that could give him an additional hold over me. Charlie was capable of all kinds of skulduggery.

It was 1:30 when I got home. I stuffed the various articles I would need for my sea outing into an old backpack, then unlocked the door to my mother's room and snatched up the bundle of my father's letters. Shortly after two, I was at Jazhek's store.

He indicated the little sailboat I was to hire. "You'll enjoy her," he promised. But his gaze wandered to the new boat lying alongside in the final stages of construction. "That one will be a real beauty," he assured me. "When I get her completed, I'll take you on the maiden cruise."

I admired Jazhek as a master craftsman. He did more than simply construct boats: he breathed life into them. His latest was another masterpiece; he worked on her in his free time, and when she was completed, he aimed to put her up for sale. "She's my old age insurance," he said. "I only hope the Holy Mother finds me a buyer worthy of such a beauty, someone who can appreciate the heart and soul I've put into her."

The yacht was perfectly built and eminently seaworthy. The hulk was forty-four feet long and twelve feet in the beam. The cabin, its wooden paneling lovingly polished, was fitted to house four passengers comfortably. The washroom was far superior to that of any vessel of a similar size. The second cabin in the bow, built to house two additional passengers, was equally well designed for comfort. Jazhek showed me the boat's advanced signals system. "She'll be safe in the roughest seas," he said. "She's got a perfectly even keel." He gazed about him with pride. "She's the best I've ever built."

Reluctantly, we left the near-completed boat, and I boarded the small sailboat. Jazhek remained standing on the jetty, his figure visible long after I had cast off and pointed the bow out to sea. There was a good wind and the sail billowed out immediately. I concentrated on the complexities of steering and navigating, which drove all other troublesome thoughts from my mind.

Evening fell with the swiftness of a hawk swooping on its prey. Abruptly, the sunlight gave way to dusk, which thickened into heavy darkness. The sailboat was nearing the little anchorage I had pinpointed. I was familiar with its approaches, which I now navigated with ease using the beam of the bow spotlight. Having fixed my position, I lowered the mainsail and started up the engine to turn the boat around slowly. Easing her into the anchorage stern first, I silenced the engine and hurried to the bow to fling the anchor into the inky water. The thick rope tightened, bringing the boat to a standstill, after which I folded the sail into its blue casing.

Only now did I permit myself to step down into the cabin. I lit the gas burner to heat up the kettle, and while waiting for it to boil, I carefully unlaced my backpack to extract the precious bundle of letters. Spreading them out on the table, I lingered over them, staring at them without touching. Then I lit the heater, and as the cabin warmed up, I pulled off my short heavy jacket and settled myself as snugly as possible on the narrow bench, with a large mug of coffee grasped in my fist.

I began to read, and I could not stop.

Never before had I encountered letters so unashamedly written with their author's lifeblood. There were letters that resounded from end to end with the cry of distress of a man torn between love for his woman and his "national duty." There were references—some direct, but the majority oblique and cryptic—to perilous projects, to secret operations and mysterious missions. Names of prominent Zionist leaders, Arab dignitaries, and colleagues who shared in clandestine activities cropped up here and there. One frequently recurring name was that of Mussa Eini. I wondered about the man with a name that melodiously blended both Hebrew and Arabic.

I forced myself to read slowly, so as not to miss the finest shade or innuendo, within the lines or between them. I was enthralled by the awareness that my hands held the surviving essence of my father's spirit. Beyond their revelations of a boundless love, the letters provided fascinating testimony to a fateful era, poignant with the sense of approaching catastrophe. I could never have imagined one individual capable of harboring within himself such turbulent concern for the fate of his people, as though his shoulders alone bore the burden of historic responsibility.

I laid down the last of my father's letters. Totally exhausted, I remained slumped on the bench for a long time. I was worn out, perplexed by my own inadequacy in grasping the overwhelming passion of this pair of lovers who, in one of their last nights together, had created me. I found myself forlorn and helpless in the confrontation with my father, and I hovered between two worlds, that which had been and that which was to come, feeling far from certain I could ever bridge the gap between them.

4

Early Sunday morning, when I moored at Jazhek's pier, I was still weary, as though returning from an ocean crossing. The exploration of my parents' love affair had exhausted me no less than a long and punishing voyage.

I returned home just after seven. The first thing I did was to replace the bundle of letters in the closet drawer. Then I flung off my clothes and headed for the shower. I washed at length, shampooed my hair, and got back under the stream of hot water, allowing it to run over me until the mirror was misted with steam.

My thoughts turned to Ariadne. Were it not for her, I might never have experienced this private earthquake I was undergoing. Our encounter at the restaurant on Forty-sixth Street had not been fortuitous, I concluded: she had entered my life as the instrument of some secret destiny.

I dialed her number. "What are you doing right now?"

"Waiting for you."

"I'll be over within the hour."

Her door was open and she stood there awaiting me. I relished the sight of her beauty. Hers was the palest skin I had ever seen, its velvety texture highlighting her chestnut hair, her green eyes, the artless red of her lips. She was wearing a white blouse, cut in the high-collared style fashionable in fin-de-siècle Europe, its lines accenting the curve of her breasts; her narrow hips were set off by the sweep of a full-length skirt.

She led me into the library, where she poured coffee into two fine porcelain cups. She handed me one. "I was glad when you called," she said softly. "And I'm glad you came over." She laid a hand on mine; her touch was gentle and I sensed a sudden weakness as the heat flowed from her body to mine.

"Dammit, I'm tired!" I growled, and we both burst out laughing. It was probably the most unforeseen thing I could have said at such a moment of mutual candor. "I was out sailing in one of Jazhek's boats," I explained. "I haven't slept for two days."

She regarded me impishly. "What kept you awake?"

For a moment, I imagined myself back on board the sailboat, staring down into the dark water at my own shadowy silhouette. "It was—exceptional—fascinating." I launched into a detailed account of everything I had learned about the awesome mystery of my father and mother and their tragic love. I had never before spoken of my father to anyone but Aunt Bertha; but never before had I experienced such intimacy of spirit as I sensed with Ariadne. I told her of how I reached out to touch him; of my exploration into the inner world of a man only a trifle older at the time of his mysterious death than I was now. I told her about the letters and how they had brought my father back to life, with their oblique references to the battles he fought and the comrades-in-arms with whom he shared his dream.

Ariadne sat motionless, her eyes shining with a tenderness reflecting her unspoken sympathy. She took a deep breath, as though awakening from some hallucinatory dream. "I was right," she cried, her triumph bringing a flush to her pale complexion. "Everyone has a story, but some stories are out of the ordinary, full of twists and turns—" She took another deep breath. "Your story is filled with extraordinary people." She was excited, as though she had just caught a glimpse of those figures whose actions had shaped my destiny. "You can't stop here; you know that, don't you?" It was a simple statement, not a question. "You must learn everything you can about your father."

I nodded. At that moment, I had no idea how to proceed; in any case, it would be a long time before I had fully digested the revelations contained in my father's letters. "I'm not sure . . ."

Ariadne's smile was gentle. "I can imagine how mixed up you must feel. You've just discovered the key to a door which will lead you back to your origins. Her eyes were bright, their green hue suddenly interlaced with gold. "I'm pleased for you. Everything you learn will be fascinating."

"You and your intuitions," I mocked gently.

She was not put off by my doubts. "I sense that everything you're experiencing is in some way connected with your father; if you want to unravel the things you still find incomprehensible, you must learn everything you can about him."

"Sounds like 'Introduction to Psychology, lesson one.' "

"Maybe it does," she conceded. "I envy you."

I regarded her quizzically. "Why?"

"While my father was alive, he took me on journeys to wondrous places. I'm only twenty-one, and already I can look back to a rich past and relive those superb expeditions over and over again through my slides." She shook her head. "But that's as far as it goes. As it ever will go. There'll never be any more trips quite like those. But you—you're about to set off on your most exciting expedition, with the most astounding discoveries yet to come. And I'd love to share them with you."

"I think of you as my partner," I said.

"A junior partner," she corrected, with a note of reproof.

"What makes you say that?"

"You're very particular about what you choose to share with me. You're very cautious; there are certain things you prefer to conceal."

"What are you driving at?" Her remark, I suspected, had not been entirely innocent. Not for the first time, I entertained the uneasy feeling that her interest in me stemmed from reasons I did not fully understand.

Ariadne ignored my question. "If I were in your place, d'you know what I'd do? I'd go to Israel."

I stared at her thoughtfully. "I've never been there."

61

"Then it's about time you went. You're off to Saudi Arabia anyway; what's to prevent you from stopping off, either going or coming back? You're no longer poor; you can afford to do things you've only dreamed of."

She laid a hand on my shoulder. "Promise you'll go, Daniel," she said, her voice husky.

Her appeal went straight to my heart. Drawing her to me, I embraced her, and she responded as I had hoped. Her lips parted, warm and soft, to meet mine.

"I want you," she whispered, taking my hand and leading me to the great canopy bed.

Our lovemaking was slow and tender. I exulted in the exploration of Ariadne's body, learning its soft topography. Poised over her, I thrust gently, sinking deep within her. Together we ascended every rung of desire until we peaked in a climax of our shared passion.

We lay still, Ariadne's head on my shoulder; there was so much to say and yet we reveled in a silence more sublime than any other pleasure. Then, the telephone rang.

Without concealing her irritation, Ariadne lifted the receiver to her ear. A look of surprise appeared on her face. "It's for you," she said.

My heart must have missed a beat. No one knew I was here, apart from Aunt Bertha. If Bertha was calling the number I had left her, it had to be important.

"I'm sorry to disturb you," she apologized.

"It's okay."

"Charlie called. He said to tell you he's waiting for you at the Warwick."

I thanked her, then passed the receiver back to Ariadne with a shaking hand. The forthcoming encounter with Charlie revived all my fears. I knew exactly what he was coming for, just as I knew with terrifying certainty that obedience to his instructions would require me to undertake tasks I was no longer capable of.

Ariadne surveyed me with concern. "What's wrong?"

"Nothing," I replied cheerfully. But plenty was wrong.

I spotted Charlie the moment I entered the bar. He was seated at our regular table at the back.

Over a decade had elapsed since our first meeting here at the Warwick. Charlie had hardly altered in appearance during the intervening years. His countenance remained horsey; only his strangely shaped jaw had changed, adopting a more pronounced angular slant. His sparse hair retained its original brown, and his high forehead showed only a few wrinkles. His mouth still curled up at the corners in the characteristically crooked grin, expressing a blend of skepticism and cunning.

Reaching the table I seated myself facing him. A plastic carrier bag occupied the adjacent chair. In response to my glance, Charlie's smile broadened, giving his face an impish aspect. "For the seals," he reminded me.

He always stopped off to buy fish on his way in to town from La Guardia. The weather was pleasantly springlike, and he obviously intended we take our usual walk to Central Park. On many of our previous encounters, Charlie had insisted on taking me to the park's zoo; he loved watching the seals as they darted about their pool. It was a lifelong passion, as I knew from his own accounts. In his childhood in Monterey, California, his favorite pastime was going down to the beach to play with the agile sea lions perched on the huge rocks offshore.

"How are you?" he asked.

"Fine."

"Fine? That must mean you're still seeing that beautiful girl." He sipped his coffee without taking his gaze off my face.

I remained silent.

"She really is out of the ordinary. What did you say her name was?"

"I didn't."

"You didn't," he conceded. "But I managed to hear it all the same." He smiled. "Ariadne. What a beautiful name. Unusual too. Her background must be artistic to an extraordinary degree."

"Don't crowd me, Charlie," I growled. "If I catch you poking your nose in where it isn't wanted, you may have to file an accident report."

He subjected me to a long stare, which led him to guess correctly. "You mean it." His voice was soft. Knowing how well I had been trained, he also knew that if I came after him, he would be powerless to protect himself. I remained silent. "I'm sorry you're so oversensitive. I just wanted you to know I'm keeping an eye on you."

"Why?"

"Because you're so evasive over this Beirut affair. It isn't like you."

"Go take a jump at yourself," I said. "I'm cracked, flawed, coming apart at the joints . . ."

His smile was one of disbelief. Rising from his seat, he picked up the plastic bag. "Let's go."

Spring had arrived. Clear blue skies spread out over Manhattan; the sun, no longer wan and frosty, had turned a full yellow and was radiating a warmth forgotten since the onset of winter. But my depression did not leave me. Charlie had not come from Washington just for the ride. He had me lined up for a well-defined role: I was to be his hand of retribution, and he simply shut his ears to my protests.

We walked past the little carriages harnessed to sturdy ponies before reaching the meandering path that led to the zoo. The park was crowded, the advent of spring marked by the reappearance of familiar Central Park figures: the portrait painter, the mime, and the acrobat swooping and twisting on roller skates.

Spring had attracted droves of visitors to the zoo. Dozens of children crowded around the pool where the seals were showing off their tricks and twitching their mustaches like a troupe of aquatic Don Cossacks. Charlie pushed in among the jubilant youngsters, throwing off the burden of his years. I watched him reach into his bag and bring out a fish, tossing it to one of the seals. His expression was blissful. Beaming affectionately at the children surrounding him, he began to hand out his fish.

As we walked away from the pool, he continued to chortle with satisfaction, rubbing his chin with the back of his hand. "Did you see those kids?" he asked. "Did you see how fast they learned to play with my seals?"

We reached the steps of the park cafe; he flung a yearning backward glance toward the pool and its excited spectators. The sun's rays lit up his face, throwing into sharp relief the flabbiness of his aging skin, but, paradoxically, giving him a youthful look. Abruptly, he swung around and headed for the park exit. I hastened to catch up with him.

"Look, Daniel," he said, lowering his head and glancing about as though seeking some reptile to trap, "even if you're right about reaching the termination date of your contract, there's more to it than that."

"What d'you mean?"

Charlie smirked. "If you read your contract, you'll find in subsection D11 that if an agent is engaged in some operation on the date of termination, the contract ends only on the day the operation is completed."

"That's a dirty trick." In my anger, I did not fail to recognize that Charlie was being true to his guileful self.

Charlie shrugged. "You should always read the small print. That's where all the little surprises are buried."

"I wasn't aware of being engaged in any 'operation'."

"Of course you are. Ever since October, you've known that you're on the line for this one."

I flung him a glance. His face bore its habitual sneer. "You've got me in a corner," I said, "and you're enjoying it. But in this particular instance, it won't do you any good."

Charlie stopped. "I never expected to see you chicken out."

"I have."

"Under the circumstances, you understand that you forfeit all your benefits: the bonus, the pension . . ."

"So what?"

It was a misjudgment, giving away more than I intended; Charlie seemed genuinely surprised.

He eyed me suspiciously. "You don't seem upset at losing your benefits." Then he made a surprisingly accurate guess: "Your finances must have improved greatly. Things are coming your way and you keep them to yourself? What's up, Daniel?"

For the umpteenth time, I reminded myself that the man at my side was smarter than I. I was about to answer him when I suddenly sneezed.

"You should see a doctor," Charlie said. "I'll bet you a month's pay you've been out to sea again."

I grinned. The bastard knew me only too well. "I'll be okay," I assured him, "as long as we play it by the book."

"Whaddya mean?"

"The contract. But in its entirety. You can't just pick out

those sections which happen to fit your needs. There is one clause which states that no more than four missions can be assigned in any single year."

"I get you." His tone was dry. "You've made three hits this year."

"Correct. Three. Precisely."

"And you'll take on only one more." His voice remained dispassionate.

I nodded in confirmation. At the same time, a sudden stab of pain pierced my belly. I was familiar with the feeling: it was my constant, relentless fear finding physical expression. Charlie stared at me in silence. He knew I was at the breaking point; all the same, he did not intend to let up on me.

"But the first target is only a prelude to the second," Charlie said, "and I won't agree to split this assignment. To guarantee its success, it will be entrusted to one man, and one man alone." Charlie glanced about him. "I made you an offer. If it isn't Shishakali, you're off the job. But if it is, you will tackle him. That's fair enough, isn't it?"

"The only offer I'll consider, in termination of my contract, is eliminating the source. Not Shishakali. That's all."

Charlie stared at me. "I don't seem to have much choice, do I?"

"You don't."

"Will you think it over?"

"I have other plans for my future. Who's this source?"

"Albert Mandour, a Lebanese," he answered slowly. "He was employed at marine headquarters."

"In other words, one of our counterintelligence fuck-ups?"

"So it seems. He worked as an informant of ours too, but the Syrians must have offered him a higher price."

"The old story."

"I'm waiting for some additional material that's on its way in," Charlie continued. "The plan is for you to meet Mandour at some neutral spot, not Beirut."

"Where?"

"On Tuesday you're off to Riyadh with your bosses. When you finish your business, you'll request a short vacation. Then you'll fly to Cyprus. We'll set up a meeting with this Lebanese

66

louse in Limassol. You'll have to pump him for the name of the Syrian. As soon as you've got it out of him, may Allah have mercy upon him. He's all yours."

"That's clear."

There seemed to be nothing more to say, but I was wrong. "And when you get back," Charlie murmured, "we'll discuss the Syrian."

"There'll be nothing to discuss."

"For the moment, I'll settle for the Lebanese," Charlie grinned. "You'll get the material on him before you leave for Riyadh. I'll come back and see you off in person."

"As always."

He nodded, his expression solemn. "This may be the most important assignment we've ever handled. We'll get those bastards, you and I."

When I got home, I was sick. I had a bad cold, my throat was sore, and I coughed incessantly. The family doctor prescribed antibiotics, which fortunately got me back on my feet by Tuesday, our scheduled date of departure.

That morning, I went up to Aunt Bertha's apartment to say good-bye. Bertha was excited about my trip.

"You've got an excellent opportunity right now," she declared as we made our way down to the taxi waiting out front. "Riyadh isn't far from Israel. All you have to do is change your ticket on the way back, and there you are. It won't do you any harm to spend a few days. You'll get to see the places I've told you about."

"Not this time," I said gently, "some other time, maybe." I hugged her and turned away. She remained standing on the sidewalk until the taxi bore me away.

At the office I spent a couple of hours clearing my desk. At midday, Charlie called; he had come to New York, as agreed, and was waiting at the Warwick. We arranged to meet an hour later.

The last thing I did before leaving the office was to call Ariadne to say good-bye. My schedule left me with no time to see her. She had good news for me: Oppenheimer had completed a detailed assessment of my mother's jewelry, and after setting a precise figure for each piece, he valued the collection at a total of $5,780,000!

Although I was gradually growing accustomed to thinking of myself as a millionaire, I was not indifferent to the additional three-quarters of a million dollars by which the value of my property had grown since Oppenheimer's initial estimate. All the same, the news left me with mixed feelings. I gave a dry laugh. "A few months ago, you made the acquaintance of a pauper who couldn't afford more than a tuna sandwich for lunch, and now you find yourself dealing with some Croesus who can drown himself in champagne and caviar."

"It's much simpler to be born with a silver spoon in your mouth," she admitted. "That way, you don't think about it."

"Easier said than done."

Ariadne laughed. "I know," she said tenderly, and the line went dead.

I sat there for a moment, wondering whether I should call her back. But I felt that there was nothing more to say—not at this moment anyway. And besides, I realized, flinging a rapid glance at my watch, I had only a few minutes before my scheduled meeting with Charlie.

We met at our regular table at the end of the bar. Charlie surveyed me closely. "You're pale."

"I had the flu."

Charlie nodded in commiseration. "I've warned you before, playing with sailboats is a dangerous hobby. But you never listen to me. How d'you feel now?" That was Charlie all over: a touching blend of stern father and overprotective mother.

"So-so," I replied.

He remained dissatisfied. "You look awful. When you're in Riyadh, you should get out into the sun."

"I'll be fine just as soon as the Cyprus matter is attended to."

"When you come back," Charlie suggested, "we should get together."

"Don't bother," I said. "Cyprus is the end of the road. Don't lean on me anymore, please. I hope we can part friends."

Charlie ignored my appeal. With an enigmatic smile, he laid a sealed envelope down before me. "Inside, you'll find all the material you need. Blake has apparently convinced this Lebanese punk that we're in earnest about making a deal with him. The rest is up to you, Daniel. He's our only lead to finding the man we're after."

Slipping the envelope into my inner breast pocket, I rose. "I'll see you around," I said.

5

Shortly before our plane began its approach to Riyadh airport, I left my seat in the first-class section to slip into the washroom, where I studied the contents of the envelope I had received from Charlie. It contained three different mug shots of my target and a closely typed page of background material about him. Albert Mandour was a thirty-eight-year-old Lebanese Christian from Tyre. For many years, the résumé stated, he had sold his services impartially to the CIA representative at our Beirut embassy and to Syrian intelligence; the fact that he was a double agent emerged only after the bombing of the marine base. By profession a cook and caterer, Mandour was entrusted—on the embassy's recommendation—with food deliveries to the marines, thereby gaining free access to their headquarters.

He was described as standing five feet—four and weighing two hundred and forty pounds. I foresaw no difficulty in identifying him; on top of all else, he sported a Burt Reynolds mustache.

Charlie's research extended to the minutest detail: the information even included background material to serve me in my interrogation of Mandour. I scanned the page once more and ripped the envelope and its contents into tiny scraps, which I flushed down the toilet. I speculated that, with luck, the brief summary of Mandour's identity would float down on some Saudi oil well. A kind of final mark of respect.

Moritz and Liebman had depicted Riyadh to me as an exotic dreamland, and I found their account to be no exaggeration. I had visited numerous places that bore the traditional characteristics of the East: some exercised an intoxicating fascination, others were repulsive hellholes. But I had never seen a city to compare with Riyadh. Taking full advantage of the advances and inventions that had taken civilization two thousand years to produce, the Saudis built Riyadh into a stunning urban wonder; over the past two decades in particular, it had grown to superb dimensions. It featured broad avenues; residential complexes vied with public buildings in their splendidly innovative architecture, blending Western know-how with Eastern refinement. With few exceptions, the cars filling the streets were the very latest models, with a preponderance of Mercedes to mark the triumph of the German car industry over its competitors.

The evening of our arrival, I was privileged to make the acquaintance of three representatives of the Saudi government: Sheikh Abdulla Ibn Raif, Sheikh Saud al Salem, and Sheikh Rahim Ibn Sura. These three were to be among the Saudi representatives in talks with my employers on their role in furthering Saudi economic interests in the United States. They were clothed in elegant desert splendor. Not only did they speak with splendid solemnity, but they moved with self-importance; their composure reflected an unshakable inner conviction of their own elevated status in relation to ordinary men.

All three were cunning and determined negotiators, but as Moritz and Liebman pointed out, the most formidable member of the commission was the one most noticeable by his absence from our dinner meeting. Sheikh Ibn Aziz had excused himself from attending, sending word that he was suffering from an attack of one of his chronic ailments. But even without his physical presence, his personality—and his position as personal representative of the king—overshadowed the other three committee

71

members. Indeed, whenever his name came up, it was pronounced with respect and deference.

The following morning at eleven, we held our first business meeting in a luxurious conference room situated in the offices of the Saudi Finance Ministry. This time, we were joined by Sheikh Ibn Aziz. As he shuffled in, bent over his staff, his appearance bore clear evidence of his recent illness. His complexion was gray, his features more drawn than I recalled from my first encounter with him at our Manhattan offices. As he took his seat, he proffered us a reserved greeting, cautiously expressing gratitude at our visit.

The conference table was round, thereby solving any protocol problems of status and rank; nevertheless Sheikh Ibn Aziz dominated the proceedings without formally presiding over them. We got right down to business. The first item on the agenda was the draft of an economic agreement between Saudi Arabia and the United States for the coming fiscal year. The draft, submitted by the U.S. Treasury Department, proposed closer links between the economies of the two countries. Our aim was to protect the United States from any disruption of oil supplies caused by the caprices of the Mideast's various rulers. In return for American sales of sophisticated military hardware, principally for the purpose of beefing up radar defenses along the lengthy Saudi borders, the Saudis were to enlarge their holdings in U.S. banks. They would, in addition, guarantee to retain them in our country for specified periods of time. In view of the growing tension in the Gulf, and the continuing drop in world oil prices—far below the minimum laid down by OPEC—Washington clearly hoped that this would be an opportune moment to harness Saudi financial resources to economic growth in the United States. At the same time, our aim was to expand American influence on Saudi policy in the international and inter-Arab spheres.

The discussion dragged on; I made my occasional contribution with a translation, doing my best to satisfy both sides. Nevertheless, verbal difficulties did arise, in one instance sparking off a stormy argument that was stilled only when Sheikh Ibn Aziz endorsed the terms I had originally proposed.

Clearly, he enjoyed superior status within the Saudi delegation. In spite of his evident physical discomfort, his mind was unaffected. The only overt sign he gave of his illness was when he refused the thick bitter coffee we were served, restricting himself to cold water from a glass that was continually replenished by a servant hovering nearby.

Our series of discussions concluded on Thursday, the following day being the Moslem day of rest. A number of unresolved points were postponed for our final meeting, scheduled for Saturday morning before our departure on the four o'clock afternoon flight. While this planning was in progress, I approached my employers to request a brief vacation on the way home. I explained I wished to spend a little time in Europe and would therefore make my separate way after our stopover in Rome.

With no program arranged for Friday, other than a reception in our honor that evening, we spent the day in our hotel. The Saudis found discreet but unmistakable ways of hinting that we would do well to respect their holy day by keeping a low profile. I passed the day on the terrace, getting some sun and gazing at the minarets of the city's numerous mosques.

The sensation that my life was changing beyond recognition intensified here in Riyadh. Despite the city's wealth of imported technological innovations, it had, at the same time, insulated its social structure against change. I, on the other hand, experienced an overpowering feeling of the inevitable about to overtake me, some predestined fate that could not be fended off.

Later, I watched the gigantic sun setting in the west. It would soon be time to set out for the reception at the mansion of Sheikh Ibn Aziz, and I went to get dressed.

A Mercedes limousine came to collect us from the hotel. After a half-hour drive, we reached the city's most fashionable quarter, restricted exclusively to members of the royal family and their most influential associates.

Entering Ibn Aziz's mansion, we found its halls and chambers housing some one hundred and fifty guests: Saudis, American diplomats, and local representatives of foreign commercial corporations. As the foreigners had been permitted to bring their wives, I had the opportunity to meet the sheikh's wife Adalla, a tall, attractive woman of about fifty. She acted as hostess to the Western women, while her husband entertained the men.

73

The sheikh was assisted by their son Fahed, the commander of a squadron of Saudi F-15's. In his mid-twenties, the young colonel wore his dress uniform, which set off his tall, somewhat heavy physique. His facial features resembled those of his mother and, like her, he sported a constant smile.

Sheikh Ibn Aziz was in slightly better health that evening; he paced about with a firmer stride, leaning on his staff more from habit than from bodily weakness. The sheikh's expression was relaxed, yet I noted his sharp eyes darting about, aware of everything that went on around him.

The reception was not without its entertaining aspects. The sheikh hosted his New York guests with courtesy and respect, an excellent example of that renowned Saudi pragmatism by which the Riyadh elite drew a clear distinction between Israelis, abhorred as dangerous foes, and other Jews, who were treated as honored business partners. In spite of official instructions to foreign companies to avoid staffing their Riyadh offices with representatives whose names sounded blatantly Jewish, the visit of men named Liebman, Moritz, and Kottler apparently failed to raise a single Saudi eyebrow. The attorneys' services in furthering Riyadh's political and economic links with the West were highly valued.

On this occasion, we even managed to elicit a friendly welcome from the trio of sheikhs who had been so frosty toward us on our first evening. The aging Sheikh Abdulla Ibn Raif shook hands cordially, and his younger nephews, the Sheikhs Saud al Salem and Rahim Ibn Sura, oozed charm. Sheikh Ibn Raif took us by the arm to present us to other prominent Saudis, stressing to them my employers' valuable contribution in strengthening economic ties between Riyadh and Washington.

Soon after our arrival, we were invited into an adjoining room, where fragrant coffee was served. From here, we could look out on a well-tended garden with a large pool at its center. I found myself near the spot where Sheikh Ibn Aziz and his son were in conversation with Moritz and Liebman. They beckoned me to join them.

"I have no luck with my children," the sheikh complained. "Fahed has chosen to devote himself to our air force. His sisters are studying in Switzerland and neither one of them seems in-

74

clined to bring me a son-in-law to help conduct my business. When my time comes, the desert sands will engulf everything I've built up."

"Not as long as I live!" the young flier said. "Your deeds fill our land and extend far beyond its frontiers. When the time comes, should you so ordain, I wil give up my uniform."

"Have no fear, my son," the sheikh smiled, "until that time, you must continue with your present occupation. The day may come when you will be called upon to take command of our air force—" A fit of coughing interrupted his words. Fahed directed an anxious glance at his father as the sheikh fought down his cough and, taking a deep breath, restored the color to his cheeks.

I moved away and dodged through the throng to seek a quiet corner beside the pool. A few moments later, I noticed Fahed nearby, sipping coffee from a tiny cup poured for him by one of the silent waiters who hovered everywhere. I walked over to him. "May I join you?"

"Certainly." Seated side by side, we fell into conversation. I remarked that this was my first visit to Saudi Arabia, and Fahed told me he had spent several periods of training at U.S. Air Force bases. I found him affable and much less aloof than I had expected. In many ways, he was a perfectly ordinary young man, resembling his peers in any other country. Gradually, as I drew him out, he launched into enthusiastic tales about his air force career. To my amazement, he told me he had been flying planes for twelve years, ever since he was fourteen. "My father always owned at least one plane. At present, he possesses a fleet of executive jets and helicopters."

"You must be very attached to your career," I said.

"That's just a matter of appearances. When the day comes, I'll take over the management of our family business. Till then, I want to stay on in the air force and advance as far as I can."

Fahed offered to drive me back to the hotel after the reception; on the way, he would show me the sights.

"Are you sure it's no trouble?"

Fahed smiled. "I enjoy your company. Aside from that, I'll expect my reward when I come and see you in New York."

"That's a debt of honor," I assured him. We arranged to meet when the reception ended and his father's driver came to collect my employers. Fahed now left me to return to his duties as host. In the meantime, I engaged in desultory conversation with the U.S. commercial attaché.

Finally, I took my leave of Sheikh Ibrahim Ibn Aziz and followed his son to the mansion's underground garage, where he opened the doors of a brand-new khaki-hued Cadillac.

"You are disloyal to your father," I joked.

Fahed stared at me. "That's a grave offense. What do you mean?"

"You drive a Cadillac instead of one of the Mercedes your father imports."

"Oh that!" he laughed. "In our air force every officer of my rank is issued a Cadillac for his personal use."

"You Saudis do things in style."

"No army in the world offers conditions like ours. Our armed forces are not large by Mideastern standards, but to attract the best available manpower, we must offer the most lavish benefits."

We drove past some crude mud hovels. "That's old Riyadh," Fahed explained. "We've advanced a thousand years beyond the life-style of our parents and grandparents." He parked the car and took me through alleyways transecting the primitive shantytown. As we walked, he explained the growth of Riyadh, how its development had surged ahead as soon as the Saudis had liberated themselves from foreign tutelage. By the grace of Allah, his people took control of their lakes of black gold lapping the underside of the sand dunes.

When Fahed finally dropped me off at the hotel, it was close to midnight. I thanked him for the tour, and with a friendly farewell, he roared away into the night.

I congratulated myself on making friends with the young pilot. I could only hope that Fahed's father, the ailing desert fox, would not object to his association with an unbeliever like myself. But however Sheikh Ibn Aziz reacted, I resolved to foster my friendship with his son. A man never knows when he will need an ally.

In Rome, I boarded a British Airways Boeing 707 to Larnaca. It was the first step on the mission Charlie had saddled me with, and my tremor of foreboding reflected a blend of by now all too familiar fears.

The plane landed at Larnaca at 11:00 P.M. Half an hour later, I was in a taxi careening toward Limassol. I found myself crouching on the edge of my seat in tense anticipation of a head-on collision with some vehicle coming the opposite way. The road was narrow and winding, with only one lane on each side; the pitch darkness did not heighten my sense of security, already undermined by the left-hand rule of the road bequeathed to Cyprus by its former British rulers.

It took the taxi driver just fifty nerve-wracking minutes to reach Limassol, where he delivered me, rattled but all in one piece, to the Elassia Hotel. In spite of the lateness of the hour, I found the proprietor waiting up for me. Marinos Panadis was a tiny man, but he managed to add to his stature by virtue of his vigorous, turbulent personality. He came from a tiny mountain village, where he was born sixty years ago. In his youth, he was a goatherd until the day his elder brother snatched him away from his four-legged charges, placing him in a job as bellboy at a newly constructed hotel not far away. That abrupt change in vocation marked the beginning of Marinos's success, and he never looked back.

He extended his usual warm welcome; within minutes of my arrival, I was seated facing him as he raised his glass of wine. "Once again, I drink to your health. May your affairs prosper from this visit to our country."

"May it be so."

"How long will you be staying?"

"I don't know. It depends on business."

"Stay as long as you wish. You know you're always welcome here, Daniel."

Marinos knew me by my own name because that was the way Charlie operated. Just as he insisted on his hit men going out on their missions without firearms or any other lethal devices, so he never equipped them with a false identity. Charlie was convinced that under their true names, his men would be doubly cautious in executing their assignment.

"How's your business?" I asked.

"I'm doing well for all the wrong reasons," he said. "My

business is good because the hotel is full almost to capacity. The reasons are wrong because most of my guests are refugees from Lebanon. They've come to seek a haven from the hell that's loose in their country." He shook his head gloomily. "What a shambles that is. It's like our own war, when we Greeks were fighting the Turks here on Cyprus. We, too, found ourselves abandoned, just like the Lebanese, who pinned all their hopes on the U.S. But you failed us then, and are failing them now. You lost a few hundred marines, and with the elections coming, that was bad for Reagan's public relations, so he got the hell out of that death trap as fast as he could."

"It's a lousy world," I said, feeling no call to defend my President.

"But when all's said and done, it's America that comes out the loser. Who'd be crazy enough to put his faith in your country now? You've got a cowboy in the White House, and he's showing about as much guts and fire as the peanut farmer you had there before."

I joined in his laughter, while he signaled to Johnny the barman to fill up our glasses. I stayed there conversing with him, glad of his unintrusive chattiness, which kept my mind off my own concerns and anxieties. At last I bade him good night and went up to my second-floor room. My thoughts turned to the assignment that awaited me the following day. The reality of eliminating Mandour drove a shudder through my body until my teeth chattered. The anxiety attack lasted several moments until I staggered over to the bed and dropped there in utter exhaustion, as though after some physical exertion.

It was just after eleven when I got to the seaside restaurant where Charlie had arranged the rendezvous with Mandour. In spite of the early hour, it was packed to capacity, with customers seated at the sidewalk tables soaking up the sunshine.

At my first glimpse of Albert Mandour, I almost laughed out loud. Just as in his photographs, he looked like a squashed Burt Reynolds. Prominent in a pale green jacket, Mandour sat alone at a table taking alternate sips from a tiny coffee cup and a tall glass of ice water. He was clutching a copy of *Time* magazine, our prearranged identification. This was my advantage over him:

he had no prior knowledge as to who would be coming to meet him and therefore had no way of recognizing me.

In no hurry to make myself known to him, I continued to stroll along the crowded sidewalk, taking careful note of my surroundings. Filthy carrion of Mandour's type was liable to bring a whole flock of poisonous snakes and scorpions in his train. My inspection failed to detect any unwanted hangers-on, but I still delayed approaching my target.

Around twelve o'clock, Mandour lost patience. Rising from his seat, he paid his check and left the restaurant. Outside, I found no difficulty in spotting the pale green jacket, and in spite of the crowd, I managed to keep him in sight until he entered a small hotel nearby. I sat down on the concrete parapet, posing as another bored tourist, while keeping my eyes on the hotel's peeling gray facade.

After a few moments, Mandour appeared on a small third-floor veranda. His room, I noted, was the last one on the right.

This, I decided, was the appropriate moment to grant him the privilege of making my acquaintance. I strode into the hotel and took the aging elevator to the third floor, where I headed down the corridor to his door. I tried the handle cautiously. It was locked, but that constituted no obstacle. I brought out my wallet and extracted a credit card, with which I forced the latch until it slid back soundlessly. A moment later, I was inside the sordid little room, closing the door behind me. I looked about. The open washroom gave off an unsavory odor, and no one had troubled to straighten up the rumpled bed with its grubby sheets. A battered suitcase stood beside the bed. The pale green jacket was flung carelessly over a chair. I slipped a hand inside it until I located the Beretta in the left-hand pocket.

I extracted the magazine, replaced the gun where I had found it, and stepped toward the open window leading out to the veranda. Over the back of the easy chair, I spotted Mandour's head slumped to one side and heard his gentle snoring.

"Monsieur Mandour?" I murmured softly.

His reaction was stunningly swift. Like a steel spring uncoiling, he flung himself out of the chair and crouched on his stubby legs in a defensive posture. "Who the hell are you?" His voice was hoarse.

"My apologies for intruding like this."

"How did you get in?" His shoulders bunched, as though he were about to fling himself at me. In spite of his chubbiness, he was well built and muscular.

"We were supposed to meet, weren't we?" I said, pulling out my own copy of *Time* magazine. Mandour's body relaxed and the color came back to his face. With the back of one pudgy hand, he wiped the sweat from his brow. "I'm surprised," he muttered in French. "I expected you at the restaurant. Why didn't you show up?"

"I'm truly sorry. I got there just as you were leaving."

"Why didn't you come up to me right away? Why did you wait?"

I turned up my palms helplessly. "I didn't want to approach you in the street."

"How did you get into the room?"

"I knocked, but you must have been asleep."

Mandour's suspicious glare melted. "Welcome," he proclaimed finally, extending his right hand. His grip was powerful. He waved me to a seat and perched on the edge of the bed near the chair where he had thrown his jacket. Ready to go for his gun, if need be, I thought, imagining his surprise should he decide to use it.

"You are—the American?" He paused to indicate that he was waiting for me to introduce myself by name.

I chose to ignore the hint. "I am the man you are to meet. I understand you have something to trade."

"I may have." He lit a cigarette with a gold-plated Dunhill lighter and took a nervous puff. "Yes," he repeated, "I may have something."

"I hope the goods are high quality."

"The quality depends on the price."

I was familiar with his furtive look: Mideastern trading practices followed certain well-defined rules, which I would have to obey.

"You want to fix the price first?" I asked.

"If the price is right," he said unhurriedly, "somebody may have something to offer you."

"I thought you brought the goods with you."

80

"Don't worry," he said. "If the price is right, my partner will deliver."

"How can I trust someone I don't even know?"

"Trust me!" He laid a hand on his forehead in the traditional Levantine gesture of a man putting himself on oath. "I'll see to it." There was now no trace of his original hoarseness; with the return of his self-confidence, his voice had reverted to its natural high, clear pitch. "You must know that I'm on very close terms with your people in Beirut."

He was also on "close terms" with the bastards who blew our marines sky-high. "So I've heard."

"From Blake?"

I smiled inwardly; this was his piece of bait to establish my identity beyond any doubt. He was cautious.

"You mean John Blake."

"John—?" He hesitated, waiting for something more.

"John David Blake," I concluded, verifying my credentials.

"Precisely."

I realized he was now prepared to get down to business. But I was in no hurry. I knew Charlie expected me to make sure the information we received was precise and reliable.

"I'd like to hear a little more about your partner," I said. "We have to make certain he's as dependable as you are."

"Don't you trust me?"

"Every word you utter is sacred," I assured him solemnly. "But there may be questions about your partner."

"I get you." He nodded. "He's first cousin to someone who works with the Iranians."

"The Iranians?" I echoed, raising an eyebrow.

"The group around the Black Ayatolla."

His irritable tone delighted me; he was beginning to lose his cool, and that was precisely what I wanted. "Lajwardi," I filled in.

"Precisely, Assadulla Lajwardi, the one-eyed monster." The Iranian clergyman, head of the shahids—the Shi'ite suicide squads operating in Lebanon—was indeed the evil symbol of the bloody revolution still rocking Iran. He was personally responsible for the execution of thousands of his countrymen and was equally notorious for his violent hatred of the United States. He got his nickname in 1975 when he was partly blinded by the accidental detonation of a bomb he was assembling. It was to be used in an assassination bid against the head of the shah's secret police, the Savak.

"What is the link between your friend's cousin and the shah-ids?"

"It's similar to my own links with your marines." His smile was smug. At that moment, I would joyfully have wrung his neck to erase that smirk and with it the man who had helped in that vile massacre. "He's in charge of food deliveries to the Iranian base. He knows everyone there. He even knows the true name of the shahid who drove the car bomb into the headquarters."

Mandour gave the precise location of the Iranian camp, describing its internal setup with enough precision to indicate that he himself was a frequent visitor there. I was now satisfied as to the thoroughness of his acquaintance with the facts; had I thought he knew the name of the man responsible for the car bombing, I would have squeezed him dry then and there. But I believed him when he said that he had yet to receive the name; his partner was evidently taking every possible precaution.

"How much does your partner want for his information?"

Mandour's face darkened with fury. "Don't play games with me!" he muttered hoarsely. "I told Blake the exact figure." His gaze was hostile. He obviously entertained little affection for Americans.

"Your partner demands an enormous sum." I endeavored to control my voice. The inevitable haggling had begun; it was vital to convince him that we were dealing in earnest, without giving him any inkling that we were aware of his treacherous role in the car bombing.

"My partner won't accept one cent less than the price I agreed upon with Blake."

"Fifty thousand is a lot for a scrap of information."

"You don't say! But he could have asked for a hundred thousand. Two hundred thousand." Nervously, he stubbed out his cigarette. "I'm here to make a deal, not haggle like a trader from the souk. You want that name. I know how badly you want it."

"Don't tell me what we want," I said calmly. "You know that

any day now somebody else will turn up and offer us the same name for less money. A whole lot less. We're in no hurry. It can take another day, or a week, or a month. So what?"

Mandour coughed suddenly, violent spasms shaking his body. I could see the bastard was rattled by my stubbornness, which he had not foreseen. "I'll tell you what I'll do. I'll try and convince my friend to settle for forty-five." He was on the point of laying a hand on my shoulder, but changed his mind at the last moment. I don't think I could have tolerated his touch.

"We're still a long ways apart. The most I can okay is thirty-five." I chose my words to impress upon him that I was the one who would fix the sum, to reassure Mandour that, in coming all the way from Beirut to Limassol, he had not wasted his time. He was now face to face with the man who made the decisions.

He got the message. "We're men of the world, you and I." His tone was respectful. "Let's find an honorable way of tying this deal up." He fell silent, awaiting my response. Matters had reached an advanced stage; when your opponent starts handing out compliments, it is a sure sign of progress. "We'll settle on a fair price. Forty. That's my last offer. Give me something on account, and I'll go to Beirut and bring you the name. How does that sound?"

"I need time to think about it."

Mandour seethed. "I don't understand you people! I was convinced you'd turn the world upside down to identify the man—"

"Maybe," I interrupted brusquely, "if you had the name right now, I might be able to convince my bosses." Holding my breath, I awaited his response.

Mandour breathed heavily. The money was within his reach. If he was after nothing more than a fast buck, he would go for my offer, toss me some name, fictitious or not, grab the cash and vanish. But his hesitation proved that he was in earnest. Moreover, he was after something he prized even higher than the money. "Okay." His lowered eyes signaled capitulation. "What's your last price?"

"Thirty-five," I said. "Not a cent more."

He frowned. "We might have ourselves a deal," he said hesitantly, "but—"

"But what?" This was it: he was about to bring out his last card.

"I have one further request."

I remained silent, forcing him to make the run.

"Blake can tell you how faithfully I've served him," he said. Had he known what I knew about him, he would have not adopted that particular argument or his tone of aggrieved innocence. "But now I have to get out of Lebanon. Me and my family. You've got to help me."

"You'll have the money," I said, pretending not to understand what he was driving at. "You can go anywhere you choose."

"I don't want to go just anywhere."

"Are you hinting at something specific?"

He gazed at me; had he been a dog, he would have been wagging his tail, begging to be stroked. "I want an immigrant's visa to the United States. For myself, my wife, and the children." His voice was soft. He had come to his main objective. He must have read my thoughts, because he summarized his demand with an unusual show of candor. "No visa, no deal. You get me?"

Short and sweet. "I don't know. It's not easy."

"If you set your minds to it, you and your superiors, I'm sure you can find a way." His tone was mild, but there could be no doubt about his determination.

"You give us too much credit."

"Plenty of guys I know got visas for services less valuable than mine."

I considered punching him between the eyes, there and then.

Suddenly, he leaned over, grabbing my hand in supplication. "This isn't a matter of haggling, believe me. It's not just me who's in danger by working for you. What about my wife and children? It's only a matter of time before the Syrians get on my track, and then I'm—" He drew his other hand across his throat.

I pulled my hand away. "These things are very complicated to arrange," I said. "True, the decision is up to me, but still . . ."

"Please!"

"You ask too much."

"I've served your country faithfully." His voice shook. "Blake can tell you . . ."

84

"Give me a couple of days."

He was all afire now. The bargaining was at an end. "That's my price," he cried. "Thirty-five and the visas. Are we in business?"

This was the fateful moment, and I couldn't let it slip by. I had him by the short hairs. All I needed to do was hand him his dream, which would be short-lived anyway. I hesitated a few seconds longer. "You'll get your visas," I said finally.

"I'll never forget you!" he assured me. "As long as I live!"

"How do we proceed?" I demanded, getting back to business.

"I'll go back to Beirut," he replied eagerly. "Within a few days, I'll return with the name of your man. I should be here by Saturday morning. If I don't make it, wait one day more. But I'll be back, even if I have to swim all the way."

"Satisfactory," I said. "I suppose you want something for your expenses?"

"I didn't want to press you." He cleared his throat modestly. "But a token would be appreciated . . ."

I gave him two thousand dollars. As his trembling fingers counted the bills, I knew I had him in the trap. He was all mine now.

Mandour could not contain his joy, swearing to me that the United States of America would profit immensely by the welcome it proffered to a Lebanese family of extraordinary merit. His outpourings disgusted me; in my mind's eye, I saw the long line of flag-draped coffins.

Back at the Elassia, I stepped into the bar for a drink, hoping to erase the foul taste from my mouth. I felt weary and defiled. As Johnny poured my vodka, Marinos came over to fill me in on the latest news from Lebanon. Leaders of the country's rival ethnic groups had convened that day for a peace conference under the auspices of the Syrian president; the purpose of the meeting was to form a new government with a pronounced pro-Syrian bent. Grinning, Marinos assured me that the Lebanese would achieve peace only when their various warring factions had finished killing off one another. "They're nothing but marionettes, dancing on strings pulled from Damascus. The Syrians are the only ones who profited from the Lebanese civil war.

Everyone else lost—the Palestinians, the Druse, the Maronites, the Shi'ites. And d'you know who lost the most? You Americans. And your Israeli buddies."

"You don't hold a very high opinion of the Israelis," I said.

"On the contrary, but something's gone wrong there these past few years. They aren't the same people they were once."

"What do you mean?"

He selected his words carefully. "I don't think they themselves know what it is they want. I'm not even certain they want peace. Maybe they believe the best thing they can achieve is something that is neither peace nor war."

I always found Marinos's political analyses fascinating. His office was filled with newspapers in five languages, and he always kept his guests updated. I wanted to hear more from him. At this moment, however, he was called away to the phone, and I headed for my room.

After a long and leisurely shower, I lay on the bed and watched some third-rate movie from a local T.V. station. A restless feeling overtook me. It would be several days before Mandour returned, forcing me to hang about idly. I shuddered at the thought.

Distracted, I recalled my talk with Marinos. His words about Israel echoed in my mind. What was it he said? "Neither peace nor war." So like my own situation of "neither here nor there." An interesting parallel and hardly surprising: after all, I was linked, by more ties than I cared to admit, to that controversial land whose borders lay only a few hundred miles away. Both Bertha and Ariadne, each motivated by different reasons, had urged me to visit Israel.

And they were right, of course.

It came to me in a flash, with an utter certainty that left no room for further doubt.

Seizing the telphone, I called down to Marinos's office.

"What can I do for you?"

"Get me on a flight to Israel tomorrow."

"What time?"

"The earlier the better."

I knew I could rely on him. I lay back on the bed, staring up at the ceiling. In only a few hours, I would set foot on the soil where my father was born; the thought inspired me with a profound excitement. I retained vivid memories of my father's letters. Between the lines written in his vigorous hand, I seemed to see the vistas of the land he depicted with such poetic fervor. I wanted to see the white city, with its golden sands; I wanted to embrace the concrete pillar bearing the flying camel that soared to meet the sun.

It suddenly struck me that the man from Tiberias was no longer some faceless entity: I had begun to fill in the outlines. But that was not enough to satisfy me. I wanted to learn more about him. I wished to know how he lived, and how he died.

6

Just before one o'clock, the plane commenced its gradual descent. From my vantage point at cloud level, I saw the blue sea lapping the beach of Tel Aviv.

As the plane landed, there were only a few wisps of cloud surrounding us, but by the time I emerged from the terminal, the weather had changed. The sky was overcast with a heavy bank of dark clouds, and a sharp wind arose, bringing with it tiny raindrops. The ancestral land of Israel was proffering me a somber welcome.

I stood at the arrivals exit, grasping my valise and wondering what to do first. But my doubts were resolved by an instinctive decision. I strode over to a waiting taxi and, speaking to the driver in Hebrew, asked how long it would take to get to Tiberias.

"Two hours," he replied, staring at me in puzzlement. "How come you don't know? You must have been out of the country a long time."

"Many years," I smiled. It was only a half-truth.

Initially, as the road bisected the closely populated coastal plain, the architecture presented a medley of towns and villages. After a time, our route took us inland among low hills that sported a sparse green covering of winter vegetation. Vivid patches of wildflowers presaged the onset of spring, their bright colors catching the occasional flashes of pale sunlight that broke through the clouds.

I found the sights before my eyes intermingled with half-forgotten images emerging from hidden recesses at the back of my mind, like the stirring of some ancient folk memory, or like glimpses of ancient snapshots, fading and yellow. Buffeted between reality and fantasy, I sank into a surrealistic haze.

Soon we would be approaching my father's birthplace. Even before my first sight of Tiberias, I knew that my image of the town was outdated; here, as elsewhere, progress would have wrought deep changes. All the same, as the road swept over a hilltop and began its descent toward the Sea of Galilee, I was surprised by the large ugly apartment buildings that dotted the road. Halfway down the hill I caught a glimpse of the city built by Herod to exalt the name of his lord and master: Tiberias. Ruined masses of masonry recalled the name of my father's family, Dur. The word carried a special significance in the Semitic languages: in Hebrew it was taken to mean "circle," while in ancient Accadian, it denoted the defensive wall encircling a city.

As the taxi glided downhill into the center of the town, I experienced a strange mixture of emotions. Questions crowded into my mind. What would I unearth here? My father's letters contained references to various individuals whose names I had carefully noted. If I were lucky enough to track them down, they might offer me a thread by which to begin unraveling the mysteries crowding my mind. Still, I sensed a profound unease at the prospect of my imminent encounter with the unknown.

My hotel stood in the northern portion of the town, close to the shore of the lake; from my balcony I gazed down at the water and then across to the Golan mountains beyond, towering up like a wall into the highlands.

To the right stood the older section of Tiberias. My elevated vantage point gave me a good view of its houses built of black stone, hewn from the hills above. I stood there for a long time, filling my lungs with the air my forefathers had breathed. At this moment I became, for the first time, fully aware of having truly returned to my origins. But with that consciousness came a sense of alienation, as though something within me resisted the magnetic draw that threatened to reduce me to nothing but one more link in a chain of events spanning the centuries.

After a shower and shave, I slipped into a light gray suit, then located the hotel's information desk. I asked the clerk if he was familiar with Mussa Eini, the name that figured prominently in my father's letters.

"Mussa Eini?" The man smiled broadly. "The Eini family is an institution in Tiberias. You might say they're a chapter in the town's history." With that glowing recommendation, he directed me to Mussa Eini's restaurant on the lakeside promenade.

Were it not for the babble of Hebrew and the Oriental music blaring out from a pair of loudspeakers, I might easily have imagined myself to be standing at the entrance to a traditional Greek taverna, on the beach of some Aegean island. The resemblance was heightened by the stone building, which looked like a replica of the venerable arched structures one encounters on the islands.

I asked a waiter where I could find Mr. Eini. He nodded toward the far end of the restaurant. Approaching, I found a young man in his early twenties: his name was indeed Eini, but he turned out to be Rafi, the grandson of the Mussa I sought.

"Where can I find your grandfather?" I inquired. "I understand he's an authority on Tiberias and its history."

The young man smiled and invited me to follow him. He guided me out and around the building, where we reached a broad flight of steps with a highly embellished cast-iron railing. The stairs led up to an enormous terrace, which we traversed to reach an ancient blue-painted wooden door. Its metal knocker was shaped in the form of a roaring lion. Rafi knocked on the door and, without awaiting an answer, pushed it open and stepped inside. We entered a large lounge, filled with furniture of heavy wood darkened with age. The divans, standing only a few inches above floor level, were covered with Persian rugs. Similar rugs hung from the walls, flanked by ancient carbines, lances, and swords.

But what caught my eye immediately was the sturdy figure seated at a desk at the far end. He had a remarkable form. The bald pate in the center of his head gave his skull an egglike appearance. The sparse remnants of his hair were iron gray, but his eyebrows were black and bushy, as was his well-tended mustache. It was difficult to assess Mussa Eini's age; knowing him to be my father's peer, I assumed him to be in his late sixties, although he looked younger. He nodded a greeting and rose to welcome us.

"This gentleman wants to ask you some questions about Tiberias," Rafi told his grandfather.

"Tiberias?" Mussa Eini's voice was a low rumble.

"When it comes to stories about the town, you have no equal when you are in the mood."

Mussa Eini plucked the tip of his mustache. "Telling stories about Tiberias isn't a matter of mood, it depends on who's listening." His gaze settled on my face. "So, young man, you want to hear about Tiberias. Which Tiberias?"

"What do you mean?"

"Tiberias that is, or Tiberias that was?"

"Tiberias that was."

Rafi left us to return to the restaurant. After he had gone, his grandfather eyed me curiously. "What's your name?"

I told him.

"Kottler? There's something familiar about it." He inspected me. "Are you new here?"

"I'm an American. I'm here on a visit."

"You speak Hebrew like an Israeli."

"My parents were ardent Zionists," I replied truthfully, if not with total candor.

He regarded me from beneath his bushy eyebrows. "Well," he said, "if it's Tiberias you're interested in, you've come to the right man. Why don't we drink to that, you and I?" He strode to the far end of the long room.

While he was rummaging among his bottles, I examined

the framed photographs standing on his desk and hanging from the walls. They were old and yellowing for the most part; many depicted my host in his younger days. In one, he appeared mounted on a rearing steed, in a pose similar to the one I recalled from the framed snapshot in my mother's room. But in contrast with the tall slim figure of my father, Mussa Eini, in youth as in old age, was broad-shouldered and thickset. One of the pictures showed him standing beside a thirties-vintage pickup truck, grasping a rifle almost as long as he was. He wore some kind of uniform that included a sheepskin hat. Another snapshot had him standing among a group of solemn young men dressed in similar uniforms.

There were several photographs of Mussa Eini with prominent Israelis. One, bearing a personal dediction, was with Moshe Dayan.

"He was one of my best friends." I turned to face him. He was bearing a tray with a bottle, two glasses, a jug of cold water, and a dish of ice cubes. "What a man he was," he said. "Moshe Dayan was of this land; he belonged to it as much as any of its rocks." He filled the glasses, adding water until the liquor turned milky white. "This is arak. A true drink, better than cognac or whiskey. Believe me."

I was a stranger to him, yet he welcomed me to his home as an honored guest, displaying all the traditional flourishes of Eastern hospitality. Raising his glass, he muttered a toast and took a gulp with evident relish. "Well, Mr. Kottler, what is it you want to know about Tiberias?"

"Anything and everything." I was resolved to conceal my identity as long as possible, and thus refrained from asking specific questions about my father. I wished first to hear about the general climate in which he had spent his childhood and youth.

As though reading my thoughts, Eini launched into a long account of his own youth and of the characters he recalled from those times. His rich, spicy Hebrew was interlaced with a wealth of Arabic proverbs and sayings; he was endowed with a power of description, depicting events and personalities with vivid strokes. He described his early childhood in the Tiberias of the twenties, during the early years of the British administration. Little had changed from the days of Turkish rule, when it was nothing but a remote township in a far-flung corner of the vast Ottoman Empire. Tiberias remained a straggling assortment of black stone houses, scattered at random across the hillsides that dipped down toward the Sea of Galilee.

"There were always plenty of fish," he recalled with a smile. "That was our staple diet—fish from the Kinneret." Mussa Eini referred to the Sea of Galilee by its poetic Hebrew name, which described its harplike shape. Then, as now, the lake provided a livelihood for many of the town's inhabitants. He spoke lovingly and at length of the fishermen of Tiberias, sturdy taciturn men who knew the lake as they knew themselves: where to cast their nets to reap its rich bounty, and where to skirt its hidden rocks and treacherous shallows.

"How many inhabitants did the town have at that time?" I asked.

He shrugged. "Who knows? Four thousand or so, could be more, could be less. No one went to the trouble to count. Jews and Arabs lived side by side." He flung me a fierce glance, as though challenging me to disagree. "That's the way it ought to be. It's been like that since time immemorial. After all, we are all from the seed of Abraham."

He related how the two communities in Tiberias coexisted, separate and yet bound together by close ties of trade and friendship. Naturally, there was occasional friction between them. Such confrontations could be bitter, sometimes sparking off acts of violence. But the conflicts were generally resolved after the age-old manner of the East, with patient mediators—men of standing from both communities—working together to find an honorable compromise.

He spoke for close to an hour, while I listened enthralled. Suddenly, he broke off. "Is there something specific you want to know?"

Startled by his unexpected question, I chose my words cautiously. "There's someone who used to live here, a man who had close links with a relative of mine."

He stared at me. "Are you writing some kind of book? A family chronicle?"

Embarrassed, I mumbled something like "I might . . ."

"And who is this man you're interested in?"

"Yosef Dur," I said softly.

I was startled by his reaction. It was as though he had been slapped across the face. He froze in his place for a long minute, perched there with the immobility of a marble statue. The color drained from his face and his eyes narrowed. "What was that name again?"

"Yosef Dur."

Mussa Eini smiled faintly. "No, you've got it wrong. Not 'Yosef.' Never 'Yosef.' " He shook his head. " 'Yussuf' we called him. The way the Arabs pronounce the name. He grew up among the Arabs, so it was natural to call him 'Yussuf.' That is, when we didn't call him by his nickname."

"Nickname?" I asked in surprise.

"That was Arabic too. 'Badwi.' We called him 'Badwi.' "

" 'Badwi,' " I repeated slowly. "The Bedouin."

Mussa Eini nodded, the same faraway look lingering in his eyes.

"I heard you knew him well," I prompted.

"I knew him like a brother, as though we'd popped out of the same womb." He frowned. "You said something about a family connection?"

"Indirectly . . ."

"Kottler!" Eini said, smiting his forehead with a clenched fist. "That's why the name sounded familiar. That American wife of Yussuf's—her name was Kottler. Are you related to her?"

His direct question placed me in a dilemma. Desiring Eini to speak without reservation, I was reluctant to reveal my identity; but I did not want to lie outright to this sturdy son of Tiberias. Under the circumstances, I opted for a white lie. "She was related to my father."

"Was? She's dead?"

I nodded wordlessly, observing him closely.

"She's gone too. Like Yussuf." He sighed. "Like Yussuf . . ." His eyes were half closed; he leaned back in his armchair, evidently carried away by a wave of nostalgia. "Yussuf Dur . . ."

I began to prompt him. "The two of you must have been about the same age."

Mussa Eini nodded. "We were born in the same year, in the very same month. Sixty-eight years ago, in 1916, here in

Tiberias. I was born in this house, and he was born at his family home up on the hilltop. We grew up together, we played together, we went everywhere together. We became inseparable." He smiled wanly. "As I told you, two brothers. Apart from the army years, we were always together, right up to the time he set out on his last mission."

Eini fell silent. Abruptly, he rose from his seat and strode over to the window, staring out at the lake. "That was our playground. We swam like fish, both of us. As though we were spawned in the water. We thought God had created the lake specially for our private pleasures. In those day Tiberias was just a big fishing village."

He beckoned me to join him at the window and pointed to a mass of black masonry. "That wall was built around the town in the eighteenth century. Whenever some new ruler laid hands on Tiberias, he tried to build a wall. And d'you know what? All the walls crumbled, every one. With one exception—those hills— the wall that God erected—and that has defended this town for two thousand years."

"As long as the exile of the Jews."

He glanced at me reprovingly. "Not all the Jews were exiled. There have always been Jews in the land of Israel. There were always a handful who refused to leave the country. Some were killed, but we were never uprooted. Many Jewish families have lived here without interruption for thousands of years. The Dur family has always lived here."

"Always?" I asked, startled. "All these centuries?"

"Ever since the days when David offended God by sinning with Bathsheba. Ever since Solomon, the bastard son of their forbidden love, built the temple in Jerusalem. The Durs never left here."

"Here?" I pointed downward toward the lake.

"There!" Eini's finger indicated the lake's eastern shore, where the dark hills stood out starkly against the blue sky. "Up in the Golan mountains, that's where the Durs lived for generations, as far back as anyone can recall—tall and agile and daring. And Yussuf was just such a Dur, like his father and his father's father before him."

"Did you know his father?" It was a startlingly novel thought:

95

somehow I had never before thought of my father having parents of his own.

"His father? Do you think I'm talking about a friendship embracing no more than a single generation? The Einis and the Durs go back a long, long way. I knew his grandfather and grandmother. I knew his father, Yehoshua, and his mother, Sarah. Sarah!" He raised his head. "What a woman she was! What a beauty! Even as a child, I could never take my eyes off her. She was tall and slim, with bright red hair. You should have seen her when she went riding with Yehoshua. What a couple they were, on their fine prancing horses!" His face clouded over momentarily. "And what a price they paid."

His cryptic remark was beyond me. I prompted him to tell me more about Sarah Dur.

"She was a superb horsewoman. She could hold her own against the best of the Bedouin riders. I remember as if it were this very morning, how she used to drive into Tiberias in her carriage drawn by a powerful mare, to pick up supplies to carry home. After her purchases, she would come to our home to gossip with my mother, and Yussuf and I would go down to the lake. And then she would call him and off they went, in that little carriage, back up into the hills. I always dreaded the moment I'd see Yussuf leave. He was my favorite playmate and I loved him more than my own brothers."

Mussa Eini heaved a deep sigh. "He was a true son of the desert, an aristocrat of the wilderness, just like the Bedouin. He even looked like them, had their way of thinking, spoke like them. I've heard few Arabs speak their language with a perfection approaching his. There wasn't a regional dialect he didn't know—Syrian, Palestinian, Egyptian, or the local variants. As a young man, he would sometimes dress up in Arab robes, with the headdress and all the other garb, including crossed cartridge belts. You would have sworn that he was an Arab. And he was exceedingly knowledgeable about horses. As a young man, he traded in them. British officers often commissioned him to buy horses for them. At times he would take me along on one of his buying expeditions among the desert tribes. Before my very eyes, he would turn into a Bedouin, a Jewish Bedouin. Come over here and I'll show you." He pointed to the snapshot where he posed with his uniformed companions alongside the ancient pickup truck. "Here, next to me. That's Badwi!"

I bent forward for a closer examination of the fading photograph. It showed my father with greater clarity than in my mother's picture of him. His appearance bore out Mussa Eini's description: he was tall, and even the heavy uniform he wore could not conceal the muscular suppleness of his body. His face was long and thin, its expression conveying a trace of yearning; his gaze was sharp and incisive. Like Mussa Eini, he sported a mustache that gained prominence from the contrast with his ascetic features.

"He certainly caught the eye." Mussa Eini paused, a roguish smile on his lips. "He attracted every girl for miles around. On occasion, we would ride over to Nahalal to visit Moshe Dayan—or so we claimed—but in fact, we went to see the girls from the agricultural school. When we got to Nahalal, we would trot around on our fine horses to make sure we were noticed, so that news of our arrival would reach the school. That evening, a group of girls—half a dozen or more—would sneak out of school to come and find us. Badwi and I would take them off into the fields and light a fire. Badwi would sing the songs of the nomads. Sometimes he'd bring out a flute whose tones went straight to the heart." He winked impishly. "More than one girl's heart was broken on an evening like that . . ." He gazed into the distance. "That year, 1936, Yussuf and I celebrated our twentieth birthdays. We didn't know then that our youth would come to an abrupt end."

"The 'incidents'?"

Mussa Eini nodded. "It was no time for boys and girls to sit around open fires. We were all threatened by a far more sinister blaze."

My own studies had taught me about 1936, the year that marked the end of coexistence between Jews and Arabs in Palestine. As tension grew between the two peoples, the Arabs took up arms to prevent the emergence of a Jewish national home.

"What happened to you? And to Yussuf Dur?"

Mussa Eini squared his shoulders. "I was called to serve with the local units of the Hagana, the underground Jewish militia. Yussuf joined the Hagana's intelligence arm. They made good use of his knowledge of Arabic and his knack for posing as an Arab."

"He was a spy?"

My brusque question evoked no immediate response. Mussa Eini dropped a couple of ice cubes into my empty glass, replenishing it with arak until the milky liquor filled it to the top. "You could call him a spy," he conceded. "There was plenty of work for a spy at that time. The Arabs were waging a holy war against the Jews. Jewish villages were fired upon, and our transport suffered harassment on the highways. The situation grew worse by the day. We were limited in arms and manpower, and we had plenty of vulnerable targets to protect. There was the Levant Fair in Tel Aviv, for example. It was a major project, a showcase for the new industries Jews were building up. We knew the Arabs would do everything in their power to wreck it—by force, if necessary. Yussuf was sent by the Hagana to tour the Arab villages to see what was brewing. He put on his disguise and set out on his mission. It didn't take him long to learn that an armed gang was preparing to attack the fair. Acting on Yussuf's information, the Hagana alerted one of its units, and when the attack came, our boys were waiting. The attackers fled in disgrace. But since there was danger of further raids, Yussuf was ordered to stay at the fair and keep his eyes open."

"He kept them wide open," I grinned. "That was where he set eyes on—I mean, that was how—my relative Rachel Kottler happened to meet him."

"Meet?" Eini smiled. "You call that 'meeting'? It was more like a head-on collision! Like the explosion of a meteor."

"I know she was very taken with him . . ."

"She may have been 'taken,' " Eini placed scornful stress on the word. "But he was bewitched by her. Bewitched out and out!"

"Did you meet her at the time?"

"Not in the flesh. But I met her through Yussuf, because when you were with Yussuf, you sensed her presence. He was utterly possessed by her, as though some spirit had taken up its abode within his soul."

"He must have talked about her a lot."

"Yussuf wasn't talkative. He rarely uttered her name. But

he came back from the fair a changed man. From that day on, there was no other woman for him. He lived like a monk. She was much younger, little more than a child, but when she returned to the United States with her family, he didn't give up. He settled down to wait for her." He gazed at me. "Even when they were far apart, there was a unique bond which united them. On one of the rare occasions when he consented to talk to me about her, he said something I shall never forget. 'Rachel and I,' he said, 'we are twin spirits.' "

He paused, his eyes closed, his head resting on one hand. "You ask if I met her? I did. But it took twelve years. Everything was disrupted by the war in thirty-nine. I joined the British army, and so did Yussuf, but we served in different units. I saw nothing of him till the end of the war. When he finally got out of uniform, his only aim was to find his Rachel. He delayed just long enough to scrape together the money for the fare, and he was off to New York. But then late in forty-seven, the fighting broke out again here and he came right back. A few months later she arrived too." He took a sip of arak. "I went to Haifa harbor to meet her. I'll never forget that moment. I was a grown man at the time, long married, with children of my own. I knew all about women. I'd seen plenty in my time. But when I set eyes on Rachel, as she was stepping down the gangplank, I thought to myself, 'Ya Yussuf! Oh my brother! You certainly knew what to pick!' " Eini shook his head. "She was no great beauty. I've seen prettier. But she was all woman. A woman who drives you out of your mind just by looking at you."

I shifted in my seat, hard put to camouflage my unease: it was the first time I had ever heard my mother described as she appeared to another man. "Why was it you who met her at the port?"

"Because Badwi wasn't there!" Eini said. "Because he had gone to Yemen on a mission for the Mossad, so of course he couldn't come to welcome her. She had made her way from New York to find him—and he wasn't there! I'll never forget the pain in those great wide eyes when I told her. She said nothing, but the expression on her face was enough to break my heart—" He paused before resuming, his voice so low as to be almost inaudible. "To break my heart, because I knew then, before she

99

realized it, before she sensed or guessed or imagined it, I knew what it was she faced."

"What did she face?"

"Another love," he whispered. "A love stronger even than the love he bore for her."

"But you said he never . . ."

"Oh no, it wasn't another woman. I told you, after he met Rachel, other women didn't exist for Badwi. No, his other love had no human form, but that didn't help, it only made matters worse, because it utterly enslaved him."

"I don't follow you."

Mussa Eini raised his eyes. "Yussuf and I, and the men of our generation, we were all born with a love which overshadowed all others. It was a love for this land. For the Galilee and the Negev, for the Judaean Mountains and the Jordan Valley, for the splendors of the hills and the glories of the valleys and the radiance of Jerusalem."

He paused, out of breath, his gaze again directed toward the window and the mountains beyond the lake.

Finally, I broke the silence. "What—what did she do then?"

"What could she do? She waited. For some time, I don't remember exactly how long. Sat around, waiting and hoping. Until finally, one day, he returned." Mussa sighed deeply, as though reliving his own relief at this happy outcome. "I don't have the words to describe their joy. It radiated from them, enveloping everyone who knew them. After that, the next step was inevitable. Within a very short time, just as soon as the formalities could be arranged, they got married. The ceremony was held at his home, the ancestral Dur home on the hill. God, what excitement there was! Badwi's friends came by the hundreds, from all over the country, arriving without formal invitation— who sent out formal invitations in those days?—just summoned by the rumor that flashed over the grapevine. 'Badwi is marrying his American sweetheart!' What a party that was! What a celebration! A day and a night and another day . . ." He shook his head. "Nobody thought of tomorrow. Not Yussuf, marrying so late in life, and not Rachel, who had waited patiently, obstinately, desperately, never giving up hope, until that day when he would be hers and hers alone."

The smile faded. "Only he wasn't hers alone. That was her mistake, and it became evident when he was called on another mission for the Mossad, with everything that entailed. That was when it really began to get to her. His other love, I mean. She couldn't understand. I sensed her anguish and shared it, but there was nothing I could do to help. She crumpled under the weight of a jealousy such as no woman should ever have to endure."

He sighed again. "One day early in fifty-two he told her he was leaving on a mission which promised to be long and dangerous. Rachel begged him not to go. It was as though some second sense warned her she would never see him again. She even came to ask my help, imploring me to talk him into giving up his work. But I couldn't do that because, like Badwi, I was convinced that duty came first. That was the way we all thought in those days."

Mussa Eini lowered his head. "The tension between them became intolerable. Finally, I went to see Badwi. I said, 'Yussuf, my brother, even the Bible says that a newlywed man should take the year to build his own home. Beyond that? God is great and He will illumine our path.' He heard me out patiently. But then, in his own quiet way, he told me why he couldn't. 'In my work for the Mossad,' he said, 'I am responsible for laying down a certain strategy. It has to do with a matter of greatest importance for the future of our country. Unfortunately, there's been a mishap, and it's up to me to put it right. It's something I can't leave to anyone else. Just like the army, Mussa, the commander marches at the head of his men.' That was all he said. His mind was made up and he refused to reconsider."

"What did he tell you about his mission?"

"Nothing beyond what I've told you."

"Didn't you ask?"

His smile was condescending. "When you're dealing with a man like Badwi, you don't ask. If he wanted to tell you something, he told you."

"So you know nothing more?"

He shook his head. "One day, he slipped across the border into one of the Arab states. After that, it was as though he'd vanished. No news, no sign, nothing."

"And she—Rachel—?"

He averted his head. "Shortly after his departure, she left too. She never even came to me to say goodbye. I can't blame her. Her agony was intolerable; she felt she had been abandoned."

Eini stopped. We sat there, sipping arak, each drawn into his own thoughts. I could hear his gentle breathing. Without a word, he refilled our glasses. The alcohol was beginning to affect me; my tongue felt heavy and swollen. But I continued to sip the arak; I needed the liquor to summon up the courage to ask the question that seared the tip of my tongue. "Tell me," I said slowly, trying to meet his gaze, "how could he go away and leave his wife pregnant?"

My question startled him. "What sort of a story is that?" he said, drawing back as though I had delivered a blow to his jaw.

"That's what I heard . . ."

"You heard what?"

"That she was pregnant when she got back to New York."

"Out of the question!"

"Well," I said hesitantly. "That's what I heard. But maybe I misunderstood . . ."

"Of course you misunderstood! People talk a lot of nonsense." Suddenly, his eyes lit up. "And anyway, if she were pregnant—whatever became of the child?"

We were getting onto dangerous ground, and I doubted my ability to negotiate it successfully. Quickly, I sought some way of closing the subject. "Maybe she had a miscarriage." I took a deep breath. Quite aside from the effects of the arak, what I had just heard was quite sufficient to throw me off balance. If Mussa Eini was right, Yussuf Dur set off on his final mission never suspecting his wife was pregnant. In all probability, she herself was still unaware of it when he left. Perhaps I was the fruit of their last night together. Who knows—?

"The stories people believe . . ." Eini muttered indignantly, in evident despair at the folly of the world. "It's all talk. But I like you. You've given me an opportunity to dredge up all those memories and I'm grateful for that. So tomorrow, if you like, I'll do more than just talk. I'll take you to see for yourself, with your own two eyes. Be ready first thing in the morning."

I got the hint: he was weary and I had taken up enough of his time. I thanked him and took my leave. Eini scarcely gave me a glance, and his goodbye was absentminded. At the door, I turned my head and caught a final glimpse of him as he crouched in his chair, his chin resting on his hand.

As I made my way back to the hotel, I too allowed my thoughts to wander to faraway times and places. I was still dazed by Eini's vivid account and the figures he had brought back to life. I felt like a traveler returning from some distant galaxy to my own familiarly drab world.

When I woke up, sunlight was streaming into my room. I stood up, my balance unsteady from the dazzling light no less than from the aftereffects of the drinking. I walked over to the window, propping myself against its frame, and gazed out at the lake that shimmered in the morning sun like a burnished copper buckle. I stayed there for a few moments, drinking in the fresh morning breeze and staring at the sun as it mounted over the hills, precisely as my father had seen it as a young man.

At 7:30, Rafi Eini came to the hotel to call for me. At his grandfather's behest, he had taken the morning off work to place himself at the disposal of his guest.

"I understand you had a long session last night," he said, as he drove down the steep street. "I hear you have an interest in one of granddad's old buddies." His tone was indifferent; still, it failed to conceal an underlying curiosity.

"There's a distant relative involved," I explained, keeping my gaze on his face.

He paused just a moment too long before answering. "That's interesting."

A few moments later, Rafi led the way up the steps behind the restaurant to Mussa Eini's apartment. He was up and awaiting us, eager to impress me with the culinary blitzkrieg by which Tiberians launch their day. At the arched window stood a long table laden with jugs of fresh juice, orange and tomato, flanked by a tall carafe of ice water and a pot of steaming black coffee. Alongside stood dishes with an assortment of fish, cheeses, and every imaginable variety of newly picked vegetables, supplemented by two baskets overflowing with fresh rolls and pita.

"Come on, young man," Eini roared with an insistence that would have done credit to Aunt Bertha. "Dig in."

When I had eaten my fill and gulped down the last of my coffee, the three of us marched down the steps and settled ourselves in Rafi's car. Rafi drove, and I sat beside him, while Mussa sat in back. "I used to drive myself," he said in my ear, "but this *jakhash*, this young ass . . ." he pointed at Rafi, "thinks anything we old-timers did, he can do better."

After leaving the town boundaries, the car sped along the lakeside, heading south, then gradually swinging around to the east. There the road diverged from the shoreline and we began to climb into the foothills. After a rapid ascent, we emerged on the upper plateau, where Rafi found a suitable spot to stop.

We got out of the car and I gazed about me. I saw a broad, unbounded expanse, reaching into the hazy distance, with dark outcrops of black rock overshadowing the deep purple soil. Mussa picked up a chunk of rock, holding it out to me. Obediently, I grasped it in my hand. The stone was a dark gray and hard as flint. "It's heavy," I observed.

"More than heavy. It's solid. You can't break it." He picked up another piece. "Look at it. It was formed eons ago by some elemental eruption, when the earth heaved and thundered until it brought forth this—this unflinching, unyielding, intractable rock." He surveyed the landscape. "That was how the Durs were forged, adamant and inflexible, embedded in the soil just like these rocks."

"Was this where . . ." I paused, hesitating to utter my father's name, "where he grew up?"

Mussa Eini nodded. "On this harsh, inhospitable plateau, learning its secret ways, how to endure the enmity of its rocks, and how to reap the rich profusion of its soil. Here he ran and played as a child, and here, while yet little more than a boy, he became a man—a Dur. He withstood the fire and survived."

I listened, puzzled by his cryptic references. "Fire?"

He seemed not to hear my question; he was in a reverie, his eyes again contemplating distant sights, from distant days. When he finally spoke, his voice was barely audible over the monotonous howl of the wind. "The fire that seared his soul one fearsome night, leaving him stunned and orphaned. Did I say 'fire'? 'Pestilence' would be a better word, a pestilence in human form." His voice returned to a more normal tone. "Yussuf's father raised horses, as I told you, and his trade was sizable. But the pick of his stable, the most splendid animal you could imagine, was his own mare." The gloom of Mussa's expression was broken by a fleeting smile of admiration. "She was no ordinary horse. She was a raging tempest. She was pitch-black, with a white star at the center of her forehead, which is why Yehoshua named her 'Morning Star.' Sheikhs and emirs begged him to sell her. But Yehoshua refused them all. That mare was his joy and comfort and the embodiment of his masculine pride.

"There was one Bedouin sheikh who offered astronomical sums. When Yehoshua rejected his repeated offers, the sheikh swore a double oath—to possess that mare and to punish Dur for his presumption. One night, the sheikh sent a gang of his men to seize the mare. Yehoshua fought valiantly, but they overpowered him. In the course of the fight, they saw that they had been recognized by Yehoshua, who could easily deduce who had sent them. To protect the sheikh, and to cover up the traces of their crime, they slaughtered the entire family before fleeing to the desert.

"By some miracle, they overlooked Yussuf. The little boy crept behind the great clay oven and cowered there that whole dreadful night. The following morning, Dur's Arab laborers came upon the horrifying scene. Seven bodies were scattered throughout the house. Yussuf's grandparents, his father and mother, his two brothers and his baby sister. Finally the laborers came upon Yussuf, still crouching behind the stove, paralyzed with shock."

I experienced a strange emptiness. Somehow the atrocious deeds he described failed to move me. I could sense no connection with the victims; logically, I knew them to have been my flesh and blood, but logic brought no attendant emotion. My father still remained remote and intangible; how, then, could I grieve for his parents? And yet, I felt an urge to know more. "What happened then?"

"The laborers were very gentle. When Yussuf had recovered somewhat, they put him on a horse and brought him up here, to the mountains, to an Arab family friend, Yehoshua's closest business associate. Like Yehoshua, he too traded in horses and camels. The trader took the child into his household and raised him with his own children. Several times a year, he would send him to us, to the Einis, for the Jewish festivals, because he knew we were Yussuf's own people. The Arab trader wanted the boy to grow up as his father would have wished. But whenever Yussuf came on those visits, he never once set foot in his family home. He knew he must not return to that house before he had fulfilled his sacred duty."

Goom, I thought to myself.

"The *goom,*" Mussa echoed my unvoiced word. "Blood vengeance. Yussuf was brought up never to forget for a single moment that he would be called upon one day to wash away the blood of his dear ones with the blood of their murderers. His Arab guardian trained Yussuf well, teaching him everything he needed to know for the discharge of that debt.

"On Yussuf's sixteenth birthday, his guardian called him and told him the time had come. Yussuf was provided with everything he required—a fine horse, a lance, a rifle and revolver, and enough money and food to sustain him in the desert."

"But he was only a child!"

Mussa's gaze dismissed my objections. "You never knew Yussuf. At sixteen, he was a full-grown man. He knew precisely what he had to do. He had often gone with his guardian on expeditions into the desert; he knew it by day and by night; he knew its ways, its lore, its people.

"Yussuf set off, scouring the desert in quest of his prey. He was away a full year. When he returned to the Golan hills, he arrived at the house of his guardian and walked in without a word. Still not speaking, he presented himself before his guardian and held out the sword of the Bedouin sheikh who had sent the murderers. He had discharged his debt."

"What an awesome feat," I murmured. "How did he . . . ?"

"He never told me. Or anyone else. The story got around, of course, and people looked up to him, even though he was a mere youth. That was when they took to calling him 'Badwi,' and the name stuck."

Badwi, I thought. I followed Mussa Eini's gaze, scanning the dark stony landscape that had molded my father. A light push jolted me abruptly out of my ruminations. I looked up to find Mussa Eini standing close by. Wordlessly, he beckoned to me to return to the car. Silently, I followed him.

Rafi started the engine and the car cruised down the hillside until it turned onto the lakeside road, following its curved path until we were again in Tiberias. But Rafi did not stop; he drove on until we emerged to the north, where he spotted what he was seeking. A gap in the avenue of trees marked the beginning of a track leading uphill. The track was scarcely wide enough to allow the vehicle through, and its rough surface testified to its infrequent use.

We were halfway up the incline when Mussa pointed ahead to an ancient stone wall. It surrounded an equally venerable building, its upper two stories tapering forward into an enormous terrace resembling a prehistoric altar. Leaning forward, Mussa laid a hand on my shoulder. "This is it," he said. "The home of the Dur family. That's where they lived as far back as anyone can remember."

Rafi stopped the car beside the wall and we got out. With Mussa leading the way, we stepped through the heavy wooden gateway, painted a bright blue to fend off the evil eye. I glanced up at the house. "It still looks lived-in," I said, staring up at the crumbling facade.

"You can thank my grandfather for that," Rafi Eini grinned.

I directed a puzzled glance at Mussa. "I come here every now and then," he confessed.

"What for?"

"A house is like a living being; it has to be cared for, otherwise it dies. Before Yussuf set out on his last mission, he begged me to help his young wife look after the house. At first, I did just that, but then, not long after his disappearance, she went away too. So I was left with these." He fished out a bunch of keys. "Ever since, I've been taking care of the house. I hoped that one day she would return. I come around, open the blinds, clean up. But the main thing is to give the house the feeling of a human presence."

Mussa led the way up the wide stone steps to the great terrace, which was roofed over with heavy wooden beams. Just as Mussa had described, there was a splendid view of the Sea of

Galilee and the surrounding hills. Here, I thought, on this terrace, my father and mother were married; here they stood beneath the canopy while its four poles were held upright by the sturdy arms of men like Mussa Eini.

It is difficult to know where and when and at which particular burden of stress a man will surrender to his emotions. But standing there, on the threshold of the home of my father and my father's father, I was on the verge of revealing my true identity to Mussa Eini. Still, I bit the words back, flexing my jaw muscles till they were stiff.

Mussa unlocked the door and flung it open. I walked in behind him, inhaling the musty odor of the aging structure and its moldering furniture. Mussa opened the blinds, letting in a flood of clear light. With the fresh air that poured in, the house soon lost its enclosed smell, returning to life as though it had never been abandoned or uninhabited.

Mussa showed me the massive furniture, the great upholstered divans, the fine hanging rugs, and the heavy desk. He pointed to the faded photographs on the walls. One, in the center, showed a figure in the robes of a Bedouin sheikh, seated proudly on a noble horse that lifted its head as though it too were posing for the photographer.

"That is Eliyahu Dur, Yussuf's grandfather," Mussa said. "He was known throughout the province as 'Abu Hamsa.' "

"Meaning 'the owner of the gun that shoots five.' "

Mussa Eini looked at me in surprise. "Do you know Arabic?"

"Yes."

He broke into a flood of Palestinian Arabic; I replied fluently in the same dialect. "If I hadn't known you came from New York, I would have taken you for one of ours," he said.

I was flattered by his admiration, but I noticed that my mastery of Arabic had given a jolt to his grandson; Rafi was studying me closely, as though somehow suspecting that my present guise was meant to fool. He said nothing, but I noticed that he stayed close beside Mussa, listening carefully to his responses, no less than to my questions.

Now Mussa drew me over to the desk, where he rummaged through the drawers to bring out an assortment of faded papers written in Arabic, Turkish, English, and Hebrew. There were land deeds and bills for the sale of horses and farm products;

there were birth, marriage, and death certificates, and a wealth of other documents. I helped Rafi drag armchairs out to the great terrace, while his grandfather rearranged whatever he had displaced during our tour of the house. "You're making a very thorough study of Yussuf Dur," Rafi said.

"His wife was a relative of mine."

"Is that the only reason?"

"Could there be any other?"

Rafi shrugged. "How would I know?"

Mussa came out to join us, and we seated ourselves to watch the landscape change color and hue with the shifting shadows. Then Mussa Eini plunged once more into his recollections of those fascinating times long past.

He related what he knew of Yussuf's exploits in the British army during the war. Initially, Badwi served in Burma with the special units that operated far behind the Japanese lines. Later, toward the end of the war, he was posted to Europe. When the fighting ceased, Yussuf joined the 'Avengers.' That was the name of a shadowy organization of Jewish soldiers from various armies who cooperated with former members of Jewish partisan groups. Their job was to hunt down Nazi war criminals and officers of the SS and Gestapo. During Israel's War of Independence, Yussuf would set off into Arab territory on solo missions, infiltrating the headquarters of the various Arab forces and returning at dawn, bringing valuable information about enemy plans. "Much of what he did then remains confidential," Mussa said. "He set up contacts and built channels of information which continued to serve Israel for many years. Some may still be functioning to this day."

"What a pity he isn't here to see the results of his work," I said. "Where did he die? And how?"

"That's the most difficult question you could ask. Don't imagine it hasn't troubled me all these years. No one, none of his friends or companions, knows anything about his last mission or how it ended. All we know is that he vanished."

"Didn't you try to find out from the Mossad?"

"I did. I asked everywhere, pulled every string I could reach. So did Yussuf's other friends. All we got were vague answers. 'He fell in the line of duty'—that's all."

For some unaccountable reason, I turned my head suddenly

to find Rafi staring at me with unconcealed hostility. But as soon as he caught my eye, he averted his gaze.

Something was going awry. I had a gnawing feeling that Rafi suspected the motive behind my interest in Yosef Dur was not as innocent as I had presented it. I hoped his distrust wouldn't lead to any dangerous complications.

7

The outline of my father's house merged into the shadow of the hillside as the taxi climbed the steeply inclined road out of Tiberias. Utterly weary, I stretched out on the back seat. Darkness was falling, and clusters of light pointed out the positions of the various villages and settlements along the way to Tel Aviv. But I had no interest in them; my thoughts were elsewhere, in another place and another time.

It was shortly after my fifteenth birthday. I was seated at the table, facing my mother, in the small lounge of our Brooklyn home. The table had been prepared with punctilious care. Everything was in its proper place: cutlery, china, and glasses, all set out on the fine cream-colored tablecloth reserved exclusively for festive occasions. On a nearby shelf stood the candlesticks that, together with their matching pair in Bertha's apartment, had been acquired when the Kottlers visited Jerusalem in 1936.

The room shone like a finely polished gem, and little wonder: my mother had spent the entire day scrubbing the floor, washing the windows, and rubbing the furniture to a fine sheen.

For that evening's meal, she had insisted we wear our best outfits, and I obeyed, even though I detested the garments she bought me. I played the game entirely by her rules.

Seated at the table, I found it hard to take my eyes off her. The flickering candlelight created soft shadows that danced and curtsied across her features. Her face was set in the dreamy expression of surrender to something that transcended my understanding. A stranger would never have guessed that this elegantly dressed hostess was mentally unbalanced. She attended to everything with perfection. That particular evening, she was dressed handsomely. As was her custom, she wore no jewelry, and merely a trace of makeup; her use of cosmetics was characterized by a touch as light and delicate as her own person. Her skin was pale and smooth, and her white, swanlike neck remained miraculously free of wrinkles. In the warmth of that spring evening, she wore a white dress with a modest décolletage, set off by matching white linen gloves reaching up beyond the elbow.

The meal marked my mother's return from her first trip to Miami, where she had gone to care for the mysterious cousin who, I now believed, was in fact an aging and dotingly open-handed lover. It had been her first excursion from New York since her return from Israel fifteen years earlier, when she carried me in her womb. She had spent a week in Miami, returning, to everyone's amazement, an utterly changed person. The moment she stepped out of the taxi that brought her from the airport, her manner was all affability and sweet patience, as though she had been born anew.

I plied her with questions about her journey. Her replies were detailed and charming, with a wealth of amusing anecdotes. She had a subtle sense of humor that I witnessed all too seldom. But this particular evening she was at her best: incisive and witty.

Nevertheless, I was hazily aware of being excluded from whatever she had experienced during her absence. I perceived that some of her answers were craftily worded to conceal something. But her dissembling was less than perfect, and in spite of my adolescent obtuseness, I was not totally insensitive. I realized that, in her own bizarre manner, she was seeking an oblique way of sharing with me—and with me alone—some grand revelation. Whatever it was, she stopped short of putting it into words.

She's nuts, I concluded at the time. A lost soul awaiting a deliverance that would never come. Like a swift jab of physical pain, I felt a stab of pity for her. I had an urge to burst into tears, for myself no less than for her. I understood that my mother had been robbed of some glorious splendor. And that she, so soft, so gentle, so devastated by her misfortune, was too weak to raise her voice in protest.

Only now, nearly seventeen years later, as the taxi sped toward Tel Aviv, did I succeed in tying together the threads. My youthful instincts had not misled me: my mother had, indeed, been despoiled of her love, that first love whose glory nothing exceeds. Mussa Eini had been right; in the struggle for my father's allegiance, she had lost—to Israel. My God, I wondered, how was she, with her fragility of spirit, ever capable of living here? Then, as now, it was a land whose soil erupted in fountains of violence, blood, and hatred. A land that devoured its sons.

I found no room within me for equanimity. I abhorred this land for everything it had done, to my mother and to me. My hatred was so powerful that it sent a shudder through my body. Now, as I followed my father's footsteps, in his own land, I experienced a deeper confusion in my conflicting emotions toward him. At one moment, I hated him; in the next, I loved him.

But alongside his almost superhuman figure, I saw the fragility of my mother. All she had had in life was one tiny corner that she cultivated and cherished. All she sought was to love her man. Perhaps her greatest gift was her ability to love with that total devotion that brings a man and woman together in a communion of body and soul. She loved with all her being, until the loss of her man destroyed the delicate balance of her mind. Seated now in the taxi, I saw her face before me again, as she smiled her enigmatic smile, looking at me without seeing me.

I chose to stay at the Sheraton, which the taxi driver recommended, situated as it was within easy walking distance of almost any place of importance in Tel Aviv. Having deposited my bags, I returned to the lobby and walked over to the information desk.

"I want to get to the site of the Levant Fair," I said.

"Levant Fair?" The young clerk seemed puzzled.

"It was in 1936 . . ." I paused. "An international fair. You must have heard of it."

"I'm sorry; I can't help you." He turned and referred me to his superior.

Entering the office, I found a man in his fifties, courteous and affable. He listened patiently to my question, nodding when I reported my failure to elicit any help from the desk clerk.

"You must forgive him," he said. "He wasn't born in this country and knows little of Tel Aviv. Very few people remember the country as it was in the old days." He sketched out a little map. "All you have to do is walk out of the hotel and head north all the way up Hayarkon Street. At the end of the street, turn right, to a traffic light. At its left you'll find the entrance to the fairgrounds."

Outside the hotel, the street was full of the noise and bustle characteristic of all Mideastern cities. I walked along Hayarkon Street, gazing about me. Along the beach to my left stood modern hotels; to my right, the road was occupied by two- and three-storied buildings whose facades were peeling from long exposure to the sea air. Their ground floors had been converted into stores selling everything from watches and jewelry to antiques. Interspersed among these were the elegant offices of international airlines.

But whichever way I looked, I found not the slightest trace of the white city featured in Aunt Bertha's accounts: no remnant of the little white-washed houses or of the tree-lined avenues running down toward the azure sea.

I reached the northern section of Hayarkon Street, which housed a colorful and odoriferous assortment of pubs, Chinese restaurants, steak houses, and cafés.

The changes time had wrought became insignificant as I anticipated my imminent encounter with the winged camel. I glanced ahead impatiently. There, between the traffic light and the old wall, I would locate its soaring silhouette, poised as it had been for decades past.

The winged camel may have been there. Once. But not now. There was no camel. No pillar. Nothing. I had not erred. I was indeed standing before the rusting gates of what was once the majestic entrance to the fair. But all that remained of the small piazza that had centered about the pillar with the winged camel was an ordinary traffic light and a busy street.

My disappointment left me with a sense of emptiness. I crossed to the other side of the street. On the right, near the short bridge spanning the Yarkon River, I found a small pub. I took a seat and ordered a large beer. The other stools were occupied by a smattering of bored men; the small tables were taken by young couples.

The barman filled my glass. "This beer is unequaled," he said.

"What's so special about it?"

"It clears your mind of anything you want to forget. That's where it has the advantage over whiskey or brandy. It doesn't get you drunk, but it does an equally good job of obliterating."

"Thanks for the tip."

"You're welcome."

"Do you know this part of the city well?"

"Sure." He brought me a plate of olives. His name, he said, was Ya'akov, but the clients called him Yak. He was in his late fifties, balding and round-faced. His expression was friendly, and his frequent smiles brought out a boyish dimple on his right cheek. "I was born around here."

"It must have changed since those days."

He laughed. "That's an understatement."

"You must know about the Levant Fair, over there on the other side of the street."

Yak whistled in surprise. "It's been some time since I heard anyone mention it. You're going back a long way."

"What do you know about the fair?"

"What don't I know? My family came to live here in 1934. My father managed the crews erecting the exhibition pavilions. I remember it all."

"And its emblem?"

His gaze turned toward the traffic light. "The architect who designed that camel was a friend of my father's. I remember

115

when they cast the pillar. It must have been about thirty feet high. When it set, they mounted the camel. It was made of stainless steel and must have stood about ten feet high. The camel was so lifelike, I can't tell you! When the sun's rays caught its wings, you could really fancy that it was about to fly." He poured himself a beer. "When I started going out with girls, we used to meet there. How could I ever forget it? I was standing beneath it one night when I was fourteen and got my first-ever feel of a tit. I got so excited I almost came there and then."

"Those were the days," I agreed.

"But they came to an end when they took down the camel."

"When was that?"

He scratched the back of his neck. "About seventeen years ago. There were cracks in the pillar, and anyway the municipality wanted to widen the road. So they found a simple solution for the winged camel. They took it down, and that was that."

It was after midnight when I left the pub. Crossing the street, I halted at the spot where the column once supported the camel on its flight. I stared at the dark sky. Up there, at least, nothing had changed.

I began to walk toward the hotel, making my way past the tumult of the restaurants. After a few minutes, I reached the park, which occupied the area between the street and the beach. I decided to walk to the seashore where my mother had spent so many magical hours with Yussuf Dur. The park's central path was well lit. I sauntered down until I reached the heavy wall of rocks overhanging the beach. I paused there, gazing down at the white-capped waves as they lapped the shore. After a moment or two, I clambered down to where my feet sank into the soft sand—I crossed the beach until I reached the water. The damp sand offered a better foothold, and I began to walk south toward the hotel.

Overcome by weariness, I slept till eight the following morning, waking to find my room bathed in dazzling light.

The information clerk told me how to get to the municipal museum. The twenty-minute walk along Ben Yehuda and Allenby streets took me past the bustling sidewalks of Tel Aviv's downtown commercial section, which, like its counterparts in other major cities, turned out to be far too narrow and crowded to accommodate the traffic. The roar of the buses and commercial trucks, the swift purr of cars, and the high-pitched clatter of motorcycles all blended into one incessantly agonized growl, as though the heart of the city had been wounded.

It was only when I turned off into Bialik Street that I caught a glimpse of Tel Aviv as it had been before being covered over by the gaudiness of modern facades. Although the street was partly blocked by a line of parked cars, its houses had been preserved as they were at the time of their construction long ago. The end of the street widened out into a small square filled with brightly colored flowers. The square was designed to permit access by carriage or car to the old municipality, a graceful building laid out along the classical lines of Levantine architecture. Twin flights of steps led to the main entrance on the second floor.

The interior had been converted into a compact and tasteful museum. I wandered around, gazing at the various exhibits, which depicted different periods in the city's history. There were pictures of the city's founding fathers congregating on the sand dunes to cast lots for the choice of building plots in the new town. I studied photographs of the main streets during their construction and of newly planted trees just beginning to sprout leaves. Tel Aviv had been a small town with a great vision. There were pictures from later years, with the houses more numerous and the trees grown to full height. There were photos of children born in Tel Aviv and of the new immigrants who poured in, wearing the European clothes of the twenties and thirties. They were the survivors fleeing from the barbarians, bringing with them the aroma of the coffeehouses of Berlin and Vienna.

Events of the past arose before my eyes. Long lines of camels carried sand from the port area to the new construction sites, the beasts seeming to move straight at me, as though their long gawky legs were about to step right out of the picture. I saw photographs of Jewish laborers building the first jetty of Tel Aviv's miniature port. No seagoing vessel could enter its open anchorage; instead, the ships cast anchor offshore, and their cargoes were ferried in by flat-bottomed lighters. Nevertheless, this section of the coast became known as "the port of Tel Aviv."

When I had concluded my tour of the museum, I approached its director to inquire whether there was any material on the Levant Fair. I was in luck: the museum had photographs of it. I leafed through them with trembling hands, knowing precisely what I sought. Finally, I found it: the fair's emblem— the flying camel which I had hoped to find at its original site. I stood gazing down at the photograph. To me, it represented a vision taking on clear form. The camel was beautifully designed, a dream given artistic life. The East awakening from its slumbers. It appeared to be lifting off, its wings spread out, its neck curved, forelegs folded up beneath its belly and the hind legs preparing to spring off the column, which was its sole remaining link with solid earth.

After that, there was nothing more I wanted to see. I walked out of the museum into the afternoon sun.

It was late evening when I got back to the hotel. I had stepped over to reception to pick up my key, when someone behind me laid a cautious hand on my shoulder. Wheeling about, I found myself facing two men: one in a police uniform, the other in civilian clothing.

"Excuse me sir," said the uniformed one. "Are you Daniel Kottler?"

"I am."

He exchanged glances with his red-haired companion. "May I see your passport?"

"Just as soon as I see your identification."

"Certainly," he replied courteously, holding out his police ID. In return, I reached into my jacket and brought out my passport, which I handed him. The policeman opened it, and, after a fleeting glance at the photograph, passed it on to his companion. The latter inspected it carefully, and then, without a word, slipped it into his pocket.

"What's all this about?" I demanded with the assurance of a man who knew he'd done nothing wrong. But I began to worry when the policeman ignored my question and subjected me to a rapid frisking, without, of course, finding any weapon. After that, he took the key to my room and handed it to the civilian, who turned away and headed toward the elevator. Obviously, he was on his way to conduct a search.

I became uneasily aware of the curious stares of the hotel employees, who eyed me with misgiving. The policeman escorted me to a corner seat where we would be less conspicuous. I tried to draw him into conversation, but he replied with such evident reluctance that I finally let him be. He had clearly received instructions to say nothing and was following them to the letter. Ten minutes later, the civilian returned; his face was expressionless, but I knew he had found my room clean of anything suspicious.

"Let's go," said the redhead. "We have a matter that needs your clarification." The policeman nodded to me to rise.

Suddenly, I remembered other eyes staring at me and a piece clicked into place. Rafi Eini, I thought, you did your work well.

Outside, a white Ford Escort awaited us, with a driver in civilian clothes. None of the car's occupants said a word as we drove north along Hayarkon Street. After less than a mile, the driver swung right; he soon swerved again, advancing slowly along an unlit avenue until finally he drew up at the local police station. We climbed the steps to the second floor, where I was ushered into a small room. The uniformed policeman had disappeared.

I was shown to a seat at the end of a table, placed alongside a second table. Behind this one sat another man, also in civilian clothing. The redhead introduced him to me as Mr. Zinger. He was in his forties. His teeth clutched a cigarette holder, which he sucked incessantly in an evidently desperate attempt to stop smoking; his fingers, I noticed, were stained yellow from nicotine. The redhead, who entered behind me, brought out my passport and laid it down on the table before Zinger, who was obviously his superior.

The passport was brand-new, having been issued by the CIA's consular section only a few days prior to my departure. Once again, I blessed Charlie for his precautions, which included the incineration of my old passport; otherwise Zinger would have seen numerous visa stamps testifying to my visits to countries hostile to Israel. But he noticed something all the same.

"I see this passport was issued just before your present

journey," he said drily. "Don't tell me this is your first trip to Israel."

I hesitated. I still had no idea how matters stood, and until I did, there was no point in exacerbating the situation. I knew all about interrogation techniques, and this one did not sound like standard police procedure.

"You'd better cooperate," Zinger said with a weariness for which I could not blame him. He had evidently waited long after his regular working hours before his men succeeded in netting me in the hotel lobby.

"I'll ask you again, Mister Kottler. How many times have you been here before?"

"This is my first time here," I said, "and I've done nothing wrong."

He shook his head from side to side, as though rebuking me for fooling with him. "You're a very cool liar. Your Hebrew is perfect, like that of a native-born Israeli. You may even have spent lengthy periods of time here, and this 'new' passport is merely the latest in a long series."

I didn't answer. Silence seemed the best response.

"Whom do you work for?"

"I don't know what you mean."

"Play it your way." He stuck the holder back between his teeth, chewing it angrily.

"I am employed by two New York attorneys," I said at last. "I'll give you their number. You can call them right now, and they'll tell you anything you want to know."

"Are you an attorney?"

"No. I'm a translator. Arabic-English and English-Arabic."

"Your employers—do they have dealings with Arab states?"

"Affirmative."

"What were you doing in Saudi Arabia?" The question was sudden: he was trying to catch me off guard.

"I was there with my employers on business."

"What business was that?"

"You'll have to ask my employers." I smiled smugly. "I'm not authorized to discuss their affairs with you or anyone else."

"I could make trouble for you."

"I know. But I hope you won't."

"Want some coffee?" he asked, with an abrupt change of tone.

"Yes, please."

Zinger flung a glance at the redhead, who got the message and stalked out of the room. "What brings you to Israel?"

"Curiosity." I shrugged. "You know. Jewish roots."

"Convincing, but there's just one difficulty." His smile was patient, indicating that he was perfectly capable of sitting there and talking to me for hours. "With your Zionist background and your perfect Hebrew—how come you never paid a visit before this? Why now? And why did you arrive here directly after a visit to Saudi Arabia?"

"The trip to Riyadh gave me an opportunity to stop off here."

"Really?" His expression remained unaltered, but I sensed his rising impatience. "Tell me about it."

"My ticket to Saudi Arabia was covered by my employers," I said. "All I had to do was pay for the detour."

Zinger made no comment; the redhead had returned with a plastic tray bearing three cups of coffee. Gingerly, I sipped; it tasted like recycled sewage, and I shoved it away in disgust. "Your working conditions are appalling."

Zinger laughed, sipping his coffee with evident relish. "You know what men will do out of patriotism."

I now knew precisely whom I was dealing with. I had been picked up by Israeli counterintelligence. From the seat occupied by the thickset man with the cigarette holder, I suddenly saw Charlie's horsey features smiling at me. "Patriotism," the man said. Men of that ilk always have a divine mission and a deep-rooted conviction that they are the last of the patriots.

"So," Zinger resumed blandly, "you took advantage of your paid trip to Riyadh to fulfill your long-cherished dream of visiting Israel?"

"That's right."

He nodded, his smile almost friendly. "That's a fairy story, complete with marzipan coating, and your passport doesn't quite confirm it. When you left Riyadh, you couldn't fly here directly because Israel and Saudi Arabia are belligerents. So you had to go by some intermediate stopover. Right?"

I nodded, knowing what he was driving at.

"But, that isn't exactly the itinerary you followed. Athens is the intermediate stopover. But you didn't fly directly to Athens."

"I never said—"

"Of course you didn't," he snapped. "How come you flew by way of Cyprus? Another 'opportunity'?"

"The best connection I found went by way of Rome to Cyprus. If I hadn't taken that flight, I would have found myself stuck in Riyadh for days." I tried to make my tone convincing. But the link between Riyadh and Cyprus made me vulnerable. Cyprus was one of the principal forward operational centers for the Palestinian underground, and the Israelis knew it. "You can see it all in my passport—Riyadh, Larnaca, Tel Aviv."

"I'm not blind," he said. "Your passport proves that you stayed over in Larnaca far longer than the time required to pick up a flight to Athens. What were you doing in Cyprus, Mister Kottler?" He paused, and when I made no response, continued. "I'll tell you what you did. You met your controller for precise instructions on your mission in Israel." He brought his fist down on the table with a thump. "So you're an innocent tourist. On your first visit to Israel. Is that your story?"

"That's right."

"Well then, tell me how a tourist on his first visit to Israel doesn't take a taxi to Jerusalem, or Bethlehem, or Tel Aviv, or Nazareth, but instead, heads for the world-renowned metropolis of Tiberias. The Paris of the Levant." After that plunge into sarcasm, his voice grew grim and threatening. "We know every step you took since you arrived. You were followed all the way. I'm giving you one more chance to cooperate. It will make matters easier. For us. And for you."

He thought he had me trapped, and his grin showed it. I knew he was lying; no one had followed me on my arrival at Ben Gurion, just as no one but Marinos had prior knowledge of my departure for Israel. All the same, the man facing me was acquainted with my every move since I set foot in Israel. With Rafi Eini's unwitting help, I was nearing the source where I could find the answers I was seeking.

"You think I'm a spy," I said placidly. "But the only reason for your suspicion is my interest in one of your operatives who died many years back."

My unexpected ploy caught his attention.

"Is that all you have to say?"

"That's all."

"Oh no!" His voice was low, as though we were engaged in an exchange of intimate confidences. "You aren't going to get off that easily. We're just at the beginning. Why are you so interested in that man? And why is whoever employs you so eager to find out about him?"

"You're wasting your time," I said. "I have nothing more to say to you."

"Okay." His grin was evil. Rising, he seized my hand, his stubby fingers squeezing it as though intent on cracking my knuckles. "You go around the country asking all kinds of strange questions about a former senior Mossad agent. Are you a journalist?"

"No."

"A writer?"

"I told you . . ."

"I know precisely what you told me. You're a simple translator employed by two Jewish attorneys from New York. You visited Riyadh, went on to the terrorist center in Cyprus and from there to Israel, directly to Tiberias, to ask questions about a man who was one of the Mossad's top agents." He breathed deeply. "Why? You're probably going to tell me again it was a quest for your roots. I don't believe that story."

I did not budge. I knew he would ultimately lead me to the man I wanted to meet because no other choice would remain open to him. "I have nothing more to say to you," I repeated coolly. "There's only one man I'm prepared to talk to, and he'll get all the answers."

His reaction surprised me. "Just one man?" he said calmly.

"That's right."

His expression displayed contempt, but there was an underlying note of puzzlement. "Tell me who."

"The head of the Mossad."

His eyes widened. "Would you mind repeating that?"

"Sure. The head of the Mossad."

I could see that he was thinking it over. My refusal to flinch before him made him treat me with caution. "You're very sure of yourself."

"That's not the issue. If you want to get this matter settled quickly, bring me to the head of the Mossad."

"You'll tell him everything?"

"Yes."

He lowered his head. He was obviously undecided, but I sensed he would follow my advice, if only for want of an alternative. After a long moment, he straightened up; I could read his decision in his eyes. "I'll look into it," he said, rising. "In the meantime, you'll be taken somewhere so you can shut those bloodshot eyes of yours."

I was escorted to the basement of the police station, to a room with one narrow bunk, a malodorous mattress, and two thin blankets. As I flung myself down, I heard the door being locked from the outside.

I did not fall asleep immediately; instead, I tossed about, torn between weariness and my anticipation of what lay in store. Certain highly placed people were perturbed by the link between my arrival from an Arab country and my inquiries about Yussuf Dur, alias Badwi. I wondered what it was precisely that upset them and why they were so uneasy about a mysterious episode that had come to an abrupt end thirty-two years back.

The following morning, my interrogators came to release me. They took me to a washroom to relieve myself and scrub away the residue of my fatigue. After that, they escorted me to a heavily curtained police patrol car. I was placed on one bench; my interrogators sat facing me.

"The meeting you requested is on," said Zinger.

"I appreciate your efforts." My tone was even in spite of my agitation.

"It had better be productive," he growled, jerking the cigarette holder from his mouth to point it at me. "Make the best of it."

That was my intention, precisely.

Finally, the driver slowed to a stop and turned off the engine. When he came around to open the doors, I found myself in a subterranean car park. My escort led me to an elevator, which took us up to the fifth floor; there, Zinger and the redhead guided me down a long corridor. At its extreme end, we entered a small office occupied by a woman in her thirties, her hair tied in a bun and her face set in a severe expression. She waved us to be seated. I found myself on a small couch, while my escorts stood facing me. They maintained a strict silence.

After a time, one of a battery of telephones on the secretary's desk emitted a soft ring; she lifted the receiver and listened wordlessly. Putting down the phone, she turned in my direction. "Please be good enough to come this way."

I accompanied her to the connecting door. My two escorts remained motionless. The secretary opened the door and stepped aside to admit me. As soon as I passed, she closed the door.

I found myself standing in a broad room whose walls were paneled in dark brown wood. The man seated behind the large desk was instantly familiar, having been until recently one of the best-known figures in Israel's military command. He sat flanked by photographs of Israel's successive defense ministers, from David Ben Gurion to Moshe Arens.

He invited me to take a seat in one of the armchairs facing his desk. "I understand we have matters to discuss."

"Yes." I was uncomfortable at finding myself in his presence. His military exploits had won worldwide renown, and some of the battles he had conducted were studied at military academies. He was noted as an excellent field commander and a superb operational planner. In a recent *New York Times* article, the writer named him as one of the minds behind both the Entebbe rescue operation and, several years later, the raid that destroyed the Iraqi nuclear reactor.

"You've been giving us a lot of trouble," he said, his eyes boring into me. His head was large, with a broad face. He had long ago parted company with most of his hair, and the straggling remnants adhered to his skull like soft fluff that seemed on the verge of sliding off. Beneath his blue eyes hung little pouches of sagging skin, indicating a chronic lack of sleep.

"I'm sure you're now convinced of my identity," I said.

"Your cover as a translator is of no interest to me."

I felt as though I had just been kicked in the crotch. I

suddenly realized how thoroughly the Mossad had its moles embedded in Washington's deepest and most secret recesses. It was an awesome thought, doubly so when I considered the probability that Charlie's moles would alert him to my personal embroilment—how much I would give to make sure it remained 'personal'!—a simple screwup I would be hard put to explain away. As it was, my relations with Charlie were sufficiently tense and hostile, without my getting mixed up with the Mossad.

The general's blue eyes continued to study me. "You wouldn't expect us to act in any other manner?"

"No," I conceded.

"A man arrives here from an Arab state and wanders about asking questions about a man who was a senior Mossad operative. You would have done the same."

"Your inquiries are liable to put a noose around my neck," I said.

"We'll do our best to make sure it isn't pulled tight—if this meeting achieves positive results." His eyes narrowed. "You said you would provide me with information. I expect you want something in return."

"Yes."

"Go ahead." He offered no deal of any kind.

"I want to know what Yussuf Dur's last mission was and how he was killed."

The expression on his heavy features did not change; but a gleam lit up his eyes momentarily. "You seem convinced that you will not only get the information you seek, but also walk out of here a free man."

"That's right."

"First things first. What is the link between the CIA and Yosef Dur?"

"The CIA has no connection with Yosef Dur."

He ignored the answer. "Is the CIA investigating Yosef Dur for some third party? A client of some sort?"

"No sir. The CIA is not connected with my inquiries. I do not represent the CIA."

"Whom are you working for?"

"Myself."

He did not change his position, but I sensed that my reply

was the last thing he expected. "I'm not here to waste time," he said.

"I value your time, sir, but I want to know whether I'll get the information I require in return for the information I give you."

He did not reply immediately. His face remained frozen, but I could almost hear his mind racing. "This matter is far too serious for petty tricks," he said finally. "If I'm satisfied that the information you request can be released, I shall do so."

I appreciated his response. But it meant I now had to talk. I groped around for the right words. "It's a family matter."

The general altered his posture, endeavoring to camouflage his impatience. "Family?"

"That's right."

He scanned the sheet of paper that lay before him. The page must have been a summary of the information from my father's personal file. "I understand you claim some kind of kinship with Yosef Dur's late widow."

That last fact did not come from the Mossad's "Yosef Dur" file. I knew it came from a confidential report submitted by Rafi Eini.

"Yes." I felt weary, as though I were a thousand years old. "Rachel Kottler—was—my mother."

"In other words . . ."

"I am the son of Yussuf Dur."

The silence that ensued was the longest and heaviest I had ever experienced. Sweat poured down me, as though I had stayed too long in a sauna. The general's expression was not difficult to decipher: he was utterly dumbfounded.

"Your name is Kottler, not Dur." He was not trying to trap me, merely seeking clarification.

I took a slow breath. "My mother did not want me to grow up bearing his name. Maybe she didn't want me to face questions about why I should be called Dur when her name was Kottler."

He was in no haste to respond. With measured movements, he opened a drawer and pulled out a bulging file whose binding had once, long ago, been blue. It must have been my father's personal file. I never expected it would be so thick.

For several minutes, I watched the furrows deepen on the

general's brow as he leafed through the file in silence. Finally, he completed his study and closed it. "I find no confirmation for your claim that Yussuf Dur and Rachel Kottler had any joint offspring."

"I wouldn't expect you to. Not in that file."

"Why not?"

"My mother wanted no link between me and Yussuf Dur." I paused. There were certain matters I preferred not to touch upon in the presence of this man. "My mother left Israel in the third month of her pregnancy. She never notified the Israeli Defense Ministry of my birth. She didn't apply for any allowance on my behalf."

He glanced down at the file. "There's nothing here. Not a hint. That's rather bizarre."

"My mother was a bizarre woman," I said. "You can find evidence of that in the file."

As I foresaw, he now resumed his study of the file—this time, out of undisguised curiosity.

"What you're saying," he drawled, "is that you are Daniel Dur."

The dryness spread from my mouth down into my throat. No one had ever called me Daniel Dur. Even in the privacy of my own thoughts, I had never thought of myself under that name. Daniel—Dur. The name echoed and reechoed, reverberating in my head.

I nodded.

"You are Daniel Dur," he repeated. In his eyes, I detected a gleam of human comprehension. Things suddenly seemed easier for both of us. I was no longer a suspect, and he was no longer considering me from his vantage point as head of the Mossad.

I had to fight back my unease. This was no ordinary run-of-the-mill confusion. I was the center of a mysterious something that dominated my life; it was as though long ago, at the moment of my birth, someone had activated a remote control mechanism that directed my every step. And the master switch lay—right here. My mind was confused, with powerful undertones of self-pity.

"I want to know . . ." I was about to repeat, but he was already aware of what I wished to know, so I stopped.

He cleared his throat. "This development was unforesee-able," he said.

"That's how it stands, I'm afraid."

"These musty files can hardly match up with real life."

"No, sir."

His broad face lost its alien aspect, becoming familiar, as if I had known him all my life. I watched him take advantage of the brief interval to reorganize his thoughts and take in my unexpected revelation. Formally, he had yet to recognize me as the son of the man from Tiberias; he evidently wished to check up on one or two points. For the first time, he smiled. "It looks as though I'll have to write one further entry in this file."

I nodded.

"If you don't mind waiting in the secretary's office . . . ?"

"Certainly." He had his job to do, and it was up to me to wait. I left his office and returned to my seat at the center of the small couch, where I found myself under the questioning gaze of my two escorts. My grin must have looked ridiculous.

"What's happening? What's the next step?" Zinger's questions were directed at me, as though I were the one to decide what we should do now.

"He told me to wait here."

Zinger obviously failed to understand what was going on, but he maintained his tone of ominous menace all the same. "It's your funeral," he said darkly, with a vigorous nod of the head.

A soft buzz from the intercom saved me the trouble of a reply. The secretary picked up the receiver. As she listened to the man in the adjoining room, she flung me a look of aston-ishment. Then she lowered her gaze and uttered a laconic yes.

She addressed my escorts. "You can go. He's staying." She jerked her chin at me.

"Is that all?" Zinger asked.

"Yes."

The first to rise was the redhead who had arrested me at the hotel. His expression reflected undisguised confusion. Zinger rose too, staring at the secretary, but she had returned to her desk work. He touched his companion's shoulder, and the two men strode toward the door. "We weren't rough on you," he said, turning.

"No," I conceded. "You weren't."

As soon as the door closed behind them, the secretary raised her head. For the first time, her features bore a smile. She offered coffee, and I accepted.

The hands on the clock advanced slowly, and I allowed my thoughts to wander until the secretary beckoned me to follow her. I found myself reentering the general's office; again, he waved me to one of the armchairs. I had no idea what inquiries he had made during my wait outside, but the results must have been satisfactory. He appeared to be more relaxed.

"So you are Daniel Dur," he said, picking up the conversation at the point where we had left off.

"Kottler . . ." I fell silent. I had no clear words for what was happening; my emotions were carrying me away once more.

"I suppose the more you learn about your father, the greater your awareness of your loss. It can't be easy trying to get acquainted with a father you never knew."

"It isn't," I muttered.

He must have sensed the emotional upheaval I was undergoing. "In this country, cases like yours are not exceptional." The soft tone and pained expression reminded me of a father engaged in a heart-to-heart talk with his son. "This state has been in existence for thirty-six years. They haven't been peaceful years. It's been one long, drawn-out war. Many of the men who fell in that war were fathers with children too young to retain any clear memory of them. There are others, like your father, who went off to their last battle never even knowing that the wife they left behind was pregnant."

"Then I'm just a routine phenomenon," I said.

"That's one way of putting it," he answered, his tone chiding me for my sarcasm. Abruptly, he changed the subject. "I hope you've found what you're seeking."

"Oh yes," I agreed readily. "Mussa Eini was very helpful." I looked at him wryly. "So was his grandson, Rafi."

He did not overlook the irony in my voice. "You and I came to meet by a roundabout route," he admitted. "But that may have been the only way . . ."

I wanted to add that my discoveries had served only to deepen the gulf dividing me from my father. There can be no intimacy with a man if he overshadows you. Perhaps it was all a misunderstanding, and there was no kinship between me and Yussuf Dur.

"I never knew your father," the general said. "I'm from a younger generation. It was only when I entered the higher ranks that I heard occasional mention of his name. Everyone spoke of him as a kind of legend. I understand he was an exceptional man."

"So I hear from those who knew him."

"When you were younger, did you have any idea of his exploits?"

"I did, in an indirect way. My grandfather used to refer to him as 'der Spion.' "

"What did you mother tell you about him?"

"Nothing."

"Why?"

"On account of her Great Wall of China." He stared at me. "She didn't want me growing up like him," I explained. "In view of what I've discovered, I can hardly blame her."

"You're angry," the general said.

He was sincere. I believed that. But I found no words for a reply, and then I suddenly gave way to an irresistible urge. Leaping to my feet, I raised my arms and executed a number of rapid glissades, with graceful precision, as though I had just this minute been practising. "How was that?" I asked.

"That was your Great Wall of China?" he asked.

"Dead on," I grinned. I walked over to his desk, resting both hands on it. "Were you ever taught classical ballet? Of course you weren't. But I was. The aim was to make my walk graceful and gentle, so that it would bear no resemblance to the stride of the man nicknamed Badwi. How many hours did you spend at a piano, banging out minuets? Did you ever spend hours on your knees alongside a crazy mother, scrubbing and scrubbing and scrubbing the floor of your home, over and over again because that was the only way of scrubbing away the memory of that stone floor in the stone house facing the black mountains of the Golan?"

The general's wise eyes regarded me steadily. "I'm sorry," he said finally. I am sure he was. I dropped back into my seat. "Are you all right?"

"As far as that's possible . . ."

"She drove you out of your mind," he said gently.

I laughed. "I don't blame her. He was to blame—Badwi. And all of you. You too, general. Don't look at me like that. You, too!"

"Do you want a drink?" he asked softly.

I nodded gratefully. He stood up and walked over to a cabinet. For the first time, I saw the full length of his figure. He was just below average height, but he appeared taller. He had the sturdy build of a farmer; his shoulders were square and broad enough to bear a heavy sack of wheat. He drew out a bottle of French cognac and two glasses from a cabinet. I think he needed the drink no less than I did. We sipped the cognac in silence. Gradually, my agitation died down. By the time I tossed down the last of the cognac, I was back under control.

He gazed at me. "A drink always helps when the pressure is on." His smile was slightly abashed.

"People always feel hassled when they're around me," I confessed. "There are times when I hate myself for it. Like now. So what do you think of the legendary Yussuf Dur's offspring?"

"You have a problem."

"You're telling me?"

"It's the second generation syndrome—the generation that follows the founding fathers. The sons always feel insignificant."

"I never thought of it in those terms."

He refilled my glass. "It's like that everywhere. When you're an heir to greatness, you're convinced there's nothing left for you to accomplish. It's all been done. You look at the first generation and you see giants. You even get to believe they created the universe."

"Great men don't beget great men."

"I understand how you feel," he said. "I hope you come to terms with yourself."

"I hope so, sir."

He grinned. "Stop calling me 'sir.' You're a member of the family. Whether you like it or not, you are Yussuf Dur's son. I'll call you Daniel and you call me David." He shook his head reflectively. "Life plays strange tricks. . . . Your links with the CIA, for instance."

His remark hit me hard. It was a salutary reminder, recalling who he was and who I was. He had his secrets from me, and there were things I would have to conceal from him. I was worried about the risk of running afoul of Charlie; I could imagine the skeptical expression on those horsey features if I tried to explain this visit to the head of the Mossad.

I fixed my eyes on the general. "I would appreciate it greatly if no hint of that were to leave this room."

"Let's forget the subject."

"I already have." I took a further sip of cognac. "Now there are certain things I want to know. What was Yussuf Dur's last mission? How did he die? What happened to his body?"

He shrugged. "I'm afraid I'm not the man to help you."

"There must be somebody!"

He hesitated. "Someone *was* with your father during his final hours."

I felt my heart pound. "When can I meet him?"

The general glanced at his watch. "He'll be landing at Ben Gurion Airport within the hour." He was uneasy, possibly because he himself was forced to confess his own ignorance about the long-forgotten episode dominating my thoughts. "His name is Yehuda Duek," the general offered reluctantly.

"What more can you tell me about him?"

He hesitated again before breaking into a grin of shamefaced complicity. "As little as I possibly can," he replied with refreshing candor, and we both laughed at the mutual mistrust so natural between members of intelligence-gathering organizations. "My secretary will take you to lunch while I see to one or two things. After that, I'll introduce him to you."

"I appreciate your help."

"It's the least I can do for you," he said. "By the way, I have something of yours." He drew out my passport from a drawer and handed it to me.

I thanked him and stuffed it into my pocket. His soft gaze followed me to the door.

The general's secretary was named Naomi. Belying her tight bun of hair and her grim exterior, she proved to be easygoing and friendly. We left by the main entrance. It did not escape me that there were no further precautions to prevent me from pinpointing Mossad headquarters, whose precise location the Israelis kept a secret. My credentials having been established, my hosts were evidently convinced that I could be trusted.

At my request, Naomi took me first to a barber, where I had a shave and a facial massage that restored my spirits. By the time we reached the restaurant, I felt much better. No sooner had we taken our seats than the table was loaded down with the usual Mideastern assortment of salads and grilled meats. "You have to be well looked after," Naomi explained.

"Why?"

"The general said you're one of the family."

I contented myself with a gratified smile. It was vital for me to establish my credibility with her: a member of the family hears things that are concealed from strangers.

It was an enjoyable meal. I pushed my concerns to the back of my mind and permitted myself to relax. Naomi, too, appeared natural and unreserved. She even mimicked the embarrassed expressions of the two interrogators when they were instructed to leave. My own recollections of them, recounted to the best of my ability, made her smile.

"You even have the same brand of humor as our people," she said.

"My humor is very ordinary."

"Do you always underrate yourself?"

I nodded.

"Why?"

"To avoid disappointments."

She laughed merrily. I was getting there.

I began sawing at a slice of braised meat. "When is Yehuda Duek expected?"

"We'll probably find him in the general's office when we get back."

"I expect he's returning by way of Paris."

"Oh no, Zurich as usual . . ."

"He's an old friend of my family," I said hastily, anxious to distract her attention from her unwitting revelation.

But I was not quick enough. It took her only a moment to realize that she had erred. "I'd prefer not to discuss him or anyone else," she said. "You'll soon be able to ask him anything you like."

"He's still on the same job, is he?"

"Why don't you taste your mousse?" she said. "It's excellent."

It was, indeed.

Naomi dawdled over dessert and spent a long time sipping her coffee. Obviously, she had been told to keep me away from the office as long as possible.

It was close to three when she finally suggested we walk back. Immediately, she ushered me into the general's private office.

Everything remained as it was before, except that the armchair where I had sat previously was now occupied by an elderly man, seated with his back to me. His age was instantly evident from his white hair. Its whiteness was neither snowy nor silvery; instead, it showed a yellowish tinge, of a kind I have encountered only in men of great age. But as he stood up and turned his head around, I blinked in surprise. His face bore a fresh expression, and his eyes were alert and bright, like those of a young man. Approaching him, I noticed the delicate cast of his features, which also reflected a youthfulness I had not expected. His eyes were gentle, and a smile raised the corners of his mouth. His gaze engulfed me. He did not simply focus on my face or on my eyes, or on any other part of me; instead, he took in my total being. His look of perplexity indicated that he had yet to digest what he had just heard about me from the general.

I caught a shadow that flashed across his eyes, its duration no more than a fraction of a second. But that was enough to shake me. Even though it had already vanished, I was unlikely to forget the terrible fear it conveyed. His lips parted, as though about to say something, but no words emerged.

I halted a short distance from him. He was a head shorter than I was. In his youth he must have been one of those stockily handsome men who always draw attention. His eyes were light brown with flecks of yellow. His facial complexion was smooth. Had I not known who he was, I would have taken him for a man of forty-five who had experienced some terrifying nightmare that had turned his hair white.

His thin lips parted again, and again he said nothing. All the while, his kindly eyes continued to examine me.

The general addressed me. "As I told you, Yehuda Duek was the last of our men to see your father alive. Whatever questions you have, he's the one who can answer them."

Duek's soft eyes flickered again in a second of terror, as though he had seen a ghost. I have seen dying men with a similar look of dread in their eyes. But he was alive, vital, sturdy: his neck was young, as were his hands, the skin taut and free of wrinkles. And yet, there was a look of fear.

"So you're Badwi's son." Like his eyes, Yehuda Duek's voice was soft and caressing. He interspersed his words with brief pauses; it was not a stammer, rather a kind of hesitation. In time, I recognized it as his regular speech pattern. He exchanged a rapid glance with the general, conveying some secret message whose significance escaped me.

"You're still here," I said dully, as we seated ourselves. I meant: still working for the Mossad.

His smile did not waver. "Badwi's son," he repeated, his face retaining the expression of wonder it had worn since the first moment he set eyes on me. "None of us knew your mother was pregnant when she left the country."

"None of you kept contact with her over the years," I said.

Duek shrugged. "We tried," he said. "Many times. But she didn't want to have anything to do with us."

" 'Us'?"

"I tried to."

"When?"

He reflected briefly. "Nineteen years back. I was in New York at the time, and I tried to call. She refused to talk to me. I spoke to her sister."

"Bertha."

"That's right. She begged me never to try again because every call from us only threw Rachel deeper into her depression. What could I do?"

"Do you see any resemblance to his father?" the general asked Duek.

"They do have something in common," Duek said. "The shape of the face mainly." He studied me with solemn eyes. "But

136

if I didn't know you were Badwi's son, I would never have guessed."

I grinned. "God knows who I take after then. I've always been told I don't look much like my mother. Now I hear I don't resemble my father either."

"You're taller than he was," Duek said. "But there's something in your walk that reminds me of him. Your tread is light and springy, like his."

So much for wasted ballet lessons, I thought. Duek wouldn't understand the irony. "You knew him well," I said.

Once again, Duek's eyes darted toward the general. Their glances were beginning to get on my nerves, as if they were communicating in some secret code they did not want me to understand.

Duek smiled. "Badwi was my superior from 1946, right after his release from the British army. I was with him for over five years. We started by smuggling Jews out of Iraq, Lebanon, and Syria. With the nationalist wave in the Arab countries after the war, Jews became targets for robbery and murder. So we had to get them out of there. On our first mission, there were five of us, with Badwi in command. We were all terrified. I'll never forget those nights. Every time I heard an owl hoot, I almost wet my pants. But Badwi carried us through. Few men could compare with him as a leader. The daring and courage shown by him and others like him were what made the Jewish state possible."

"You're prejudiced," I said.

Yehuda Duek shook his head. "I've never pretended to be objective about Badwi. How could I be," his voice dropped suddenly, "when I have only him to thank for being alive today?"

A chill ran up my spine. "What do you mean?"

"Badwi saved my life."

I braced myself to hear the true account of my father's death. "He saved your life," I prompted.

He ignored my remark, intent on telling his story in his own way. "Ben Gurion instructed us to extend our intelligence network across the Arab states. That was no mean undertaking. At that time, we had three principal sources of information— Arab mercenaries, local Jews living in Arab countries, and a few agents of our own. That was all we had. The information we' got was less than adequate. Badwi knew that the existing setup would never enable us to meet Ben Gurion's challenge. Paid agents are often more trouble than they're worth. They tend to be untrustworthy. Jews living in Arab countries could do little because they were inexperienced and closely watched. As for sending in our agents, that provided only a small part of what we were after."

"On top of which," the general observed, "there were painful setbacks . . ."

"For which our men died," Yehuda Duek completed the sentence. "Some died violently, others were executed in public in central city squares. Those were—moments—of—horror."

I could sense his agony. I wanted him to talk about my father and those fateful final hours, but Yehuda Duek was no man for shortcuts. I had to be patient until he could bring himself to speak about the subject he so evidently dreaded.

He breathed slowly, trying to order his scattered thoughts. Gradually, his face lost its pallor. When he spoke again, his tone was suddenly dry and factual, as though he were delivering an academic lecture. "We sought a formula for an intelligence gathering operation which could be relied upon for more than a limited time. We had to think in terms of years, not of days or weeks. Above all, we had to find a way of planting eyes and ears in our enemies' innermost councils." His gaze seemed to settle on some invisible point just above my head. "It was Badwi who made the crucial decision. He opted for a method just then gaining renown in the world's intelligence services—deep penetration. The mole. The agent who infiltrates an alien society, under a perfectly devised false identity. He works his way up into the highest level of military and political decision makers, lying low for years if need be, until he is in a position to start transmitting . . ." He glanced at me momentarily, before his eyes went off again into the distance. "We had never worked like that. Some of our policy makers doubted the feasibility of such a technique, mainly because we had no experienced candidates for the part of moles.

"But Badwi insisted that we had no other choice. Not that he neglected our other channels. But he knew they were of limited value. When Badwi believed in something, he was incredibly persistent. On this subject he was as obstinate as a mule, immovable as a mountain. The man who headed the Mossad at that time was behind him, and together, the two of them fought off the opposition. At the same time, they selected the first four candidates."

"And you were one of the four," I ventured, eliciting a nod of confirmation.

"In January 1950, I flew to Argentina, masquerading as an Iraqi immigrant by the name of Nuri Jareh, a job trader. I went to live in Buenos Aires among immigrants from the Arab countries. Within a few months, I had formed friendships with local traders of Arab origin. When I set off for Baghdad at the end of the year, they gave me warm letters of recommendation to their relatives as well as to highly placed people in the government. In Baghdad, I rented an elegant villa. I began to build up commercial links which I continued to expand. At the same time, I cultivated social ties with highly placed persons in the police, the army, the Foreign Ministry, and the Treasury. And I did not neglect my image as a Moslem. I would invite my Iraqi friends to join me in my devotions as I crouched on a prayer mat with my face toward Mecca. By such tactics I established my position among Iraq's social and political elite." Duek took a deep breath. "It's easier told than done," he remarked wryly. "I was under constant psychological pressure."

"I can imagine," I said. I knew something of the intolerable burden borne by men who undertook such perilous assignments.

"What I've described so far," Duek resumed in the same factual tone, "is the background so that you can understand what went wrong. For all our sophistication, we were novices." His smile was rueful. "Young men always imagine they are smarter and more experienced than anyone else. We were no different. Where we slipped up was overlooking my past."

"Your past?"

"My family emigrated to Palestine when I was fifteen," Duek explained. "But before that, we lived in Egypt, in Alexandria. That was my undoing. As part of my trading activities in Baghdad, I completed a deal with the Iraqi army for delivery of gas masks. When the contract was signed, I had my picture taken with the quartermaster general, Abed Amar. The picture appeared on the front page of a Baghdad newspaper. Somehow or other, a copy of that paper reached Alexandria. An officer of Egyptian intelligence saw it. As a boy, that officer lived in my neighborhood; we even attended the same school." His tone remained impersonal, as though relating some curious accident that had befallen a total stranger. "The moment the officer saw that photograph, he recognized me. Within hours, a cable reached the head of Iraqi intelligence."

"It was a one-in-a-million chance," the general commented.

"Be that as it may, that mischance was my downfall." The dispassionate tone had vanished. Duek attempted a smile but produced nothing more than a twisted grimace. "The Iraqis didn't waste any time. They were adept at inducing a man to talk by application of certain refined arts such as ripping out fingernails, breaking toes, and crushing testicles. But they didn't get a confession out of me."

Now I understood the origins of that mysterious flicker of terror I had seen earlier in his eyes, terror that would dog him for the rest of his life.

But he was again composed, speaking with a cool restraint as though the tortures he had endured at the hands of Iraqi counterintelligence had been inflicted upon someone else. "After many weeks and months spent trying to squeeze me for information, they put me through a mock trial. They didn't let me utter a word. The travesty ended with a sentence of death by hanging. I was taken back to the central prison to the top security wing and dressed in the red robes of convicts awaiting execution.

"In Baghdad, no one is in any hurry about carrying out hangings." His tone remained even. "After sentence has been passed, there's plenty of time. In this case, the Iraqis had an additional reason for delaying my execution. I was worth more to them as living testimony to their triumph." He smiled contemptuously. "Each postponement revived my hopes. I trusted our people here to save my life. While I was in the death cell, I learned that an English attorney had arrived in Baghdad and hired a local lawyer to get me a new trial. Our people set up a story about my true mission having nothing to do with espionage, that it was aimed only at furthering religious education in the local Jewish community. It goes without saying that they failed to get my sentence quashed. But their appeal led to a further postponement of my execution."

I gazed at him. "And all this time, you were in the condemned cell?"

Duek nodded. "Dressed in my red robes. That was to remind me every minute of every day that my end was imminent. If you ask how I managed to cope, it was my unshakable conviction that my colleagues in Israel would never abandon me. My Iraqi interrogators used to mock me, telling me my friends had deserted me. But I believed in Badwi and his superiors, all the way up to Ben Gurion." He shrugged. "As I learned later, I wasn't wrong. From the moment he learned of my arrest, Badwi undertook personal responsibility for getting me out. He flew to London to hire that attorney and supervised the legal efforts in Baghdad—to buy time until he found some loophole to extricate me. While the two attorneys worked on my appeal, Badwi came to Baghdad to set up contacts with the prison governor.

"Then one night, one of my interrogators came to my cell to notify me that my execution had been set for the following Thursday. There had been other moments when I had given up hope, but this time I plunged into the abyss. That night, I was convinced that I'd never get out alive.

"At one o'clock in the morning, two soldiers came up to the condemned cell and called my name. I was surprised. No one had ever been taken away to execution before dawn. I feared that the Iraqis had dreamed up some special kind of sadistic refinement. As they led me out of the cell, I must have stumbled. My legs just didn't seem capable of bearing me. I wanted to beg for my life, but there was no one to appeal to . . . The other convicts blessed me in the name of Allah and His Prophet Mohammed.

"Only when we left the wing did I grasp that something unusual was happening. I wasn't taken to the courtyard. Instead, they led me to the wing which housed the prison offices. I couldn't understand why. I thought I had been taken out early to leave time before my execution for one more session in the torture chambers. My state of uncertainty and fear made it difficult for me to breathe. At one stage, as we were climbing the stairs to the second floor, the soldiers had to drag me until I could get together enough strength to walk unassisted. I felt as though I were dead already.

"Finally, we reached a long corridor with a high ceiling. I recall that particular detail because I remember thinking it was almost as high as the heavens. At the end of the corridor a door opened into a large room. Behind a black desk sat a balding square-faced man with a clipped mustache—the prison director, Aref al Bechar. To the inmates of the prison, the man was a demon. But now, he was looking up at me and smiling! I couldn't believe my eyes! No one had ever seen Aref al Bechar smile. But his smile didn't make me feel any better—on the contrary, it only added to my sense that my sufferings were not yet at an end."

Duek paused, a strange light in his eyes. "But then I heard a voice. A voice I had dreamed of day after day, minute after minute, constantly, endlessly. At first I thought that my fears of what lay in store for me had fired my fantasy and that I was hallucinating. But I wasn't. There, at the side of that menacingly black desk, sat Yussuf Dur.

"A million thoughts raced through my mind. My gaze met that of Badwi, and his eyes simply engulfed me. I stood there, shaking like a leaf, incapable of uttering a sound."

Yehuda Duek fell silent, exercising every ounce of will-power to overcome his agitation. I was not alone in being moved by his account: I saw the general's gaze focused on the aging man, his eyes narrowing to hold back the pain.

"I didn't know then how on earth Badwi had done it," Duek resumed, "but the fact was, he had, and he was there, seated at ease in the office of Aref al Bechar. He didn't need to say anything to reassure me. His mere presence meant life for my body and my tormented spirit. Then Aref al Bechar rose from his seat to greet me. Can you imagine? Here I was, in my red robes of death, being honored by the prison director as though I were some eminent personage! He stood there, holding out a box of cigars and offering me a cup of coffee. One of his men was already crouching at my feet to unlock the shackles. I felt like a corpse resurrected.

"There was another man in the office, the English attorney. Badwi instructed me to go with him to the airport. He himself, he assured me, would join us in Europe. He was to leave on a different flight, just as soon as he had tied up all the loose ends. I had a thousand questions, but I knew I wouldn't get a single answer just then. I remember him looking confident and self-assured. It was the most shattering moment of my life. I just didn't know what was happening to me. Standing up, I wanted to embrace him, but he just held out his hand for a friendly handshake. 'Everything is going to be fine,' he said.

"The attorney took me to another room, where I changed into a new suit someone had ready for me. At six-thirty that morning, we took off in a KLM plane bound for Holland. I only breathed freely when the pilot announced that we had left Iraqi air space. You may not believe me, but my sole thought at that moment was of Badwi."

Yehuda Duek waited for me to speak, but I was unable to utter a sound. The pains in my neck were severe, as though my vertebrae were cracking.

Duek drew a deep breath. "I knew that no one but Badwi, with his boundless imagination and daring, could have engineered such a miracle. And I was living proof, seated there in that plane, alive and free and heading for home.

"When we reached Amsterdam, the attorney insisted that we take the first El Al flight for Israel. I expected to wait for Badwi. But I trusted him, never imagining there could be anything wrong.

"We arrived the morning after my rescue. I was given an emotional welcome by relatives and friends. It was a moment of delirious joy. But within a short time, I fell into a profound depression. I'm often overcome by the same feeling to this day." His face was pale again, full of stress and anguish. "The next morning I glanced at a newspaper headline and broke into a fit of uncontrollable trembling. The headline read that on the previous day an Israeli spy had been hanged in Baghdad."

I sensed the waves of fever rushing through my body till my lips seemed about to split from the heat; then my skin turned to gooseflesh. Gone was my former impersonal detachment. Yussuf Dur no longer remained a faceless stranger. At certain points in Duek's account, I experienced the momentary delusion of having become my own father.

Duek's tone conveyed desperation. "I thought I was delirious from the long, drawn-out tension. I held the paper in my hands, but I couldn't bring myself to read it. At that moment, I knew something had gone terribly, terribly wrong." His imploring eyes sought mine, begging my understanding. "When Badwi squared the deal for my release, his side of the bargain wasn't only a bribe. It was his life in place of mine."

Yehuda Duek blinked, as though trying to remove some obstruction from his eyes. "Only a man like your father, with his fierce sense of duty and commitment toward his subordinates, would undertake such an act."

Rising, I strode over to the great window to look out at the green treetops swaying gently to and fro. I raised my head. The sun was sinking, coloring the sky yellow. A breeze from the sea stole through the open window, sending an involuntary shudder through me.

I was torn, wounded in spirit. Nothing could ever rival the account I had just heard in bringing me close to my dead father. Nevertheless, a profound gulf of alienation lay between us. Our roots—his and mine—lay in different soils. The air we breathed was not the same air—our psyches drew on different sustenance. His soul was disturbed, abnormal.

My nausea grew. I clung to the windowsill, gripping it with my fingers till the nails pierced the wood. "Shit," I mumbled.

"What did you say?" someone asked from behind.

"I said, 'shit.' " I was not speaking to myself alone; my words were directed at the two men behind me, my father's colleagues who were far more than mere colleagues: they were flesh of his flesh more certainly than if they had been his blood kinsmen. I was no kinsman of his. "He was a shit. That's what he was."

"He was a man of exceptional quality!" Yehuda Duek cried.

"Sure," I snapped, whirling to face him. "And I'll tell you what that quality was—pure horseshit!"

Duek lowered his head.

"He was crazy and irresponsible," I hissed. "My mother was right when she tried to turn me into something unlike him. But she didn't succeed in castrating me and that's a pity. It would still be better than—that man of yours. He was crazy. One hundred percent nuts." I stared at them. "What kind of people are you?"

Duek raised his head. "We . . ." he said hesitantly before relapsing into silence.

"You're crazy too. Just like him. High quality, patriotic shit." I turned away again to regard the treetops standing out against the yellow sky. My eyes were blurred. Without turning my head, I addressed them softly. "You know what they say about a man executed by hanging. The moment the neck is broken, he has one final erection and spurts out the last of his sperm . . . An interesting phenomenon, isn't it?" I turned to face them once more. "What happened to his body afterward?"

"He was buried there," Duek whispered.

"Where?"

"In Baghdad. In the British military cemetery alongside soldiers who died in World War Two."

"Can you find out precisely where it is? I want to visit the grave."

Yehuda Duek hesitated. His eyes again flickered with that momentary flash of terror I had already seen. But I grasped suddenly that this was not terror: it was anxiety, profound and boundless. He exchanged glances with the general, and again I felt they were conversing in some secret silent language. Duek turned back to me, his expression now relaxed and confident, as though some clearcut decision had been reached. "But you see, you don't have to go to Baghdad. Israelis don't abandon their casualties in enemy territory. Even if it takes years, and even if retrieving a sack of graying bones might endanger someone's life."

"It was a very delicate operation," the general said in a dry, professional tone.

"It was completed at the time you took over this job," Duek reminded him, wiping the back of his neck. "It took us many years of hard work before we found someone high up in the Iraqi government who could be bought." He raised his head, but did not look at me. "Badwi's remains were brought back here."

"And given burial with full military honors," the general added, "at the Kiryat Shaul military cemetery. We'll take you there tomorrow."

.   .   .

The general and Yehuda Duek proceeded to map out the schedule for the rest of my stay in Israel. That evening, Duek would come to the hotel to take me to his North Tel Aviv home. My visit to the cemetery was set for the following morning immediately prior to my departure. The timetable having been arranged, the general's driver drove me back to the hotel.

I was exhausted almost to the point of insensibility. Ordinarily, I would wash away my weariness in a shower, but this time the hot steam failed me. I remained wide awake, my thoughts far away behind the bars of a distant cell where I saw the spare, swarthy figure clad in its ominous red robes; then I saw it encased in a white sack, dangling from a rope before the inflamed eyes of a bloodthirsty mob. The vision was so vivid that the lapping of the sea waves on the beach below sounded in my ears like the roar of the multitude screaming for the blood of the condemned man.

I sprawled face upward on the bed. My eyes were open, fixed upon the ceiling. I wanted to erase the vision of the hanging man, but he refused to go away. My anguish remained with me, immutable. I suddenly grasped what agonies my mother must have experienced on all those countless occasions when her imagination soared. She must have conjured up my father's death in a thousand forms, each more horrifying than the last. The strongest personality would have cracked under the terror and stress, and she—she was so delicate and fragile. Where was God when she needed Him? What does God do in His absence, I wondered . . .

It happened instantaneously, in a sudden flash. In the flickering of an eyelid, I perceived a figure, visible only in outline.

My father was in the room, seated in front of me.

I sat up in alarm. I was hallucinating, I knew. All the same, the figure appeared solid. I stretched out a hand to touch it, but my hand passed right through the immobile form, leaving me dazed.

The figure remained so real that my words erupted of their own accord. "You raving lunatic," I whispered to my father. "What did you do to her?"

He merely sat in the armchair, silently rocking back and forth.

. . .

A short time after Yehuda Duek picked me up at the hotel, we reached a quiet suburb of modest little houses surrounded by small, well-tended gardens. We were met by Duek's wife, Aviva. She was in her mid-fifties, with warm eyes and an engaging smile, and she welcomed me like a beloved nephew. It was all done in the familiar style of my Aunt Bertha. Sit over there. Taste this. Have a drink of that. It'll do you good. It was all I could do to clamp down on my more aggressive instincts. In her own well-intentioned way, she proclaimed their admiration for my father, declaring that they regarded me as a part of him.

Aviva asked about my personal biography. I boasted that my upbringing had been out of the ordinary, like that of no other child on our block. I assured her I had enjoyed experiences undreamed of by any of my peers. She asked whether my childhood had been normal. I told her that, apart from my mother, all the other members of our little family were outstandingly normal. As the bright hope of the Kottlers, I had exceeded all expectations by attaining the post of translator at a prestigious law firm on Park Avenue. Impressed by my mastery of Hebrew, she asked whether I had studied the language at school or had learned it as a child, from my mother. In view of the emotional stress I was suffering, my replies were impeccable.

It was close to midnight when I took my leave of Aviva Duek. Her husband drove me back to the hotel. When he dropped me off, I detained him briefly. "I appreciate the efforts you and the general are making on my behalf."

"You're Badwi's son," he said. "Don't forget that." Without waiting for my response, he slammed the car door and drove off.

He and the general reached the hotel at exactly 9:30 the following morning. We shared breakfast, although conversation was difficult and strained.

At 10:30, I paid my hotel bill and picked up my valise. We headed for the general's large American car; he sat in front, alongside his driver, while Yehuda Duek joined me in the rear. It was a gray day: although there was no cloud formation, a layer of mist blocked out the sun's rays. After heading north, the driver turned off the main highway onto a narrow road, climbing a small hill before reaching the entrance to the military cemetery. There were large parking lots on either side, but at this hour of the morning, they were occupied by no more than half a dozen cars.

My cemetery visits had been limited to four. The first was when Zeideh died; the second time was when we laid Bobbeh in the ground alongside him; the third was when my mother was crushed to death by a car; the fourth and most recent was when Uncle Sam died. Sam's was the gentlest of deaths, as befitted a man who had walked through life on tiptoe. One night, he woke Bertha to tell her that his best moments were when he came home to her from the store. After that, he fell into a sleep from which he never awoke.

I remembered the Jewish cemetery in Brooklyn, its great gray gravestones arranged in no particular order, all bearing the Star of David. Here, in the military cemetery, I found difficulty in picking out the gravestones. My initial impression was of a vast, unbroken expanse of green. It was only on further inspection that I noticed the long lines of unimposingly uniform stones, scarcely projecting above the earth. They lay flat, like pillows put down to sweeten the repose of the dead. Each stone bore the emblem of the Israeli army; below that, the dead man's name and rank, the dates of his birth and his death. Judging by the dates, most of them were mere boys when they fell. I saw an elderly woman crouched with her cheek against a gravestone, as though she were lulling a child to sleep.

The silence was complete. The grounds were in full bloom. Birds hopped along the branches of the trees, whose roots drew sustenance from the decomposing bodies.

At the far end of one of the rows of gravestones—it may have been the fourth or fifth—there seemed to be a memorial ceremony in progress for some newly interred soldier. My eye caught a detail of paratroopers standing at attention, while nearby stood a bespectacled chaplain with a rust-colored beard. Only when we approached did I suddenly grasp that the red-bereted soldiers had been brought here in honor of my father. I froze in place. I wanted only to see the spot where the man from Tiberias had been buried; nothing more. I wanted the encounter to be intimate, to include no one but him and me. But the two intelligence chiefs had mounted a full military ceremony, as though I required a ritual introduction to my glorious father. As though the sanctity of this moment would somehow be marred if the solemn occasion were not shared by official representatives of the Israeli nation.

Shit.

Why didn't they get the hell out of there, I wondered. But I maintained an impassive expression that gave away nothing of my inner feelings. I stood upright, mustering as much dignity as I could as I strode between the rows of paratroopers. Finally, I reached my father's grave.

I remained stiff and unmoving, anxious to avoid embarrassing the young soldiers who stood nearby, grasping their rifles; they deserved to feel that they were not wasting their time. The general and Yehuda Duek took up positions just behind me. The chaplain now planted himself beside me, inaugurating the proceedings by launching supplication to the Almighty for the soul of Yosef, the son of Yehoshua Dur, who, while in the service of his Israeli homeland, was hanged by the wicked. The meaningless words reached my ears and bounced off into space. Finally, the chaplain presented me with a prayer book, pointing out the text of the Kaddish, the prayer for the dead. Unwilling to defy tradition, I mumbled the words without thinking, obsessed by my fear that the moment I concluded the paratroopers would let loose a commemorative salvo.

When I finished reading, the chaplain stepped up and squeezed my hand, advising me to seek comfort in the reconstruction of a strong and impregnable Israel. He added that I was truly fortunate, since I could draw solace from knowing that my father had died a hero's death, sanctifying the name of Israel. I toyed with the idea of hitting him, but the general and Yehuda Duek came and stationed themselves between us.

I said I would appreciate being left to spend a few moments alone at the graveside. My wish was fulfilled with gratifying promptness. A young lieutenant barked an order and the paratroopers marched off without firing a shot. In my heart I congratulated the Israeli army on its frugality with ammunition.

I stared down at the gravestone and the large wreath with

its band of black cloth inscribed in white: "From your colleagues at the Defense Ministry."

"You son of a bitch," I muttered to the square headstone. "I hope you never find rest. I hope this grave gives no comfort to your rotting bones." Out of the corner of my eye, I saw the general and Duek staring at me; seeing my lips move, they must have thought I was murmuring some private prayer for my father's soul.

I was overcome by a sense of empty futility. I stepped backward and turned to face the two men who had been waiting with such patience and tactful consideration for the son communing with the memory of his father.

We began to pace between the long lines of gravestones, with their borders of greenery and patches of bright flowers. Emerging from the cemetery, we seated ourselves in the general's car. The driver swung out onto the highway leading to the airport. He drove without haste, even though my plane was due to take off within an hour. There was a heavy silence in the car, as though its occupants sensed that mundane conversation might dispel the solemn atmosphere of the cemetery. After a half-hour drive, we reached the passenger terminal at Ben Gurion. Someone from the airport administration ushered us into the VIP lounge. The general asked if there was anything I needed. I told him I would like something to read on the flight. "Science fiction," I added. The general murmured something to the attendant, who hastened away. Moments later he returned with a cheap paperback. I glanced briefly at the title: *Voyage of a Million Years*. That seemed to fit the bill.

It was time to leave. Within moments, I was at the foot of the gangway, flanked by the general and Duek.

"You had some painful experiences here," the general murmured. "You leave behind you friends whose hearts are always open to you."

"I know."

"Any time you need something, just say the word."

It was Yehuda Duek's turn now. He subjected me to a prolonged stare, as though the sight of my face somehow conjured up the agonizing experiences of his own distant past. "Come back to us," he said finally.

I turned away. With light strides, I climbed the steps to the open cabin door, where a hostess took my valise and ushered me to my seat. I had been placed beside a window, but I did not look out at my escorts, who lingered below on the tarmac. I pulled out the book I had just received and plunged into the first chapter. As the plane began to advance along the runway, I was already under way in a space cruiser hundreds of light years from Earth. It was a voyage from which I felt no inclination to return.

8

On disembarking at Larnaca, I immediately rented an orange BMW. I drove to Limassol and drew up at the Elassia. Marinos was not to be seen; the hotel was buzzing. Men and women of various ages scuttled about, surrounded by clusters of pale, nervous children. As I registered, the woman clerk indicated them with uplifted chin. "Refugees," she said. "They've arrived on a ferry from Sidon."

When I got to my room, I spent a few moments shortening the cord of the reading lamp, hoping nobody would notice. I needed a piece of wire to proceed with the plan I had in mind for Albert Mandour. That done, I walked out of my room and promptly ran into Marinos, who invited me to join him in a drink at the bar. "To your good health," he said, raising his glass of white wine. His eyes, drawn into narrow slits by his smile, glinted warmly. He indicated the crowded lobby. "As I predicted, the Lebanese peace conference was a failure. They're still killing one another."

Marinos was called away to take care of a Lebanese woman overcome by labor pains. I sauntered outside to the parking lot, where I had left the BMW. I raised the hood and fiddled around inside. It took me less than ten minutes to set up my little booby trap, leaving one end of the wire unconnected until the moment I would prime it. I locked the car and set out on foot toward George's steak bar. George had spent several years in Dallas, returning with a certain expertise on the preparation of any imaginable variety of beef. When I got there, I learned that George had left for Rhodes, where he planned to open a similar restaurant. However, his mother served me in his place, conjuring up a steak of superb tenderness. While waiting for coffee and dessert, I stepped over to the phone and called the car rental company in Larnaca to notify them that the BMW had been stolen. My announcement caused no alarm. The clerk assured me that the missing car would probably be recovered within a few days; in the meantime, they would send me another vehicle the following morning.

By the time I finished my meal and steppped out of the steak bar, night had fallen. I reached the beach, where I set out on a brisk five-mile walk. After several days of near inactivity, I needed the exercise; I walked vigorously, intent on achieving that state of physical exhaustion without which I had no hope of throwing off my depression.

When I got back to the hotel, the receptionist stopped me. "There was a call for you from the United States," she said. "The caller left no name." She held out a piece of paper. "He asked me to give you this number." Thanking her, I glanced quickly at the familiar figures: Charlie's private phone number.

It was not Charlie's custom to call me when I was in the midst of a mission; the rare exceptions cropped up only when it became urgently necessary to provide me with additional instructions or information. Was that the purpose of this call? Had he decided after all to spare the life of Albert Mandour? I went to my room and asked the hotel operator to get me the Washington number. I found time for a shower and a change of clothes before the call came through.

"You were looking for me," I said without any preliminaries.

"Just wanted to know that you're still on Cyprus."

Irony was in place. "I seem to be," I said in a reserved tone. Something was wrong. "Is there any change?"

"No. When do you expect to get back?"

"If everything goes according to plan, I should conclude the deal tomorrow. That means I'll be back Sunday night."

"Okay. Hope it all works out."

"Is that all?"

"Be seein' ya," he said and hung up.

I stared at the receiver. Charlie's even tone notwithstanding, there was something afoot: he never placed calls needlessly. He had asked if I was "still" on Cyprus. Why "still"? There could be only one answer: Horseface already knew I had taken off a few days for my own affairs, and my absence obviously disturbed him. Did he know of my tangle with the Mossad? And if so, did he know the reason for it?

I abandoned my speculations, deciding that if Charlie had any questions, he would pose them in his own good time. I stretched out in an easy chair with my sci-fi novel, making a determined effort to direct my thoughts to the bizarre denizens of distant galaxies. Instead, my mind focused on Tiberias and Tel Aviv. The figures hovering before my eyes displayed a greater affinity to the winged camel than to any other flying machine.

At 10:30 Saturday morning, I drove the "stolen" BMW to the little restaurant on the narrow promenade where Mandour and I had agreed to meet. Parking nearby, I took good care to lock the car, but not before I connected the loose end of the wire to the car's ignition.

I was still standing beside the car when the Lebanese approached from the other side of the street. I waited for him to take his seat at the front end of the restaurant, scanning the area to make sure he had no unwanted comrades in tow.

Convinced that Mandour was unescorted, I entered the restaurant and settled in the adjacent seat as though we were old friends.

"Everything okay?" He gazed at me with the servile look of a street mongrel.

"The money's okay," I said.

"And the other?" His voice was thick. He was tense, and

154

his eyes were moist. Evidently, a visa to the United States was his last hope.

"Well . . ."

He grabbed my hand. "Without that, the deal's off!"

"You're impatient," I said, drawing my hand out of his. "The other matter is also arranged."

He gasped like a marathon runner. "Arranged?"

"As we agreed."

"May God protect you always!" He seized my hand again. "May He guard you and your dear ones."

I managed to jerk my hand away before he could press it to his fleshy lips. "As for your part of our deal," I said, making my tone intentionally ominous, "you've taken care of that, of course."

"Of course," he beamed. "Of course!"

I had no time for his affability. "The name," I demanded.

Mandour glanced about anxiously, as though still mistrustful. He stiffened as the waiter approached. We ordered coffee and the man went away.

"The name," Mandour mused absentmindedly.

Son of a bitch. "That's right," I said softly, almost courteously, as though I had all the time in the world.

"My payoff," he said. "How will it be handled?"

"D'you see that orange BMW?" I jerked my chin toward the car, parked about a hundred feet away.

He turned his head. "I see it."

"Here are the keys." I laid the bunch on the table. "As soon as you leave me, you'll take the car back to the rental office at Larnaca Airport. When it's returned, you'll be handed a locked valise containing one-half of the money."

He grinned. "While I'm on my way there, you'll have time to find out if there's any such person."

"That's right."

"I'd do precisely the same," he complimented me. "What about the other half?"

"You'll get that from Blake at the Beirut embassy."

"And the visas?"

"Blake has appropriate instructions."

"So that's that," he murmured.

155

He had swallowed the bait. The rest would be easy. "Yes, that's that."

Mandour lit a new cigarette from the stub of his old one. He flung an avaricious glance at the orange car. His nostrils widened, as though in need of additional oxygen. He had picked up the scent of money. "Satisfactory," he said.

"You will forget you ever met me." I found sudden difficulty in breathing, as though I had suffered an onset of asthma. Mandour scented money, but my own nostrils had picked up the stench of death.

"You can trust me," he assured me. "I never set eyes on you." The waiter approached with our coffee. As soon as he had moved away, Mandour reached for the bunch of keys.

But I was swifter; my fingers grasped his wrist. "Not so fast," I said. "Now. Who are we talking about?"

Mandour leaned toward me. "Rif'at Shishakali."

"You're sure?" The question was superfluous. He was merely confirming what Washington already suspected.

Mandour spoke solemnly: "By the lives of my children." His voice shook. "You're my only hope of salvation from that hellhole. Do you think I'd play any tricks? I tell you it was Shishakali who planned the car bombing. The Islamic Jihad wouldn't have dared such an action without an okay from Damascus."

So, Shishakali was the target! The Syrian was a mystery man, rarely seen in public. He was a former commander of Syrian air force intelligence—the senior position in the Damascus intelligence community. But in recent years he was rarely mentioned by the Syrian media; this fact provided indirect confirmation that in all probability he was a special envoy for President Assad.

Shishakali saw the world in terms of black and white: white was for Syria's Soviet patrons, while black stood for the United States and its ally Israel. He had recently made it clear that he would regard it as a personal triumph if he could humiliate America. That was undoubtedly his intention when he gave his blessing to the Iranian shahids' plan to devastate the U.S. Marine headquarters in Beirut. I reminded myself that the attack could never have been mounted without the inside information provided by my table companion, Albert Mandour. I felt myself overcome by revulsion. I wanted him to get out of there. To disappear. "I hope your information has been checked and double-checked," I forced myself to say.

Mandour's calf eyes gazed at me moistly. "Shishakali's your man. If I'm deceiving you, may I die here and now!"

"We'll run a thorough probe," I said. "If it's negative, I don't envy you." I stared at him narrowly. "Now, you remember what you have to do?"

"Yes, sure." His face beamed.

"Take the keys and get out."

Mandour grabbed the bunch as we both rose. Outside the restaurant, he paused, evidently intending to repeat his effusive thanks. But I left him no time, instead crossing to the other side of the street. I found a convenient vantage point from which I could watch as retribution caught up with the man who had helped blow our marines to smithereens. Charlie would appreciate the surprise I had set up, I thought with satisfaction.

Mandour hastened toward the BMW. At first he had difficulty sliding the key into the lock, but after a brief tussle he managed to pull open the door. Bouncing into the seat, he leaned forward, resting his body on the steering wheel while he fumbled with the ignition key. He finally turned the key, and flames instantly enveloped the entire length of the car.

Cypriot policemen came rushing up, but they were helpless to put out the blaze. Even after the fire died down, they would be faced with an almost equally impossible task. It would require herculean efforts before anyone would succeed in identifying the remains of Albert Mandour.

On reaching Kennedy, I called Bertha to let her know I was on my way home. "I've got news for you," I added.

"Oh Daniel!"

"Are there any messages for me?"

"Yes," Bertha said. "Here's the first, from me: I can't wait for your news. Second, also from me: welcome back. Third: Mister Liebman asked you to call him. Fourth: a call asking when you'd be back. From Ariadne."

"Ariadne?"

"That's right." Her voice bristled with excitement.

My first call was to Ed Liebman. He sounded genuinely pleased to hear from me, and asked courteously about my European vacation. I answered him with a few meaningless words, assuring him the holiday had done wonders for my constitution and had erased all trace of my recent flu. Liebman was glad to hear of the improvement in my health; the Riyadh office was approaching the operational stage, and I would soon be required to return there to take care of on-the-spot preparations. In the meantime, there were a number of letters on my desk awaiting translation into English. If it were no imposition, he would be grateful if I could take care of them first thing in the morning. I promised to do just that and hung up.

Next I called the Dakota number, but there was no reply, so I hailed a cab and rode to Avenue Z.

The weather remained chilly; receding winter was putting up a desperate rearguard action against the approach of spring. At exit 7 we left the highway; two minutes later, the driver pulled up to the familiar building and I got out. I spotted Aunt Bertha at her window perch. She waved and flashed me a broad smile before disappearing inside. By the time I had raced up the stone steps, the front door was open. She gave me a hug, then drew back to look at me.

"You got yourself a tan!" Releasing me, she led the way up the wooden staircase. "You look as though you've been on vacation."

"That's just camouflage."

"Pretty good camouflage." She looked at me again more closely. "Are you okay?"

"It was a long flight. I'm tired."

I launched into a description of my impressions of Saudi Arabia, but she showed no special interest. She had something else on her mind.

"You did go," she said finally.

I regarded her evenly. "Yes."

"Tell me about it."

I did not want to talk about Israel at that moment. There was so much seething inside me. I glared at her. "The land you cherish in your memory is no more," I said with a dull rage.

She sensed my pain immediately. "What happened to you?"

I ignored her question. "It's all gone!" I said. "That exotic land with its little white houses, and its sea bluer than blue, and the sand dunes of pure gold dust between the blue sea and the white houses. That's all baloney, Bertha; none of it exists anymore."

"I'm sorry," she said, as if she herself were to blame for my disappointment. "Time leaves its imprint everywhere."

"Except in your memories," I said. "The only place I found your Tel Aviv was in the museum."

"I wasn't dreaming." Bertha's face was pale. "I'm sorry you found no trace . . ."

"Even the flying camel is gone."

"What happened to it?" she whispered.

I shrugged. "The camel itself was stainless steel, so it remained intact. But the concrete column cracked. It had to be taken down. There's a traffic light there now. You know, red-yellow-green . . ."

"I'm very sorry I can't ease your pain." Sorrow deepened the furrows in her face. I felt a measure of relief: I had found someone to share my anguish. She gazed at me sadly. "I thought that if you went there . . ."

"There'd be a miracle?"

She nodded. "I hoped you'd be able to piece it all together. All the pieces . . ."

"There are no pieces, Bertha. Just powder. Dust. Pulp." I picked up my suitcase and headed for the stairs.

I closed the door to my apartment and picked up the telephone. Once again, there was no reply at the Dakota. I undressed and took a shower, then dialed again. This time Ariadne's "hello" was hasty and short of breath. She had just that minute come home, she explained. And yes, she had missed me. It was a reassuring declaration.

I told her briefly about my journey to Riyadh. I described the Saudis' pomposity that served to camouflage the cunning that had made them into the true masters of the Western world.

Ariadne laughed. "You sound good. You must have all kinds of stories."

"If you'd gotten home earlier, you would have had a first-hand report this evening."

"I'm sorry you didn't find me."

I longed for her. Her voice caressed my ear. "You left a message for me," I said.

"Right. Mister Oppenheimer called last Friday. He's been in touch with d'Orly's of Zurich."

"The jewelry! Was any of it bought from them?"

"Every single piece."

My neck muscles tautened. "Who was the buyer?"

"He didn't ask."

"Why not, dammit?"

"A reputable jeweler doesn't ask a question like that," she explained. "If Oppenheimer had asked, he wouldn't have been told."

"Did he get anything out of them? Anything tangible?"

"They told him the dates when the various pieces were sold."

"Better than nothing. What were they?"

She read out the dates. The first one was in June 1967; the last was in 1972, about two months before my mother's death. I read them back to make certain I had them down accurately. The information seemed trivial, but I thanked her all the same.

"What are you doing tomorrow?" she asked hesitantly. I could sense the expectation in her tone.

"I'm afraid I won't make it to lunch. It's going to be a busy day. What about five-thirty at your place?"

"Sounds good." Her voice was low and I felt she wanted to add something, but she remained silent. After that, there was nothing more to say beyond good night.

I gently laid down the receiver, running over our conversation in my mind. She was obviously pleased at my return and eager to see me; I could sense her warmth. I desired her profoundly and intensely, above all perhaps because she had awakened in me some unknown and unsuspected strain of gentleness no one else had ever discovered.

With an effort, I turned my thoughts away from Ariadne and gazed down at the sheet of paper before me. The dates covered the last five years of my mother's life, the years of her mysterious assignations with her aging lover in Miami. How did it work, I wondered, deliberately tormenting myself. What was

160

the procedure? Whenever she was due in Florida, did her lover phone his jewelers in Switzerland to order a gift, a payoff for her services in Miami?

In Miami?

A sudden suspicion flashed through my mind. True, she always *left* for Miami. But who says—

I went to her closet, rummaging through the drawers until I found a large brown envelope containing three passports. I tore off the elastic band that held them together and opened the one with a green binding—evidently the earliest. Date of issue: 1936. Inside, I saw the face of a pretty girl, with long hair falling down past her shoulders: my mother at fourteen. The second passport was dated 1948; the features in the snapshot bore a far closer resemblance to my mother as I remembered her; even the cheap passport photo with its fading tones could not diminish her radiance.

It was the last and most recent passport I was interested in. I found the date of issue: 1967—the year she started her regular trips to her ailing relative in Florida and the first year to appear on the list of jewelry sales. I turned the page, looking for exit and entry stamps.

Zurich.

And Zurich.

And again Zurich.

A shudder ran up my spine.

I struggled to read the blurred dates on the consular stamps. Not all were decipherable, but even those were not difficult to guess; a comparison with the list Ariadne had dictated proved that whenever a piece of jewelry was purchased, my mother was there. In Zurich. She never went anywhere near Miami!

Her distant cousin Reizel, lonely and neglected on her Florida sickbed, was nothing more than a smokescreen for a liaison no less romantic or turbulent than the one she had with my father.

I returned the passports and noticed another envelope that I had overlooked before. It was stuffed with papers of all kinds. There were airline receipts: New York–Zurich, Zurich–New York, first class. There were brochures describing five-star hotels in every capital in Europe. Ticket stubs from the theater, always for the best seats. Boxes at the ballet, the opera. Menus embossed with the names of the finest restaurants.

Were these the places frequented by my mother, the impecunious woman from Brooklyn who scarcely managed to make ends meet? Her own modest income could never have supported such extravagance. All she had to live on was her monthly pittance from the Israeli Defense Ministry, a sum barely adequate for our basic living expenses.

Obviously, her lover had been far more generous even than indicated by the jewelry.

The shadowy figure of my mother's lover continued to occupy my thoughts for the rest of the evening. I could not get him out of my mind. Several times during the night I awoke to find myself wondering about him. His identity remained a mystery, but there was nothing mysterious about my obsession with him: my curiosity was fueled by jealousy. It was as though I had begun to champion the cause of my dead father, powerless to defend his tragically doomed love.

It was a painful, turbulent night. Past was confused with present, the present intermingled with the past. My mother and her lover remained in my thoughts until morning came at last, permitting me to drag myself from my rumpled bed and set off for work.

A few hours later, I was called in for a meeting with Moritz and Liebman. They briefed me on the significant expansion in the company's relations with clients—private as well as official—in Saudi Arabia and the Persian Gulf states. With income from that quarter growing, the two attorneys were in high spirits, and their elation made them generous. In view of my growing responsibilities, which would now include frequent trips to Riyadh to supervise the functioning of our new office, they had decided to award me a 10 percent raise.

I returned to my office to continue my work. In spite of the bonus I had just received, my concentration faltered. My thoughts wandered from the translations as I pondered the turmoil and confusion that had overtaken me in recent weeks. The translations took far longer than usual, and I had to stay late to complete them.

It was after six when I reached Ariadne's apartment. I kissed her, burying my head in her hair.

"Did you miss me?" she asked.

"I never so much as gave you a thought."

She laughed. "And I thought you'd come back a changed man."

"Whom did you expect?"

"Let me take a good look." Her hands clasped mine, sending warmth through my body. "Your eyes haven't changed," she said. "Gray and sunken under those dark curved brows of yours. The nose hasn't changed either, and your cheekbones still give you that hollow look. But above all, your lips—"

"What about them?"

"They're still hungry and sensual."

"Anything wrong with that?"

"They make you look as though you're constantly on the alert. Sexually, I mean."

I laughed. "That means I haven't changed."

"I'm glad you haven't," she said softly.

"There were moments when I thought I was about to," I said. "I expected a sudden metamorphosis into a full-fledged Israeli."

Her green eyes widened. "You did go!" she said. "I want to hear all about it."

I launched into the story of my visit to Israel and my search for my father's past. It was a full report, though there were details I withheld, including my arrest. She listened intently, asking only an occasional question.

When I told her how I stood beside my father's grave, Ariadne's agitation mounted, her mood changing abruptly. "Why are you getting so emotional?" I asked.

She bit her lower lip.

"It was a ludicrous scene," I continued. "There I was, standing over the remains of an Israeli nationalist, a man with confused ideas about providing a sanctuary for survivors of the Holocaust. A man who prized all that patriotic crap more than his own life, even more than the woman he loved. So I stood there. That was all. What is there to get worked up about?"

"Because it's touching, that's why."

"Touching? It was disgusting!"

"I don't understand you!" she shouted. "How twisted you get when you try to hide your feelings."

I tried to soothe her. "I was just trying to explain how I felt."

"No you weren't! I know you well enough. If there had been no one else there, you'd have kissed your father's stone." Her cheeks had an angry flush. "But you have to put on this strange act." She paused. "I want to hear more about Mussa Eini. About Yehuda Duek. They sound remarkable."

"Oh, they're remarkable all right," I said. "If they thought it would serve their nationalist ideals, they'd gladly bring the whole world tumbling down about their heads."

Ariadne's eyes glinted. "You make them sound like a bunch of Nazis."

"There's some truth in that."

"You're out of your mind!"

I shook my head. "Nationalism always contains a grain of destructiveness. Men lose their sanity when they place nation above all else."

"That doesn't make them Nazis."

"The comparison was yours, not mine. All I'm saying is that I can't understand men like my father—they fall somewhere between heroes and criminals."

"Depending on your viewpoint."

"He's no hero in my eyes."

Ariadne understood perfectly well what I was implying. She gazed at me with compassion. Finally, she left the subject, making a conscious effort to clear the air. "We haven't even had a drink yet," she said.

The change of subject came as a relief. "Cheers," I said, hoisting an imaginary whiskey glass.

My feigned gaiety did not fool her. "There's something troubling you in particular," she said. "What is it?"

"It's the information from Oppenheimer. It confirmed a suspicion." I made a wry attempt at a grin. "I don't know who my mother's lover was during those last few years, but whoever he was, he certainly gave her the royal treatment."

"It must have been exhilarating for her—to be treated like a princess."

"Not a princess, Ariadne. To this man, she was nothing less than a queen." I told Ariadne everything I had learned about

164

my mother's secret European excursions. "I wish I could find him. I wish I could learn his secret. What was there about him, Ariadne?"

"I can't help you," she said. "You have to help yourself."

"I'm confused," I said. "My head is bursting. These past few weeks, I've learned two things—one, that my father was some kind of a paragon, a superman straight out of a Jewish Olympus. Two, that my mother emerged every now and then from her batty seclusion to a life of royalty with a rich lover. And where does that leave me?" I raised my arms in a helpless gesture. "I'm just a miserable bastard. No, that's not quite accurate. I'm *two* miserable bastards. Two Daniels. One, naïve and evil, the other wise and cowardly." I flung her a challenging glance. "Can you imagine those two Daniels united into a single person? I'd be naïve and smart and evil and cowardly. Everything a man needs to become a card-carrying fascist. So where do I go from here?"

"One thing is clear," she said. "You'll never find peace until you solve your riddles."

She rose and took me by the hand, leading me along a winding corridor to a room I had never seen before. It had only one window, facing out on the dark trees of Central Park. The center of the room was occupied by three slide projectors, each one set up to face a different wall. At her beckoning, I stretched out on the heavy Persian rug with its scattering of cushions, supporting my head on my hand.

The next moment, I found myself surrounded by the vacant, wandering expressions of the denizens of the gutters. Ageless men. Formless women. Inmates of the dead alleyways, the filthy rooms, the miserable slums. I watched with a blend of disgust and fascination. Only the sharpest and most discerning of eyes could have penetrated those dark and secret crannies of human degradation. The Ariadne who had taken these photographs bore little resemblance to the woman I knew.

"You're torturing me," I said softly.

She flung me a mute glance.

"You're doing this intentionally," I said. "You're trying to make my anguish insignificant."

She pressed the control buttons, and three more faces flashed onto the walls. There was a blowup of a man about my own age. He looked as though he had lived a thousand years. Even though he was still alive, his eyes were dead.

The slides showed Ariadne as a genuine and sensitive artist. I waved a hand at the oversized portraits. "This is you," I said.

"This is what I want to be."

"Your insight frightens me."

She smiled in comprehension.

"Other lands, Ariadne," I begged. "Other lands, other people . . ."

At my urging, she rose and replaced the carousel with different slides. She set the projectors running again, this time with pictures of Mikonos, Hydra, and Milos, then flicked the controls of her stereo to fill the room with Greek music. She lay down beside me.

The room caught fire with the bright rays reflected from every wall. Ariadne cast her spell, bewitching me with the magic of the islands and her nearness to me.

I embraced her gently, slowly giving way to my passionate desire for this woman I loved so dearly. She responded with equal fervor, our bodies uniting in affirmation of our need for one another.

Everything we did or said that night bore a profound significance for both of us. But as the darkness began to fade, I sensed a change.

"There's an old tradition about the last watch of the night," Ariadne said, a strangely somber note in her voice. "It's said to be the hour for lovers to make their confessions."

"Anyone who makes a confession must feel sinful, irrespective of the watch." I grinned at her. "To me, you don't look like a sinner."

"Wait till you hear what I have to say."

Ariadne's expression made me feel uneasy. She remained silent a moment longer. Then she raised her head and gazed at me. "Our meeting, it was no accident."

I stared at her, bewildered.

"When we met at the luncheon counter, there was nothing fortuitous about it."

My laugh was forced. "It sounds like a riddle."

She grimaced. "I was following instructions."

I responded with unthinking swiftness; my hand seized her arm, bringing a soft moan of pain from her lips. Her complexion had turned pale to the point of translucence. "The last watch makes your imagination run wild," I said.

The gruff violence of my tone must have taken her by surprise. "I'm sorry," she said. "I want you to know the truth."

"It wouldn't do to have some lie between us," I sneered.

My barb struck home. "That's just it. I didn't want anything like that to stand between us."

"You didn't act on your own initiative?"

She shook her head.

There was no need for her to elaborate. I sensed the vile stench of the CIA rising about me. I was familiar with the technique. All her intuitions, her divinations, her inspired guesses about my background—all these were no spontaneous manifestations or occult gifts; they were the outcome of thorough briefings and carefully memorized details of my biography. I remembered Charlie once saying something about the possibility of Ariadne getting hurt. That figured: at this moment, I was the one liable to hurt her. I forced myself to speak with control.

"I want to hear it all, Ariadne."

She nodded, but it was some time before she could speak. She was evidently perplexed by the change in me. She must have realized that the man who faced her now was neither tender, nor gentle, nor considerate. She seemed afraid, as though she had finally recognized my other personality.

"Talk," I said, trying to moderate my tone. "I don't want to see you hurt."

She hesitated. "I didn't mean to do you any harm."

"I want to hear your story," I said coldly. "All of it."

She nodded submissively. "Remember what I told you about the time after my father died?"

"I remember some of it."

"All I had left was this apartment and very little money. A few months ago, it had dwindled to two thousand dollars."

"Quite a problem." My tone was intentionally callous. "Was there nobody to help you solve it?"

"I had no one. Not a soul. The only person who stood by me was Sheila. I went to seek her advice. A few days later, she called to say she wanted to introduce me to someone who might be able to help. A government employee. I asked how he could help, and she said to trust her. The following day, she appeared with him."

"What was his name?"

"Abner. He didn't give any other name. He was courteous and pleasant, almost fatherly. He said he understood my predicament. He told me he might have a proposition which would enable me to keep this apartment, as well as give me financial security. He didn't go into details. A week later, he came to see me again, asking all kinds of questions about my background. Again, he went away without telling me anything definite. He came and went in this manner until I almost gave up hope of something practical coming of it all. I was in despair. At that time, it was only Sheila who kept me going."

"Didn't you realize Sheila's role?"

"Not then. I hadn't the faintest notion. It was much later before I caught on. Finally, after several meetings with Abner, he came up with his proposition. It was very tempting. He didn't refer to the CIA by name—he called it 'my organization'—he said it would cover the upkeep of my apartment for the next five years. In addition, I would get three hundred dollars a week. For my part, I was to strike up friendships with certain persons and to obtain information about them. The whole proposal was totally unexpected. I had never considered anything of the kind. I asked for time to think it over." She paused reflectively. "Of course, I wasn't stupid enough to overlook the risks I'd be letting myself in for. But what other choice did I have?" She broke off with a shrug. Her eyes begged understanding. But my expression remained stony.

"Abner began to teach me how to go about it. My role, he said, was to act like a bee. I was to flit from flower to flower, gleaning whatever grains of information I could extract before bringing it back to the hive. Do you get the picture?"

"I do indeed." I was also beginning to recognize a familiar voice.

"I was scared, but Abner reassured me. He told me that

the strongest of men, however firm their character, would always make fools of themselves with a woman like me."

"And you fell for all this?" I said. "How naïve can you be?"

She smiled. "Maybe I was stupid."

"And then?"

"He—Abner—told me to befriend you. He told me exactly where I would find you."

"And gave you some tips on how to approach me?"

She nodded, flushing.

"What were you ordered to find out?"

She drew a deep breath. "Abner told me to focus mainly on your income and its sources. He wanted to know if you threw your money about. He asked me to find out who your friends were. I was to learn anything I could about your past."

"What did you report to him?"

"Everything, at first," she confessed, evading my eyes. "But when I got to know you, I couldn't bring myself . . . I just made up all kinds of things that went along with your stories."

"I suppose you told him about the jewelry?"

"Not a word!" she protested. "By that time, I was determined to tell him as little as possible." She broke off, evidently uncertain whether I believed her.

I stared at her, refusing to let up. A sudden thought struck me. "When was it exactly that this—er—Abner—set you onto me?"

"Two months ago."

The timing figured. The moment I told Charlie I wanted out, he had made me one of his targets. "You're sure of the date?"

"Positive. It was the day I signed the contract."

"Contract?" I froze. "What contract?"

"My contract with Abner's 'organization.' If, at any time over the next five years, I fail to fulfill my side of the deal, all rights to the apartment and its contents will revert to the government. In return for retaining possession, I undertook to obey all instructions. My reward, in addition to the apartment and the weekly allowance, includes a twenty thousand dollar bonus to be paid after five years' work."

"Excellent terms," I said, feeling bruised and betrayed. "You claim you've only worked for this Abner over the past couple of months?"

She nodded.

"Why should I believe you?" I said. "For all I know, you could have been in this sordid little job of yours for months. Years even." Watching the blood rush to her face, I hated myself for attacking her, but I could not restrain myself. "You did it very well. I'm sure you had a long list of successful assignments before you ever got to me."

Her eyes were moist. "Not only were you my first assignment," she whispered, "you were my first love . . ."

I realized what I had done, but it was too late. "I didn't mean . . ." I stared at her, pitying her for allowing herself to be trapped but pitying myself for the demolition of my own illusions about this woman who had touched the innermost chords of my soul.

When Ariadne spoke, her contempt was disconcerting. "For your information," she said, "I notified Abner that I intend to cancel the contract."

"And he just smiled and said, 'This is one contract you can't cancel without losing.' "

She glanced at me sharply. "That's right. How do you know?"

"It's his standard reply."

Her eyes widened, registering fear, even panic. "You know him?" I nodded and her confusion grew. "You mean—you're one of them?"

I nodded again. My association with the bastard, Abner, and his "organization" was probably the last revelation she had anticipated.

"What else did Abner say when you talked about calling off the deal?"

"He just shrugged and said, 'Okay by me.' Then he told me, come April first, he'll invoke the final clause."

"Meaning throw you out of your apartment."

"Right."

"He won't," I said confidently. "That contract isn't worth the paper it's written on." I smiled at her, trying to make my confidence infectious. "You can trust me. Abner can't rob you of what is legally yours. I know him well." My fury at Ariadne

170

had melted, and I sensed an overwhelming rush of tenderness for her. I leaned toward her, cradling her in my arms. Still hurt and bewildered, she pushed me away at first, but her resistance was short-lived and she nestled agaist me, shuddering. We remained in that embrace for a long moment. "Trust me," I repeated.

9

The next morning, I went on with my routine tasks, but my mind remained preoccupied with Ariadne's predicament. Aunt Bertha called to tell me Charlie had phoned from Washington. He would be arriving in New York that evening. Bertha's message came as no surprise: Charlie invariably put in an appearance within a day of my return from any of his assignments. These were "debriefing sessions," devoted to drawing conclusions and learning lessons, all to be included in his reports to his superiors. I would also return my stamped passport to Charlie. We never used the same passport twice.

"You'll be staying in town overnight?" Bertha asked. I often wondered what she thought of Charlie. I doubted that she still believed he was an academic colleague sharing my interest in Mideastern studies. "Can I expect you tomorrow?"

"I'm not sure. A lot of urgent business has piled up."

I could hear her sigh of disappointment.

It was much later before I succeeded in reaching Ariadne to tell her I would not be coming over. "If I can get away, I'll call you."

"I'll be home," she said simply. "Take care of yourself."

Such cautions were not her style. "Is something wrong?"

"I don't know." She hesitated. "I have an uneasy feeling."

"Everything's going to be fine."

"I hope so." She sounded unsure.

Charlie reached the Warwick just after seven; but he did not join me at our usual table. Instead, he stood in the doorway, beckoning me to come with him. Before leaving Washington, he had reserved a quiet corner table in an Italian restaurant a few minutes' walk from the hotel.

It was only when we were comfortably seated that we began our conversation. Charlie told me I looked well. Then, as he grappled with his spaghetti bolognese, he began to ply me with questions, as always, brief and strictly to the point. First, he wanted to know about my stay in Riyadh. My replies were factual, punctuated by my own tussle with a dish of shrimps in garlic. I had not forgotten his bizarre call to the Elassia hotel or his inquiry if I was "still there." Had he expected me to defect?

"I understand you'll be going to Riyadh quite frequently now," he said.

"Looks like it."

"Things are working out according to plan. You'll have free access to Saudi Arabia, to all the Gulf states."

He was baiting me, assuming I would continue to work for him. Cautiously, I examined his features. In spite of his relaxed expression, I did detect some change. For one thing, his whiskey glass was standing to one side, untouched; he was drinking nothing but water. His aim was obvious: while keeping his own mind clear, he was hoping to get me drunk.

"You'll have to find someone else in that part of the world." I spoke clearly and distinctly, but he continued to toy with his spaghetti as though he had not heard. "I'm not sure I'm staying on with Moritz and Liebman. If I give up my job, you'll be free to install another one of your boys there to take advantage of their Saudi contacts." Charlie calmly continued to chew, as if he had not heard me. "And don't say I didn't warn you," I said. "It may not be long before I leave."

"When do you plan to go to Riyadh again?"

"Could be next week." I took a sip of water. Realizing I had caught on to his game, a glint of humor lit up his eyes. "I'll be dealing with the practical arrangements for the new office."

"I must say," Charlie said smugly, "it was a good idea planting you in that office."

"You're not listening to me. Limassol was my last assignment. I've discharged my contractual obligations and you know it."

He smiled. "That was a fine trick with the BMW."

"I had a good teacher."

"The teacher had a good pupil."

I did not like the look in Charlie's eyes: it was veiled and distant. My conviction grew that he was up to something. I couldn't be sure what his trump was, but I had an uneasy feeling that he would use Ariadne in his plans to trap me. I didn't want him to know that I had discovered his connection with her: I had yet to work out a way of extricating her from his contract.

"What was he like, this Mandour?" Charlie asked.

"Despicable vermin. Typical of Lebanon. No past and no present."

"No future either," Charlie reminded me.

"A loser."

"Don't sound so sorry for him. He sold our boys down the river." He stared at me. "Lately you've begun to lose sight of priorities."

"I've changed, Charlie."

"Don't think I haven't noticed," he said dryly. "What did Mandour tell you?"

"The man we want is Shishakali."

He did not seem surprised to learn that his own prime suspect was, indeed, responsible for the deaths of our marines. "Let's go for a walk," he said suddenly.

Charlie liked walking; it cleared his mind. When he set out on one of his strolls or went to fling fish at the seals in Central Park, it was more than nostalgia for his lost childhood. This evening, as usual, he steered our course toward the park, walking in silence, head to one side, hands clasped behind his back. I sauntered beside him, waiting for him to break the silence. Finally, he began to ask about Shishakali. Charlie resembled a regurgitating cow with his habit of chewing and rechewing familiar information until he had sucked out its essence. I answered his questions again; it was a topic we had gone over repeatedly.

Shishakali was mixed up in every kind of shady dealing, taking advantage of his official position to organize large-scale smuggling of gold, diamonds, and drugs. He ran them in or out of the country in accordance with fluctuations in the market. He had an unsavory reputation in Syria: his fellow countrymen said that when he entered a snakepit, the snakes fled for cover. With that, the Syrian president regularly entrusted Shishakali with his country's most sensitive dealings with other Arab states. He had recently served as liaison between Damascus and Riyadh on matters arising from the Lebanon conflict.

"Which proves how influential he is," Charlie said. "We know how much importance the Syrians attach to Lebanon."

"He's invulnerable in Damascus," I said. "He couldn't be better protected in a nuclear bunker."

"In that case, where would you try for him?"

"Wherever he thinks he has the least to fear."

Charlie hummed some toneless melody; he was in a strange mood. "Where would that be?"

I had fallen into the trap. "You know very well," I said. "Riyadh."

"I like the way you think," Charlie said quickly. "Riyadh's the best place, for three reasons. First, he thinks no one knows when he's expected there; two, there have never been political assassinations of foreigners in Riyadh; three, the Saudis are very much aware of points one and two." He grinned with self-satisfaction. "At most, they'll run some routine security checks to satisfy Shishakali's sense of his own importance."

Charlie was trying to draw me into a discussion of the operational details, but I chose to remain silent. I was determined to have nothing to do with the assignment.

"I wish this were behind us," Charlie said, continuing to toy with his plan as though my consent had already been given.

I continued to remain silent.

"We've taken some humiliating knocks in recent years," he went on. "They've inflicted enormous damage on the organization. The responsibility for salvaging our credibility is left to men like you and me. This may be the most important assignment you've ever been given, Daniel. It's for all of us."

"I know," I grinned. "It's for the President, so he can sleep well at night."

"Make all the wisecracks you want." He slapped me on the shoulder, but his expression remained gloomy. "It isn't for the President. It's for America. So the families of those dead marines know they haven't been forgotten. So the entire nation knows that our arm is long and mighty. And it's for us, Daniel, for you and me and men like us. We have to prove we aren't impotent."

"Listening to you is like hearing the beat of the drum."

He refused to give up. "You've been with us for ten years. That's quite a slice out of your life. So when the next test comes, I'm sure you won't fail."

"Stuff it, Charlie. Mandour was my last assignment."

"Last but one," he corrected evenly. "The last one guarantees your pension. And the bonus too. You wouldn't want to forfeit your benefits?"

"Don't act tough," I said. "You wouldn't steal my rights."

He smiled. "I know how much you need every penny." Unwittingly, he had confirmed that Ariadne had not revealed the discovery of my mother's jewelry.

"Money isn't everything," I said.

"You've become strangely indifferent to it. Did you win in the lottery?"

"Mind your own business."

"Your business is my business." He stopped, turning to face me. "Everything you do is of interest to me. Like your change of itinerary last week." His tone was razor-sharp. "And your unscheduled visit to Israel."

That was it. Just what I had dreaded. "That was a private matter."

"You don't say! Going AWOL in the midst of a mission? You've never indulged yourself like that before."

"Mandour had gone off to Beirut to bring the information. That left me with five days to kill. So I went to Israel."

"Why Israel?"

"I've never been there before."

"I see." His blue eyes became watery; from past experience, I knew that Charlie's humanity was dwindling. I could only hope that my tangle with the Mossad had not been reported to him. As it was, his knowing of my visit to Israel put me further into his bad graces. "Was the journey interesting?" he asked.

"Depends on your viewpoint."

"Why so modest, Daniel? Anyway, your viewpoint interests me."

"I went in search of something."

"Did you find what you were looking for?"

"My trip to Israel was totally unconnected with the Cyprus mission. And I completed that assignment to your full satisfaction."

His expression was thoughtful. "That was quite a fuss you raised over there," he said.

I held my breath. Although I knew there were Mossad moles within the CIA, I was unaware Charlie had planted any of his own inside the Mossad. Evidently, they had supplied him with a full account of my encounter with Israeli intelligence. "What are you driving at?" I asked.

He ignored my question. "Your journey was unscheduled, you say?"

"That's right."

"No one could have known of your intention of arriving there?"

"Correct."

"Didn't you mention it to anyone as a possibility?"

"I spoke about it with my aunt. In fact, it was her idea. Bertha wanted me to find my roots."

"What for?"

"She's made me feel like a mongrel. Half American, half Israeli."

"An interesting crossbreed," Charlie said. "Half Lion of Judah, half American eagle. No one expected you in Israel?"

"That's right."

"Then who scheduled your meeting with the head of the Mossad?"

I shuddered inwardly. He did know. "The whole thing has to do with my father."

"Your father?"

"I told you that he was an agent for Israeli intelligence, that he was killed during a mission."

"Yes, I remember that."

"I went to Israel to try and find out about him and how he died." Briefly, I told him of my voyage of discovery and of the facts I had learned about my father's death.

"So that was the reason for your mysterious trip," Charlie said slowly. "Exploring for a bag of moldering bones. Sentimentality is one of your greatest weaknesses, Daniel. There are times when you are so Jewish."

"There are times when you sound like a lousy anti-Semite."

"It's a matter of upbringing, isn't it? Your visit to Tel Aviv worried some people in Washington."

That was another heavy salvo. I seized his arm. "What are you after?"

"I'm trying to solve a puzzle," he said. "You're not impulsive enough to throw away a hundred thousand dollars just to avoid one final mission. You're not the kind of man to treat a government pension like peanuts. This sudden rejection of materialism," his irony was unconcealed, "comes directly after your visit to Israel. What did you find there? Thirty pieces of silver?"

My heart missed a beat. "I haven't been bought, Charlie."

"No?"

I stared at him. "If I don't take on the Shishakali mission, you'll cheerfully hang me."

"That's right. I'm just looking for a central square that would do you justice."

"What's that supposed to mean?"

"Like father, like son," he murmured. "Every man has his secret ambition. I think I've just stumbled on yours."

"Leave me alone."

"No way. You always had one single ambition in life. It had to do with your father, your shadowy, unknown father. The man of mystery. A mystery you've always wanted to unravel." He laughed suddenly. "Your search even helped you choose your academic studies—Semitic languages. The languages *he* spoke. You were looking for your origins all right. But you weren't looking for your land of origin. You were looking for your balls."

"That's a ridiculous hypothesis. Half-baked psychology."

"Scary, is it?" He refused to let up. "You don't want to admit to the immature motives of an adolescent. One of the few things you knew about your father was his intelligence work. When you decided to join the organization, wasn't it out of an unconscious desire to emulate him?"

"I couldn't," I said. "I don't reach as high as his ankles."

"And that eats you up, doesn't it?"

"The world I grew up in is nothing like his world. I'll never be like him. He was a genuine nut. I'd never allow myself to be hanged in place of someone else." I made an effort to smile. "You would, though, Charlie. You're like him."

"You may have something there. So, you had an interesting stay in Israel." Charlie tacked swiftly, hoping to take me off balance.

"What do you mean?"

"Your meeting with the head of the Mossad. And Yehuda Duek, his second in command." He stared at me, guessing correctly what was running through my mind. "That's right—he probably holds your father's old job." He cocked his head to one side. "And these two important men, with so much to do and not much leisure to spare, spent so many valuable hours talking to you, Daniel. How do you account for that?"

"My father was one of their most brilliant operatives. Don't forget that."

"I forget nothing."

It was a warning: he had heard my story and believed it— up to a point. But his suspicions of me, and of my involvement with the Mossad, were far from stilled.

As though to stress that he was leaving matters in suspense for the time being, Charlie said nothing further until we reached the hotel. He invited me to the bar for a nightcap.

The liquor was a welcome tonic, smoothing away some of the tension of the past hour. Charlie too was more relaxed after his walk, and I tried once more to talk him into assigning the Shishakali mission to another agent.

"You're wasting your breath and my time," Charlie replied.

I refused to give up. "I have this premonition that I won't come back alive from another mission."

"I don't buy it. Not from you."

"I just want to live," I said helplessly, sullenly conscious of floundering in his net.

"If you're so concerned about your own welfare, you'd better reconsider the Shishakali assignment. It wouldn't be too healthy for you if certain persons in Washington get strange ideas about your loyalty to the organization."

"A lot of unfounded suspicions," I snorted.

"Which you have one way of disproving—by taking on Shishakali."

"I can't do it, Charlie."

"You will," he said, and ordered another round of drinks.

At breakfast, I found Charlie at one of the far tables. He gave me a quizzical glance. "I'm returning to Washington today. If you need me, you can reach me at home."

"That's very generous of you."

He glowered. "What does that mean?"

"I've never been authorized to call you at home. Do you expect dramatic developments?"

"You can never tell." He grinned, but his expression gave away nothing.

I opted for a frontal assault. "Are you laying some trap for me?"

He looked offended. "Heaven forbid. You and I, we need one another."

"I wonder."

He went, leaving me with a sense of dejection that bore me down like a rock.

The office brought me little relief. At eleven, I called Ariadne, but there was no answer at her apartment. At twelve, I headed for the Forty-sixth Street lunch counter. I waited in vain: she did not show up. Back at the office, I dialed Ariadne's number once more, but there was still no reply; I got the same result at five. Had Charlie, in fact, decided to use Ariadne to twist my arm?

At five-thirty, I got to the Rendezvous, where I found a quiet corner table. There was no sign of Ariadne. I went to the phone. I held the receiver in my hand for a long time, even though I knew there would be no reply this time either.

I dialed Charlie's home number in Georgetown. After a brief moment, I heard his soft "Hello?"

"It's me, Charlie."

"To what do I owe this call?"

"I'm taking you up on your offer."

"Oh."

"You show foresight."

I heard his soft chuckle. "What can I do for you?"

"Where is she?" I demanded.

"Certain subjects are unsuitable for discussion over the phone." His voice was tranquil. As I suspected, she was in his hands.

"I have just one request." I enunciated the words slowly and clearly, to hold down my rising anger. "I want you to tell your thugs that if she gets so much as a scratch, I'll know where to find them."

"You sound concerned."

I remained silent.

"I understand you have something to discuss with me," he said.

"Without delay!"

"Okay," he said. "Grab the first shuttle and get on down here."

The seals' slippery playmate hung up. I cursed. The unusual intimacy that had grown between us had lulled me into hoping that he would show me a trifle more understanding. I should have remembered that I was dealing with a venomous spider.

The thought of Ariadne in the hands of Charlie's hoodlums threw me into an impotent fury. I remained standing beside the telephone for several minutes, as though paralyzed. I had never experienced such a murderous rage. I could have killed him. It was a normal reaction on the part of a man who knows the woman he loves is in danger. But for someone dealing with Charlie, it was a symptom of weakness.

10

Charlie did not meet me at the Washington airport. He was not a coward. Even at the risk of his own life, he would not back down from an open confrontation with me. Why, then, was he not here?

But, then, Charlie was complex. At best, my thinking extended two moves ahead; but Charlie, being a grand master, invariably planned three or more, which was why I could never be a match for him. Why should he come to the terminal in person when the simple chore of escorting me could be entrusted to the quartet of sturdily built gentlemen presently approaching me from four different directions. I scanned them swiftly. Three were courteous enough to hold back while one approached and addressed me: "Mister Kottler, you will come with us."

I went along quietly.

In a way, I was relieved now that things were out in the open. Still, I cursed myself for my stupidity in blundering into the trap. My mistake had been a glaring one. I thought Charlie was holding Ariadne to force me to agree to one last mission.

But such tactics were not in character for Charlie. Ariadne had served him as nothing more than bait to lure me to Washington; any other form of summons might have forced me under-ground. Indeed, if my current reading of the chart was correct, Charlie had chosen to play his other trump, the one inscribed "Mossad."

We marched toward the parking lot, the eight-armed del-egation surrounding me. They must have had instructions from Charlie to treat me with caution; they shepherded me along like some unpredictably ferocious beast.

Everything was being done to make me feel insecure. In-stead of being taken to an ordinary car, I found myself rudely shoved into a sealed commercial van with no windows. I had no inkling as to our destination. Nevertheless, my escorts continued to take precautions. Two of them sat up front while the other two settled themselves beside the rear door.

Although I had no idea where they were taking me, I knew the "organization" was well supplied with safe houses in the city and on its outskirts. Of one thing I was certain: I was not being taken to Charlie's Georgetown residence. Another point equally certain: whereas only a few minutes back I was a free man—one moreover licensed by the United States government to kill on its behalf—I was now in custody, suspected of being a col-laborator with a foreign government.

The drive must have taken about twenty minutes. When the van stopped, the driver leaped from the cab and came around the back to open the doors. The other two beckoned to me, and I stepped out. A rapid glance pinpointed my whereabouts: I was on Avenue C, only a short distance from the White House.

I was taken to the sixth floor of a barrackslike building. We marched out into a broad corridor, at the end of which one of my guards opened a door to usher me inside. There were a number of unoccupied desks with typewriters nestled under dustcovers—the employees had evidently left for home. From here, I was led into a smaller room, windowless and furnished with a plain table on either side of which stood a pair of simple wooden chairs —a standard interrogation room. My guards or-dered me to hand over my wallet, watch, and key ring, then marched wordlessly out of the room, leaving me alone.

My dejection grew when I spotted the closed-circuit television camera at ceiling level; I was obviously to be under surveillance. With nothing better to do, I settled myself into one of the chairs, to relax as best I could.

Many hours passed. Without a watch and with no glimpse of daylight, I lost track of time. Every now and then I nodded off.

It must have been sometime in the early morning when the door opened to admit a beefy man in his forties. The Bulldog, as I instantly christened him, was dapper and well tended. His sparse hair, carefully brushed and combed, adhered to his scalp as though glued on; his smoothly shaven cheeks and the cheap but pungent after-shave he exuded gave one the impression he had come directly from the hairdresser. An elegant suit, carefully tailored to fit his generous dimensions, completed the picture.

He seated himself at the table and opened a briefcase to bring out a miniature tape recorder, a notebook, and a pen. I wondered whether Charlie was not overreaching himself with this little pageant. It struck me as a waste of public funds. He would have to do better than this if he figured on getting me back.

As though wearied by the mere thought of the interrogation that lay ahead, Bulldog's eyes displayed a dull absence of curiosity; he had been delegated to do a job, and that was all that he intended to do. He yawned. It must have been well past his bedtime. "I'm sure you know why you're here," he said. His voice was pleasant, the tone just short of friendly. "Since we're both professionals, let's get right down to business."

"A sensible suggestion," I said, with what I hoped was equal conviviality. "What is it you hope to hear from me?"

Bulldog's smile remained fixed. "Let's start from the moment of your departure from Riyadh, and we'll run right through your itinerary, up to your return to Kennedy."

I felt as though I had been taken back to the interrogation center in Tel Aviv. Bulldog's expression bore a likeness to that of the moon-faced Israeli with the cigarette holder—the international brotherhood of inquisitioners.

"There's only one man I report to," I said. I might as well get my stage directions from the director, instead of wasting my time on one of his script girls.

184

"But you'll talk to me," Bulldog said. "I'll ask the questions and you'll provide the answers. Which flight did you take out of Kennedy?"

I said nothing.

"Did you fly in the company of your employers, Moritz and Liebman?"

Still nothing.

He continued to press his questions with a steady obstinacy, while I maintained an equally obstinate silence. My taciturnity did not appear to provoke him. Like me, he knew it was only a matter of time before I made some response. He was neither violent nor threatening.

Bulldog continued to read out the questions listed in his notebook. He asked about Riyadh and the various Saudis I had met; about my stay on Cyprus and my links with Marinos and the Elassia Hotel.

It was a slow procedure. Every time he asked a question, Bulldog paused to await my reply, apparently eager for me to give it my earnest consideration. I ignored his questions, and he ignored my silence, pressing on with total indifference to my indifference.

He asked about my dealings with Mandour. Then he moved on to the "gap," as he termed the time that had elapsed between Mandour's departure for Beirut and his return to Cyprus.

"What made you suddenly decide to go to Israel?"

I stared at him, trying to make up my mind whether or not his ears displayed the shape characteristic of his breed.

"You've taken frequent visits to that region." He glanced at his notes. "Egypt, Lebanon, Greece, Cyprus, and Rhodes." He yawned; his fangs were enormous. "You never went to Israel before. Why now?"

The question was apt. But I had no intention of admitting that two women had influenced my decision. He went on with his questions, evidently scripted by Charlie after our conversation in New York.

"While in Israel, you were given precise instructions on your future tasks. Who briefed you?"

I remained silent.

"When did you first establish contacts with the Mossad?"

He looked tired. When I maintained my silence, he added, "We have a detailed report of your movements over the past six months. We also know you've been working for the Mossad for a considerable period. So you'd better start singing."

I refused to sing.

Bulldog paused. I thought I detected a glimmer of anger in his eyes. Was his patience beginning to crack? "You *yids*," he said finally, "are all the same." Like him, I had been finding difficulty in keeping my eyes open. But his anti-Semitic gibe jolted me awake. "You kikes serve two masters; that's a well-known fact. One in Washington, the other in Jerusalem. Except that the one in Jerusalem is the one you obey."

The all-American bigot. There must have been some visible anger in my eyes because he gave a self-satisfied grin and folded his arms.

"That's God's own truth; only you don't like to hear it, do you?"

My lack of response was a lucky break for both of us.

It dawned on me that my predicament was worse than I had imagined. This interrogation was well in excess of anything Charlie would set up to strong-arm me into line.

Bulldog left for a break, and I was able to nap. When he returned, I noticed he had found time for a fresh shave. As he entered, he flashed me a friendly smile and brought out his paraphernalia. "Well?"

"I told you. I'll talk to Charlie. No one else."

Bulldog guffawed. "You are one for laughs." He leaned toward me, his expression suddenly earnest. "Fuckin' yid."

This was not a pretense. The man was an anti-Semite, and I had had all I was going to take from him.

"I need the washroom," I said.

"For my part, you can burst."

"You don't have to take me to dinner," I said, my voice low. "But you do have to show me some decency." I flung a glance at Charlie in the control room. If he were watching, he would know something was about to give. Bulldog had to be taught his proper place.

"You wanna piss, huh?"

"Yes."

"Troubling you, is it?"

I remained silent.

"And it gets worse all the time?"

"You're right on that."

"You'll see how much better you'll feel after you talk; I'll take you to the washroom for a good long piss." He flashed me another smug smile, while I directed an imploring glance at the camera.

Time passed. The pressure on my bladder grew. The pain at the pit of my stomach was acute. Bulldog continued drawling his questions; but as the agony increased, I no longer heard his nasal intonation. If this went on much longer, I would have to give him the satisfaction of wetting myself.

At some point, he must have grown tired. I think he was sick of me.

"You're a weird cat," he said finally.

I shrugged.

"I know what I ought to do. I should hand you over to someone who specializes in handling kikes."

I continued my self-imposed silence.

"You were born on September sixth. Right?"

I remained silent.

"A Virgo," he said, pointing a triumphant finger at my face. "A treacherous Virgo! On top of being a Jew! More reason not to trust you. I'll tell you a little more about yourself. You're emotional. That's a well-known fact about Virgos. Also, you're concerned about your image. And you're inconsiderate of others. But above and before anything else, you're deceitful. A two-timing Judas. And being a Christian, I know all about Jewish treachery . . ."

The combined pressure of my discomfort and the endless crap pouring from his mouth was more than I could bear. I rose, pushing back my chair.

"You'll see," I said, rushing to a corner where I could turn my back on him and on the T.V. camera. I yanked at my fly.

Bulldog leapt from his chair. "You'll piss when you get permission!" He grabbed my shoulder and spun me around.

The urine spouted forth in a high arc, hitting him in the face. I proceeded to swing the jet about, playing it up and down

187

like a garden hose, etching snakelike shapes all over his elegant suit. "What the hell!" he roared, trying to distance himself from me.

"Sorry," I said, grinning at the camera.

"You're out of your fucking mind!" Turning, Bulldog raced from the room, leaving his briefcase on the table. I leafed through his notebook, where I found the questions written out word for word, just as Charlie had dictated them.

The door opened. As I expected, it was Charlie. He stood there staring at me, his countenance set in a scowl.

"You may come in," I said encouragingly, with a wave of a hand to my crotch. "I'm all done."

His smile was at its thinnest. He closed the door behind him and walked over to the table. "You are undoubtedly crazy," he said.

"In my family, it comes with the genes."

"You've convinced me."

"I hope you enjoyed listening to your racist bulldog."

"He wasn't quoting me."

"I'm touchy on that point. You should have warned him. Not that he looks like one of the greater intellects on your staff."

"I can't blame him," Charlie said, taking the chair I had formerly occupied. "He was just trying to needle you into talking."

"About what?"

"About why you went to Israel, now of all times, after passing up all those other opportunities."

"Supposing I were of Italian extraction, would you suspect me of treason if I visited Italy? If I were Irish, would you get suspicious if you heard me call Ireland my home?" My rage flared. "Why am I different from a Puerto Rican? Or a Pole? What did I do wrong? I went to my father's country to find out how he got himself killed. Is that a crime? I went to the Mossad, his employers, to seek help. Is that such an outlandish procedure? Whom did you expect me to approach? The turkey breeders' association?"

Charlie watched me coolly. "Why now?"

I shrugged, drawing my arms up to my sides. "I don't have any clear-cut answer. For a whole range of reasons."

"I'm in no hurry." Charlie made no attempt to camouflage his skepticism. "Why don't you think about it till you can come up with something a trifle more convincing."

"I've been trying to do just that ever since I got here."

"Your performance is disappointing. Though you piss in a fine arc." He rose and turned toward the door. "When you make up your mind to tell me about your links with the Mossad, call me."

His fingers were on the doorknob when I caught up with him. "Where is she?"

"You're really in love," Charlie said.

"I asked you a question."

Fury flashed in his eyes. "Believe me, Daniel, you have far graver concerns than her welfare."

"You're going a bit far," I said. "If you think this is the way to make me eliminate Shishakali . . ."

His astonishment was genuine. "What the hell are you talking about?"

It was what I had dreaded. His response told me that I had been far off the mark.

"Treason, Daniel." His voice was harsh, ruthless.

"That's bullshit, and you know it."

"How often have you been to Israel?"

"Once and once only. I swear it."

"Have no fear," he said relentlessly. "We'll find out about your other visits sooner or later." Before I could stop him, he walked out of the room, leaving me dazed.

Moments later, the door opened again and two men came to escort me along a corridor to a small apartment. Like my former quarters, it was windowless and soundproofed, but by comparison with the interrogation room, it was a five-star hotel. It contained a narrow bunk and, most important of all, a washroom with a shower. I stood under the stream for a long time. Then I flopped onto the bed.

Borne down by my weariness and stress, I must have slept for many hours. When I awoke, I had absolutely no idea of the time or of how long I had been detained. I was starving, my belly as empty as a moon crater. However, this was something Charlie had taken care of. Whoever was watching **me** over the closed-circuit T.V. must have seen me awaken; within moments, the door opened and one of the guards entered with a tray: steak, roast potatoes, salad. The plate was flanked by a pot of coffee and a cup.

When the plate was empty, I poured myself some coffee and reflected on my situation. One point struck me immediately: Charlie was still determined to avoid using violence, assuming I would talk of my own accord when I was ready.

I considered his accusations of treason. My only mistake was to have traveled to Israel while assigned to deal with Mandour. However, that was nothing more than a minor error of judgment, at worst. But Charlie seemed convinced I was lying to him about my links with the Mossad. It was a grave charge. In spite of sporadic joint operations, the CIA perceived its Israeli counterpart as a hostile entity.

What made matters doubly ironic was that I had never made any secret of my reservations about the Israelis. I had no great love for them and professed no affinity with them. But Charlie seemed to regard my criticism of Israel as nothing more than a smokescreen. He probably suspected I had taken advantage of my CIA missions for parallel assignments on behalf of the Mossad.

A long time passed before Charlie returned. He was elegantly dressed in a black tuxedo. After a moment of surprise, I burst out laughing.

"Going or coming?"

"Coming," he shot back.

"Did you enjoy the party?"

"It was a violin recital," he said. "A lady friend bought a couple of tickets to hear Shlomo Mintz."

"The rookie of the Israeli mafia."

He stared at me. "Mafia?"

"That's the term music columnists use for Israeli musicians, like Pinchas Zukerman, Itzhak Perlman, Daniel Barenboim. Mintz is the latest."

"I never knew you were so knowledgeable about music."

"We've never talked about anything but our work," I grinned. "For my part, I never knew you went out with women."

"Son of a bitch," he muttered. "Let's get back to the subject."

"Ten years of talk, and this is the first time you've ever accused me of being a double agent."

He was not an easy man to throw off balance. "I'll be straight with you." He folded his arms. "If I weren't in possession of certain information, your story about the search for your father would've hit me like a real Hollywood tearjerker. But aside from the sentimentality, your story stinks from coast to coast."

I stiffened. Charlie drew back a step, evidently alarmed by my expression. "You're calling me a liar?"

He shrugged. "That story of yours about your meeting with the Mossad's two top men—did you really expect me to buy it?" He leaned toward me until I could see the network of fine wrinkles at the corners of his eyes. "When did you dream that one up? As soon as you realized that we were on your trail?"

"Someone here wants to burn me alive, Charlie. Why?"

"You're wrong. My information is absolutely reliable."

I noted the word "reliable." My guess had been correct: Charlie did have a well-placed Israeli source. "If I were you," I said slowly, "I'd run a check on your mole inside the Mossad."

It was a stab in the dark. Charlie blinked, neither confirming nor denying. "What are you trying to imply?"

"The information you got is accurate, but slightly misleading. Which makes it look like it's *your* mole who's serving two masters."

"That's a serious charge."

"I can't prove it," I admitted, "but I swear that everything I've told you is true."

"The facts are straight," he said. "Can you disprove them?" There was a note of appeal in his voice, as though he were begging me to clear myself.

"I didn't sell out."

"There was no need." His voice was harsh. "You were sold out to the Israelis from birth."

We were getting nowhere. I took a desperate plunge. "Tell me why you alerted your mole in Tel Aviv, and I'll tell you the whole truth."

His eyes reflected a blend of curiosity and mistrust. "D'you mean it?"

"Yes."

191

He gave me a reproving glance. "Every exaggeration is dangerous. That's a rule you overlooked."

"Where did I exaggerate?"

"That story you told about Yehuda Duek. How he was uncovered by the Iraqis and sentenced to death, then saved at the last minute by your father—"

"Who was executed in his place."

"What melodrama!" Charlie's sarcasm was brutal. "An event of worldwide interest. The sort of story that would hit the headlines anywhere. Am I right?"

"That's precisely how it was." I felt a choking sensation in my throat. I hated to show my feelings to Charlie, and the necessity to do so riled me.

"It's one hell of a story," he said. "It's also a lie."

I was dumbfounded. "What are you driving at?"

"I asked our archives department to comb through the files for 1952. Good basic procedure, right? There had to be something there."

I nodded dumbly.

"Would you like to make a guess what they came up with?" His pause was a challenge.

I stared at him. "They must have found far more than I told you."

He shook his head. "Wrong."

"I—I don't . . ."

He waited for me to fall silent. "I'll tell you what they found, Daniel." His smile was thin and cruel. "A goose egg. Zero. Nothing at all."

"That's—that's out of the question." I wanted to yell, but all that emerged was a whisper. I had lost control of my vocal chords. "I met him. Yehuda Duek. You—you know who he is. I—he sat facing me, just as you are now. And he told me how he was about to be hanged. And how Yussuf Dur appeared at the very last moment. He—he told me—every tiny detail . . ." I broke off, vainly scanning Charlie's face for the faintest spark of sympathy. His empty eyes regarded me as though I were a stranger. "Your people must have found something. Some indication."

"They went through every file for that year." He shook his

head relentlessly, "There is absolutely no mention anywhere. Not a goddam word. How do you explain that?"

I tried to meet his gaze. "I can't."

"I'm glad you admit it." He rose. "Your cover story was just too good to be true. We've cracked it. You know what you can anticipate." His look was unbending. "You're on the butcher's hook, Daniel. If you talk, I might—I just might—manage to get you off. Tell me precisely what it is that Duek and the general have in mind, and I'll see what I can do for you. But if you don't . . ."

The ensuing silence was interminable. Abruptly, I sprang to my feet. "I've got it!" My voice was hoarse with agitation.

He looked at me suspiciously. "Don't try to stall. This is no time for gimmicks."

"A grave is no gimmick!"

"What grave?"

"My father's grave," I cried. "It's in a military cemetery."

"So you tell me," he said dryly.

"They—the Israelis—waited twenty-five years before they managed to retrieve his remains, but they did get them back. And they buried him in their military cemetery. With a standard headstone, like they set up for all the other soldiers."

"So what?"

"The headstone!" I insisted. "The headstone is inscribed with his name and rank." I paused to swallow. "And the date of his birth . . . ," my voice rose to a shout, "and his death. His death! Don't you see?" I stared at Charlie, looking for some sign that he believed me.

His expression remained blank, but his eyes flickered. Neither of us stirred. We remained like that for a long moment before Charlie spoke.

"That's an interesting point."

"It's easy to check out."

He glanced at his watch. "It's six in the morning in Tel Aviv. Our man at the embassy there will be overjoyed to get this assignment." He was already at the door. "That cemetery—where is it?"

"Just outside of Tel Aviv. At Kiryat Shaul."

He laid his hand on the door handle.

"Charlie," I said urgently, "just one thing more . . ."

He paused.

"A man doesn't simply vanish without leaving some explanation." I had no need to elaborate.

He smiled. "Your aunt has been told that you're here for a series of urgent meetings."

"She's a smart woman."

"So I believe. I told her you couldn't come to the phone because you caught cold and lost your voice. I asked her to notify the office about your sudden indisposition."

The story was plausible enough. Charlie could easily make a person disappear into thin air.

After the door closed behind him, I remained standing, my mind going over the details of our exchange. I felt a great relief. My ordeal was nearing its end. Within hours, Charlie would be back with an apology.

But why had the American press neglected to highlight the 1952 drama in Baghdad? Why was there no word about my father's execution? I recalled Yehuda Duek's account of the headline he had seen in the Israeli paper. How could such an important international event—involving major world leaders—pass without mention in the United States? The Arab press would have gone overboard in reporting the stunning triumph of Iraqi counterintelligence. Why was none of it picked up by the American papers? The omission was more than bizarre; it stank to high heaven.

Nervous and irritable, I strode back and forth, turning on my heels with an angry inclination of body and head. I could not find the patience to wait for Charlie to complete his check and acknowledge the error of his previous assessment. Finally, probably to the relief of my unseen watcher, I slumped down on the bed, where I soon feel asleep.

I awoke with a start. Charlie was standing over me, dressed in an ordinary business suit, with a wet raincoat dangling carelessly from his shoulders. His features were inexplicably expressionless.

"I've been waiting for you," I said.

"You were fast asleep. I've been standing here for several minutes. You never stirred. There must be something defective about your reactions." His face was weary, making him look suddenly much older.

"What brings you here?" I asked, with a feeble stab at humor.

"Nothing to brighten your day."

One glance at his face was enough to tell me he would have rather been anywhere else but this room. "I just got the report from Tel Aviv."

"What's wrong?"

"Everything." Thrusting a hand into his inner pocket, he brought out a telegram, which he held out toward me. "Here, read it for yourself."

Never before had my hand moved with such furious deliberation. My fingers closed around the paper, unfolding it in the same motion. The message was terse. THERE IS NO SUCH GRAVE. That was all. I read it through again. My death warrant.

Charlie turned toward the door.

"Charlie!"

He turned back slowly. I now believed without a shadow of doubt that he was not to blame for my predicament.

"Tell me, do you imagine for a single moment that I'd be dumb enough to come up with a story so easy to disprove?"

He looked at me, undecided. "I don't get it either," he confessed. "How do you explain it?"

"I don't. I haven't the faintest clue."

He laid a hand on the doorknob, but made no further move to leave. "You're too fond of yourself. You aren't the kind to get yourself into unnecessary trouble. It's a trait of yours I've always respected. And that's what makes me uneasy." He turned again.

"Don't go!"

"What good will it do if I stay?"

"Let's talk. The two of us might be able to unravel this thing."

He sighed. "Then how do you account for this—this 'mystery of the vanishing grave'?"

"Give me seventy-two hours to check it out."

He shook his head.

"I've given you ten years of service!" I cried. "Haven't I earned three days?"

"It's out of the question," he said, "unless you can convince me there's some justification for taking the risk."

I had nothing to add. "I'm no double agent," I said doggedly.

"So you say."

"One last try," I said. "Let me tell it to you all over again, step by step, every single thing I said and did during my four days in Israel. Maybe I've overlooked something."

He hesitated, conscious that this was one final throw, with little prospect of success. But he evidently wished to help me because his hand released the doorknob.

"Okay," he agreed. "Talk."

I went through my account again, relating every detail, each nuance, every word I had heard or uttered. I omitted nothing. But it was fruitless. Charlie heard nothing that would contradict the evidence against me. His eyes showed a faint flicker of interest when I told him of my father's encounter with my mother in the shadow of the emblem of the rewakening Levant. But its human interest aside, the episode was of no practical assistance. He shook his head sadly when I approached the end of my account, describing how the general and Yehuda Duek drove me to the airport.

"They treated me like a long-lost son. The moment they realized who I was, they scarcely left me alone. I know it sounds sentimental and overemotional, but that's a Jewish characteristic."

"It's a boomerang," Charlie said. "'Long-lost son' you said? That explains what made you place yourself at their service. As flesh of their flesh."

It was sharp reasoning. A hand was thrusting me ever deeper into the quicksand. "But you didn't wait for me to go to Israel. You've had your eye on me for months."

He rubbed his chin. "You mean the 'bee'?"

"Yes. Ariadne."

He nodded apologetically. "No disrespect meant. I put her onto you as part of the regular procedure."

"What procedure?"

"When an agent tries to get out of an assignment, we have to check up on him as though he were back at the recruitment phase."

"So you sent Ariadne to test me?"

"She's a tough cookie, that one. She was prepared to jeopardize her apartment to protect you."

"Get off her back, Charlie. She doesn't know a thing about me."

"Not even why you developed this sudden interest in your Israeli antecedents?"

I smiled. "In a way, it all started with her." His glance was mystified. I elaborated. "She encouraged me to search for my family history. You see, it was on account of Ariadne that I began rummaging in my mother's jewelry box . . ." I told him all. Even to my own ears, it sounded like the ramblings of a madman. "And that was what prompted me to go to Israel," I finished.

"You took your treasure trove to some expert?"

I gave him Oppenheimer's name and address. "Okay," Charlie said with a grimace, as though dismayed by his own show of weakness. "I'll look into it." He turned to go.

"Charlie." I seized his sleeve. "If you find I've told the truth, there's just one thing I ask . . ."

He stared at me. "I know." He nodded. "Seventy-two hours to go look for a grave." He grinned skeptically; his shrug testified to a boundless scorn for my optimism. A moment later, the door closed behind him.

The door opened once more. My visitor was Bulldog, double chin and all. He remained standing in the doorway, inspecting me cautiously, paying particular attention to my hands.

"Okay, Kottler, get up."

I hoisted myself off the bed. "Hi," I said. "I see you've changed to a different suit."

"The game's over." He pointed an admonishing finger at me. "Put on your jacket and come with me."

"Where are we going?"

"Charlie wants to see you."

I slipped into my jacket. "What time is it?"

"Six-thirty." He retreated into the corridor, keeping a safe distance from me. Two guards were standing nearby.

"Morning or evening?"

"Evening," Bulldog growled as we approached the elevator.

"What day?"

"Friday."

"Shit." I had been detained two entire days. But now I sensed that the wind was changing in my favor. Bulldog was answering my questions without any sign of disapproval from the two guards.

We climbed into a car waiting outside. No one told me where we were going, but I had no difficulty in following our route: we were headed for Georgetown. Soon, the car pulled up outside a small house. Bulldog, seated behind me, jumped out and opened my door for me. "Last stop." He handed me the envelope with my possessions. "You're on your own now." He ducked back into the car.

I remained standing there, savoring the warmth of the Washington night and a fine springtime drizzle. The aroma was intoxicating—the scent of freedom. I scanned the outlines of the street's modest little houses, which were joined to one another in a long line, like railway coaches. I walked up three steps to find myself facing a wooden door; it bore a small copper plate inscribed: "M. R. Donnevy." I had never known that Charlie sported a middle name; there was always something new to learn about him. I pressed the doorbell and waited.

Charlie opened the door. He was dressed in a blue silk houserobe and furry slippers. I laughed.

"What's so funny?"

"You look like Sherlock Holmes in retirement." I stepped into the tiny hallway.

"You're in a good mood."

"I have good cause as you well know."

He grinned, acknowledging the hint. "You look as though you could do with a shower and shave. When you're through, come into the kitchen." He indicated one of the doors. "I've ordered dinner."

I headed for the bathroom. He had seen to everything: fresh underwear, a pale-colored shirt and blue summer suit, each garment a perfect fit. After a shave, I showered with great relish, scrubbing myself with the perfumed soap laid out for me. Then I put on the new clothes, flinging my soiled garments into Charlie's laundry basket. For all I cared, he could keep them. I retraced my steps and entered the library. On the carved wooden desk stood an antique telephone. I dialed Brooklyn and felt a great relief on hearing Bertha's voice. "You must take better care of yourself," she said. "Scarcely over one cold and you go and catch yourself another." She had evidently swallowed Charlie's explanation for my absence. I told her I would be back in New York the following day and we said good-bye.

I found Charlie in the kitchen engaged in laying out a Chinese meal. He uncorked a bottle of wine.

"Yes, Daniel, you're a rich man. Not quite a Rockefeller, but you do have several millions more than I." He filled two glasses with wine, handing me one. "No intelligence organization in the world could have paid so much for your services—unless, of course, you were hired to assassinate the President of the United States." I must have turned pale, because he laughed. "No, Daniel, that's one assignment I don't think you could handle." He began to dish out the food. "You posed quite a problem. I was left with no choice. I hope you understand."

"Maybe I do. But what if I hadn't convinced you of the flaws in your theory?"

Charlie laughed. "Robs you of your rest, does it?"

"It would rob you of yours."

"That may be so." He placed an overfilled plate before me. "Best Chinese restaurant in town." He was uneasy, and I enjoyed watching him squirm. It was the first time I had ever seen Charlie lose his self-assurance.

"Charlie . . ."

"Hm?"

"I don't believe for a moment that you've got a mole planted inside the Mossad."

"Why not?"

"Because a genuine mole wouldn't have misled you."

"What makes you think I was misled?"

"You were given carefully selected items—'disinformation.' Whoever did that wanted you to crucify me."

"You may be right," he said. "To tell you the truth, the more I think about the information we received—and what's come to light since—the less I understand what the hell's going on."

"How did you find out about my meeting with the Mossad?"

"From one of our people in the Tel Aviv embassy." He frowned. "But why should they want to trip you up?"

"Now you're asking," I replied evasively. I wanted to hear his view before expressing my own. "Where was the leak?"

"My man says it came from a source which has never let him down. An indirect channel used by either side when circumstances require."

"You never had cause to doubt his reliability?"

"None at all. It looks as though someone in the Mossad considers you a threat."

"That's a sobering thought." I brought up the other subject that I had been wrestling with. "I'm still concerned about what you told me. Why was there no mention of the Baghdad hanging in the American press? How come your man found no trace of my father's grave?"

Charlie refilled my glass. "The welcome you got from Duek and the head of the Mossad was definitely out of the ordinary."

"What do you mean?"

"Sounds like they went far beyond what could be expected of them, even if they consider you a prodigal son. It would've been quite enough to entrust you to the care of Yehuda Duek."

"You think they were putting on an act?"

He shook his head. "It sounds as though you took them by surprise. For some reason, they improvised." Charlie's words came slowly. "They tried to bluff you by palming off some phony story. Why?"

"Could be . . ." I shook my head, perplexed. "Maybe something to do with the remains of Yussuf Dur." My throat felt dry. "The Israelis give the impression of being one big family. They'll go a long way to prove their loyalty to one another. They *had* to convince me that they didn't leave the body of one of their men on the battlefield."

"And the grave?"

"Tangible proof that my father's remains hadn't been abandoned." But even I did not believe this explanation.

"We're groping in the dark," Charlie said. "But I still don't think your theory is right."

"Do you have anything better?"

Charlie grimaced. "They never left you alone," he murmured.

"We've been into that."

"They never left your side. They stuck with you until they got you onto the plane and out of the country. You had their undivided attention. Not because they were overcome at seeing you. Not from a flood of irresistible emotion. They didn't want you digging any deeper into the story of your father's death. They didn't want you to find out that somebody had bungled."

"Bullshit!" I made a weak attempt to grin.

"And that mistake was serious—it cost your father his life." He glared at me challengingly. "Someone decided it would be better to leave Dur's place of burial unknown." He toyed with his glass, rolling it around between his palms.

I remembered Duek's wise eyes, his sensitive look; I pictured his pallor when he spoke of his dead colleague. I wanted to cry out that the last man in the world who would wish to harm Yussuf Dur was Yehuda Duek. But then I also remembered the nervous glances he exchanged with the general—glances that expressed a subtle fear.

"The grave was there," I said helplessly. "Your embassy man must have missed it." Charlie's theory led to only one possible conclusion. If he were right, someone in the Mossad was determined to hide all information about that historic drama, several of whose participants were still alive. Perhaps Duek was not the only one involved. The idea terrified me.

"The grave," Charlie said firmly, "was part of a diversionary operation. It was planned with utter cynicism, and it was done to distract your attention from the true facts."

"That's going a bit far."

"Then let me go further. I think the Israelis deliberately set out to trap you."

I shook my head dumbly, refusing to believe his theory.

"Their intention was to make us aware of your meeting with them. As soon as they learned you were one of ours, they set up their snare."

"I don't get you," I said.

Charlie was gloomy. "They trapped you into telling me a story you'd be unable to prove."

"Lay it all out, Charlie." Thoughts were buzzing through my mind, but I had to hear him translate them into explicit terms.

"Let's consider how they operated. All of a sudden, you appear out of nowhere. Your appearance, your questions—you were a threat to certain members of the Mossad. So, you had to be silenced. But it needed to be done smoothly, and they didn't know how to do it until they learned that you work for us. As soon as they discovered that, they hatched their little scheme."

"Do you really believe all this?"

His look had only the slightest hint of reproach. "I'm only saying out loud what you know yourself."

"Go on," I prompted.

"First thing they did was slip us information to put you under suspicion of working with the Mossad. The second part came while you were still there, as their 'honored' guest. They gave you a piece of evidence they could later erase. By the time you came to use that evidence to explain your contacts with them, the grave would have disappeared. Your explanation couldn't be proven. In other words, they set you up with no direct involvement on their part."

"To be successful, they still had to have someone give me the final shove," I said.

"That's the part that troubles me," Charlie agreed. "Whoever set up this whole scheme—in fact, whoever was responsible for Yussuf Dur's death—also tried to cast *me* in the role of executioner."

The ensuing silence was lengthy and painful. "I have to get to the truth," I said.

"I know," he said gently.

"I've got to go back there. You know that."

"It had occurred to me." He walked over to a cabinet, opening its top drawer and extracting a brown envelope, which he handed to me. Inside, I found an El Al ticket to Tel Aviv; departure time was 9:30 the following night. Charlie watched me as I read the return voucher. The date was open. "I can't give you more than three to four days."

I pulled out a brand-new passport, issued only a few hours earlier. "A new passport for every operation," I said.

He grinned. "As ever."

I studied the ticket and passport. "You know I can't leave without seeing Ariadne."

He stretched in his chair. "Any time you like."

"Where is she?"

"At home. Safe and sound." He flashed me a sly grin. "You'd gladly skin me alive, wouldn't you?"

"When did you release her?"

"When you were on your way here, she was already on a flight back to New York." He grinned again. "I know when I'm beaten. I'm not always as smart as you take me for. One thing I didn't take into consideration was the old, old story . . . You've got a sharp eye, Daniel. She's a breed unto herself."

"Keep your hands off her!"

"In my own time, boy. Just as soon as you and I straighten out the last of our differences." He glanced at his watch. "I'd better drive you to the airport." He went upstairs to change out of his robe into street clothes. I walked over to the phone and dialed the Dakota.

"Hello?"

"Hello, Ariadne," I said softly.

"Daniel!" I heard a sharp intake of breath. "Are you all right?"

"Of course," I said, trying to sound in high spirits.

"I was so worried . . ."

"I'm sorry."

"You just disappeared . . ." Her voice betrayed her tension.

"It happens occasionally, Ariadne."

"I wouldn't have worried if I hadn't known what I know now. Your connection with those people . . . You understand what I'm trying to say?"

"I understand."

"Especially after the other night. I realized I was wallowing in a swamp and that it was dangerous—for both of us."

"There's no reason to be worried." I again feigned cheerfulness. "I had to go away on business for our mutual friend."

My explanation was met with a long silence.

"Where are you calling from?" she finally asked.

"From his house."

"I see . . . Did he tell you that he called me to Washington?"

"He did. About that problem of yours—I told you, there's no reason for concern. I'm taking care of it. But we'll talk about it when I get there."

"How soon?" she asked anxiously.

"Tonight."

Charlie came down the stairs, dressed in his regular gray business suit and holding the raincoat I had left on the rack. "I don't want you to forget anything here," he said with an impish grin. "I wouldn't want to be linked with any unfortunate accident you're liable to have."

"Very funny." We left the house and strode toward his white Volkswagen Rabbit.

"Life gets tedious if you don't keep a sense of humor." He opened the car door for me.

"I never know when you're being serious."

Charlie started up the engine. "That's the idea. When you do business with me, you have to stay on your toes."

"It's hard staying on your toes for ten years."

He made no response. "Play it cool in Tel Aviv," he advised finally. "They made one attempt to get rid of you. They didn't succeed the first time, but that doesn't mean they won't try again."

"They won't try anything while I'm over there," I assured him. "A major scandal is the last thing they're interested in."

We had reached the terminal entrance. Charlie pulled up and I opened the door. He extended a hand and I shook it. "Take care," he said. "They're gunning for you."

"I'll bear that in mind," I promised, slamming the door.

It was close to midnight when I arrived at Ariadne's apartment. Our love play washed away the last remnants of the stress I had undergone during the last several days, offering relief from the depression that had plagued me ever since leaving Charlie. We were both exhausted, physically and emotionally. Neither of us wanted to spoil the peace we found together by talking. We lay side by side, motionless until we drifted into sleep.

When I opened my eyes, the large room was awash in daylight. From every side, I found myself under the gaze of stiff-backed boyars. The dispossessed Russian aristocracy seemed to

204

have formed a guard of honor to protect the midnight passions of their princess, the last of their line—even as she moaned in the arms of the son of some fool from Tiberias. A fool who had allowed himself to be hanged in place of someone else.

Ariadne woke now. Her eyes were wide open, their green hue heightened by the morning sunshine. She raised her head and rested it on my shoulder, her breathing quiet and regular. We lay side by side for a long time, fingers intertwined, reveling in a luxurious silence that crowned the intimacy of the night.

We showered together, sharing the streams of water. Ariadne soaped my entire body. Her long fingers discovered my ticklish spots, and she burst into giggles as I wriggled and squirmed. Finally, forced to flee, I raced through the cavernous apartment, she chasing after me like a splendid nymph turning the tables on her randy satyr. She cornered me in the bedroom, where, under the watchful gaze of the Russian Imperial Court, we made gentle love for a long time. Then we went back into the shower.

"Hold me tight," she begged. Obediently, I clasped her to me.

I was about to say something, but I forced myself to remain silent. She must have noticed my expression.

"What's troubling you?"

"What do you mean?"

"There are times when I lose you. You vanish and reappear and vanish again. A moment ago you were gone. What's wrong?" She turned off the faucet.

"Troubles."

"Let's talk, Daniel."

"Why did Abner call you to Washington?" I asked, watching her towel herself dry.

"I thought he was going to make me leave the apartment," she said. "But it wasn't that at all. He felt that my latest reports on you were not quite accurate, and he wanted an explanation."

"What did you tell him?"

"That he was wrong." She slid into her skirt. "He probably didn't believe me, but he didn't say so. He just treated me to an excellent dinner, and then drove me to the airport to catch a plane back to New York." She talked on about the time she had spent with Abner, still not realizing she had been used as bait to draw me into Charlie's trap. I knew she expected me to tell her about my own meeting with Abner/Charlie; she wanted to know whether she could keep the apartment. I assured her that my talk with Abner had been friendly, that she need have no concern over her contract; she would soon be released from all her commitments.

I also told her that I was flying to Israel again that night.

"Why?" she asked.

I did not reply. "Let's make a deal," I said.

"What's the offer?"

"If I evade your questions, please don't press me. Just let it pass."

"But you'll answer eventually?"

"Maybe."

A short time later, we left the Dakota and headed for the park. Spring had erupted. We were not alone in the park; its pathways were crowded with children on skates, skateboards, and bicycles.

"Abner is wrong about you," Ariadne said suddenly.

"He is?"

"He says you're square. You aren't. But you are the most bashful man I've ever met." She turned toward me. "Those times at the luncheon counter, it was all I could do to keep myself from laughing as I watched you watching me. You were too shy to make the first move."

"Oh, come on!" I cried.

"But it's true, isn't it? Women make you shy."

"Yes, they do," I conceded. "But in your case, it was on account of being a law-abiding citizen. I thought I'd better not get involved with jailbait like you."

Laughing, she brushed her lips against mine, before breaking away to race lightly across the grass toward a stone bridge. I could have caught up, but I preferred to hold back and watch the perfect movements of her body. She looked as though she were hovering over the grass.

Suddenly, for no apparent reason, she stopped in mid-step. She stiffened, her body bending forward, and then tumbled to the ground. I bent over to find her clutching her right knee, her face contorted with pain.

"It's my knee," she gasped.

"What can I do to help?"

"Sit here and hold me. It'll pass in a few minutes."

I did as she asked, watching sweat run down her face. She leaned back against me, while I gently kissed her forehead.

"I so wanted to dance," she said. It was the first time she had ever referred to her aborted career. "There were nights I didn't sleep. Because I was dancing. I would lie on my back with eyes wide open, dancing. At times, I'd jump out of bed and dance all over my bedroom, on my own. Dancing was my language."

"I know."

She gazed up at the blue sky. "I wanted wings."

"I know what you mean," I said. She turned her head to stare at me curiously. "There were times when I too dreamed of growing wings." I looked about me at the people in the park. "They have their dreams too. I don't know anyone who hasn't."

A smile lingered about her lips. "And I thought it was just me. What a pity."

"Why is it a pity?"

"Don't you think it natural to wish for colors to set you apart from all the others?"

"It may be natural, but it isn't important."

She looked at me in surprise. "How can you pick someone out in a crowd if he doesn't have a color of his own?"

"You don't have to worry about it," I said. "You're definitely different."

"How?"

"You continue to dream."

"Doesn't everyone?"

"I'm afraid not."

"What about you?"

The sky was very clear. I could not detect a single cloud. "It would be splendid to fly now," I said. Ariadne did not reply. She stood hesitantly flexing her leg. "The knee seems fine," I said.

"Sometimes it swells up." She took a small step. "It's okay now." She smiled. "Don't worry. It may be weeks or even months before it gives me trouble again."

We continued our walk through the park, not talking. As we approached the zoo, we heard children shrieking with glee.

"Have you ever seen the seals leap for fish?" I asked.

"When I was a child, my nurse brought me here to watch them being fed. But when it comes to tossing them fish, there's only one man who does it in style."

"Who?"

"Abner," she replied unsurprisingly. "He brought me here several times."

"I know a man very like the one you describe," I said. "Only he isn't called Abner. His name is Charlie."

"Who's that?"

"Abner's twin brother."

She grasped the irony. "You mean . . ."

I nodded. "Abner goes by many names. You know him by one. I know him by another. He has at least a third." I watched as one of the seals clambered easily onto a concrete platform projecting from the water. "But besides loving seals, he's capable of being extremely cruel."

She noted the earnestness of my tone. "You're afraid of him."

"I may be."

"You don't trust him."

"Let's put it like this—I prefer him in his role of providing fish for the seals."

She tried to smile, but her expression remained gloomy. "I, too, am scared of him at times. I wish I could get him off my back."

"Stop worrying about the contract. I promise you . . ."

"Daniel . . ." she said, but stopped, probably guessing that I knew how frightened she was and that she was putting all of her trust in me.

11

The El Al Boeing 747 landed at Ben Gurion airport at 6:20 P.M. It was Sunday, April 1. I checked in at the Sheraton and stretched out on the bed to try to catch up on the sleep I had missed on the plane. It was late in the afternoon and I had a bad case of jet lag, but sleep evaded me. I was convinced that Charlie's analysis was right—somebody had tried to use him to destroy me, to maintain a cover-up on some thirty-two-year-old misdeeds. If I could verify the disappearance of Yussuf Dur's grave, and the absence of press coverage of the Baghdad hanging, it could mean only one thing; the entire military leadership of the newly independent state of Israel had made a major miscalculation, and my father had paid for it with his life.

It was almost midnight before I managed to fall asleep, but at five I awoke, alert and ready. I spent twenty minutes exercising the stiffness out of my back, then sat on the veranda to consider my next moves.

At eight, I caught a taxi and directed the driver to Kiryat Shaul. At that time of morning, most of the traffic was streaming into the city, leaving our outbound route clear. It was not long before the driver pulled up outside the cemetery gateway. I asked him to wait, then entered the grounds. There were no visitors; the only people I saw were gardeners watering the flowerbeds. I remembered two trees near the spot that had been pointed out to me as my father's grave. It did not take me long to reach the place. I stood there, staring at the spot where I had been transfixed when I had read my father's name inscribed on the headstone.

There was no such stone to be seen.

I inspected every grave in the area. My search was fruitless. I walked further along the path, inspecting the tombstones along the cemetery's northern wall. But I found nothing.

The conclusion was inescapable: the remains of the man hanged in Baghdad's central square had never been interred there. I had been the victim of a clever act of deception, cynically planned and executed by men who claimed to cherish my father's memory.

I walked back to the taxi and asked the driver for the address of the nearest newspaper office.

"There's *Yediot Aharonot*," he said. "On Petah Tikva Road."

"Take me there."

Our progress was slow, but we finally reached the parking lot behind the newspaper building. I headed for the reception desk and inquired after the archive department. A moment later, I was on an upper floor, where an elderly woman stood behind a long wooden counter. She ushered me to a table upon which she laid bound folders containing all the 1952 editions of the daily.

Each issue had no more than eight pages. One by one, I read through them, looking for some mention of the trial of an Israeli spy in Iraq or of the hanging in Baghdad. There was not a word about the execution of my father. To make absolutely sure there had been no mistake about the dates, I went back to the elderly woman and requested the 1953 files. There, too, I found nothing.

Returning to the counter, I thanked the woman for her assistance. "Unfortunately, I haven't located what I was looking for."

"If you tell me what it is, I might be able to help you."

"I'm working on research into the early years of Israel's independence," I explained. "One of the subjects I'm interested in is an espionage affair. It happened sometime during the fifties."

She shook her head. "Our military correspondent could help you, but he's out covering a terrorist incident." In reply to my inquiry, she elaborated. A Palestinian suicide squad had attacked passersby in downtown Jerusalem. "The military correspondent went up there to cover the story. I'm afraid he's unavailable."

I thanked her and walked away. I was almost to the door when I heard her call me back.

"I just remembered," she said. "One of our veteran employees is here—he's given up day-to-day reporting now, but in his younger days, he was our military correspondent. His name is Eitan Elad. Would you like to meet him?"

It was like winning first prize in the lottery. A swift inquiry over the internal telephone soon located Elad, and moments later, I was face to face with an elderly man with a long narrow beard and thinning gray hair. He inspected me, his head inclined forward as though about to butt me. Behind his eyeglasses, a pair of piercing eyes caused me to choose my words carefully. He asked about the subject of my study.

"The Jewish exodus from the Arab countries. During the early years of Israel's independence."

"Interesting," he said. "Is it on behalf of some institution?"

I nodded. If I was going to lie, I might as well make it a good one. "The Mideastern Studies department of Columbia University."

"I'll be glad to help you," he said, "very glad. It's always a pleasure to assist a scholar who takes an interest in my field." He smiled. "I often find myself discovering information of which even I am ignorant. It's a reminder that my own knowledge is far from complete." His delivery was interrupted by an occasional stammer, for which he compensated by repeating some word or phrase. "So you're interested in the Jewish exodus from the Arab states. Any country in particular?"

"Iraq."

"Iraq," he repeated. "Iraq was very chaotic during those years. Is there something specific you're after?"

"There is," I said eagerly. "When the Jews of Baghdad were starting to leave, in late fifty-one and early fifty-two, an Israeli spy was arrested there. He was tried and hanged."

"Hanged?" He gazed at me in surprise. "Are you sure of your facts?"

"I got the story from someone who lived there at the time. That's why I'm checking up on the details."

Elad shook his head. "You were misled. A number of Iraqi Jews were tried and executed on charges of espionage for Israel, but no Israeli was hanged there."

With nothing left to lose, I decided to try a gamble. "I'm referring to the Duek affair," I said. I held my breath as I awaited his response.

Elad's smile was condescending. "Now I get you. I get you." His fingers drummed on the tabletop. "Duek, of course. But that's a different story, a totally different story. It has nothing to do with the events of fifty-one or fifty-two."

"Are you sure?"

"I remember the Duek affair," he said. "The Duek affair." He frowned. "It began—let me think—yes—in 1957. And dragged all the way into 1959."

"I don't understand," I said, puzzled.

"You must have gotten the whole story mixed up. Let me try and untangle it for you. It was fascinating, quite fascinating. After Egypt's defeat in 1956, the Egyptians refused to admit their army had been routed. They blamed their defeat on penetration of their councils by Mossad moles. The Arab states were in a panic. They became obsessed with hunting Israeli agents. At this precise time, Yehuda Duek was sent to Iraq to organize the evacuation of local Jews. It was feared that if they remained there, they would suffer terrible persecution. Iraqi counterintelligence soon unmasked Duek. He was tried and sentenced to death by hanging. By hanging," he reiterated. "Duek spent a year and a half in the condemned cell. His execution date was constantly postponed; the Mossad managed to get to various VIPs in the Iraqi government. Israel offered Iraq a large ransom, and also warned of serious reprisals if Duek were executed. Ultimately, in some mysterious fashion, the Iraqi government was persuaded to release Duek in return for delivery of one thousand trucks from Germany. Since the Iraqis needed the trucks far more than they needed Duek, the deal went through."

"Then—there was no execution?"

"I told you. Duek was released."

"And they—the Iraqis—they didn't hang any other Israeli?"

"Certainly not!" Elad exclaimed. "The whole affair was concluded without the loss of life." He sprang from his chair. "Wait a moment, I've got something to show you."

Before I could respond, he had vanished, leaving me confused. The more I thought over what I had learned, the more I was inclined to share Charlie's view that Duek was in collusion with the head of the Mossad to perpetrate a gigantic cover-up. This explained their desire to get rid of me. It was a frightening thought, but I pushed it to the back of my mind as Elad returned, carrying photostatted sheets.

"I brought you these," he said, laying the photostats of press clippings on the table. "There are plenty more, but I picked out the three most concise, the most concise I could find. Take a look at the headline—that says it all."

"ONE THOUSAND TRUCKS FOR ISRAELI AGENT," I read. The subhead elaborated: "Israel Persuades Iraq to Free Israeli Accused of Espionage; Baghdad Gets Trucks from Germany." The reporter was Eitan Elad. Just below his name appeared a photograph of a much younger but easily recognizable Yehuda Duek.

Elad pointed to the other two clippings. "These are pieces I wrote about Israel's efforts to extricate the Jews of Iraq. Very important operation, very important."

"Very important," I echoed without any ironic intent. "The truck deal, though, that's intriguing."

"Intriguing, indeed. I once thought of writing a book about it."

"Why didn't you do it?"

"I wish I could. It's out of the question."

"What's to stop you?"

"All kinds of difficulties."

"But the story has been published. It's out in the open."

"Far from it! Only a small, a very small portion, has been made public."

"Surely it can't still be confidential?"

Elad waved his hand at me. "It seems that the time has yet to come for a full account. From what I understand, it was a very complex operation. It involved public figures in Israel, West Germany, and Iraq. Everyone concerned is closemouthed about it. Very closemouthed." He gazed at me. "I wasn't the only one trying to obtain additional material. Some of my colleagues also sniffed around. But just like me, they ran into silence."

"And you discovered nothing?"

"Believe me. This is the kind of story which may stay buried until the resurrection of the dead."

When I climbed back into the taxi, I was breathing heavily, as though I had just completed some strenuous physical exertion. But the heaviness I felt was merely a manifestation of my despair. After my visit to the cemetery, I believed I was on the track of some mishap that had cost Badwi his life. Now, I sensed that I had caught wind of a story whose dimensions were far wider than an isolated mistake.

As a consequence, I felt increasingly anxious about my safety. If, as I guessed, I was on the verge of some revelation, it explained why the heads of the Mossad had to rid themselves of me, the son of the legendary Badwi.

At the hotel, I was suddenly ravenous. I had a meal at the restaurant, then returned to my room. I lay on the bed, my thoughts racing. Solving the riddle seemed to require more skill and experience than I possessed; I doubted whether even Charlie was equipped to unravel it. It must have been my personal connection with the long-forgotten episode that led me to the foolish belief that I could get to the bottom of it. I decided to try a direct approach.

It was just before five when my taxi drew up outside Yehuda Duek's home. I mounted the stone steps and pressed the doorbell. The door was opened by Aviva Duek. She did not seem surprised at my reappearance. She smiled with a friendliness bordering on genuine affection. "Come in," she urged, as I mumbled an explanation about returning to Israel on business matters. "Does Yehuda know you're back?" she asked.

I presumed my presence in the country had been reported

214

to Duek shortly after my arrival at Ben Gurion. "I'm not sure," I said.

"We'd better notify him. He sometimes stays late at the office." She stepped over to the phone, and within moments she was talking to her husband.

As on my previous visit, Aviva Duek proved a gracious hostess. She spoke of that morning's "terrible incident" in Jerusalem. One of the terrorists was killed on the spot; two others were captured by police within minutes of the attack. "That's life in Israel," she said.

We soon heard the car pull up in the driveway. A moment later, the door opened and Yehuda Duek stood in the entrance, looking at me with something between a smile and a frown. He crossed the room to kiss Aviva's forehead before extending a hand to me. "Welcome back," he said. His complexion was gray; in spite of evident efforts to remain controlled, he looked tense. He and his colleagues must have been taken by surprise by my return. I had forced him into a corner, but I reminded myself that he was smarter and more experienced than I could ever hope to be.

He joined us for coffee and cake, chatting casually as though he and I were in collusion to conceal from Aviva the fact that I held a bomb whose fuse was already smoldering. "I feel like a walk," he said. "I usually stroll on the beach in the evening. Would you like to join me?"

"With pleasure."

We drove west as far as the bare sandstone downs overlooking the beach. The sea waves were little more than ripples at this time of early evening. The sky was still yellow as the sun neared the horizon, setting the clouds aflame.

"There's a superstition in the east about yellow skies," Duek declared.

"What are they supposed to signify?"

"Trouble."

He was not looking at me; his regard was directed toward the horizon. The glow of sunset highlighted his weary features.

"You knew I was back," I said.

He forced a smile. "You got here sooner than I expected."

"But my name was on the list given to your passport control.

215

You must have had good reason." I stopped. "Why didn't you come looking for me? I left a clear trail. I'm staying at the same hotel. I went to visit the cemetery."

"Why trouble to look for you?" He shrugged. "It was only a matter of time before you'd come looking for me."

"So it seems."

"It's a strange thing—time." He closed his eyes momentarily. "You never know how time is experienced by someone else. You never know how much time is necessary for a certain process to come to fruition. And when you need to act, you never know how much time you have."

"It's one of the great riddles."

"It never leaves my thoughts." His voice was low, as though soliloquizing. "Time constituted an entirely different dimension when I was in prison. I thought about it then. I wondered what it does to people and how it functions. When we understand it, I think we'll come close to comprehending the significance of our existence."

I let him ramble on freely. It was a tricky moment, for him no less than for me. His philosophical speculations were his way of releasing stress. He paced along steadily, occasionally stooping to pick up a piece of stone or rock, studying its shape and colors before allowing it to slip between his fingers. "You are persistent," he said finally.

"That's one way of putting it."

"Persistence can boomerang if it isn't backed up by wisdom."

"I had to come back."

"I know." He paused, evidently uncertain how to proceed. "What made you sense something was wrong?"

"I'd be lying if I claimed to have been the first to notice."

"Somebody else was smarter than you?"

"He put two and two together, and the result he came to was regrettable."

"That somebody must have been Mike Donnevy."

"That's a good guess."

"I suspected things might not work out. But I didn't expect him to react so fast."

"Why don't we start from the beginning?" I suggested.

"There are many beginnings."

216

"I mean the unvarnished truth."

"I could argue that the truth too possesses many aspects," he said, almost bashfully. "But you'd accuse me of confusing the issue."

"Let's stick with the basic truth."

"The basic truth is very simple. We were not perceptive enough to guess you might be capable of facing it."

"That whole charade—what did you hope to gain by it?"

"Gain?" he said in surprise. "My only concern was sparing you unnecessary pain."

Had I heard him correctly? What "pain" did he refer to? The events that happened years ago caused me less pain than the attempt he had made to cover up the mistake that sent my father to his death. "We seem to be going around in circles. I'm convinced you were trying to hide something from the past."

Duek turned toward me. I could make out the gray pallor of his complexion. "That sounds like you're accusing me of something."

"That's exactly what I'm doing."

"What's the charge?"

"I have reason to believe you're determined to cover up the truth about Yussuf Dur's death. You may even be the sole living person acquainted with the truth." At that moment, I detested him. "You were in the condemned cell. That fact is undisputed. Apparently my father did save your life. But he wasn't hanged instead of you. His death was evidently the result of some bungling for which you and the Mossad were to blame. I want to know how he died."

Duek smiled wanly. "I see you've done your homework. In that respect, at least, you are your father's son."

"*You are your father's son.*" No one had ever spoken such words to me, and they made me shudder. "I want to know how my father died," I repeated. "One thing is certain—he wasn't hanged in Baghdad or anywhere else."

"Or anywhere else," Duek said.

"Then why lie if you have nothing to hide?"

"Your appearance threw me off guard. I was stunned. I arrive on the flight from Zurich, and all of a sudden, I'm informed that the son of Yussuf Dur is waiting for me in the

217

general's office . . ." His voice faded until it was almost inaudible. " 'Who? Yussuf Dur's son? Where in God's name did he spring from?' Then I met with the general and learned the details. I knew of the questions you had asked the head of the Mossad, and I knew it would be up to me to provide convincing answers."

"Why didn't you tell me the truth?"

"There are good reasons."

"Can't you even tell me what his mission was?"

"This was where we made our initial mistake. Instead of telling you the facts—however painful—we modified them. You might say we embroidered them."

"How did Yussuf Dur die?"

"I don't know."

I stared at him. That was the answer I least expected. "And you don't know where he's buried?"

"No."

It was worse than I had foreseen. "In fact, you merely wanted to stop my prying further."

"True." He smiled in embarrassment.

"But the farce you staged for me at the cemetery wasn't enough. That was only part of it, part of something even more despicable."

He was an excellent actor. His eyes widened in astonishment and he stared at me as though seeing me for the first time. I could only admire his steadfastness.

"Watch out," he said quietly.

"Why should I? What do you have to say after putting a noose around my neck and leaving someone else to pull the rope?"

"What are you talking about?"

"I'll tell you." Step by step, I led him along the path Charlie had been sharp-witted enough to mark out. I told him how close I was to being condemned as a double agent and ending up as a corpse dumped on some roadside.

Duek did not interrupt. The gathering darkness prevented me from reading his expression. "Now I see," he said, when I had finished. "On the face of it, Mike Donnevy's deduction appears correct. But we never hatched any such plot. Even at my meanest, I wouldn't have gone to such lengths."

"What would you have done?"

"I would have chosen to tell you everything that could be disclosed. No more, but no less."

"How did Mike Donnevy learn of the link between me and the Mossad?"

"It must have been our fault."

"What happened exactly?"

"It was a string of errors, that's all. During your interrogation, you gave various details about your identity. They didn't jibe with the fact that you had come directly from Saudi Arabia or that you started to ask about Yussuf Dur. There were two hypotheses. One, that you were on a mission for the Saudis, and two, that you were on a mission for the CIA. We made soundings in Washington. It turned out that you did belong to the CIA. But in the meantime, the moles started burrowing—in Tel Aviv as well as in Washington."

We paced on in silence while I turned over Duek's story. I had two choices—either accept it, or condemn him. In my heart, I wanted to believe him, but wishing was not enough.

After a while, Duek spoke again. "I don't know how to convince you that I'm telling the truth. But I assure you there was no negligence involved in your father's death. There are certain facts I can't elaborate on. But I also assure you that you were the victim of an unfortunate set of circumstances. That's all. Nobody was trying to push you off the edge. I certainly wasn't. After all, you are the son—the son of . . ." His voice broke, and he took a deep breath to control his agitation. "While the general's secretary took you out to lunch, he and I considered the problem. One thing was evident—we simply couldn't afford to let you continue your prying. We had to set your mind at rest. It's well known that we don't leave our wounded or dead on the battlefield, that we do everything possible to retrieve them. That was how we hit on the idea of the grave at Kiryat Shaul. As for my story—we thought that one up to convince you that you knew all the facts. We simply took a painful episode—something I did genuinely experience—and moved it back a few years. It could be regarded as a partial truth."

"And the ceremony at the graveside," I demanded harshly, "what was that for?"

Duek winced. "We thought you'd never be satisfied till you knew where your father was buried. That was why we erected the headstone."

"But why did you remove it afterward?"

"The stone was temporary. We expected you to come back some day, and by then we'd have placed a permanent headstone there for your benefit."

"You knew about my return the moment I arrived yesterday. Why didn't you repeat the trick?"

"What would have been the use? We knew the CIA had sent someone to check the cemetery. We didn't want another investigation."

"Would it harm you?"

He hesitated no more than a second. "It might." He coughed nervously. "I'm sorry for what happened—we meant well."

Abruptly, I turned and grabbed his arm. "I have to know how he died," I said. "And why." I was back in the labyrinth. My path to the truth was blocked by one stocky, white-haired man. I could have killed him.

"Let me go," he said quietly.

"I've got to know!"

He remained composed. "I have a spine infirmity," he said softly. "You're hurting me."

I let go of his arm. "Go to hell," I cried.

"I can't help you. No one can."

"Please . . ." I said, knowing that my words would do no good.

"There's something you must do," Duek said. "Stop tormenting yourself over Badwi."

"I'm trying."

"If your father is really important to you, then you must stop prying. There are certain people in Washington who are far too inquisitive for our liking. You must not arouse them any further."

"What are you worried about?"

"Every intelligence service keeps certain things to itself. There are secrets to which no statute of limitations applies."

"What's the link between the statute of limitations and my father's remains?"

"There are instances when a grave is occupied by more than one corpse."

He was giving nothing away.

"You see me as an outsider, don't you?" I said.

My challenge brought him to a halt. "You're Badwi's son," he said simply, evidently convinced that those words said it all.

"What does that mean to you, that I'm his son?"

"Everything." He began to walk, head down, toward the car.

He drove me back to the hotel. We remained silent during the ride. After he pulled up at the curb, we maintained the same silence, merely exchanging a handshake that neither of us wished to release. I was about to close the car door when I heard his voice. "One day, perhaps . . ." He may have said something further; if he did, I failed to hear it over the roar of the engine as he pulled away.

I headed for the hotel bar, where I ordered a double vodka, hoping the liquor would help ease the stress that plagued me. I must have spent a long time at the bar; it was only when I began my third vodka that a sudden flash of understanding almost made me leap from the stool. "The statute of limitations," I mumbled aloud. The statute of limitations, as it applies in most Western countries, lays down a certain time limit after which all official information, no matter how highly classified, is released. Publication may be further delayed under emergency regulations, as in cases where disclosure may harm some individual.

The idea that struck me was stunning. It was Duek I faced, and Duek alone. Even the general now heading the Mossad—Duek's "superior"—was only a dummy, controlled and dominated by Duek. In this particular affair, Duek was the final authority. And Duek was motivated by an unbounded fanaticism that served him as vindication for every step he found necessary. The end justified all means—including the preparation of an empty grave for a living man!

There was only one course open to me. I called him.

"Yes?" Duek's voice was low.

"It's Daniel."

"Aren't you asleep?"

"I want to see you. Now."

He hesitated. "I had a long day. Suppose we leave it till morning?"

"By morning, I want to be on a plane to New York."

"All the same . . ."

"You may be curious to know certain facts about the thousand trucks." I paused, awaiting his response.

At length, it came. "I'll meet you in the hotel lobby in half an hour."

I saw him as soon as he entered the lobby. He had changed his gray suit for jeans and a sports jacket. His face was pale, but his expression appeared calm. In the course of his lifetime, he had coped with stress situations at various levels; outwardly, at least, he looked tranquil, balanced, and assured. Like him, I maintained an even expression. Our confrontation had reached a climax. He would continue to protect his secret, and I would do everything in my power to force him into revealing it.

"Let's talk in my car," he proposed.

I nodded and we went outside without a further word. Duek drove south, through Tel Aviv's decaying older neighborhoods. At one point, he turned west before resuming his southward route to reach the ancient alleyways of Jaffa. He turned off the engine, but made no move to get out of the car.

"Why here?" I demanded.

"At painful moments, a man returns to the womb." He nodded toward Jaffa's crumbling houses and narrow alleys.

His forthrightness surprised me. "So this is a painful moment," I said. "And the womb?"

He pointed to the slum below. "My family lived here when we arrived from Egypt. It's a place where I feel more collected. So you want to talk about the trucks."

"To hell with the trucks! You know exactly what I want to hear from you: why, after thirty-two years, the case of Badwi is still a highly classified secret."

"You don't give up, do you?"

"I can't. Could you, if you were in my place?"

"I'd do just what you're doing," he admitted.

"I've never given up on him," I said. "Even though there were years when I wasn't allowed to mention his name, I've never

222

stopped wondering about him. My Zeideh had a name for my father," I added.

"A name?"

"Zeideh was the only one who ever referred to him—called him 'der Spion.' He resented him. The grudge was what converted him from a Zionist to an anti-Zionist."

"Why?"

I shrugged. "Zeideh couldn't understand my father's loyalty to the ideal of a Jewish homeland. He couldn't condone a loyalty that led to the betrayal and abandonment of his daughter and grandson."

"Did you ever talk to him about Badwi?"

"Never. Badwi only existed in my imagination. I used to envision myself in some distant land, mounted on a horse, riding alongside a man with a faceless body. My mother had only one photograph of him. It showed him on a rearing stallion, but his face was hazy. My faceless father . . ."

"What anguish." Duek gripped the steering wheel, his shoulders suddenly tensed.

"Do you know that I almost killed you today?"

The starlight showed Duek's fingers tightening on the wheel.

"It wasn't a sudden rage," I told him. "I was quite cold-blooded about it. I wanted to kill you for what you did to me."

"I'm not surprised," he said soberly.

"I was very close to doing it this evening."

He remained motionless, saying nothing, as though frozen in place.

"Very close," I repeated.

"That isn't why you called me out in the middle of the night."

"I called you on account of the trucks. The ones that bought you your life."

"You've come a long way."

"How was the deal concluded?" I demanded.

"What are you driving at?" For perhaps the first time since we reached the ridge, he met my eyes.

"I want to know the details. Who handled the deal? Who got the trucks from Germany to Baghdad? Who conducted the negotiations with the Iraqi government? It had to be someone with the widest possible connections among the Arabs. Someone willing to risk his own life to save yours—even though there was no call for him to sacrifice himself."

"What do you want from me?" Duek broke in, evidently unwilling to hear any more.

"You know very well."

"I can't help you."

I admired his control. "I have a right to know."

"I can't tell you," he repeated weakly, and before I could reply, he had opened the car door and hoisted himself outside. I saw him stand before the car, his mouth open, as though trying to fill his lungs with the night air.

I got out of the car and stood beside him.

"That's the Andromeda rock," he said, pointing toward the harbor. "According to legend, that was where she was shackled."

"I have no one else to turn to," I said.

"Perseus arrived mounted on Pegasus. He released Andromeda from her bonds."

"Release me from mine."

He turned to me. "I can't."

"Go to hell," I said.

"What do you know about Mike Donnevy?" he asked.

I was taken by surprise. "Next to nothing."

"He's a brilliant thinker," said Duek. "A loyal friend—and a dangerous enemy."

"He's very clever," I agreed.

"Mike Donnevy has never left a riddle unsolved. In our profession, we call a man like him an 'archaeologist.' He digs. Layer after layer. Do you know what post he occupies in Washington?"

I shook my head.

"He's not only in charge of the liquidation section. Over the years he's advanced to a position where that section is only one small part of his domain. He now supervises coordination between the CIA and friendly intelligence services."

"What has that got to do with my father?"

"I'll explain," Duek said. "Suppose one of the Arab ambassadors in Washington complained to the President that whenever a secret military agreement between his government and

224

the United States was concluded, it immediately fell into the hands of the Israelis. What would be the first deduction? That somebody in the CIA was playing footsy with the Israelis." His smile was thin. "But suppose that were proved wrong?"

I remained silent, but I was beginning to understand.

"Suppose there's no top-level Washington source leaking secrets to Israel. Another explanation could be that an Israeli mole is operating either in the U.S. or in the Mideast. As a result, the two agencies—the CIA and the Mossad—are at logger-heads."

I nodded.

"The U.S. government must convince its Arab friends that their friendship is appreciated no less than Israel's. The Americans act without hesitation—they try to ferret out the Israeli mole."

"So you suspect Mike Donnevy of being on one of those archaeological digs of his?"

Duek shrugged. "He knows we had an operation going in the fifties to plant moles in Arab countries. So he advances one step further. He combs the archives for names of our agents who became inactive during that decade. All those names go into a computer. In the process certain details warrant special attention, such as the name of someone thought to be dead who, in fact, has disappeared without leaving any trace . . ."

Duek's eyes remained fixed on me.

"Mike Donnevy forgets nothing," I admitted. "Years ago I told him that my father had been a Mossad agent. I told him he was killed on a mission. He never mentioned the fact again. At least, not till recently."

"Till recently," Duek echoed. "When he began focusing on you. He did precisely what I would have done in his place. When he learned that no one knew anything about Badwi's final mission—beyond the fact that he didn't return—he began to delve and dig all around you—you, Daniel Kottler, Badwi's son—in the hope that you'd lead him to something."

The elderly man was right on the mark, I thought. The moment I made my first mistake—evading the Shishakali assignment—Charlie hit upon the idea that Shishakali was my father, the man from Tiberias. He probably interpreted Shishakali's anti-American activities as part of his cover. He knew that Shishakali had access to almost all military secrets of the Arab states. That was why he refused to believe me when I pleaded shattered nerves. That was why he set Ariadne to spy on me. A series of innocent coincidences, compounded by the questions Charlie was pursuing, had set off a chain reaction. And the implications for the Mossad were potentially explosive.

Duek's breathing was heavy. "Donnevy won't let up unless we can make him think he was wrong about the identity of the mole."

"In that case, words won't be enough. What's needed is something tangible." I knew what Duek hoped to hear from me. Whatever the cost, he wanted me to eliminate Shishakali in order to rid myself of Charlie's suspicions.

Turning away, I paced along the edge of the ridge. I had to be alone. After a few steps, I stopped to lean against a projecting rock, suddenly so weak that I could go no further. I now knew what lay behind the truck deal. My father—my shadowy, faceless father, the father I had never known—was alive, and that awareness had brought my defenses down. I sat down on a low rock.

After a long time, the pounding at my temples moderated and my breath grew more regular, but I remained incapable of clear thought. The mosaic had fallen into place. But without Duek's help, I had no hope of ever finding him.

"Continue to think of him as dead," Duek said. He approached out of the gloom, laying a hand on my shoulder. "The problem is far more complex than you know or even imagine. You have to consider the other people involved."

"What are you trying to tell me?"

"Leave the curtain where it lies. Don't try to lift it."

"I must see him . . . once . . . just once. He's come to life for me, the man who gave me life. I want to lay my hand in his. He's there, Yehuda."

"Light years have passed since his disappearance. It's a changed world. He's a changed man."

"Changed? How has he changed? What image do I have of him? I know how he looked to you. I know how he looked to Mussa Eini. I know how he looked to Zeideh. But you have no

226

idea how I see him." I took a deep breath. "A man has to possess rare qualities to live as a mole among his enemies. He has to be one of them, without ever forgetting why he's there . . . There's just one thing I know—he's alive, like you and me . . ." My voice trembled and I broke off.

Yehuda Duek did not take his eyes off me. I expected warmth and encouragement, but in spite of the soft tone, his words were callous. "You're wrong," he said. "He is no longer living. The man born under the name of Yussuf Dur died the day he began to live a false life under another name, in another country. The man who was your father is buried inside the living body of someone else. He is no longer alive, Daniel, neither by your definition nor by mine."

I heard him out patiently. When he stopped, I shook my head. "I find myself living with conflicting facts and in conflict with the facts. All my life, I knew him to be dead, but imagined him alive. Now he is alive, and you're asking me to think of him as dead. How do you expect me to do that?"

Duek seated himself beside me on the wide rock. "Yussuf Dur was twelve years older than I was. He was my model. He never sent anyone else on a mission when he could go himself. He provided the example for others to follow." There was a half-smile on his lips. "Maybe what set him apart was his conviction that what he did would serve generations to come."

We sat in silence, listening to the waves lapping at the coast. From the city opposite, the lights began to flicker out. I glanced at Duek beside me; it struck me that I could have been sitting there with Yussuf Dur.

In referring to Yussuf Dur, Duek was not relating to mere hearsay: he spoke of Badwi as though they had face-to-face contact, in the present, not in the distant past. Duek had to be the link between the Mossad and Yussuf Dur. As head of Israel's intelligence-gathering operations in the Arab world, he was my father's one remaining connection with his homeland.

It was suddenly obvious. Duek's regular journeys to Europe were for the purpose of meeting with Dur, to receive his reports.

"You see him frequently," I said.

Duek sighed. His head slumped forward. "You're only torturing yourself," he said.

I remained silent. After a lifelong search, I had found my father, only to lose him again.

"That was where he got to know my mother," I said, pointing toward Tel Aviv. "The sand dunes were golden, the houses were white as sunlight. And there was a flying camel. Every night, it would soar away off its column. It would return each morning and resume its perch facing eastward, toward the dawn."

"I remember it," Duek said. "There are certain relics of those days which I try not to remember. Their disappearance is painful."

To the east, the darkness was lifting. A soft gray light spread, slowly at first, and then with greater swiftness. As the light grew sharper, Duek seemed to age. Rising, he walked toward the car.

I knew he would say no more about Badwi; not now, nor at any time in the future.

12

When I cleared customs at Kennedy, I drove directly to the Dakota. Ariadne was picking out a selection of photographs for the "Man in Torment" exhibit. All three slide projectors were in operation, each wall reflecting ravaged, anguished faces.

I had never seen her so euphoric. These were no mere photographs she was about to exhibit, she confessed; for the first time, she felt that she was going to reveal her inner self. On the library walls were blown-up segments of a single portrait. Brow. Lips. Eyes. Part of the profile. Chin. A hand supporting the forehead. Like a mosaic, broken down and waiting to be reassembled, they were single shots, giving one the impression they were taken with an unsteady camera. By depicting the face in this manner, Ariadne had achieved a bizarre effect; these dismembered sections revealed the very essence of her subject.

She placed one of the photographs on the desk, a closeup

of the eyes. They bore the tranquil look of a man who had come to terms with fate: a philosopher's gaze. I felt sorry for the man. His loneliness seemed total.

Still, there was something more important to discuss. I asked her to tell me precisely what Charlie had said during her visit to Washington.

"What made you suddenly think of him?"

"I never stop thinking about him."

"Is there a particular reason?" She seemed disappointed by my response, as though having expected me to say something else. I knew her thoughts were elsewhere, among the portraits that surrounded us.

"Did he want to know what I told you after my return from Israel?"

Ariadne smiled. "It was hard to tell. He was drunk."

"Drunk?" I exclaimed, astonished.

"He was downing drinks one after another. He was so befuddled I didn't attach any importance to his questions. He's charming when he's drunk. He has this blend of gentle humor and the macabre. He kept talking about the dead."

"The dead?"

She laughed. "You're looking at me with the same surprise he must have seen on my face when he talked about your parents. He asked if you mentioned your father."

"Did he want to know anything specific?"

"He wasn't asking so much as—well—babbling." She smiled. "You won't believe this, but he seemed convinced that your journey to Israel was some kind of . . . ," she paused, seeking the right word, "séance." She broke off, embarrassed. "Don't take it too seriously. It was a combination of scotch and his morbid fantasies that gave him such a macabre notion."

"Which was?" I prompted.

"He said he was convinced you'd gone to Israel to meet a ghost." She picked up the picture of the hand supporting the brow. "That must have been when I snapped this."

I was dumbfounded.

She pointed to the rest of the pictures. "Didn't you recognize the face?"

I shook my head.

"I thought you had. That that was why you mentioned him."

"Charlie," I said. "I never imagined he'd make such a fascinating subject."

"He has an unusual face. I couldn't resist snapping him. Almost every time I had a meeting with him, I took along a concealed camera for a shot or two." Her glance was amused. "And you didn't even recognize him!"

I failed to identify him because she had captured a Charlie that I never knew: Charlie poised to unearth a mole.

I had to leave. I did not tell Ariadne that I was going to meet Charlie. She made no secret of her disappointment. Her gentle look had faded.

"You may not think I'm brilliant," she said, "but you don't have to treat me like a dummy!"

"What are you talking about?" I was puzzled; Ariadne was too gentle to adopt such an abrasive tone without good reason.

"You know perfectly well!"

"No. Tell me."

"Nothing special," she said. "Just that I'm sick of being your sex object. And nothing more!"

"You know you mean much more to me." I placed a hand on her shoulder; only now did I feel the trembling of her body.

"Don't you think I sense what's going on?" She took a deep breath. "There's something going on between you and Charlie, and that something is endangering your life."

I grinned feebly. "Nonsense."

"I'm no fool, Daniel. From the moment I was told to watch you, I realized that you were in trouble. And now I care what happens to you. To us. These probes into everything to do with you, all this prying into your affairs—it's all aimed at drawing you into some trap. I must know what it's all about."

"You're imagining things," I broke in.

She was enraged. "Don't patronize me!" She removed my hand from her shoulder, her eyes warning me to hear her out. "All you offer is a one-way street. That isn't sharing, Daniel. That's one side being enslaved by the other, and it's not the kind of partnership I want!"

"I can't talk about it now," I said.

231

"I want to help you!" Her voice rose to a near shout. "You need help. Please! Charlie's a snake. Everything he does is calculated. What does he want of you? Can't I help you?"

"No, Ariadne. No one can do anything for me. Not now, anyway." I wanted to touch her with a reassuring hand and restore our intimacy. But she drew away and opened the door, standing aside wordlessly as she waited for me to walk past. I sensed there was much more she wanted to say, but she remained mute, evading my eyes.

"I'll call you later," I said, pausing in the corridor.

She was closing the door behind me. "You're welcome to call—just as soon as you feel you're ready for a genuine relationship."

Then she shut the door.

Charlie was waiting for me at our regular table. He welcomed me back with a strong handshake. "We've got things to talk about," he said.

"We always do."

Charlie studied me. "You look tired."

"The flight was eleven hours nonstop."

"You went back into the lion's den."

"Don't make such a big deal of it. From my point of view, it was a profitable trip."

"I guessed it would be."

Charlie's single statements always contained unspoken meanings, but I decided to ignore the bait. "I'm convinced that what almost led to my undoing was a set of coincidences."

"You must find that reassuring," he said. "Tell me about it."

I did—with certain deletions. "You know the Israelis," I said lightly.

"How do you mean?"

"They're sentimental. They only fabricated the grave because they assumed I'm as emotional as they are. They wanted to give me proof that my father had not been forgotten. The grave was supposed to assure me of the efforts they made to bring his body to Israel."

"Why were they in such a hurry to dismantle it?" he asked. "Didn't they think you'd come back?"

"Sure. They planned to erect a permanent headstone, but your man from the embassy took them by surprise. He came to inspect the cemetery the day the provisional stone was removed in preparation for a permanent one."

Charlie nodded. "How do you account for the matter of the press?"

"The press?"

"How come we found no mention of the Baghdad hanging?"

"That was a lapse on their part. An oversight."

"They slipped up?"

I told him how Yehuda Duek had stitched together two separate episodes to present my father in a heroic light. "They didn't want me to feel that his death was in vain. In fact, he got sick on a mission to Iraq. He died there and was buried in some village. That's why no one knows where his grave is. That also explains why the press didn't mention the story in 1952. You'd have to look up the 1959 files to find it. They never imagined someone would check up on the discrepancy . . ."

Charlie remained silent, weighing my account. Finally, he leaned back in his chair. "I'm glad we got that one unraveled." He smiled genially. "Now what do you say we have dinner and celebrate your safe return?" He glanced at his watch; when it came to eating, he was a stickler for punctuality. "I ordered a table at the Russian Tea Room."

"I appreciate the meal," I said, raising my glass of chilled vodka. "It's a fine gesture on your part."

"Gesture?"

"To mark the end of our professional association."

Charlie smiled pleasantly. "My boy, we'll celebrate that notable event when it materializes."

"It already has," I insisted, "in the form of a sadly abused orange BMW."

"Don't trouble yourself with matters of the past. There are plans for the future which you and I should consider."

"I have no plans for the future," I insisted. "At least, none I want to share with you."

"You'd do well just to listen."

"Why?"

"It has to do with the fate of a certain little bee."

I swallowed abruptly. "Ariadne? What about her?"

"She may find herself buzzing far from New York."

"You son of a bitch!"

His expression grew serious. "She's shown a duplicity which has led some of us in Washington to predict a great future for her in the organization. It isn't every day we run across a young woman with such valuable qualifications. I don't know anyone so well-fitted to penetrate the circle of aristocrats in Europe. The ones frequented by Russian diplomats. After all, she's a princess—and a Russian princess at that. Our bee may soon find herself sucking nectar from some very select blooms."

"You've always been a lump of shit."

"Your language is in deplorable taste."

"Do you expect me to let you force her into becoming a whore?"

My response brought a smug smile to Charlie's face. "I hope you spare me the painful necessity of putting her through the standard procedure."

"Go to hell."

"If you don't, she'll go through the mill. She may indeed end up a whore. She has enough quality to become one of our greatest successes, and the credit will be all yours."

He paid the bill and led the way out of the restaurant, all the while continuing his verbal harassment. "You need only one look to see that Ariadne's got class. She's well-bred, authentic . . ."

"Cut it out, Charlie!" I stopped in the middle of the street and grabbed him by the shoulder. "I want to buy her contract."

"You're kidding."

"Name your price." I tightened my grip. "I'll pay whatever you ask."

"Her contract isn't for sale."

"You've always said that everything has a price." I let go of his arm and we continued walking.

"I know you're rich now," Charlie said evenly. "But you aren't rich enough to buy her contract. All the same, if you want to free her, there is a way . . ."

"I need time to think it over," I said finally, knowing what he meant.

Charlie shook his head. "Sorry. You don't have time. You've got to make your decision now."

"What's the big rush? Some new development about Shishakali?"

Clearly gratified, Charlie's eyes twinkled. "I'm glad to hear you talk like a man of experience."

"You must have reliable information."

He nodded. "From a source in Saudi Arabia. Shishakali has been summoned to Riyadh. The Saudis are worried about this latest escalation between Israel and Syria, and they want it stopped. The Saudi side will be represented by one of your employers' clients, Sheikh Ibn Aziz. Shishakali is expected in Riyadh within the next few days. I'm sure you understand that this is an opportunity we can't ignore."

I nodded.

"I was sure you'd see it my way," Charlie went on. "Shishakali will be at the hotel you stayed at last time. We can book you a room on a lower floor, directly underneath his suite. You may find it useful." Charlie flashed me a friendly smile—"I'm offering you a quick and elegant way of acquiring Ariadne's contract."

"You have the soul of a hyena."

His look was amused. "If you don't want to take up my offer, that's your affair. Your love for the lady is no reason for you to allow yourself to be railroaded. And I'll be happy to help Ariadne, since you seem unwilling to lend her a hand. After all, it is traditional in your family for the men to abandon their women . . ."

Charlie's malevolent oration ended in a sharp cry. I lunged forward with my right foot, kicking at his left ankle with the point of my shoe.

"Go to hell," he hissed. "Fuckin' son of a bitch."

"Your language is deplorable." My smile was frosty. "I could have killed you. Never talk to me like that again. Don't ever defile my father's memory, you copper-bottomed son of a bitch."

"You're right." He attempted a smile. "Let me lean on you."

I placed myself alongside him, and he laid one hand on my

shoulder. "I owe you an apology," he said. "I opened my big mouth too wide."

"That's not a mouth you've got," I said. "It's more like a sewage main. But we're going to clinch the deal here and now."

He eyed me cautiously. "You mean it?"

"Give me her contract."

"You know it all, don't you?"

"I know you've got the damned contract with you." My tone remained chilly. "That was the bait."

"I trust you'll carry out the assignment satisfactorily."

"I'll do my best."

Now that he had me, he reverted to his normal role of strategic supervisor. "The trickiest part will be getting out after you do the job."

"The Saudi control network?"

"Precisely. It's one of the tightest in the world. You won't find it easy to slip through. Whatever happens, you could do with an adequate alibi. You might try using your connections with the Ibn Aziz family to help you out there." He thrust a hand into his inside jacket pocket to bring out an envelope, which he extended to me. "It's yours. From this moment on, she's a free woman."

I sighed. "So that's that."

"Every path comes to an end." He brought out a second envelope with a new passport to replace the one I had used for my last trip to Israel. "One further point, Daniel. This is no ordinary killing. This is retribution. Not for a moment can you forget those marines. Shishakali was their butcher two hundred and forty-one times over. His death must not be trivial."

"I'll remember," I promised. We had reached the Warwick entrance.

"I'm sure it will work out. And I know you'll make it back. As always."

"Don't be so sure." Without awaiting his response, I strode away, leaving him standing there. I knew he was looking after me, but I did not care what he was thinking or what he felt toward me. I wanted to be by myself.

This time, I decided to leave without any word to Ariadne or Bertha. What could I tell either of them? That I was about to vanish again? That I had no idea when I'd be back or, indeed, whether I'd ever be back at all.

It was one of the longest nights I had ever experienced. Every time I dozed off, I was beset by fantasies. In between the dreams and the brief bouts of light sleep, I lay on my back, staring up at the ceiling with demented eyes.

Yehuda Duek had advised me to let the dead lie in peace, but the truth about my father had come as too great a shock to be absorbed lightly. It was sinking into my system, setting off a series of delayed reactions, like recurrent dreams. I did not know how to adjust to the fact that my father was alive.

Finally, I padded to the washroom for a long shower, followed by a shave. I brushed my teeth vigorously, as though the motion of my arms would liberate me from the fantasies of the night. Then I got dressed.

I drew out the contract between the organization and Ariadne Alexander—the contract in which Charlie had played the role of intermediary and pimp. I quickly glanced through it. It was a remarkable document, illustrating how a slave may be acquired and manipulated by a cruelly capricious master.

I proceeded to rip the contract into tiny shreds, which I then dropped into the toilet, flushing it twice until not a scrap remained.

At the office I found a number of letters and documents from our clients awaiting my attention. Among them I noticed an envelope at which I only glanced. But the glance suddenly turned into a prolonged stare as I caught sight of the embossed emblem representing the company's name.

My thoughts ran wild. Unless I was being carried away, the emblem of a winged camel was a lead I dared not ignore—even if it turned out to be nothing more than mere coincidence.

Restraining my agitation, I weighed my course of action. I had to pose one simple question. If the answer were negative, I risked bitter disappointment; but if it were affirmative . . . ?

Time and time again, my hand reached for the phone; but each time I drew it back. Suppose I were proved wrong. One thing I desired above all was to protect myself from further pain.

Finally, I picked up the phone and dialed the number. A

moment later, the secretary put me through and I heard Paul
Oppenheimer's mellow tones. "It is indeed some time since we
last spoke," the jeweler said. "Is there anything I can do for you,
Mister Kottler?"

"I think there is. I've run into a minor legal problem, and
I need your help."

"Over the telephone?"

"I'd prefer to meet you in person."

"When would it be convenient for you to come to my office?"

"I'd be grateful if you'd see me right now."

"Certainly," he said. "I look forward to your visit."

Ten minutes later, I was ushered into his office. Oppenheimer was of that rare breed of professionals who give the
impression of having no worries. Their courtesy is impeccable.
Their expressions are invariably relaxed. Their voices convey
unruffled calm and confidence.

"I suppose you've reached a decision as to the disposal of
your collection?" he said.

"Not quite. But the jewelry has posed a certain problem."

"I'll do everything in my power to assist you in solving it,"
he promised evenly. "Were the purchase dates of any help to
you?"

"Indeed, they were. But they raise a further difficulty."

"What is that?"

"I need to find out whether or not the name of the purchaser appears in the records of d'Orly in Zurich."

The jeweler's face clouded over. "As I explained to Ariadne,
my profession calls for considerable discretion. It's a basic prin-
ciple with me. I'm sorry, Mister Kottler, but my position remains
unchanged."

"I'm not asking you to break your rules," I said. "There's
a legal tangle connected with the inheritance, and to settle it, I
need the name of the purchaser. I understand your need to
proceed with discretion. If I had any anxiety on that score, I
wouldn't trouble you with my request."

Oppenheimer's expression grew somewhat more relaxed.

"My mother acquired the jewelry legally," I said. "I hope
you have no doubts on that point."

"None at all! Your mother's name appears in d'Orly's book as the person for whom the jewelry was purchased."

"You are also aware that I am the legal heir."

"No question about that either."

"To meet the requirements of the tax authorities, I have a letter which testifies that the jewelry was bought for my mother by a certain person. All I want is confirmation as to his identity so as to avoid unnecessary bureaucratic difficulties. So you see, Mister Oppenheimer, my request doesn't flout conventions. I'm not asking you for a name. All I need is one word, either *yes* or *no*."

He gazed at me searchingly. "In other words, you will give me a name, and I am merely to confirm or deny his link to the jewelry."

"Precisely."

It was the first time I had ever seen Oppenheimer grin. "That's a fascinating idea. In effect, we are not breaking the rules, merely bending them slightly . . . Mister Kottler, I'll do it."

"I appreciate your cooperation."

"In that case, it only remains for you to give me the name."

I leaned forward, drew up a notepad that lay on his desk, and took up a pen. Then, with my heart beating wildly, I carefully spelled out the name in block capitals. Rising from my seat, I tore off the page, handing it wordlessly to Oppenheimer. He glanced at it briefly, with no change of expression, and rose, circumventing the desk to escort me to the elevator.

"I'll be in contact with you within a few hours," he said, shaking my hand.

Those hours of waiting were wearisome. I sat in my office, doing nothing; it was a break with my self-imposed rule to find some occupation whenever under stress. I felt almost paralyzed, my mind empty of all thought except for sporadic reflections that got me nowhere. Every now and again, I looked at the large embossed envelope, my conviction growing that the clue it offered was more than mere coincidence. The facts all pointed in a single direction. By a wild stroke of luck, I might have located the man who had burrowed his way into the very entrails of the Arab world. But in spite of the unambiguous nature of my conclusions, I commanded myself to lower my expectations. Oppenheimer's answer might yet change everything. I brought out the slim blue folder the jeweler had prepared, with the detailed valuations of each piece of jewelry. Every page bore a photograph of a different piece. I leafed through until I found the page I sought; then I sat there for a long time, staring at the snapshot. I was engrossed in my inspection when the door opened.

"Is something wrong?" my secretary asked.

I shook my head. "Everything's fine."

"Didn't you hear the phone? I put a call through to you."

"Who was it?"

"A Mister Oppenheimer. He said it was urgent. Shall I call him back?"

I shook my head. "I'll do it."

I dialed the number, overcome with the feeling that all my muscles had suddenly withered.

"I'm sorry I missed you." Oppenheimer's voice was clear and excited. "In response to your question, my answer consists of one single word . . ."

I heard it with a sense of unreality, feeling far from sure he meant what he had said. "Would you mind repeating that?"

"I said yes, Mister Kottler."

I replaced the receiver gently; then I laid my head on the desk and cried. I had, at long last, identified my mother's mysterious lover.

As usual, Bertha sat at the edge of the veranda, facing the setting sun with eyes half-closed. My unannounced arrival took her by surprise: I had not called her since my return. Her confusion grew when she noticed the taxi waiting for me opposite the house. She bombarded me with questions: When had I gotten in? What happened? Why hadn't I called? How did I feel? I replied patiently but briefly. As for the waiting cab, I explained that I had to reach Kennedy within the hour, to catch the flight to Riyadh.

"Something's wrong, isn't it?" No one knew me better than she did.

I sat down on the stone parapet facing her. "I don't have much time," I said. "There are lots of things we're going to have to talk about later. But at this moment, I have just one single question."

"You've located the flying camel."

I nodded.

"What is it you want to ask?"

"Since when have you known?"

She hesitated. "I think I knew right from the start, right from the very first time he called." Her voice wavered. "When I realized who it was, I—I—it was one of the most moving days I have ever lived through."

"Did she tell you?"

"No, she didn't. She never told me. But it all happened so suddenly, I could read it in her face. It must have been about an hour after you went off to school. She came to the kitchen for a cup of coffee. She was strangely unsettled. 'I don't feel well,' she said, 'something is troubling me.' Again and again, she mentioned that something was wrong. Her face was gray, and she looked very old. 'Those days—they haunt me,' she complained. She very rarely mentioned those days, for fear of gettng overexcited. It scared her, the idea of being hospitalized again. I reassured her as best I could. Then, suddenly, the phone rang and a man's voice asked if Rachel was home. He gave no name and I didn't ask; afterward, though, it occurred to me that I'd heard his voice before. I went off to collect the laundry. It took me several minutes, and when I got back to the kitchen, she was standing by the phone, her face radiant. In that short time, she was back to her former self, the way I remembered her as a girl. At that moment, I knew exactly what had happened.

"There was nothing I could say. I couldn't ask any questions. But it was written in her face." Bertha paused, tears brimming at the corners of her eyes. "I've never seen her so beautiful. She was young again. What astonished me then, and what still makes me wonder, is that she didn't look surprised. As though she'd always known that he would reappear."

"You never gave me the slightest hint."

"What would have been the use? As far as you were concerned, he was dead, and that's how he wanted it to remain."

"Do you know who he is?"

She shook her head. "I only know that in those five years, he gave her what other men don't give their wives in fifty."

I did not want to understand. I detested him. "Do you know where he is now?"

Bertha shook her head.

"Did you ever speak to him again?"

"Only once," she said. "It was a week after she was killed. Remember, she was due to leave a few days later? For Miami. She didn't make it. When he called to ask about her, I told him what had happened. He didn't say a word. I heard only his breathing. Or maybe what I heard were sobs."

"Has he contacted you since then?"

"Never. He may be dead. Many years have passed. He must be going on seventy."

"He isn't dead, Bertha," I said. "Not yet."

She scanned my face. "You know who he is," she said, a tremor running through her body.

"I do." I rose. "I have to go," I said, kissing her forehead. She was icy. "Why are you scared?"

"Don't go looking for him," she whispered.

"Why not?"

"If he senses that you're a threat . . ."

"Don't worry." Once again, I kissed her and turned toward the stairs.

"Daniel!" She seized my forearm. "You don't know him . . . He's living a different life . . . Let him remain dead . . ."

I turned to her, my voice low with reproach. "It was you who insisted I go there. To get acquainted with the land of his birth. To know who he was. And now?"

"I meant the dead man," she said; she was pale, and her eyes were wide with terror. "I didn't mean for you to find him alive. I never imagined you'd find him."

"I must see him."

"He's dangerous, Daniel. Don't forget that!"

"I won't."

She made as if to run after me, but held herself in check, remaining poised on the top step, her frozen stance seeming to reflect a coming to terms with the fact that there was nothing she could do to stop me.

13

From Kennedy, I called the Saudi airbase where Fahed Ibn Aziz was stationed, and notified him of my imminent arrival in Riyadh. He sounded pleased, promising to meet me at the airport.

I reached Riyadh at midday. Fahed was there, looking quite handsome in his pilot's uniform. He greeted me warmly. Within moments we were seated in his Cadillac, speeding toward the city. On the way he explained to me why he was back in Riyadh. "It's my father," he said. "He's sick. He needs an operation, but he's terrified of surgery—he's fearful of the effects of the anesthetic. He'd rather die than go under the scalpel."

"I'm sorry to hear it," I mumbled.

"He lives on painkillers," Fahed resumed sadly. "He refuses to go to the hospital. He wants death to take him at home."

I experienced a sudden surge of curiosity. "Fahed," I said, "tell me about your childhood—yours and your sisters'."

I had obviously touched a warm spot, for he smiled at once.

"I had a wonderful childhood. We—my sisters and I—we were very close with our parents."

He had grown to maturity along with his country; its tremendous economic boom began shortly before his birth. By then, his father was already a wealthy man as an agent for Mercedes.

"How did he acquire the agency?" I asked.

"I don't know the details. A few years after World War Two ended, he knew the time had come to modernize our desert nation. Since the Europeans were then rebuilding their own industries, he decided to become the local agent for their products. One of the agencies he acquired was Mercedes."

"He had vision."

"He is one of the wisest men I know. And farsighted. More than thirty years ago, few men predicted the tremendous boom we would soon experience. At that time, our roads were primitive. Only the royal family and its circle of a few elite owned cars. The idea of modern transportation only caught on here in the early fifties, and my father saw it coming. As soon as oil revenues started coming in, the desert changed, and my father was among those who profited."

As we continued our drive from the airport, we discussed Fahed's childhood, which he had spent surrounded by affection and wealth. The sheikh would often take his family on trips to Europe. Fahed had happy recollections of the elegant European hotels where they had stayed. "Those were family shopping expeditions," Fahed explained. "My father took other trips alone, taking care to remain unrecognized, because he preferred to travel around Europe without attracting unnecessary attention. He felt that remaining inconspicuous was good for his contacts with European businessmen."

But Fahed's youth was not simply frivolous, he asserted. He remembered how his father took advantage of these trips for quiet moments to instruct Fahed about Allah, and about His Prophet Mohammed and the message of Islam.

"We Saudis are known for our devoutness," Fahed said as we approached the hotel. "But not everyone grasps the spirit of the Koran. My father is among those who are wise enough to understand the truth of the Prophet's message."

We pulled up outside the hotel. Fahed accompanied me up

to the room that had been reserved for me by one of Charlie's assistants. It was on the eighth floor. I assumed that Rif'at Shishakali would be occupying the suite immediately above it, a floor reserved for VIP guests of the Saudi kingdom.

Fahed inspected my room and pronounced himself satisfied. Its balcony looked out on Riyadh's most prestigious quarter. He asked whether he could be of any assistance to me during my stay in Riyadh. I told him the purpose of my visit, that I had brought along signed copies of the contract drawn up by my employers, which were to be delivered personally to Sheikh Ibn Aziz. I was also prepared to discuss the sheikh's plans for entering the construction industry in the United States. Lastly, I had been charged with finding a local architect to undertake the design of our projected offices. "As for your meeting with my father—you may have to wait a day or two," Fahed apologized. "He's busy with preparations for a summit conference with the Syrians. With regard to the architect, there is one I know well. He's a Palestinian by the name of Ahmed Atlan, an excellent man. I'm sure he'll be delighted to take on the job."

Fahed then took his leave, explaining that he would have to hurry to join his father at prayer. He would call me later, after he had contacted the architect.

Late that afternoon, I received the promised call from Fahed. The architect agreed to meet me right away. Fahed offered to come at six to take me to Atlan's penthouse. Atlan turned out to be a man in his forties, of medium height and somewhat plump. His face was round with large, coal-black eyes. His hair showed almost no trace of gray. We dined at a table placed on the balcony. Atlan was an affable host and an entertaining conversationalist. After the meal, he showed us slides of offices he had designed for various corporations in Riyadh and elsewhere in the Arab world. His style was a blend of Western modernity and the more ornate style characteristic of the Mideast. I judged him eminently qualified to meet my employers' needs. I briefed him on the required layout of our office, and he noted down all of the points I raised. He promised to come to the hotel the following day and take me to his office, where we could discuss the plans in detail.

Thanks to Fahed's suggestion, I had found just the man I

needed. Atlan and I managed to solve most of the outstanding problems over lunch the next day at a French restaurant. After our meal, we returned to his office, where he drew out several large sheets of paper and began to sketch the outlines of the design he had in mind. We agreed that he would complete the initial drawings and send them to New York for final approval.

It was dark when Atlan drove me to the hotel. I immediately noticed unusual activity at the hotel entrance; four armed soldiers were posted outside, and two young men in black suits conducted an identity check of everyone entering the building.

"What's going on?" I asked my companion.

Atlan smiled. "Someone prominent must be coming to the hotel."

"The Saudis seem to be exercising great caution."

"They're noted for that. They don't want to run any unnecessary risks. It could be embarrassing . . ."

I said good-bye to Atlan and walked toward the hotel entrance. It had been more than a simple lack of courage that had made me hesitate to take on Charlie's assignment. Ahmed Atlan was right. Riyadh had never permitted any harm to come to its Arab visitors. That was why Charlie's men avoided any operations in the Saudi capital, choosing instead to carry out their missions in other cities. The organization's operatives in Riyadh confined themselves to intelligence gathering for various branches of the government. The CIA had an unwritten law against taking any action liable to lead to unnecessary friction with the oversensitive Saudis.

All of which made my current mission so exceptional; the unwritten law was going to be breached in order to avenge the deaths of our marines.

The Saudi security men were thorough but courteous. The name Kottler must have been new to them; consequently, they merely noted it in a small book, together with the date of my arrival in Riyadh. This done, they returned my passport, wished me a pleasant visit, and permitted me to enter the lobby.

So far, my activities in Riyadh had consisted of establishing and buttressing my cover; I was now about to start practical preparations for my more important assignment. My first step was to place myself in the lobby in order to check on what was happening and, with luck, to catch sight of the man in whose honor such tight security was in force. I bought a newspaper and settled myself in a deep armchair that offered me a good view of the elevators. I knew that the one on the extreme left was reserved for the exclusive use of guests occupying the ninth floor suites, and so I focused my attention there. According to the information Washington had received from Damascus, Rif'at Shishakali was expected in Riyadh that very day.

Soon, I saw four Saudis entering the private elevators. Fifteen minutes later, the elevator door reopened, and the foursome emerged, accompanied by three other men. Two of them, young and sturdily built, were evidently bodyguards. Rif'at Shishakali himself looked older than the few photographs obtained by the organization. Shishakali must have been in his mid-sixties; his brow was deeply furrowed and there were dark rings under his eyes. His Saudi hosts and bodyguards surrounded him as he strode toward the entrance. His step was measured and masterful. Four additional bodyguards now appeared from various corners of the lobby, reinforcing the protective screen flanking Shishakali's entourage as it made its way toward the exit. I watched closely, taking careful note of the faces of the security men, Syrian as well as Saudi.

As soon as the group had departed, I slowly folded up my newspaper, rose, and sauntered over to the elevators. I emerged on the eighth floor and after a swift glance around, rushed to the emergency stairs. Climbing one flight, I reached the ninth-floor door, opening it just a crack for an inspection of the broad, ornate corridor. Halfway down the hall, two young men were sprawled in leather armchairs. In the absence of their charge, they were relaxed and at ease, but their presence confirmed Charlie's information about Shishakali's suite; it was indeed directly above my room, making it possible for me to climb up from my own balcony to that of the Syrian's.

My principal concern was the tight security network that would be activated the moment Shishakali was liquidated. The only way to delay the inevitable danger would be to create the impression that his death had been accidental. In any event, I needed to establish a credible alibi to account for my actions at the time of his death. In any other country, I would have been able to rely on my position as a representative of a foreign law firm. But that would not work in Riyadh, where every foreigner had to provide a precise explanantion for his presence. If the security network closed in before I got out of Riyadh, I had to be ready to account for my whereabouts at the time of the "mishap."

A few minutes after seven, Fahed called me. He wanted to hear the results of my meeting with the architect. I told him that our meeting had gone extremely well, and that I had decided to hire Atlan. "Good," Fahed said, obviously pleased. "You'll be well served."

"What about my meeting with your father? I must see him soon. I would like to hear his comments and convey them to New York."

Fahed hesitated. "Tomorrow, maybe. He is exhausted."

I had a sudden inspiration. "Do me a favor, Fahed. I'll give you an envelope for your father and just wait outside while he takes a look at the material. If he then agrees to see me, fine. If not, we'll postpone the meeting for another time."

"I think that will be fine," Fahed agreed after a moment. "I'll be over in half an hour to collect you."

He pulled up outside the hotel at quarter of eight. I noticed immediately that he looked troubled. "What's the matter?"

"Are you sure you can't postpone your meeting with my father?"

"I'm sure of one thing," I said. "Your father is waiting for this material." I pulled out the envelope and laid it on the seat beside Fahed. "If he decides it isn't urgent, I won't wait for an answer."

"Is that all?" He looked relieved. "If it doesn't take too long, we could get together with a few friends later. How does that suit you?"

"Fine," I replied.

Fahed prattled on about his friends. I listened to his stories with all the concentration I could muster, but I soon began to feel hemmed in and short of breath. Fahed's chatter was getting on my nerves, like the buzzing of a swarm of insects.

I was immersed in my own thoughts of the forthcoming encounter. The prospect simultaneously attracted and terrified me. I felt nauseous. Lowering the window, I allowed the fresh breeze to whip across my face. Fahed did not notice my discomfort as he concentrated on his driving. Dammit, I was scared and, instead of subsiding, my nausea only grew.

The car drew up outside the Ibn Aziz mansion and I leapt out, glad to plant my feet on solid ground. "Follow me," Fahed called out, running up the marble steps.

We crossed the great hall and emerged onto a terrace overlooking the swimming pool. "Have a seat down there." Fahed pointed to the poolside tables. "I'll order some coffee while you wait."

He strode back into the house, the envelope in his hand. I watched him go, fighting off waves of nausea once again.

A servant approached with a tray bearing a cup of bittersweet coffee and a glass of cold water. Minutes passed and Fahed did not return. My sense of time was probably warped; indeed, all my senses seemed to have dulled. My mind was void of all thoughts, of anything, just as I had experienced when waiting in my office for Oppenheimer's call.

I jumped when a hand was laid on my shoulder. I turned my head with a swiftness that surprised Fahed. "You are not well?" he asked with concern. "Where were you? I called you several times but you did not seem to hear."

"Just deep in thought," I replied lightly. I forced my lips into a smile. As on so many other occasions, I felt I was making a fool of myself. "There's a stillness here in the mansion. It's as though we're in some gigantic tunnel where time has stood still."

"It's the silence of the desert," Fahed explained. He seated himself in the chair beside mine. "I delivered the envelope, but I doubt that my father will be able to see you."

"Did you stay while he opened it?"

Fahed shook his head. "I just laid it on his desk. He'll read it when he feels a little better. He looks quite pale."

It was now or never: once I had liquidated Shishakali, I would have to get out of Riyadh as soon as possible—leaving no opportunity to see the sheikh.

Fahed suddenly raised his head and looked up toward the veranda overhanging the terrace. Following his eyes, I saw what he had seen.

There, at the head of the stairs, stooped over his staff with one hand grasping the railing, stood the sheikh. He was poised there, motionless, his fragile body seeming to hover in space like an apparition. His staff and flowing robes made him appear like some biblical patriarch as he stood outlined against the sky.

Fahed sprang to attention in deference to his father, and I too rose to my feet. The old man remained quietly in place at the head of the stairs. Suddenly, I experienced an extraordinary tranquility. The physical discomfort that had plagued me in anticipation of this encounter began to fade. I breathed freely and my heartbeat slowed to a normal tempo. I wondered whether he would come down to greet me or whether he expected me to mount the steps.

The moment was broken by Fahed. Surprised by his father's appearance, he took a step toward him. But the sheikh lifted his hand from the railing in a mute command to halt. At the same time, he turned his gaze toward me and lifted his head, beckoning me to approach. I negotiated the steps one by one, mounting steadily to meet my father.

I ascended slowly, my progress at an even pace until I came to a stop one step below him, an arm's length away. He stared at me for a long moment, and then, with a visible effort to stifle his pain, turned and shuffled slowly toward his office. I followed, taking care to stay one step behind.

We entered the spacious study. With enormous effort, the sheikh lowered himself into the seat behind his desk. I stood some distance away. For the first time, we were alone, this stranger who was my father and I, each of us equally alien to the other. His curiosity seemed as keen as mine, but there was no need for explanations: a photograph of my mother's winged camel coronet lay face upward on the desk.

His health had worsened since our last meeting, markedly changing his appearance. His tortured features were a paler shade of gray, the skin reflecting an internal decay. His cheeks and temples were sunken, and his thin nose projected sharply over lips whose bluish color testified to continual pain.

I suspected he was unable to see me distinctly. Perhaps he distinguished nothing more than a shadow—a shadow who claimed to be his son with rights equal to those of his beloved Fahed.

The sheikh continued to fix me with a strange stare, as though weighing in his mind which of his sons could claim the birthright: this Isaac who stood before him, or the absent Ishmael waiting below. I wanted to tell him I understood his thoughts; yet I hesitated to break the silence that said more than could be expressed in words.

In that mute confrontation, we groped inwardly toward one another, sniffing each other out like beasts that recognize their own kind through a primordial sense. I had never experienced a sensation more primitive than the consciousness of this intimacy. With a sharp awareness that could wound us both, we acknowledged our kinship.

I tried to identify some familiar line in his features, some wrinkle or expression that would identify the man who had grown up beside the Sea of Galilee with Mussa Eini. I sought some trace of the boy sent out by his foster father to scour the desert to avenge the murderers of his family. I looked in vain for the man I loved and hated, admired and despised, at whose feet I would willingly hurl myself were he only to beckon. I wondered whether I should fling myself at him and shower him with gentle embraces and words of tenderness. I wondered whether I should tell him how much I had longed to meet him. But I swiftly rejected the idea: he was a man who would expect me to bear myself like a man, with self-restraint and reserve. Men do not exhibit their emotions. They do not shed tears. Dammit. I had accumulated tears enough to weep for hours—to scorch my face and scar my flesh.

I wanted to curse him until each white-hot word wounded him, to remind him that he had sanctified country above all, erecting an altar to which my mother and I were bound and offered up to the knife. He was mad and she was crazy, and I carried within me their insanity.

My legs trembled. He sensed what was happening and commanded me to be seated. I obeyed without protest because it was the first time he had treated me—albeit without words—as a son. At that precise moment, with that simple gesture, he had established our relationship as it would be henceforth. There was a change in his eyes. They grew clearer; for a moment, they were free of the shadow of death.

He stared at the envelope I had brought from New York,

bearing the address: Sheikh Ibn Aziz, Winged Camel International Construction Corporation, Riyadh. Then he looked at the photograph of my mother's white platinum coronet.

"You found it," he said in Arabic.

He did not address me in the Hebrew language I had hoped to hear. The torrent of his emotions had been pent up in him far too long to be let loose now. I understood him well. He dared not release the superhuman tension under which he lived, not even now, as his life ebbed away.

"Yes, I found the flying camel," I said in Arabic. His expression remained unchanged, though he must have guessed then that I knew what the emblem signified.

"You came a long way," he said.

I wanted to say, "Son of a bitch. Do you have any idea how far? Or of my anguish?" But I merely muttered, "Son of a bitch" under my breath. He stared at my lips, reading there what I wished to cry out loud.

"If it helps you to curse me, go ahead," he said quietly.

I did not reply. Death was closing in on him; I would never see him again. Perhaps he looked forward to a reunion with the woman he once loved.

"When will you die?" I asked.

"Soon, I think."

"You'll be buried here."

He hesitated for a moment as brief as the flicker of an eyelid. "Yes."

"You'll be buried among Moslems."

"Yes."

"Even after your death, you've condemned yourself to isolation."

"One day, my beloved ones will be buried alongside me. I've bought a burial plot for my entire family."

"They're Moslems," I reminded him angrily. "You're an infidel. A Jew."

"God alone will make that distinction."

"Don't die," I pleaded suddenly.

He did not respond.

"We're strangers. I envy Fahed. You love him."

"Fahed is my son. So are you."

So are you. What was the significance of being his son? Could he love me as he did Fahed? Did he attach any importance to the fact that I had emerged from the womb of the woman he loved? A man cannot command his heart to sense affection for a fully grown man whom he has never seen, never cradled in his arms, never tossed high over his head. A man cannot sense a close kinship with someone of whose existence he knew nothing for so many years. This man, this father, was absent from my mother's side when the birth pangs came; he remained absent during my childhood; he did not share the pain and self-doubt of my adolescence.

A strange knot was swelling up in my throat. My voice grew thin, with an almost imploring tone. "She wanted to protect me. To keep me from growing up like you—to keep me from becoming your kind of Jew."

I began to pour out recollections about his beloved crazy wife and about my own warped childhood. I did not spare him a thing. I wanted him to experience, in the course of one hour, everything I had experienced throughout my life, in the hope that some miracle would enable him to understand that I too was his son, entitled to some measure of the love and devotion he felt for Fahed.

He listened mutely, his face frozen. Only when I told him he had given my mother nothing beyond a lopsided, crippled love did a momentary glint appear in his eyes. "What did she want of life?" I asked. "All she wanted was to spend it with you. She could never compete with your other love, even a love as abstract as a 'homeland.' She asked for so little, but even that was denied her."

When he broke his silence at last, he made no attempt to defend or vindicate himself. He seemed to harbor no guilt over what had happened. "You'll never understand what we had between us, your mother and I."

"Why did you see her again after you had disappeared?"

He remained silent.

"What a cursed life she led! She knew the nature of your last mission, yet you insisted she think of you as dead."

His eyes clouded over.

"She probably told you nothing of what she went through

in those fifteen years until that day you called her from Zurich. But during those years, you killed her countless times." I wanted to tell him how she would wake up screaming in terror, and what I felt as I awoke to those fearful cries.

"I died along with her in that road accident," he said in a voice that sent a tremor through my body. "But you will not understand that."

He was right and I said nothing. There was so much between them that I failed to understand, that I would perhaps never understand. "I have a question," I said. "If you had known she was pregnant, would you have changed your mind about going on the mission?"

A long time passed without any reply from him. His expression remained unchanged. Even now, shrunken and shriveled, his features looked as though they had been hewn from the hard basalt rocks of his childhood landscape. That face had grown accustomed to revealing nothing. But his prolonged silence reflected the bitter inward struggle he waged until he could bring himself to speak. "I've often asked myself that." He shook his head. "Knowing would have made the decision more difficult, but in the end, I would have changed nothing."

"I hope you burn in hell!" I cursed. Our eyes met. His had grown harder. He ignored my outburst as though it too were part of a fate beyond his power to change. I detected only one sign of weakness: his hands tightened about his staff until the knuckles whitened. In spite of everything, he retained some spark of humanity. But I may have been wrong: perhaps the gesture was nothing more than a reaction to his pain.

"Your mother was proud of you," he said. "She always described you as gentle and delicate. She was proud of herself for having exposed you to the world of culture."

"Is that so?" I suddenly realized that she had died without ever knowing me for what I truly was. "She was out of her mind. All of her efforts had only one purpose: to keep me from resembling you. You were of the desert; therefore I had to be alienated from the desert by a powerful shot of 'culture.' How I wanted to resemble you," I said weakly. "I thought it was fate when I was recruited to work for the government. What d'you think of that? You and I in the same line of business!"

"You are employed by the CIA." He was not questioning, merely stating a fact.

"They discovered my special aptitudes; perhaps I inherited them from you. The fact is that my dirty assignments for the organization paid my way through Columbia. The difference between you and me is in our motives. You acted out of ideals which are alien to me; I acted out of necessity because I had to rely on myself."

"That isn't true."

"You don't say!" My voice was as harsh as his. At that moment, one would have thought we detested each other.

"Your mother controlled large sums in cash," he said evenly. "There was an account for the two of you in a Swiss bank. You had no cause for concern."

"This is the first time I've ever heard of it," I said slowly. "If I had learned about that money, she knew I might catch on to other things which neither of you wanted me to know."

I stopped abruptly, remembering the tireless efforts of my mother to keep me unaware of my father's existence. I now wondered how he had reacted to learning of mine. I was the living result of one final night of passion before he set off on his one-way mission. What had he thought when he first heard of me? How did he react to such stunning news knowing that his own teenaged son was living in Brooklyn, that a child was the product of his aborted love? Did it make him happy? Remorseful? Did it fill him wih wonder? With regret? Did it so much as stir a ripple in his long repressed emotions?

"Weren't you ever curious about me?" I asked suddenly. "Did you never want to see your son?"

His face gave no sign of emotion at the accusation implied by my question. "What would have been the use?" he said dully. "While you were growing up, it would only have inflicted an unnecessary burden upon everyone . . ." His voice was suddenly faint.

But I remained relentless. "And when I was older? Did it never occur to you to come looking for me?"

The aging man sank into his private reflections; every now and again, he shut his eyes as occasional spasms of pain transformed his features. "Finding you presented no difficulty," he said. For one brief moment, his look evaded mine, as though he were ashamed of conceding that he had ever given way to sentimentality.

I wondered whether his choice of words was fortuitous. *Presented no difficulty* he said, implying that a search for me was not only considered, but that it had been in fact carried out successfully. So what? I thought angrily. Suppose he did try to locate me—what did he do when he succeeded? Again, I gave way to self-pity for the neglect and indifference of my father. But then my thoughts flashed to our first encounter at the Park Avenue office and the sharp scrutiny to which he subjected me when I was introduced. "Kottler," he had said; at the time I thought he was merely repeating the name to impress it on his memory. But surely that was a name he would never have forgotten. "There are many attorneys in New York," I said. "What made you choose Sheldon Moritz and Ed Liebman to handle your affairs?"

"Moritz and Liebman? They had extensive contacts in the Arab world, and they seemed reputable." He was not thrown off balance by what I was implying: he still had his wits about him.

He asked the question that must have haunted him from the moment Fahed brought him the envelope. "How did you track me down?"

I told him the whole story. I began with Ariadne's birthday and went on to tell him about the rest of my search, mentioning his friend Mussa Eini in the hope that the name would arouse some sign of emotion. But the dull eyes remained cloudy; his face did not change its expression and the gaunt hands did not tighten on the staff. A heart of stone.

I drew out my account, intentionally devoting much detail to descriptions of Tiberias and the Sea of Galilee. I told him how enthralled I was by the majesty of the landscape. He said nothing. I told him how Mussa Eini continued to tend the stone house on the hillside. I described how I sat with Eini on the terrace looking out at Tiberias and the Golan Heights as they were lit up by the sun.

I longed to reignite the inner fires he had quenched, but he maintained his passionless calm; in spite of everything, his back was turned on the past. His apparent indifference convinced me that the path he had traveled had concluded with an irreversible metamorphosis into his identity as Sheikh Ibrahim Ibn Aziz, with no trace of Yussuf "Badwi" Dur.

I told him of my meeting with Yehuda Duek and the head of the Mossad, and their attempt to conceal the truth. But when I recalled the prayer the military rabbi had chanted over the phony headstone, I thought I noticed a light in his eyes. Their cloudiness receded further as I related how I was given the honor of reciting Kaddish for the elevation of his soul.

The glint did not fade. "Are you religious?"

"No."

"But you did say Kaddish for me."

"I did." My God, I thought, and a shudder ran through my body. It was the first time he had lowered his guard. Perhaps he remained a Jew at heart.

"When you go there, tell them to leave my body in its grave here. It belongs to my family in Riyadh. I have lived a lie with them; I don't want them deceived after my death. I am their husband and father, and they are my flesh and blood. Just like you." He paused, his eyes boring into my face. "You'll tell them."

"I will," I said softly.

He nodded, accepting my solemn pledge. He must have guessed how moved I was and how aware of his own inner turmoil. But he intended to be brought to burial as Ibrahim Ibn Aziz. Divided in spirit, he owed his body to his children and to the Saudi wife who had loved him wholeheartedly. They had never penetrated the inner sanctuary of his soul; for that matter, neither had I. No one could ever claim his spirit. If anyone had ever touched him, however fleetingly, that person was my mother, and she was dead.

His pallor increased. The time we passed together had taken its toll. Suddenly, a muscle twitched in his jaw.

"You wanted to see me, and you have," he said.

His cold words left me speechless. The message was clear: he was drawing a line between past and future; he had had his fill of reliving the past, and would not allow himself to indulge his momentary weakness. It took me time to grasp the meaning of his undeclared resolve, but finally, I nodded to signify that I understood and would respect his wish to end this exchange.

"I have a problem," I said evenly.

"And you need my help."

I nodded.

"What can I do for you?"

"I need an alibi to cover my whereabouts during certain hours."

"For what purpose?"

"I may be arrested before I can get out of Riyadh. I need you to testify that I spent those hours in your company."

"You are speaking of an assignment which may cause you serious trouble."

"It could."

"Such operations are difficult in Riyadh. The security network is easily alerted on very short notice."

"So I understand."

"If I'm to provide you with an alibi, I need to know why."

"It would be better if you didn't."

He shook his head. "I can provide whatever you require, but only if I know your plan. You may need more than an alibi. You may find yourself in need of an escape."

"I've thought of that too."

"You have no choice but to confide in me fully."

I did not want him involved in matters he had no need to know, and I told him so. But he would tolerate no secrecy, demanding to know the details of my assignment.

"You don't have to help me if you're worried about possible complications," I said.

"Complications are to be expected. But in this case, you risk nothing more than your own neck. What I endanger, in addition to myself, is my family."

"You don't owe me a thing!" I said. "I've never received anything from you, and I don't need anything you're reluctant to give." I rose to my feet.

He tightened his grip on the staff. "Don't be a fool!"

"I . . ."

He did not give me a chance to go on. His voice dropped to a hiss. "You'll stand up when I permit you to."

His imperious tone stopped me. "Sit down!"

I obeyed. His was not the tone of a man trying to establish his mastery; it was the growl of a father to a disobedient son. The bizarre situation made me feel confused and embarrassed as I sank back into my seat.

"You know much about this country," he said, "but you don't know how different it is from others where you have operated in the past. The Saudi security network is tight. Its operatives have been trained to spring a trap with surprising swiftness. In any emergency, they are capable of sealing off the sea and airports on five minutes' notice." He paused to catch his breath. "I know what I'm talking about. You can believe me."

I nodded.

"You confided in me, even though you knew you were liable to put me in danger. You were aware of the possible implications for each of us. But you reached the conclusion—which is undoubtedly correct from your viewpoint—that you need my help. I have received you and listened patiently, because such was the manner in which you decided to conduct this meeting. For my part, I could have dispensed with the emotional introduction." He lifted his hand to stop me from leaving. "Even if you insist on being so stupidly sensitive, you will shut up and listen to me."

I said nothing.

"You're a professional. It seems that after ten years in your job, you're good at it." He knew all about me. Yehuda Duek must have briefed him. And I had been naïve enough to imagine I would have something new to tell him. "Nobody holds out that long in Donnevy's outfit if he isn't good. Your expertise led you to choose Riyadh as your target's most vulnerable spot. That's why you came here seeking help. You will receive that help when I have learned your target's identity."

Since he knew everything about me, there was nothing I could say to contradict him. In his own way, he had let me know that my existence was no longer the abstraction it had been to him during my mother's lifetime.

"Your offer of help is not simply out of concern for me," I said.

"That's your conclusion. My motives are irrelevant, except that I care about you."

259

Those words were precisely what I had longed to hear. What he had just offered me was the most precious gift I could receive. Nevertheless, I suspected that his help would be given in such a way as to also remove the threat it might pose to his Saudi family.

I relented. "I've been charged with the assassination of a certain individual. That individual is guest of the Saudi government."

"I guessed as much. Rif'at Shishakali."

"Correct."

"Rif'at Shishakali," he repeated. "Why?"

"It was Shishakali who authorized the Jihad's attack on our marine headquarters in Beirut."

He studied me at length. "A man has to be out of his mind to attempt an assassination in Riyadh. Any other place would be better. It's as though someone were trying to set you up. Did it not occur to you to try and kill Shishakali in Damascus, rather than here?" He leaned forward, as though intent on making sure I heard every word. "This mission of yours, in addition to being highly dangerous, is also irresponsible. It's as much of a threat to your own life as to that of your target."

"The people in Washington weighed the risks," I explained. "They knew I might be caught."

"I don't understand your superiors." He leaned back in his seat; a spasm of pain made his features contract. "There's something I don't understand. Somebody in Washington has gone mad. Whoever sent you should have also considered that your capture could spark off a major diplomatic scandal."

"That risk was considered, I assure you. In such an eventuality, they have a remedy."

"Which is what?"

I sensed a wave of heat run through my body. In his presence I felt like a pupil before his mentor. I told him about the passports with the incriminating Israeli stamps that Charlie could use to portray me as an agent for the Mossad. "Donnevy is no fool," I concluded.

"By no means," he said. He raised his head. "Killing Shishakali is not the only thing Mike Donnevy is after. What are you holding back?"

I swallowed. "What do you mean?"

"A man of Donnevy's caliber doesn't invest so much effort and such complex planning into a mission of this nature unless he's after something more."

"You mean . . .?" I did not complete the sentence because his nod confirmed the words I had not spoken.

"Riyadh is a trap for you. In spite of the security precautions in Damascus, your chances of getting him there are better than here. Your prospects of making your escape from Riyadh at best are slim. In that case, why here of all places? Why?"

Destiny had made us both of the same flesh and blood, and the same destiny now required us to act as allies. I told him about Charlie's search for an Israeli mole embedded in one of the Arab capitals; how his suspicions had come to rest on Rif'at Shishakali, whom he also suspected of being my missing father.

"Donnevy knows exactly where the mole is embedded," he said when I had finished.

"I don't understand."

"You don't," he agreed. "If you did, you'd know that Donnevy has laid a clever trap which you have not guessed. Donnevy suspects that the mole is emplaced in Riyadh. He hopes to use you as bait to lure him out of hiding." He breathed heavily. "Understand me, Daniel. You are his decoy."

In a single moment, the mist cleared. This man, teetering feebly on the threshold of death, remained immensely more clever than I.

"Donnevy set things up to convince you that Riyadh is the only place where you can kill Shishakali. Correct?"

"Yes."

"That's how he strung you up." He paused, wearied by so much talking. "If you manage to get out of here alive after killing Shishakali, Donnevy will see that as proof that you were helped by someone on the spot. Going one step further, he will assume that the help came from your . . . from me." The old man glared. "You've acted hastily," he concluded. "If you perform the liquidation successfully, you'll set them on my track."

"That never occurred to me . . . I never guessed that Donnevy could want you!" I felt as though I had been flung into a furnace.

He gazed at me sorrowfully. "What pressure did he exert on you? What does he hold against you?"

He had guessed my situation; his perception was sharp as a laser beam. "A woman," I said.

"Tell me about her."

I briefly told him about Ariadne.

"How did they get their claws into her?"

"The classic technique," I said. "A well-bred girl gets into financial trouble, and along comes the kind uncle to resolve her difficulties."

"Donnevy."

"Donnevy threatened to make her into a high-class hooker. The technical term is 'queen bee'—the kind that flits from one bed to another, sucking up information like nectar. I had to do something."

He understood. "You bought her contract."

"And now I have to pay." I saw his expression change. He looked younger, as if he had cast off the burden of his years. I could almost imagine that I was witnessing the return of the man from Tiberias. "I need help," I said. "But I don't want you mixed up in this."

"Do you have a plan?"

"Of course."

"I want to know what it is. When I do, I'll be in a position to decide how to give you the help you need."

I explained my plans, starting from the moment I would climb up from my veranda to Shishakali's suite.

The aging man listened with great patience. When I finished, he asked me questions that picked out every flaw in my projection, convincing me that Charlie's briefing had been faulty. For example, he had overlooked a detail that the sheikh was now quick to point out: two of Shishakali's bodyguards shared their charge's sleeping quarters. In addition, the bedroom, like the rest of the suite, was linked to a network of electronic cameras, part of the sophisticated surveillance equipment installed to protect the guests occupying the ninth-floor suites.

I threw out alternative plans, but the sheikh dismissed them all: each one would lead to my immediate capture. "Whatever happens," he said, "you must not kill Shishakali in the hotel."

"But I can't get him anywhere else. I don't have his schedule. I don't know where he'll be, or when, or with whom. I have no way of finding him anywhere besides the hotel."

"You don't," the sheikh said. "But I do." He thought a moment. "I'll tell Fahed to bring you here tomorrow night for dinner. By then, I should have worked out a solution."

He raised himself from his seat; I followed. He stood bent over, apparently on the verge of toppling forward. But he gripped his staff to steady himself and began shuffling toward the door, stopping beside me. I felt an urge to reach out and touch him; but I held back. His eyes were close to mine, his gaze unwavering. "I have no answer for the questions which trouble you. They'll plague you for as long as you live. There's only one thing I can tell you, and which you must remember. To understand my motives you would have had to live my life in the manner I lived it."

"But that's impossible," I said.

"Precisely. That's why you'll never find all the answers you seek. The questions will remain with you forever." He turned away, his voice suddenly soft and gentle. "I never loved any woman as I loved her."

I looked at this weary sick old man, and then, suddenly, I blurted out: "From your house, you can see the Sea of Galilee."

"The house is yours." He spoke with great difficulty. "The most splendid time is when the night recedes and the sky to the east, over the Golan, begins to turn pale . . . If you are ever there at that hour, remember to open the windows to the east. A cool breeze will fill the house . . . from the hills . . ."

He opened the door and stepped outside.

I woke early the following morning with a headache and took three aspirins to still my throbbing temples. I paced the room, my thoughts centered on Shishakali asleep in the bedroom overhead, protected by an electronic alarm system and two bodyguards who never left his side. I reconsidered my original plan. Dammit, the old man was right. It offered no hope of escape. It was midday before I left my room and headed down to the lobby. I waited there until Fahed came to drive me to a soccer game between the Saudi nationals and the Kuwaitis. After the game, we were to drive to his home, where I would have a further meeting with the sheikh.

"You certainly aroused something in my father," Fahed said as we drove off toward the stadium. "This morning he told me how excited he was about his American project. I'm struck by his improvement. It's been a long time since I've seen him so vigorous."

"I'm glad he takes such an interest in the corporation."

Fahed laughed. "You underrate yourself. It's your idea which has made a new man of him. Before leaving home this morning, he embraced my mother in my presence—something he never does. He seemed to be in a kind of euphoria, as though he still sees great things ahead. It must be true what they say about invalids, that their physical condition improves if they find some genuine interest in life. He really should undertake this project." Fahed grinned. "Yesterday, when you insisted on meeting him, I was very angry. But it paid off. There were moments this morning that took me back many years."

When we reached the giant stadium, an attendant ushered us to the grandstand set aside for members of the ruling class. The game commenced under mounting excitement.

A growing nervousness caused me to fidget in my seat as though I sensed impending catastrophe. As Fahed and I sat among this crowd of cheerful football fans, a menacing cloud massed on the horizon. I made every effort to control myself, to keep Fahed from noticing my unease. But as my stress increased, my knees and elbows ached as though I had endured a brutal beating.

I began to count the minutes, and then the seconds. I did not wish to spoil Fahed's enjoyment of the game; fortunately, he was too engrossed in the contest to notice my agitation. I could not get my mind off the old man. He dominated my thoughts incessantly.

His gaunt, imposing face was still before my eyes when I took my seat beside Fahed in his car. On the drive back, I was subjected to Fahed's long and detailed analysis of the game. It had concluded in a draw, an outcome that pleased Fahed; he saw it as a fine achievement for his country's team.

He was still gloating as we approached the Ibn Aziz mansion. But as the car swept through the wide gateway leading into the grounds, he abruptly stopped talking. Policemen were everywhere. Fahed paled as he brought the Cadillac to a halt. "Something's happened," he said, leaping out. Before I could get my door open, he was already talking to one of the officers. After a brief exchange, he raced up the steps. I followed. Reaching the entrance hall, I heard the sound of sobbing from an adjoining room. Servants were hurrying about nervously, concern and confusion straining their expressions.

I grabbed one by the arm. "What's wrong?"

"The master," he said, "the master . . ."

"What about the master?"

"The master," he repeated.

"Speak up!" I tightened my grip.

"There's been an accident. The master—he—he was killed."

"How did it happen?"

"I don't know. The police just came . . . I don't know . . ."

I released him and he staggered away, leaving me standing alone.

At that moment, with the tragic news still echoing in my ears, a moment of finality, I experienced a strange sense of peace. My headache vanished. I knew now what it was I had intuitively sensed in the stadium: I had divined the impending death of my father.

I walked into the large hall. In a distant corner I saw Fahed embracing his mother. They stood motionless. Adalla allowed her head to droop on her son's chest, while Fahed's head rested upon hers. For a long time, I looked in wonder at the people who were mourning the death of my father. Solitary and alien among those who had loved him, I stood aside, unable to escape the disturbing realization that now, at the fateful moment of our long-delayed meeting, when he finally understood how great was my need of him, now as before, he had vanished.

After a long time, I caught a further glimpse of Fahed; he was guiding his grief-stricken mother to the women's wing. Wordlessly, they passed near me. Adalla's face marked her silent pain, but she bore her misery with a reserve that invited respect. Fahed sheltered her gently in his arms, lovingly soothing her agony.

I waited there until he walked up to me. I offered my condolences. He raised his eyes; they glowed with a strange light, as though he suddenly grasped the weight of the responsibility that now rested upon him.

"It was the will of Allah," said my half-brother.

"Allah has His own secret ways" I said.

"Perhaps it was better so. You saw how sick he was."

"He was spared much suffering."

"A man senses the approach of his final hour. This morning, he must have sensed this would be his last day."

"Do you know anything about the accident?"

"I received a report from the police."

"When did it happen?"

"In the early afternoon. A few moments after the start of the match. They told me he was killed instantly. How extraordinary that he would choose today of all days to drive himself." Fahed inhaled deeply. "He rarely drove, and even when he did, he always made sure his chauffeur came along. But today, he told the driver he wouldn't be needed."

"Where did it happen?"

"In one of the main squares." Fahed laid a hand on my shoulder. "I'm going out there to see what's left of the car before it's towed away. Please. I'd like you to come with me."

I agreed readily. On our way into the city, Fahed repeated the details he had heard from the police. There had been no collision with any other vehicle. Witnesses had seen the limousine cruise down the hill, then suddenly pick up speed. Instead of circling the square, it crashed directly into the large marble fountain located at the center of the square. The initial police report attributed the accident to human error.

"What do they mean by that?" I asked.

"Physical exhaustion. There was a day of gruelling meetings at the governmental palace. He must have been very tired."

"That can't account for his losing control of the car," I protested. "Perhaps he simply passed out."

Fahed shrugged. "There will always be questions to which we'll never know the answers. The only thing we know for certain is that he was killed immediately, along with his passenger . . ."

I felt my face grow hot. "His passenger?"

"He was in the front seat beside my father. My father was bringing him home to dinner."

"Fahed," I said, but my voice was inaudible. My words came out in a dry croak. "Fahed," I repeated, "the man—the passenger—who was he?"

"A Syrian emissary. A man by the name of Rif'at Shishakali."

In a blinding flash everything became clear. With a single stroke, my father had accomplished my mission. And in doing so, he had put an end to the physical and spiritual torment of his own existence in such a way as to protect both his Saudi loved ones, and me, from danger. With this ultimate gesture of loyalty, he had given himself to me.

14

The jubilant children crowding around the pool at Central Park that Sunday noon surrounded a skinny, lopjawed man flinging his fish to the seals. Charlie never missed.

"Who wants to learn to toss fish?" he asked. The children clamored and begged for a chance to be allowed to try. He stood among them, chuckling, and demonstrated how the fish were to be grasped and flung to the waiting seals. Pieces of fish flew through the air, flashing in the midday sun. The seals leapt for the tidbits, their pelts glistening. Within moments, Charlie's bag was empty.

Catching sight of me, Charlie approached, making his way through the throngs of children. "Have you ever seen such agile creatures?" he asked. "None of God's other creatures can compare with them. Aren't they great, those seals of mine?" His blue eyes sparkled with emotion. Rubbing his jaw, he laid an arm on my shoulder, as though anxious to share his good spirits.

Within a few minutes, he noticed my silence. He only smiled and began walking toward the zoo exit. "You see," he said, "premonitions don't always come true. You made it back safe and sound."

"No thanks to you."

He stopped, measuring me with his eyes. "I can't claim the credit that's due to others. You're becoming quite skillful at using cars. First Cyprus, now Riyadh. Another BMW?"

"Mercedes."

"You're pro-German, I see." His grin was sardonic. "I thought you planned to get Shishakali in his hotel room."

"I didn't even try."

"Why not?"

"I would have walked straight into a trap. There would have been no need for the Saudis to come after me. Someone else would have gotten me first."

"What are you implying?"

"Your briefing was incomplete."

"How?"

"Shishakali never slept alone. Two of his bodyguards were posted inside his bedroom." I maintained my measured pace. There was a stream of pedestrians coming along the path in the opposite direction.

"That was one detail we were unaware of," Charlie said.

"So it would seem."

"How did you find out?"

"What difference does it make? As you know, I always undertake a thorough reconnaissance before charging into one of your minefields."

He smiled genially. "Which only goes to show that I picked the right man for the job."

"You knew there was a very good chance I would be caught."

He stopped again. "That's a very grave charge. And not very well considered. After all, if you were captured, it would implicate the organization. And me."

"Don't give me that crap. In the event of my capture, you were thoroughly prepared to disown me. 'Never heard of him. Never so much as came across his name.' Am I right or am I right?"

"What makes you think so?"

"Do you need to be reminded?"

"Yes," he said firmly, his blue eyes flickering as though he had been hurt by my accusations.

"Those passports—with the Israeli stamps." I took a deep breath.

Charlie scrutinized me. "The moment comes when boys become men," he said. "You were lucky. The Saudis blamed Shishakali's death on the unfortunate accident which also killed their Sheikh Ibn Aziz."

I kept my tone cold. "I didn't expect any difficulties on that score."

"Rightly so. That was one of the most elegant operations I've ever heard of. I expected you to take advantage of your acquaintance with Ibn Aziz, but it never occurred to me you'd go to such lengths to provide an alibi. Altogether, you did a fine job. I'd like to hear the details; I've a lot of questions."

"Questions?"

"Doubts," he amended smoothly. "Doubts that you could have pulled it off without help."

"And who is expressing these doubts?"

"Certain persons in Washington."

"Meaning Mike Donnevy?" I fired back. "You always were a lousy creep. As for this so-called help I'm supposed to have received—are you going to come up with that old story about my secret links with the Mossad?"

"It did cross my mind . . ."

"It's a good mind, but don't overwork it. I've no professional links with the Mossad. I never had any in the past, and I don't have any now, even though my formal ties with your organization are over. So save your breath. You won't get any answers out of me. When you go back to Washington, the only answer you'll take with you is simply this—you sent me to Riyadh to discharge my part of a deal, and I delivered. Don't forget, it was your idea to use Ibn Aziz as my alibi. The precise manner in which I took advantage of that alibi is none of your business."

Charlie did not fail to note my threatening tone, and his expression sharpened markedly. "There are a number of un-answered questions about your mission to Riyadh. I'd like them resolved, for my own satisfaction at least."

"That's your problem. I can't help you."

"For example," he went on, ignoring my rebuff, "there's the riddle of your father's death."

"You're getting old," I said. "Curiosity is a characteristic of aging."

"Not always." He rubbed his chin. "The way I operate, an episode is closed only after I've wrapped up every detail. In your case, there are a few outstanding points which puzzle me. I'd like to know how you found out about Ibn Aziz inviting Shishakali to dinner. That fact was unknown until the accident. Then there's something else I don't get. At the time of the crash, you were at a soccer game with Fahed Ibn Aziz. You devised a perfect alibi. You set up the father, and at the very moment your plans lead to his death, you are at a safe distance in the company of his son. My congratulations!"

I turned to him slowly. "You're a son of a bitch."

The epithet left him unmoved. "You're an excellent operative. You have an astounding deductive capacity, a knack for picking up minor details, then dovetailing them into intriguing combinations. You could go a long way with us."

"There are times when your imagination runs wild."

He grinned. "Only fools expect to have results by relying only on hard facts."

"And what did your fantasy come up with this time?"

He took my question seriously. "I'll be candid with you. My instinct told me that your father was not killed in the fifties as the Israelis claim. I somehow sensed that the story of his death was a fabrication to cover up his role as a Mossad mole in some Arab capital. And then, for some reason I couldn't understand, you were suddenly reluctant to undertake Shishakali's liquidation—so I started putting two and two together. Shishakali was about the age your father would have been had he lived. His past is shrouded in mystery. It occurred to me that he could be Dur. When you refused to kill him, it confirmed my hunch."

"That's a remarkable hypothesis." My tone was condescending. "Do you still stick to it?"

"Oh no. I'm satisfied it was groundless."

"What convinced you?"

"The jewelry. If you had known where it came from, you would never have mentioned it to me. But the moment your story was verified by Oppenheimer, I realized there could only be one reason for the Mossad's interest in you: they guessed you were on the verge of uncovering their best-guarded secret—the identity of their most valuable mole. That was why they did everything to throw you off the trail. Since they had no objection to the elimination of Shishakali, I knew that I had been wrong in suspecting that he was your father—and the Mossad mole. The jewelry gave me a different pointer on the mole, whoever he is. It seemed to indicate that he might have been planted in Riyadh."

"Which is why you chose that city as the site for Shishakali's liquidation," I said. "You wanted to see who would come to my rescue when I fell into the trap."

Charlie gave a shamefaced grin. "That notion did kind of creep in," he admitted.

My heart was pounding. Evidently, Charlie had no idea how close his imagination had brought him toward the truth. Even now, after my father's death, it was imperative that Charlie be thrown off the trail, to ward off possible harm to the Ibn Aziz family. "Charlie!" I cried in feigned amazement, "you were so wrong!"

"Maybe I was," he conceded. "But I'd like to explore this, even if only for my own private satisfaction."

"What's the point?"

"I wouldn't want our last encounter to end in checkmate. At worst, I'd settle for a draw."

"I understand how frustrated you must feel," I said with a smile. "But maybe I should remind you of something you once told me: where there's a fire you don't have to put out, the best thing is to steer clear of it. Why get yourself burned for nothing?"

His gaze beamed affection. "Your memory is excellent. You've been a good student."

"I've had an excellent teacher."

His eyes were suddenly flint-hard. "Which of us are you referring to?" he asked softly. "Me, or him?"

"Him?" I pretended mystification.

"That man who—er—died so many years back."

"That's a bizarre question."

"As I said . . ." He grinned. "I don't want you to go away

272

thinking you got the better of me. At most, someone smarter than either of us was one step ahead of me. Believe me, I consider it a great honor to have been left no more than one step behind. In the course of my lifetime, I've known some of the masters of the intelligence field." He shook his head. "But your father was the best."

Before this astounding tribute could sink in, Charlie turned and was marching away with vigorous strides.

Shit, I said to myself, staring after his receding figure; he may leave me with no other choice but to kill him.

Charlie vanished from my life and Ariadne's. His disappearance was as silent as it was complete. After that last stroll through Central Park, his final act involving me was the deposit of a draft for one hundred thousand dollars in my Coney Island Avenue bank account. My reward for surviving.

Following a promise to Ariadne, I arrived one morning at the Sheepshead Bay jetty, where I handed Jazhek Dizma a check, thereby becoming the owner of his masterpiece, the yacht to which he had devoted so many months of loving care.

By the beginning of May, our preparations for the voyage were completed. The night before our departure, we were Bertha's guests for dinner. Then we drove to Sheepshead Bay, where Jazhek was painting a bold name on the yacht's bow. "The Flying Camel," of course—what other name would have been appropriate?

During our ocean crossing, Ariadne did not disappoint me. From the start, she proved herself a born sailor, and by the time we reached the Strait of Gibraltar, she was proficient at hoisting sail, steering, and navigating as though she had done nothing else all her life. By taking over these chores, she left me time to complete this account. Day after day, I spent hours writing in the cabin or sitting atop its roof, paying particular attention to those episodes as yet unknown to her. She understood my urge to set it all down on paper as a way of coming to terms with my true self. I found it necessary to tear myself away from my old world if I was to achieve a full understanding of my own identity; there comes a time in every man's life when he has to study his own soul.

In the course of my writing, I found events and persons sometimes taking on unfamiliar aspects. I likewise found myself modifying thoughts and certainties that I had long harbored. My conviction grew that it was not coincidence that brought Sheikh Ibrahim Ibn Aziz to the Park Avenue offices of Sheldon Moritz and Ed Liebman. The more I thought about it, the more certain I felt it to have been a well-considered step: with his life ebbing, the Saudi sheikh reverted to his other inner identity as Badwi, resolving to catch one glimpse of the son born to him by the woman he loved so passionately.

Our voyage proceeded at a leisurely pace. We cast anchor in numerous harbors along the way: Gibraltar. Marseilles. Genoa. Naples. Piraeus. We sailed the Greek isles as far as Crete. From Heraklion, we set out for Rhodes, going on to Limassol in Cyprus. Before us lay the last leg of our odyssey.

On Monday, October 15, close to midnight, just over five months after setting sail from the Sheepshead Bay anchorage, we sighted the lights of Tel Aviv. Viewed from the sea, the multicolored lamps made the long strip of beach resemble a wreath of radiant flowers. Seen from that angle, and at that hour of the evening, the Tel Aviv of concrete and asphalt disappeared.

It was a night of total stillness. But though the smooth sea indicated that the breeze was light, we continued to advance under canvas until a short distance from the marina entrance. There, we lowered sail and I started up the engine. Once we were inside the marina, I picked out a berth to moore the yacht. After going through customs, we headed for a rental office to hire a car. We set out northward, on our way toward the Sea of Galilee.

When we reached the house my forefathers had built of the black basalt stones hewn from the nearby hills, the darkness was fading. By the time I had opened the old window shutters, the sky was afire. With Ariadne at my side, I stood on the broad terrace. As we faced the Golan highlands, we watched the sun emerge and felt the cool breeze wafting from the east.